THE VIPER

THE VIPER

HÅKAN ÖSTLUNDH

MINOTAUR BOOKS
A THOMAS DUNNE BOOK
NEW YORK

This is a work of fiction. All of the characters, organizations, and events portrayed in this novel are either products of the author's imagination or are used fictitiously.

A THOMAS DUNNE BOOK FOR MINOTAUR BOOKS.
An imprint of St. Martin's Publishing Group.

Book design by Jonathan Bennett

www.thomasdunnebooks.com
www.minotaurbooks.com

Library of Congress Cataloging-in-Publication Data

Östlundh, Håkan, 1962–
    [Blot. English]
    The viper / Håkan Östlundh.—1st U.S. ed.
        p. cm.
    ISBN 978-0-312-64232-7 (hardcover)
    ISBN 978-1-250-01127-5 (e-book)
    I. Title.
    PT9877.25.S85B5613 2012
    839.73'8—dc23
                                                2012010101

First published in Sweden as *Blot* by Ordfront

First U.S. Edition: August 2012

10 9 8 7 6 5 4 3 2 1

TO HANS-ERIK

PART ONE

I pretend to be ordinary
Just as ordinary as can be
I pretend to be ordinary
But how do people do it?
What is it they do?
What is it you do?

—OLLE LJUNGSTRÖM

Sunday, October 22
Karolinska University Hospital, Solna

He was hovering in darkness, dangling weightlessly in something that was beyond night. The world had no beginning, no end. Perhaps this dense blackness was in fact nothingness. And yet he was there, conscious that he was in motion, rocking through space. Or through nothingness.

Was this a near-death experience? Was this how it felt to teeter on the edge of life and death, a no-man's-land where one is neither one nor the other? Or was he in fact dead? It wasn't unpleasant, it didn't hurt, he didn't feel anything at all apart from the sensation of being rocked gently in a great, black void. If the rocking stopped, would he cease to exist? Was that rocking motion life itself? The end of life? But he was thinking. If he was thinking then he must be alive. Wasn't that how it worked? When he tried to pin down what it was he was thinking about he soon realized that he wasn't thinking about anything except the rocking. Could that even be considered a thought? Was there nothing more, no other thoughts that were him? He tried, tried . . . but how did you even go about trying? It was impossible. There was nothing but night and motion.

ANTONIA CAPUCCI AND her fellow nurse waited at the stretcher entrance. They peered out into the darkness, but could see little, blinded by the powerful spotlights that lit up the helipad on the roof.

They heard it long before they could see it. The engines' angry drone and the rapid thrusts of the rotor blades, cutting through the air somewhere up there in the pitch-black night.

3

"I'll call down to OR," said her colleague and walked over to the wall telephone.

Antonia scanned the notes on the clipboard yet again. Male, forty-four years old, head injury, unconscious. The words "police officer" also appeared in the abbreviated notes. The doctor accompanying the medevac would brief them in the elevator on the way down.

Then suddenly there it was, caught in the glare of the spotlights, Falck's red ambulance helicopter, roaring and whipping the air beneath it. A piece of blue string flailed across the roof in the powerful blast of air. The helicopter dropped down the final distance until it stood firmly on the landing pad. The pilot switched off the engines and the rotors began to slow.

Antonia's colleague opened the doors leading out onto the roof and the crew of the helicopter hurried to the back of the craft to unload the patient. A police officer injured in the line of duty always caused more commotion. Journalists started to call in almost at once, even though they knew that the hospital was not in a position to comment.

The patient had been flown in from Gotland, but there was no mention of that on the clipboard she was holding in her hand. She checked to make sure the ID number on the plastic bracelet she was about to fasten to her patient's wrist matched the number on the form. And then the name. Fredrik Broman. She tried to commit it to memory.

1

A bounding neon horse reflected in the dark glass facade opposite Arvid Traneus's apartment on the border between Roppongi and Akasaka in Tokyo's Minato district. Its precise gait was unclear and with each step it changed colors in a shower of stars. Its rounded babyish features bore little resemblance to a real horse. Missing was the muscle definition, the nervous gaze, and the awesome power that a live animal of that size possessed—a massive creature that could easily injure a human being without intending to.

A raven flew sluggishly between the skyscrapers, virtually indiscernible in the darkness. He had shuddered the first time he had heard that lingering shriek. In Tokyo it wasn't the seagulls that took over the city when the human population retired for the night, it was the ravens.

You got used to it.

Arvid Traneus turned his back on the October night outside the bedroom's panorama windows, the horse's never-ending gallop and the flickering lights of the city. He looked at Kass, the young woman who had just entered the room. She had tilted her head slightly and smiled sadly at him. Her black hair cascaded down over the shoulders of her red silk dress. She was holding a wineglass with both hands, in it the last of the Cheval Blanc from the bottle he had uncorked.

It was a final farewell.

The assignment had originally been intended as just a quick consulting job. As it turned out, he had ended up spending seven years traveling back and forth, and three more in the apartment; ten years in

Tokyo altogether, the last two of them with Kass. And now it was time to return home. It was over. All of it. The job, the city, the woman.

He walked up to her and she met him halfway. He took the glass from her and set it down on the ledge in front of the window. He pulled her close to him and laid his hand on her golden-brown thigh protruding from the slit in her short dress. She pressed up against him.

"Kass," he mumbled into her hair, which was decorated with shiny little bows that matched the red of her dress.

She had brightened up his last two years in the city. Made it easier to breathe in the scattered shards of free time he had allowed himself between work and sleep.

He ran his hand up between her legs and spread her hairless vulva with his fingers. She let out a loud, shrill moan. Out of arousal he thought at first, but as he continued to move his fingers in the manner she usually liked, he noticed that she had gone rigid. She had turned cold as ice.

Then came another whimper, only pitched higher this time, and definitely not pleasure induced. She gasped the way one only does when one is truly frightened.

He looked at her. She stared out at the bounding manga horse.

"Kass?"

She didn't answer.

"Kass, what is it?"

He waved his hand in front of her staring eyes.

"Kazu-mi!" he cried out. Like one might to a child about to put her hand on a hot stove.

She gave a start and looked at him with a furtive, anxious expression.

"What is it?" he asked again.

She shook her head and ran her fingers nervously through her hair so that the red bows came off and dropped to the floor.

"I don't know. Nothing. It's just silly . . ."

Yet her eyes still sought their way back to the window and lost themselves in the distance, as if she saw something else completely than the neon horse's fitful prancing.

The animated horse had not been there six months ago. He had chosen this neighborhood because it lay far from the neon lights and nightlife. It was the government and diplomatic district, where interspersed among the office complexes was an occasional stack of high-rise apartments. Not a soul on the sidewalks after seven at night. But the city was constantly changing, above and below the surface. From his window he could see four new skyscrapers rising ever higher; the cranes at the very top had shut down for the night, visible only by their blinking red aircraft warning lights.

Constant flux, interminable growth. Neon flickered. Money changed hands. Sums that made the national budget of a small country like Sweden seem like chump change flowed daily through the stock exchanges and currency markets. Multinationals collaborated, competed, and annihilated one another. And that was where Arvid Traneus came into the picture. In the annihilation. Of corporations that is.

This assignment had, following a drawn-out struggle, ended badly for the competitor, much worse than had been intended. And the slaughter was actually pointless. His employer would only be able to fill up part of the void that was left behind. The rest would just fall into the hands of some other grateful competitor.

He stroked Kass's back.

"Better now?"

"I'm fine," she said and kissed him on the neck. "Make love to me now," she whispered.

She lifted her arms above her head as he pulled off her dress with a rustle. She stood there naked in front of him, smelling of earth and rubber from the robust red wine, vanilla, and a hint of lemon from her perfume, and something else that was her own essence. Warm skin and loins.

Kass backed him up toward the foot of the bed, as she unfastened the stubborn black leather belt that he had bought just the week before. She unbuttoned his trousers and grabbed hold of his cock.

"He wants to come to Kass," she whispered, pursed her lips slightly, and let a thin string of saliva dribble down onto the head of his manhood and into her hand cupped underneath. In a quick, gentle motion, she rubbed in the saliva and he felt his legs turn to rubber.

Ten years. Had it been worth it?

For Arvid Traneus the answer was definitely yes. He had made a fortune for himself during these years. And yet that fortune was just a fraction of the money he had made for his employers, so their answer would likely be yes, too, if they would even be able to think of it in those terms. For them the contest was never over. All triumphs were temporary. They would continue to battle on for another ten years, and ten more after that.

He had been brought in to devise a strategy for increasing the company's market share by 5 percent. That was what they had agreed from the beginning. A tall order, but still specific and realistic. Then it got bigger. Their ambition grew and he was drawn in deeper and deeper, enticed by an offer he couldn't refuse; a breathtaking monthly salary and options the value of which, through his own efforts, would multiply many times over. If he succeeded.

He built up his own team. Flew back and forth to Tokyo, before finally ending up living there for the past few years.

Kass sank down onto her knees by the bed and looked at him with that wanton sideways glance that he could never quite decide whether she was feigning or not. But it didn't matter to him. If she was putting it on she was doing a good job of it, and she was doing it so that he would like what he saw, and that was worth a lot to him.

He had very nearly lost his best man because of Kass. She had belonged to Stephen first. That was how Arvid had met her. His gaze had been drawn to her constantly throughout that dinner. It can scarcely have escaped Stephen's notice. The following day he had gotten hold of her address and telephone number, and when he had called her up and suggested they meet she had answered yes at once.

Arvid was under no illusions about Kass and how she lived, but he knew that she had nothing to gain by leaving Stephen. She had done it simply because she had wanted to. Of that he was convinced.

Stephen had taken it hard. At first he had tried to reason with Arvid, get him to let her go. When Arvid refused, when he claimed on top of everything else that there was nothing he could do about it, that it had been Kass's decision, Stephen became furious. He threatened to quit, even went to the extreme of packing his things and flying back to England, though he never turned in any letter of resignation.

Arvid went so far as to appeal to Stephen's professionalism. Stephen sulked for a while, but of course he came back. He had far too much to gain to throw it all away just out of some vain demonstration of . . . well, of what . . . pride? He would only have made a fool of himself. She was just a kind of whore after all. Albeit not one you could pick up on any street corner.

She kissed his cock with gentle lips.

"Let me know," she whispered before disappearing between his legs.

She always said that. He smiled at the black head of hair bobbing back and forth down there. If she didn't know him well enough by now to be able to tell when he was about to come then that was her problem, he thought to himself.

It was actually Stephen who had come up with the idea that had made the whole thing possible, he and that blessed Norwegian computer whiz Olaisen. But it was Arvid who had been in charge when they had set the whole thing in motion. In the end it was neither marketing strategies nor product development that had brought Pricom to its knees, but an intricate scheme involving the company's shares that had been made possible by Olaisen hacking into their computer system. They had been able to peer right into the heart of their competitor. And then they had crushed him. It was a dirty trick of course, but business is always dirty, so there wasn't much more to say about it.

Kass's tongue fluttered like a butterfly of moist flesh. He ran his hands over her glistening black hair, brought his fingers together behind her neck, and held her head firmly in place. He stared out into the darkness and his pupils followed the movements of the neon horse involuntarily when he came.

After a prolonged silence, a sudden spasm that caused everything to relax, he let go and slipped out of her mouth. She slowly raised her left hand and drew the back of it across her lips and chin. Arvid Traneus looked at Kass and felt how he suddenly became filled with something heavy and black. He hadn't felt it so strongly for a long time. It almost suffocated him.

He didn't love her, but she was nice to be with, beautiful to look at, and pleasurable to make love to. She was delicate and petite, light as a feather. He could lift her up like a child. He had never heard her complain or whine or question anything. He had never seen her look at another man when they had been out together.

And yet . . . He was under no illusions. She had left Stephen to be with him. And now their time together was at an end. It was possible that he could take her with him. Though she would never ask him to. In that case, it was up to him to invite her. He had considered it, but he had another life waiting for him, besides which, she was what she was after all. It would be a strange mixture of private life and business.

Their time together was over. He would leave and she would remain where she belonged. Alone. Free. Available. Who would she move on to after him? Someone he knew? Had she already made arrangements? Would she be slipping into another man's bed already tomorrow? Look at him with that longing gaze and say, "He wants to come to Kass." Suck his cock?

He met her gaze as she looked up at him and he realized in an instant that he didn't have the slightest inkling of what was going on in her head. Was that the look of sad farewell he saw in her dark eyes, or was it just an act, like when they narrowed with desire and arousal? Was she in fact indifferent? Did she hold him in contempt? Was she smiling inside though the corners of her mouth were angled slightly downward? Was she laughing to herself?

He surprised himself. He wasn't normally a brooder. Resolutely and very deliberately he pushed the thoughts of Kass out of his mind. All these questions were pointless. They were in the midst of a parting of the ways. She was no longer his concern, nor he hers.

It must have been a moment of sentimentality that had caught him unawares. It wasn't like him. He adjusted his clothes, buckled his uncooperative belt, and picked up the red silk dress from the floor.

She eyed him with a look of mild incredulity.

He reached out and helped her up. Her skin was warm against his fingers, but the warmth and fragrance meant nothing to him now. He held out the dress.

"You'd better go now," he said.

Her lower lip, pursed just a moment ago, drew in and tensed up. Her gaze still sought out his, questioningly, as if there was something left to say.

He handed her the dress and slowly walked over to the table in the other room to see if there was any wine left in the bottle. Behind him he heard her get dressed.

2

The ring of the telephone rattled loudly through the house. It always rang louder when it was him, cutting through time and space.

Kristina hurried through the living room, into the kitchen. Her feet were damp inside her socks. She was late. She hated to be late when he called. She wanted to be well prepared, composed, her breath steady, dry between her toes. Arvid was perceptive. Always detected the slightest ripple on the surface.

She pulled out one of the Jugendstil oak chairs from the dining room table, sat down, and took three deep, focused breaths without giving a single thought to the arm that would soon reach out toward the rattling telephone, trying to remember what Noriko had said during Wednesday's session. She admired that woman's enterprising spirit. To come all the way from Washington with her husband and settle down in Gotland of all places. Within just a few months she had set up a yoga center behind Japanese rice paper blinds in a building opposite the Statoil station in Havdhem.

Two years ago, Kristina would never have dreamed of doing yoga. It was far too alien to her. Perhaps it was the fact that Noriko was Japanese, at least by extraction, that had piqued her curiosity. Japan figured constantly in her life, after all, albeit from a great distance. Her life had become rigidly structured around the daily calls from Tokyo, and in some strange way it was as if the Wednesday yoga classes with Noriko helped to balance them out, loosen things up.

She lifted the receiver. It was 2 p.m. in Levide on Gotland, 10 p.m. in Tokyo.

"Hi, darling. How's everything? All right?"

Arvid's voice was deep and composed as usual, crystal clear even though it had sped across half the world to reach her.

"Just fine," she answered.

Her voice was clear and steady, but wasn't it pitched just a tad higher than usual?

"I'm coming home," he said. If he had picked up on her voice it certainly didn't show.

"I see, when?"

She already knew that he would answer tomorrow, or possibly the day after. He always preferred short notice. If it weren't for the fact that he always wanted to be picked up at the airport he might not have given her any notice at all.

"No, I mean, I'm coming home."

She sat there silently, adjusted her grip on the phone, didn't understand.

"For good. It's over. Ended. Just like that, from one day to the next. Pretty amazing, huh, after ten years?"

She still sat there silently, as darkness enveloped her. The second hand on the kitchen clock was preparing to spring forward another step. A faint electric impulse was on its way down a wire.

There it jumped!

How long could she remain silent? Dumbstruck, she must be allowed that much, right? Not for too long, though. And then of course it was not simply a question of answering, but also what she answered, and the tone of her voice. She would have needed a score to follow, and at least two weeks to prepare. But instead she sat there, like an idiot, struck by the proverbial bolt from the blue.

The second hand took another leap forward.

She *was* an idiot, not just like one. Of course this day was bound to come. She had known that all along. Nothing could have been more certain.

Three seconds. Her time was up.

"Arvid!"

Perhaps she wasn't an idiot after all. For a moment she was quite pleased with herself. His name, spoken a little lingeringly with a slight gasp. Of course the latter was caused mostly by her having completely lost control of her breathing, but it sounded good, as if joy had taken her breath away.

"I've been so busy here that it hadn't really sunk in till now . . . It's going to be damn nice to come home. And the best thing about it is that from now on I'm completely my own man. I don't ever have to work another day in my life if I don't want to. We can live where we like, do as we please. I will never have to be away like this again, that I can promise you."

"That's just incredible."

Joy, joy . . .

She had to struggle to understand what he said when he continued. It was as if the sound in the receiver faded out, just like the light in the room had done. When Kristina finally understood what time he had to be picked up in Visby and had hung up the phone, she didn't dare get up. If she just remained sitting there she would survive a little while longer, but if she got up she would fall straight through the floor, be swallowed up by a vast blackness, and disappear forever. Which perhaps wasn't such a bad alternative, when she came to think of it.

But she wanted to live.

Who the hell was she really? She had known this day was coming after all, and yet she had chosen not to see it.

She leaned forward with her hands clasped tightly in her lap and her eyes squeezed shut in order to block out the feelings that were flooding her breast and screaming catastrophe.

"I've behaved like a fucking ostrich," she whispered to herself.

Suddenly realizing that she actually looked quite a lot like one, sitting there doubled over with her eyes closed, she straightened up and opened her eyes.

She looked out over the big, spotless kitchen, self-consciously old-fashioned in style, but actually brand new and patinated at a cost of over ten thousand crowns per cupboard. She had chosen that kitchen, nego-tiated the price, supervised its installation, caused a fuss over a door that would not close properly, saw to it that it was put right, and the price knocked down. And the rest of it: tiles, stove, fan . . . She had had time to take care of all that. Though naturally always with Arvid's consent.

She'd had years to prepare. She could have planned everything down to the smallest detail and then just disappeared one day. What was it that had made her stay? Was it that she didn't think it could be done or was she just stupid? Sure, he kept her on an allowance so she didn't have much money to speak of, but she could have put some away. If she had started . . . say two years ago, back when those thoughts first began to take shape, back when she and Anders . . . She would cer-tainly have been able to save four thousand or so every month. That would have amounted to nearly a hundred thousand in cash. How many times hadn't she dreamed about it, even made plans to escape. No! A new, secret identity . . . But had she lifted a finger to actually put any of it into action?

She started to cry, but transformed her sobbing into a cold, con-temptuous laugh. She was laughing at herself. She deserved it. She could have been on her way by now, but no.

Of course Arvid would have realized something was amiss as soon as she didn't answer the way she was supposed to, but she'd have been long gone before he'd be able to do anything about it, perhaps in an-other country, with a hundred thousand in cash that would leave no trail. And with a new name, new personal identity number, new hair color . . . He wouldn't have had a chance of finding her.

What was going to happen now? She and Anders? She would have hit herself if she could. Given herself a good hard slap across the face.

For Christ's sake, she was forty-seven years old, a grown-up several times over. What was wrong with her?

Anders! she thought, she had to call Anders.

Anders. She almost started crying again at the thought of him. She had gotten her life back, but she had carelessly gone and lost it again. How could it have happened? How the hell could she have been so . . . well, what? Stupid? Useless? Ineffectual? Spineless? Blind? It had been so strong—for two years she had been so filled with not just love and passion, she was only too well acquainted with those two sentiments, but also happiness, trust, and even . . . hope.

Suddenly she felt her chest seize up and she went completely cold. It was as if she had opened her eyes anew, even though her eyes were already open. She got up and wheezed loudly as she gasped for air.

Was it really that simple, was that really how it all fit together? Had she shut herself away in love yet again? Like an animal in a cage, grateful and content, not to mention obsessed with her daily supply of fodder, unable to see and think beyond the bars that imprisoned her?

She staggered toward the front door as fast as she could. It felt as if her windpipe had been laced shut and her heart had stopped beating. Gray spots began to dance across her field of vision. Was she about to faint? *No,* she thought. *I'm not damn well going to faint.* What kind of a fucking solution was that? Was she really that pathetic? Was that the sort of person she was? No, that wasn't her, she wasn't going to be like that. Not any more. She kicked the shoes that were lined up so neatly in the entrance hall, including Arvid's brown calfskin oxfords that he hadn't put his feet in for months, desperate to find a release for her rage. The shoes flew in all directions and the shelf on which they stood was knocked askew.

She struggled for air. It was easier to breathe after her outburst. She staggered up to the door and managed to get it open. Fresh air streamed in toward her. Perhaps it wasn't too late yet. If she scraped together all she had; cash, jewelry, that Kosta Boda vase that had been valued at seventy thousand just last year; she could put that in her bag, too. Could she sell the car, or would that get the police onto her? Was it in his name or hers? She realized that she didn't know. She hadn't even managed to find that out.

But what difference did it make? No point in whining about it, or looking back. Better to focus on her current options. Pack a suitcase with clothes, jewelry, and that damned vase. Take the car to the mainland and sell it in Stockholm, then on to . . . It was shortly past two. She could be in Stockholm in seven hours if she took the boat that left at a quarter to five. When did the car dealerships open? Say, ten o'clock. By eleven tomorrow morning all that could be taken care of.

She came out onto the front steps, took a few paces forward, filled her lungs with air, she was almost breathing normally now, stepped down onto the freshly laid footpath. And stopped.

She froze in midstep, and stared at the viper that lay coiled up on the warm limestone pathway a little more than two meters in front of her.

3.

Things can change when you're gone for a long time. Time waits for no one.

Emrik Jansson, however, did wait. He stood on the narrow stretch of paved road with the black tires of his bicycle lined up on the gray band of gravel along the shoulder. His long, white beard was yellowed with nicotine around his mouth, as were the fore and middle fingers of his right hand. He gripped the handlebars tightly with both hands. He had stopped biking over a year ago. These days he only used the bicycle for support. Better that than one of those four-wheeled contraptions you always saw the old biddies at the home wandering around with. You had to accept your fate, there was no getting around that, but you could do it with a little more decorum. He was eighty-seven years old, so there wasn't really much to say on that score. He was heading downhill. Singing his last refrain. Whistling his even-song.

A small dragonfly with an iridescent blue abdomen came buzzing along the road in fitful flight. Emrik Jansson followed the dragonfly with his gaze until it vanished out across a field. There was nothing wrong with his eyes. But his legs were unsteady and his hearing wasn't too good.

His hand trembling slightly, he reached laboriously into his inside jacket pocket and took out a pouch of tobacco. He unfastened the tape seal, rolled open the pouch, and inhaled the aroma of moist rolling to-bacco. Inside the pouch lay three ready-rolled cigarettes he had had the foresight to prepare ahead of time. Trying to roll one while holding onto his bicycle was more than his strength and coordination could handle. He took one of the cigarettes, put it in his mouth, and returned the pouch of tobacco to his inside pocket before pulling out a plastic lighter from his trouser pocket and lighting his cigarette.

Emrik Jansson awaited Arvid Traneus's return with a certain trep-idation. According to what he had heard it wouldn't be today. But you couldn't always trust the grapevine. Rumors. There had been a lot of talk over the years about Arvid Traneus and his long trips to Japan. Every so often, somebody would pop up claiming to have it on good authority that he was supposed to be on his way home, but then he didn't show up and it all turned out to be just talk. Or else he really did show up, only to leave again just a few days later.

This time was different. Word had it that he was coming to stay for good.

That's what Emrik Jansson had heard when he'd popped into his neighbor's the day before yesterday to buy some potatoes. That was how it worked. When you couldn't see something with your own eyes, there was always someone else who had the facts. And it spread. In simple phrases, said in passing. It wasn't gossip exactly, but subjects came up, names were named.

He heard a tractor approaching behind him. The driver slowed down and rolled past the old man with the bushy white beard who, despite the heat and the strong sun, was dressed in a thick black woolen suit. Beneath his suit he wore a slightly yellowed shirt that had once been white.

Emrik squinted toward the driver's cab of the green tractor and slowly raised his hand in greeting. He got a wave back. It was Magnus Hjälmrud from Kauparve, the eldest son of Hans-Göran. Emrik Jansson had taught him in school the last three years before retiring. But that was not why he remembered him. He remembered all of them. His mind didn't need any extra support. Not yet anyway. He remembered every student that had passed through the little community's school system during his roughly forty years as a teacher. He knew their names and what years they had been in his class. And if they lived close enough he knew the names of their children and parents and where they lived. He saw them drive by on the road. How they came and went. Weather permitting, he could spend hours slowly shuffling back and forth along the road. It was his self-appointed task to keep track of people and in doing so keep track of himself.

He had also had Arvid Traneus in his class. Arvid, his cousins, and his eldest child. He had seen them almost every day since they finished school. Those of them who were still alive, that is. He saw them, followed them, saw cars arrive and drive off again. Comings and goings that did not mean much to most, those who did not have the time to reflect on it and remember.

But Emrik Jansson did have time and he remembered. Today he was spending his time waiting for Arvid Traneus. But also for something else, it had to be said. Something else. He sighed heavily and looked up at the sky. *Not a cloud*, he thought to himself, *not a single dark cloud on the horizon.* But he could see them nonetheless.

HE WAS TALL and wan, standing there with his left hand shoved deep into the pocket of his washed-out black jeans. He had burrowed his chin down into the collar of his dark-blue tracksuit top, the zipper pulled all the way up. He had recently celebrated his thirtieth birthday at Norrtälje Prison. If celebrated was the right word for it. *Turned* lay closer to the truth. He had turned thirty. Nobody had cared, he barely did himself. He was out now, and that was the main thing.

The wind knocked the ash from the cigarette he was holding in his right hand and sent it dancing off in an ascending spiral along the quayside and on out over the Baltic.

He had called up an old friend, yesterday to be precise, and they had started to talk about Stefania. *He* had started to talk about Stefania. And it was then that his friend had mentioned that Arvid Traneus was coming home. At least that's what he had heard anyway, that whatever it was he had been doing over there in Japan, it was over now, and that he was coming home to Levide.

"Bullshit!"

That was his first reaction. His second was that he didn't want to know about it. What the hell did he have to do with Arvid Traneus anymore? But something else had already begun to stir inside him, that soaked up that information like a bone-dry sponge soaks up water. Inexorably it started to grow, plans took form as if by themselves, demanding his attention. And he listened, of course he couldn't stop himself from listening to *that voice,* and the more he listened the more obvious it seemed to him that this was something that had come to him as some kind of gift. That it was as if fate, which seldom, if ever, had anything good to offer him, had tapped him on the shoulder and given him an opportunity.

He let his gaze slowly drift from the sea to the big stacks of timber behind the sawmill's chain-link fence. The sea breeze had stiffened over the afternoon and his shoulder-length strands of hair were tossing about in the wind.

He took a deep drag from his cigarette. What the hell had happened? Nobody smoked anymore. When he had lighted a cigarette at the ferry terminal, people had glared at him as if he were a junkie who'd taken out his gear to shoot up. He had apologized. Of course he knew about the ban, but it wasn't second nature to him. Once he was standing there with a cigarette in his fist it just didn't occur to him. Perhaps he had apologized a little too loudly and profusely; he had felt that people had avoided looking at him, moved away a few yards, held on to to their children more tightly. Perhaps not. It was probably all in his mind. The feeling that he stood out, that he didn't quite know how to behave to blend in with ordinary people.

He tossed his cigarette over the edge of the pier. It was crazy his being here. Completely fucking crazy. Just two days after being released, he had boarded a ferry back to the place he had once promised himself he would never again set foot. "Over my dead body," he had sworn.

"Guess we'll just have to see about that?" he told himself out loud.

He was there now, and he was there for one sole reason. Arvid Traneus. He had no plan, no idea what might happen. All he knew was that he had had no choice. He had been compelled to get onto that ferryboat.

He had really believed that he had succeeded in forgetting Stefania, that she was gone from his mind forever, but during the years in prison she had stubbornly clawed her way back into his head. The very first time she had appeared in a dream, and he had woken up shocked and dismayed. After that she had remained in his thoughts, sporadically in the beginning, and then with ever-increasing frequency, until she never gave him a moment's peace. Not even for a single day. That's how dead she was.

He abruptly turned his back on the sea and started to walk away; his emotions battling inside of him. One moment an intense feeling of joy at being on his way, a searing fire like a lodestar in the night; the next moment a cold wind that caused him to shut his eyes and see himself from the outside, making him shake his head in doubt. And then the heat and the light again that with each powerful wave grew a little stronger at the cold wind's expense.

4.

The ground rocked beneath his feet. A twelve-hour flight from Narita to Heathrow and time had virtually stood still. His stomach growled and he took a big bite of the egg-white omelet he had ordered at one of the restaurants in the dimly lit transit hall. Gloomy as a November afternoon.

An egg-white omelet, steamed broccoli florets, and a few stray chickpeas dribbled with lemon-herb oil. No food for a man, but experience had taught him to eat carefully on long-haul flights. But there were other reasons for it as well. He had been forced to start watching what he ate. He had gone up in weight somewhat. It didn't bother him much, he didn't mind being overweight. But the scrawny little doctor that the fine print on his insurance policy stipulated that he visit every six months, had looked up from his test results and peered at him with a furrow of concern between his eyebrows.

He had two fixed times a week at an exorbitantly exclusive tennis club and had made radical changes to his eating habits. He hadn't amassed a fortune just to come home to Gotland and die. No, he had no intention of ending his life prematurely with his head in a pot full of mashed potatoes, butter, and caviar.*

He had indulged in a beer. Alcohol was another thing he usually avoided on long-haul flights, but now he had made it all the way to London on his final trip back from Japan. He had not come home to die, but nor had he come home to live as a monk. For him it was the perfect time to have a beer, even if it was only morning in London.

He had a tendency to become greedy. They had been too greedy where Pricom was concerned, that he had to admit. To himself, if not to anyone else. But when an opportunity presented itself, it was hard to resist not picking the bone clean. Pricom's collapse might even be disadvantageous to his employer. For a company to disappear completely from the market created uncertainty, and that was never a good thing. To just take a substantial piece of the pie instead, as much as one could handle, and leave the rest for Pricom to bravely hang on to, would no doubt have been the ideal solution. But now that's not how thing's turned out. No one blamed him. Everyone was satisfied, and it would take a while before any negative effects began to appear. By that time, they would have forgotten his name and he would cherish his fortune on the other side of the globe. In this world, everyone's gaze was firmly fixed forward.

The waiter came rushing up toward the row of tables where Arvid was sitting, and he took the opportunity to hold out his card to pay. The waiter stopped him by holding his palm out in front of him like a traffic cop.

"I'm sorry, sir, fire alarm. You've got to leave immediately."

"Fire alarm?"

---

*Translator's note: The late Swedish financier, Jan Stenbeck, who died of a heart attack at the age of fifty-nine, is said to have enjoyed gorging himself on this eccentric concoction from time to time.

"Yes, you've got to leave."

Arvid slipped his card back into his wallet and stood up holding his black leather briefcase.

Fire alarm? Strange, he hadn't heard any alarm. All around him businessmen as well as the odd backpacker stood up and moved slowly toward the exit exchanging quick glances, more confused than anxious.

"This way please, this way."

The airport staff, dressed in neon-yellow vests, tried to hurry the slow-moving air travelers along and pointed in a rather vague direction toward the far end of the hall's gray luminescence. Refreshment areas, tax-free outlets, and other shops chased out their customers, closed gates, and pulled down shutters.

He quickened his pace somewhat, without overdoing it. He hadn't amassed a fortune just to die at Heathrow, either. A fire alarm? What could it be? A terrorist bomb, an outbreak of fire, someone who'd lit their cigar beneath a smoke detector?

He shuffled along with the other passengers until they'd reached a distant wing of the terminal that seemed to be a dead end. One by one they slowed down and stopped. No vest-clad personnel anywhere to be seen anymore.

A man about his age in a suit, leather briefcase, and designer glasses, gave him a look of resignation and threw out his arms. Arvid responded with a shrug of the shoulders.

The evacuation seemed to have petered out and now there was nobody with enough sense to inform them whether they were hovering in imminent danger of their lives, or if it had just been a false alarm.

Arvid spotted an empty seat on a bench and sat down. He was filled with an absurd sensation that nothing mattered. It was a feeling that was completely alien to him. For him, usually everything mattered. Naturally things were of varying importance and had to be prioritized accordingly, but when you began to think that nothing mattered, then you were in trouble.

He wasn't getting the information he needed to make a decision. Should he run toward the emergency exit or could he return to the eternal gloom of the transit hall and order another beer to replace the one he had not been allowed to finish? Or should he just remain sitting there on the bench in some kind of limbo?

In order to pass the time, he tried to sort through his still very sketchy plans of setting up his own consulting firm. All that talk about never having to work again was of course just a ploy for talking about money without having to mention a concrete sum. He had no intention of retiring. People who strived for economic independence just to devote the rest of their lives to playing golf and lying on beaches baffled him.

The plan was to start out with a core management group of ten senior consultants and then bring in other professionals and support staff as necessary on a project-to-project basis. He counted on a planning and build-up phase of one year, during which time he would fine-tune his ideas and establish the appropriate contacts. It would be something completely different from the solo projects he had heretofore handled; not unsuccessfully, it had to be said, but having his own company would open up a whole new range of possibilities. It would probably be difficult to remain in Sweden, but he had nothing against the idea of moving to London or possibly Zurich. And this time he would take Kristina with him.

Two Asians, a man and a woman, were engaged in an intense, hushed discussion on the bench along the opposite wall. He could hear that they were Japanese and was able to place them, with 95 percent certainty, in high positions within the business community.

One of Pricom's board members had committed suicide, after first having shot his wife and their seven-year-old daughter. It was so typically Japanese—assuming the information was correct that is—they could never handle a setback. It was so feudal somehow, as if they couldn't reconcile themselves to the fact that people in a modern society climbed and fell, got up and continued climbing, constantly taking up new positions depending on choice and performance and sometimes as a result of events that lay outside an individual's control. There was no place for honor and shame in that world.

Arvid concealed an involuntary yawn behind his hand.

KRISTINA HAD RUSHED up from the kitchen table and into the living room to watch the morning show that was on the TV. The woman with the warm ginger hair, the friendly smile, and the slightly sad eyes was speaking about London. A fire had broken out at Heathrow International Airport just outside London.

Kristina felt a warm surge spread through her. There was a fire at the airport. Misfortune, terror, bombs, twists of fate, death, destruction.

Hope rekindled.

The warmth stayed with her. She embraced it, tried to hold on to it, felt how it comforted her heart, settled her soul. Images started to flash before her, images of the future. It would look much the same. She would continue to live as she had done for most of the past two years. Only she would be able to continue living that way for the rest of her life. And better still: there would be no more chilling apprehension, no more visits on short notice, no more 2 p.m. phone calls every afternoon, no more days where she counted the seconds and expected that any minute he'd scent something out, expose her with his sensitive nose and destroy everything she had come to live for. There would only be now.

"Emergency crews quickly brought the fire under control. There was no report of any casualties, but an airport representative said that passengers should count on delays of between two and nine hours."

The redhead took back the warmth. Kristina went all cold.

Hope extinguished.

Then she felt ashamed, lowered her gaze from the TV screen. First she had cheated on him, then she had wished him dead. Wished another human being dead. She felt ashamed, though she didn't think she ought to. The feeling of shame filled her once the warmth had disappeared, and all the rationalizing in the world could not stop her from feeling that she was bad. Who was she? Did she have no solid foundation?

"Am I not allowed to have any hopes, am I not permitted to wish for something better?" she said trying to defend herself. *Who am I after all, sitting here on the sofa in front of the TV, nurturing some ridiculous dream, instead of sitting on a train halfway to Bergen with that Kosta Boda vase packed in my bag and the car sold? Who the hell am I?*

She got up from the sofa, went over to Arvid's study and roused the computer from sleep mode by giving the mouse a push. Once the screen had faded up she opened Flight Tracker where she had already typed in Arvid's flight number. It was true what the red-haired lady on the TV screen had announced. Three-hour delay. He wouldn't be back in Visby until four at the earliest, later if the connecting flights from Stockholm were fully booked.

5.

The floor creaked beneath Anders Traneus as he stepped out onto the glass veranda. He didn't want to blame her, but his thoughts were going around in circles and with every lap they came back to the same place. To her. Kristina. That she really couldn't be trusted. Then he quickly stumbled on again. It was difficult to accuse someone you loved.

But he blamed himself more than anyone. He had shoved his head inside a hornet's nest for the second time. How stupid could he be? And then, inevitably, that's where he ended up: Was it stupidity or would he have done it anyway, even if he'd known how things would turn out?

Forty-seven years old. Life tapered off. Sometimes he thought he was still young. He felt young. His body was strong, showed no signs of the onset of old age, and over the last few years, he had to admit, his rather restricted life had opened up and become more filled with happiness. When he thought about how this happiness would soon be taken away from him, he felt that life did not offer much room for maneuver anymore. It was no longer very easy to change directions and start afresh. It was at moments like this that he really felt ancient.

On the other hand, he hadn't been very good at starting afresh back when he was eighteen, either. How long can someone who cast you off continue to haunt you?

Far too long.

Was that how it would end this time: a Monday at the beginning of October, while he, paralyzed, stared out uselessly across the gray-brown stubble field from the glass veranda he'd built himself.

The sun hung low in the sky and the light shone straight toward him. He saw that the entire field was covered in delicate webs of gossamer. An entire field. An unbelievable effort.

Paralyzed? Well, what was he supposed to do? Take her by force? He wasn't like that, that was more Arvid's style. Maybe that was how she wanted it. Maybe there was something wrong in her head that made her choose the one who treated her the worst? Or was that what a real man was to her: strong, ruthless?

He tried to suppress those thoughts. Idiotic reasoning. Bitterness.

He opened a window, brushed away a few dead flies from the sill with the back of his hand. The monotonous humming of the fan from Hedberg's feed silo was clearly audible today. The air stood still, as stuffy outside as it was inside.

When Inger left him he had become bitter. He had dwelled on it for a number of years. To think of all the things he had done for her. Even the glass veranda—it had been her idea, but he was the one who had built it. For her. It may not have gone so well with the rest of the house—it looked more like a modern birdhouse that had been stuck onto the big house from the twenties, but it was solidly built.

Then eventually it had lifted. Now he had to admit that she was right. She had been right to leave him. He had been fond of Inger, but hadn't been ready for her. He hadn't been able to get Kristina out of his mind, even though she had been unfaithful, even though she had jilted him. Inger never stood a chance against the memory of Kristina. And yet . . . for most of her adult life he had let her believe that he loved her. And perhaps he had done at times, for brief moments. There had been a lot of good things in their relationship . . . the children. But the feelings between them had always been lukewarm. His feelings toward her had been lukewarm.

Wasn't that also a kind of abuse, or at least an act of fraud?

Now it looked as if he'd be on his own again, in a quiet house out among the fields between Klintebys and Sanda. The children had all left home, busy with their own lives. That was as it should be. He couldn't burden them. But he felt so goddamn old.

For far too much of his adult life he had been under the impression that life would just continue. Now he had realized that that was not the case. It wasn't just that life was shorter than he had imagined. It also ended so much earlier.

WHAT WAS HAPPENING to her? It was dark. A pleasurable tickling sensation moved slowly up the length of her inner thigh, brushing gently against her vulva in two counterrotating motions, then up through her stomach, building into an intense feeling of arousal that spread through her entire body and made her start breathing more quickly.

What was going on with her? Was someone there with her? Anders? No, there was no one there. Was she touching herself? She almost became a bit embarrassed, as if she had caught herself in the act.

Where did she have her hands? Between her legs? No, one sticking straight out from her body, her forearm underneath the pillow where nobody slept, the other wedged uncomfortably behind her back. No, she was not touching herself. She had an invisible lover. She felt him moving inside her, gently and exquisitely slowly. And the tiniest movement sent jolts of pleasure surging through her entire body. It was like rapidly alternating showers of ice cold and scalding hot water, dangerous extremes constantly cutting each other off on the edge of pain, transforming torture into ecstasy.

He moved inside her and she could not resist moving toward him, close and closer . . .

But what was he doing to her? The slow, undulating movement seemed to go on forever, never turning the reversing, as if it was coming from inside, as if something were on its way out of her. She threw off the covers and sat up in the bed, completely naked, and stared between her splayed legs.

The glistening, jet-black snake eyes stared coldly into hers from the protrusions on the creature's head. Ice cold and unable to move she saw the zigzag pattern of the viper slither out from her vagina; her arousal vanished in an instant. The only physical sensation that remained felt like the cold from rocks plucked from so deep beneath the earth that they have not been touched by any warmth for a thousand years.

The scaly snakeskin glistened, greased by her vagina. It moved more quickly now that it was outside her, rustling softly as it coiled through her pubic hair, out over her stomach. She didn't feel the snake's movements, just that profound coldness rising up through her back from the depths of the earth.

It came ever closer, its head swaying gently back and forth apace with the movements propelling it forward. It reached her right breast, its black eyes seeming to see everything and nothing. It opened its gaping maw, bared its long fangs, and in the next moment it lunged. The snake's teeth sank deeply into her dark red areola and the pain . . .

Kristina opened her eyes. A few quick, panicked glances around the room to orient herself in time and space. The sofa in the living room, the afternoon sun low in the sky outside the window.

Her chest was heaving rapidly and convulsively. She sat up slowly, her left arm completely numb, her other hand reaching unconsciously for her breast beneath the sheer, white wool of her cardigan. Her mind was completely blank. Not a single thought except for the memory of the terror she had felt as the snake buried its fangs into her flesh.

Slowly she regained her composure. It was a dream, just a dream, just a dream, she repeated to herself. But what a dream! Where did things like that come from? The viper on the footpath the other day, that she could understand, but . . .

My God, what time was it? She struggled to raise her knitted left arm. Ten to four. She could just make it to the airport.

6.

Emrik Jansson stood with his back to the sun, both hands on the handlebars looking toward the main road. The main connecting road for the entire island. He was at the end of it. As far out as you could get, where the asphalt came to an end in front of a few heavy concrete blocks fitted with warning reflectors. Sure, he was way out there, but couldn't quite be discounted yet. It was as if you were allowed to sit down there on one of those concrete blocks and catch your breath for a moment before they tipped you over the edge.

Emrik usually went to sleep early and woke up early, often before night had become day. But last night he had hardly slept at all. His thoughts had kept him awake. It was silly for him to worry so much over something that, strictly speaking, wasn't any of his business, but that was probably hard to avoid when whatever could be considered your business no longer managed to fill up your time.

He was troubled and not without good reason, but what did he really expect to see or achieve by standing there like that? Kristina Traneus's car speeding past, a quick wave through the window, and then nothing more? That was about all he could expect to get out of this. A glimpse of Arvid Traneus in the same car?

Ridiculous old man, ought to go home and put myself to bed, went through his mind. He groped for his tobacco with yellowed fingers, but stopped himself. He felt weak from lack of sleep and wasn't sure whether another cigarette would brace him up or knock him onto his arse by the edge of the ditch. And if he did end up on his arse, he wouldn't be able to make it back onto his feet again without help. He knew that from experience and that was the last thing he wanted, for someone to have to come and pull him out of the ditch. Better to refrain altogether. He gripped the handlebars once more with both hands and shuffled forward a few yards. They should be popping up at any moment. Any moment now.

KRISTINA TRANEUS'S BIG SUV, a silver-gray Lexus, turned off the coast road at Klinte and continued on toward Hemse. If it was in fact her car, that is. She had gotten used to seeing it as her car having driven around in it for two years, but she was no longer the one behind the wheel.

Nearly half an hour had passed since she'd picked Arvid up at Visby airport. He had hugged her as soon as he had emerged from the exit for arriving passengers. Had pressed her hard against his big, solid frame, had to bend down when he whispered into her ear; a hoarse, growling whisper:

"Kristina, it's just you and me now."

His broad smile stretched and tugged at the skin.

She held on tightly to him, almost clung to him in order not to lose her footing. Felt how she became light headed.

"Just you and me." What did he mean by that? What did he see?

"Don't you have any more luggage?" she asked once she dared stand unsupported again and noticed his black leather briefcase and little carry-on bag on wheels.

"They're sending on the rest."

In the parking lot he held out his hand for the car keys.

"Aren't you tired?" she asked.

He had been traveling for twenty hours straight, if one counted the delay in London.

"Oh, no, I'm fine. I'll drive."

She immediately started to search for the keys in her purse.

Now he was sitting in the driver's seat of the car she had come to consider her own. They had taken the desolate route through the forest between Klinte and Levide, turned off toward Gerum and now only had the final stretch up to the farm left to go before they would be home.

"Christ, Emrik. How old is that guy gonna get?" Arvid mumbled.

Kristina hadn't even noticed the white-bearded former teacher of theirs at the side of the road; she was preoccupied with other things, plus she was used to the sight of him, unlike Arvid.

"He can barely walk anymore," she said absently.

They reached the sign and Arvid turned off toward the farm. Kristina laid her right hand on the armrest and drew in Arvid's scent through her nostrils. It was part him and part something unfamiliar, as was always the case when he returned from a trip. It was as if the smell she knew as Arvid had been diluted by something else. She had sat beside him in the car like that many times before and breathed in that smell thinking that very same thought. Yet the part of it that was him had always filled her with a powerful longing that swept away any other questions that had been weighing on her mind. If she had any doubts, they evaporated like dewdrops on a sunny July morning and all she could think about was how it would feel to be in his arms again, for the first time in days, weeks, or months. His naked arms wrapped around her naked body, hungry hands, his manhood throbbing against her belly. How she could take . . .

He coughed a few times and slowed down in front of the big house.

This time she felt none of that. She breathed in and sensed only the smell of alcohol and stale airplane breath. A hint of sweat.

What did he feel? Did she smell differently to him? Could he scent anything out?

ARVID PULLED UP on the paved driveway in front of the garage. He climbed out and went to get the bags out, but stopped short with the back door half open.

The place looked different.

He let go of the door and looked out across the garden in front of the white stone house. It was almost as if he'd parked in the driveway of the wrong house, but it was clearly his home. It was the right house, only it didn't feel right. Was it that he had been away long enough that the trees and bushes in the garden had had time to grow out? Or was it simply that he had been away for so long that his own house seemed unfamiliar to him?

"What do you think?"

Kristina. He heard her faintly, couldn't really take her in.

No, something *had* changed.

Once he'd worked it out, it was a mystery to him how he couldn't have picked up on it sooner. A stone footpath ran from the driveway over to the front door, parallel to the house. In the triangle between the path and the driveway bloomed a sea of crimson flowers, densely packed together like a thick carpet.

"What do you think?"

Kristina again. This time he heard her. Full of expectation.

"Well . . ."

He turned to look at her, but stopped short. For some reason he couldn't get the words out, just as his insipient smile stalled and died.

He turned his gaze toward the footpath and the flowers. There had been a gravel pathway there before. It had run diagonally across the lawn just where the newly planted flower bed shone an angry red.

"They're dahlias," said Kristina.

But there was something different in her voice now. It sounded more cautious.

"What's all this?" he said staring at the flowers.

She fingered the buttons on her blouse as she answered.

"I thought it would make a nice change."

Her gaze clung to him, trying to convey enthusiasm, but her wan smile was already begging his forgiveness.

"Change?"

"Yes?"

He shrugged his shoulders.

"I see," he said and lifted his bags from the car.

He took a few steps toward the limestone footpath, but stopped abruptly. He stood there completely still for a few seconds, and then, directed by an irresistible impulse, cut across toward the front door just as he would have done if the gravel path had still been there. He felt how it consumed him and controlled him, a combination of stinging disgust and anger. With heavy, resolute, but not overly long strides, he marched right across the flower bed. Stalks and red petals snapped and were crushed beneath his brightly polished black 47s.

PART TWO

O Gertrude, Gertrude,
When sorrows come, they come not single spies,
But in battalions.

—WILLIAM SHAKESPEARE

Saturday, October 28
Karolinska University Hospital, Solna

The man in the white coat bent down over Fredrik Broman and asked if he could tell him his name. Fredrik parted his dry lips, drew air into his lungs, flexed his diaphragm and his larynx in order to push out the necessary amount of air through the appropriate opening in his vocal cords. He shaped his lips. But no sound came out. Not because he couldn't coordinate all those movements and control his muscles correctly. Not because he was too weak or dazed. He remained silent because he did not know.

He didn't know his name.

And yet that wasn't quite true. He couldn't hear the words, but he saw them in front of him, not as letters but in a form that was obvious and close enough to touch, but at the same time impossible to translate into sound.

Then he came to think of the old Conservative Party leader, Gösta Bohman. Why? He was sure he wasn't Gösta Bohman. He was dead after all. Was his name Gösta? Or Bohman perhaps?

He had to say something. Had to show that he was with it in there, even if he didn't manage to transform those clear shapes into the appropriate sounds. He had to show that he was still in there.

A sinking feeling washed over him as the fantasy scenarios played out in his mind; how the doctors drew the wrong conclusions, decided that there was nothing more to be done and consigned him to a tiny room on some terminal ward where he would quickly be forgotten.

A fresh attempt. Anything. Diaphragm, vocal cords, lips.

"Bohman?" he said a little unsteadily.

The doctor smiled at him and then turned to his left toward the woman with the long, auburn hair, who was his wife.

"We're making progress."

7

Traneus's farm lay in Levide, right on the border between the parishes of Levide and Gerum, midway between Hemse and Klintehamn in southern Gotland. While most of the farms there were clustered together, Traneus's stood all by itself, on a few hectares of farmland, surrounded by forest. The rest of the property was scattered throughout the parish, divided into different parcels.

The main house was made up of two structures, one from the middle of the 1800s, the other from 1911, the latter built so that the older part formed the smaller annex of a single new house. The integrated structure was whitewashed and the roof laid with pantiles in a beautiful orange-red color that could be glimpsed through the verdant foliage of an imposing chestnut tree. Sixty or so yards behind the house stood a large barn and an old stable that had also been built in 1911.

Amanda Wahlby opened the kitchen door and stepped inside.

"Hello?" she called out, but wasted no time waiting for an answer.

She stepped out of her shoes, took out the plastic clogs from the bag she had brought with her and slipped her feet into them, hung up her jacket, and went into the bathroom to change out of her pink T-shirt into a white one with a washed-out print on the front that fit more loosely.

It was nine o'clock in the morning the first Friday in October. The sky was hidden behind a thin haze, the sun a yellow spot in the vast grayness. Amanda had been cleaning for Traneus for half a year, ever since the last cleaner had gone on sick leave due to some problem with her knees.

The routine was that she'd ring the doorbell twice. If no one came and opened the door she'd go inside, shout hello, and get started. She had a key, too, in case nobody was home, but she'd only needed to use that once since she started.

She shouted another hello on the way out to the kitchen. She lifted the vacuum cleaner out of the cleaning cupboard; grabbed some rags, cleaning fluid, a mop, and rubber gloves; filled a red pail with water and splashed two good dollops of Ajax into it.

Cleaning for the Traneuses was a good job, never much to tidy up and not much cleaning, either, really. She wondered why Kristina Traneus didn't just do it herself. It wasn't as if she had some job that took up all her time and seeing as she kept it so clean anyway . . . but then it wasn't Amanda's problem and she was grateful for the work.

She picked up the vacuum cleaner in one hand, stuck the mop under her arm, and grabbed the pail with the other hand. She usually started in the living room, vacuumed a few rooms at a time, dusted and wiped the floors, and carried on like that until she'd worked her way through the whole house, saving the kitchen and toilets for last. It usually took four hours. It was easy work but a lot of ground to cover.

She smelled it before she'd even passed the doorway into the living room. Vaguely sweet and pungent, a little sickening like . . . well, like what? Whatever it was, it was something that shouldn't be there. Perhaps just some cut flowers that had been allowed to stand too long in the same water; sometimes that could smell like the worst breath in the world. But it wasn't like Kristina Traneus to leave vases full of rotten flower water standing around.

Then she saw it. She dropped the bucket of soapy water. And then she vomited over one of the gray-velvet club chairs, unable to hold back.

8

Thwack! Fredrik's foot misconnected with the ball, sending it veering sharply off to the right instead of in toward the goal as he had intended. His colleagues on the opposing team grinned with schadenfreude.

"Take it down, Broman. You've gotta take the ball down, get control of it before you take a shot," grunted Ove Gahnström who had run in behind the left back with flushed cheeks expecting a cross pass.

Stick it up your ass, thought Fredrik, but put on a brave face.

Ove seemed to have already forgotten his screwup and was backpedaling toward his end of the field just as enthusiastically as when he'd been on offense, with the sweat glittering in his freshly cropped hair.

Some soccer nut had come up with the idea that they should start every Friday with a game of soccer as an alternative to playing floorball over at the old P18 garrison. Soccer wasn't Fredrik's favorite sport. He had never really been much of a fan, never played in any organized clubs like many of his colleagues, just kicked a ball around during recess at school. In fact, soccer was pretty far down on his list. When TV4 had run a commercial for a camera cell phone with David Beckham, Fredrik hadn't even recognized him, and had completely misunderstood the message, thought that it was some kind of gay joke he didn't get.

Fredrik wasn't much for team sports. He preferred track and field, tennis even. Team sports mostly just made him want to kick someone really hard in the shins.

They played on a dusty dirt field between Lyckåker school and the light-colored apartment buildings at Gråbo. Fredrik glanced at his watch. Fifteen minutes to go.

Simon had only recently started playing soccer at school. Despite his own lack of enthusiasm for the sport, Fredrik was glad that his son had started playing. Apart from the fact that it forced him to move around a bit it would also give him a natural rapport with the other boys. For a nine-year-old kid, the only way to gain acceptance was through soccer and a firm grasp of trivia about teams and all-star players. It seemed an inescapable fact of life.

Ove fired off a shot above the crossbar that crashed into the fence behind the goal.

Ten minutes left. He would have to pick up the pace a bit if he wanted to escape any more carping from Ove. Sara Oskarsson had the ball and was charging along his flank at high speed. She looked like a real pro in her shiny green soccer jersey and her black hair held firmly in place by two equally black rubber bands. She was really too fast for him, but he made a desperate rush and managed to take the ball away. He turned around in order to pass it to Gustav Wallin only to discover that Gustav was standing there talking on his cell phone. Someone had to be on call. They couldn't all put away their phones.

A second's hesitation was all that Sara needed. A sharp intake of air and a whiff of sweat shot past him, and then she was gone, along with the ball, but a moment later the game was over anyway. Gustav had raised his hand in the air like a soccer referee about to blow the whistle for a free kick and before he'd even said a word you could tell from looking at him that something serious had happened.

"Work!" he shouted.

Fredrik walked over toward Gustav panting. His lungs were still burning from his sprint. Gustav waited until everyone had gathered around before he gave them the details.

"Two dead bodies at a farm in Levide. It's murder, no question about it."

The other officers were still panting and catching their breath around Fredrik. Sara leaned forward and spit into the dirt.

"Just get changed and go," said Ove.

9.

"Is she the one who called it in, too?" asked Ove. He stood on the creaking strip parquet floor in the farm's ample living room and nodded out toward the patrol car parked in the forecourt.

Amanda Wahlby was sitting in the backseat and staring into the backrest in front of her. A uniformed officer was leaning in through the open door trying to speak to her.

"Yeah," said Fredrik, "She called from her cell phone, was standing over a hundred yards further down the road when the first officer arrived on the scene. Was too scared to stay up by the house, she said."

"No, well," said Ove, "that's understandable."

Ove was a sturdy man at five-ten and 187 pounds. He had weighed almost as much back when he was still an avid hockey player thirty-one years ago, but back then his pounds had a slightly different consistency and had been concentrated in other areas.

He looked at the two lacerated bodies, the woman on the floor by the couch, and the man way at the back in the far corner of the room, next to a toppled side table and a shattered lamp of frosted glass.

The room was accessed through a dining room that looked capable of accommodating twenty or more people. Immediately to the right as you entered the room, stood two gray armchairs next to a low, round table with four pillar-like legs, and a rosewood inlay in the top depicting two stags. Further inside the room stood two couches and two armchairs, all in the same light-colored fabric, placed around a brightly polished table with a white porcelain bowl as the only ornament.

"A lot of blood," said Fredrik.

"Yeah. He must be completely drained," said Ove and pointed at the body in the corner.

The man's head, which hung at an odd angle because of the partially severed throat, was completely ripped to shreds. His eyes were gone and what was left of his face was just a mass of blood and deep gashes. The hands were sliced halfway through and the rest of the body was covered in long, deep cuts. Portions of the man's entrails were hanging out from the gaping abdomen. Fredrik thought he could make out a sliver of the liver on the spilled-out peritoneum, but it wasn't easy to determine what was what. The body lay in an almost unbelievably large pool of dried blood, the trousers had become soaked a deep red.

The woman's body, on the other hand, just had a single deep cut, right across the chest, just under the heart. She had also bled heavily. Most of the blood had been soaked up by the large Persian carpet that looked like it had been passed down through generations.

The room smelled of vomit and rotten flesh. The haze outside had thickened, the day had become gray and bleak.

Ove was wearing a green windbreaker and a pair of worn-out jeans. Fredrik had left his jacket in the car, and was only wearing a dark-blue T-shirt and jeans, just as threadbare as Ove's, his service weapon attached to his right hip. Both had light-blue shoe covers on their feet.

As always, when Fredrik stood in front of dead people, he was struck by how gray and sunken they looked. All attempts at simulating death in movies and on TV were positively bursting with life by comparison. Real dead people looked more like discarded scraps. That sounded disrespectful, but that was what went through his head: refuse. All the life was gone. The bodies lying there on the floor bore little resemblance to anything human. It was a depressing thought, but it was also that very quality that made it bearable to stand there and look at them.

Fredrik raised his gaze from the two victims and gazed out through the window that faced the back of the house. He saw a well-grazed pasture with high fences beyond the beds of rhododendron and dead-headed late summer flowers that lay in desiccated piles next to a pair of garden shears with bright-red handles. The lawn was a trim and lush, deep green.

"A lot of blood and a lot of money," said Ove.

One didn't need to have read many glossy interior design magazines to realize that the Traneus family was well off. The house was big and it was obvious that someone had invested a lot of time and effort, as well as a whole lot of money, into furnishing the rooms, at least the ones Fredrik and Ove had had a chance to see. Everything was color matched and carefully considered down to the smallest detail. No sign of any Allen screws hinting at Ikea and DIY handiness.

"You think it's a robbery-killing?" asked Fredrik.

"Could be," said Ove a little lingeringly, "but I don't know how that fits in with it."

He pointed once again at the lacerated man.

Ove was right. The woman was one thing, she just had a single wound to the chest, but how could that explain the rage that had been directed at the man?

"Unexpected resistance, an unbalanced burglar," suggested Fredrik.

"Unbalanced," said Ove drumming his palm against his chest, "I don't know, he'd have to be pretty damn unbalanced if you ask me."

They heard rustling footsteps moving across the parquet floor as

Gustav Wallin entered the room. A slightly comical entrance in a well-tailored, dark-brown suit with a discrete black pattern, that clashed badly with the light-blue shoe covers.

"Do you think the horses might need water? I mean, if those two have been lying here for a few . . ."

Gustav stopped talking when he caught sight of the bodies.

"Someone's seeing to it," said Ove.

Gustav still said nothing. The first look at the victims had also caused Fredrik to go silent. If the victims' bodies were pale and mute, the room itself was positively bellowing, screaming out all the violence and hate that must have exploded in the killer.

"Do we know who they are?" said Gustav finally.

"The woman is Kristina Traneus, registered as living at this address, as for the man . . . ?"

Fredrik left his sentence hanging. The mutilated body spoke for itself.

"The cleaning woman recognized Kristina Traneus, but couldn't say who the man was," he continued. "She only got a quick glimpse of him and doesn't seem to be in the mood to come in for a closer look."

"No, well, you can hardly blame her," said Gustav. "But there is a Mr. Traneus?"

"Yes, Arvid Traneus. They have two children, according to the cleaner, but neither of them lives at home."

"So it's a fair guess that that's Arvid lying there?" asked Gustav and wrinkled his nose.

"Yeah, I guess," said Ove and ran his hand over his black crew cut, which he had apparently not yet gotten used to.

Gustav took a step to the side.

"There are three different routes you can take to get here; two from the north and one from the south, the way we came."

Ove looked up at him.

"An ideal spot for a murder."

Gustav nodded and looked down at the bodies again. They stood there silently for a long moment. A fly came buzzing around and landed on the dead woman's arm. Ove shooed it away.

"Rage . . . almost derangement and a fair bit of strength," said Gustav.

"Depends a bit on the tool, too," said Fredrik.

"The tool?"

"Well, it's not very usual for people to run around with swords, so unless the killer is a maniac with a cutlass, it ought to be some kind of a tool."

Suddenly there was something that disturbed their concentration: a voice that was speaking far too loudly and footsteps that were moving far too quickly to fit in with the ordinary activities of a crime scene investigation. All three of them reacted, by turning toward the hall and looking at the front door as someone tugged at the handle.

"YOU LET GO of me! Let go!"

It took two young, strapping police officers to keep the man, who looked like he was a bit over seventy, away from the door. He braced his feet against the ground and pushed his way forward with his shabby-looking suede jacket pulled inside out down over his shoulders.

"You've got to let me inside."

His wild eyes were fixed on the farmhouse, seeing nothing but the door that Ove had just shut behind him. His face was white with small red splotches down around his throat, his breathing was labored and gasping.

Ove, Gustav, and Fredrik hurried over to their uniformed colleagues who were struggling with the man. Fredrik tried to catch the man's eyes, stood right in his way, but the man stared right through him.

"Why do you want to go in here?" asked Fredrik, but the hoary old man didn't respond.

"You'd better answer the question," Gustav continued.

"We've tried," panted one of the officers who was trying to keep the man still.

The white-haired man started to nod over to his side, toward the two cars parked in the driveway.

"That's his car. His car's standing right there, don't you understand? If he's in there I'm going to kill the bastard, I'm gonna kill him!"

He had a powerful voice and he was shouting at the top of it, but it also sounded like his voice could seize up at any moment in despair.

Ove made a tired expression.

"Put him in a car and let him sit there till he's calmed down."

The officers gave a strained nod and struggled to drag the obstreperous, wriggling man toward the patrol car. Using gentle force, they managed to stow him in the backseat. Gustav followed after him and opened the front door on the passenger side. He leaned in through the opening.

"Who is it you think is in there?" he asked him softly, almost whispering.

"My son. That's his car. That's his car standing there."

The man's voice suddenly sounded pleading, as if he desperately wanted the five policemen gathered around him to contradict him, to convince him that he was mistaken, put him in a car and drive him away.

Fredrik and Ove stood silently off to the side, didn't want to disturb right when Gustav seemed to be making some kind of contact.

"And your son, who is he?" asked Gustav.

It took a while for the man to answer, as if he hadn't quite understood that he was expected to provide a name. His voice was dampened by the upholstery. Gustav only caught "Traneus" and leaned in further.

"Arvid Traneus?" he asked.

It was like flipping a switch. The man threw himself at the door and tried to get out. When he noticed that the door was locked he tried to scramble out between the front seats, but was stopped by the uniformed officer in the car.

"Arvid! If that's my son in there, if that's Anders lying dead in there, then it's him. Then Arvid's the one who did it. If that's my son, then he's the one. He's capable of anything . . ."

Gustav looked at Fredrik and Ove, but there was nothing in their expressions to suggest that they had understood anything more of what the man had said than he had himself.

"So you're not Arvid Traneus's father?" he asked.

"Me?" the man bellowed and spat on the floor.

Gustav recoiled.

"This is getting us nowhere," he muttered.

"Arvid!" the man hissed. "Arvid! He's your murderer."

Gustav slammed the door shut and turned his back on the patrol car, relieved to not have to sit in the car with that raving old man.

"How the hell did he find out about this?" asked Fredrik.

"Don't ever underestimate the Gotland grapevine," said Ove.

Fredrik regarded the man who one could just make out between the reflections in the side windows of the patrol car.

"Yeah, sure, but I wonder why it is that once the rumor reached him he immediately jumped into his car and drove over here to find out if it was his son that had been murdered?"

Sunday, October 29
Karolinska University Hospital, Solna

Sara Oskarsson stood with her back to Fredrik and saw the door to the hospital ward swing closed, gently and silently. Ever since she was a little girl, she had held the firm belief that hospitals had a particular smell about them, and that it wasn't an especially pleasant smell. Now she suddenly realized that they didn't smell at all. They were spotlessly clean, dust free, and odorless.

She became aware of Fredrik's breathing and turned around. He looked at her, and as she took a few steps toward the foot of the bed, caught a glimpse of herself in the mirror above the sink, of her black hair that she'd let grow down over her shoulders. Fredrik followed her with his eyes. That must be a good sign. But then again, the question was of course whether he recognized her, or was just registering movement?

It was hard for the doctors to provide a meaningful prognosis. They made it sound as if he could just as well make a complete recovery as remain in his present state indefinitely. His brain had suffered a shock and had been under pressure, and it was as yet impossible to say if he had sustained any permanent damage. But he was headed in the right direction.

Fredrik's head was shaved on the left side, the still unhealed scar from the operation covered by a compress and a white bandage that had been wrapped around his head like the headband of a sushi chef. Then on top of that, a kind of semitransparent sock reminiscent of some cool rap artist. Except for the fact that Fredrik really didn't look especially cool. But it helped to think like that, made it easier to look at him.

Fredrik was one of her closest colleagues, originally from Stockholm just like her. When she first arrived in Visby she thought that it was nice to have someone she could talk to without having to be afraid of stepping on any local toes, which was all too easy to do, she had noticed. Not so much among her colleagues at work, but in other situations. As an outsider from the mainlander and a figure of authority, she was sometimes met with double hostility.

She wasn't so sure anymore. About Gotland. Once the enthusiasm of the first year had faded, things became harder. She liked her job, there was no problem there. In the beginning she had been worried that her work assignments might prove to be too trivial, but in hindsight she could have done with a bit less excitement. Two summers ago she had stood in another hospital room in front of another colleague who lay there with a broken arm and his body all covered in bruises after a bomb had gone off on one of the ferries.

Her life outside the police station may not have seemed too bad to an outside observer. She had gotten to know some people, had one relationship under her belt, and had recently started seeing a man on a more regular basis.

But still. It was difficult to really be accepted. There was a fundamental difference between city and countryside, or small town, if you were talking about Visby. In a big city, most everyone was just as rootless and stressed—quick to dismiss you to be sure, but also curious and open to trying out something new. In a big city, life could turn on a dime, here it took at least five years for anything to turn. In that sense it was probably easier for someone from Stockholm to feel at home in Amsterdam, Berlin, or Copenhagen than in Visby. Here there were so many old bonds between people. It was as if everything was written in stone and to make so much as a single scratch on your own was almost impossible. Younger people were a little easier to deal with, but she was thirty-four now and couldn't run around like some overage groupie among twenty-seven-year-olds forever.

She couldn't claim that life in the big city was better than in a small town, but life in Stockholm was different from life in Visby, and it was the kind of different that she was used to. Maybe it was too late to learn new tricks.

She was woken from her thoughts by Fredrik suddenly mumbling off a long string of words.

"What?" said Sara without thinking.

The words were disjointed, didn't make any sense. Was it even an attempt to say anything coherent?

She got no answer to her "What?"

Just a moment ago it had felt so natural to sit down beside the bed and speak to him, but now that it was just the two of them in the room she felt unsure. The situation had become so intimate all of a sudden.

For a moment she had almost regretted offering to sit alone with Fredrik for a while so Ninni could go down and get a cup of coffee in the cafeteria or a breath of fresh air, or whatever she wanted to do. After Fredrik's, well, what would you even call it . . . fling . . . with Eva Karlén, it wouldn't be strange if Ninni felt a little uncomfortable with his female colleagues. But apparently Ninni could tell the difference between apples and oranges, because she had just nodded and smiled gratefully.

Sara had of course been forced to lie to her, but it was the same white lie that she had told everyone else, except for Göran Eide, and wasn't something that weighed on her conscience.

10.

Gustav drove while Fredrik sat in the backseat next to the previously raving man whom they had by now managed to identify as Rune Traneus. They were on their way over to see one of Rune's grandchildren, Sofia Traneus-Helin. She lived in town, Visby that is, in an apartment in Gråbo.

Rune Traneus sat silently next to Fredrik in the backseat hanging his head and staring at his hands that lay cupped in each other in his lap. He was as glum and inert now as he had been out of control just a short time ago.

Fredrik felt a sense of panic rising within him as he thought about what he would say to Sofia Traneus. Almost worse than having to notify someone of the death of a loved one, was having to inform someone that their father might be dead, but that they didn't know for sure.

Of course he couldn't do that. He would have to proceed on the basis of Rune's reaction. They had found a dead man that her grandfather for some reason suspected was his son, Sofia's father. No, that was no good, either. And then there was the car, of course. They had run a check on the plates and it was true, it belonged to Anders Traneus.

"What was it that made you go out there?" Fredrik tried asking him.

Rune Traneus didn't respond.

"I mean, how could you be so sure that you would find your son there?"

Silence. Had he even heard the question? He seemed to be somewhere else entirely.

They reached Visby, turned off toward Gråbo between the ICA

supermarket and the Sibylla hamburger grill and stopped outside one of the pastel-checkered fifties row houses on Allégatan. Across the street stood a long string of redbrick houses, all identical.

Fredrik had heard Visby residents say that "once you end up in Gråbo, you never get out" and then complain about how far away it was from the center. It was true that it was a neighborhood you never went to unless you had a reason to go there, but it wasn't more than a few extra minutes' walk into town compared to Öster, for example, and as far as Fredrik could tell it looked pretty nice.

But presumably it wasn't the charming houses from the fifties, but rather the ones from the seventies in the center of Gråbo that had given rise to the neighborhood's unfavorable reputation, thought Fredrik when he rang Traneus-Helin's doorbell.

The woman who opened the door looked to be somewhere between twenty-five and thirty years of age, and could have been a model for the essence of Swedishness, or at least the perception of it. Tall, slender—yet sturdy—flaxen-haired and blue-eyed, steadfast lips that stood guard in front of two even rows of white teeth. She had a two-month-old baby on her arm, naked except for a diaper. A girl of about three peeked out from a doorway a ways inside the apartment.

"Gramps," the little girl cried out and came running toward them, but slowed down and faltered about halfway, frightened either by the strange men or by the fact that her great-grandfather didn't seem to take any notice of her.

Rune Traneus stared vacantly at his filial granddaughter.

"Grandpa, what's wrong?" asked Sofia Traneus and then turned to Fredrik questioningly, when she noticed that she wasn't getting an answer.

Fredrik and Gustav already had their badges out and introduced themselves.

"I can't help thinking that something terrible must have happened, seeing you show up like this. Something I don't want to hear," said Sofia.

She hoisted her baby a little higher and pulled it closer to her.

"There *has* been a very serious incident, but whether it has any connection to you, we don't yet know. But with a little help we should be able to sort it out," said Fredrik. "Could we come in for a moment?"

"Sure, come in," said Sofia.

Fredrik saw how her expression changed from an initial look of confusion to one of apprehension of impending calamity. It turned in on itself and became completely exposed all at the same time. He had seen that transformation many times before.

They all went into the sunny kitchen, the girl with a firm grip at the knee of her mother's jeans. After having sat Rune Traneus down on one of the chairs at the kitchen table, Fredrik gave Sofia a quick rundown of events, in a manner that was both as sensitive as possible while at the same time being as unintelligible as possible for the three-year-old.

"Your grandfather seems to think that one of the victims could be your father. We haven't quite been able to work out why that is, nor have we found anything specific to suggest that to be the case."

Rune Traneus shook his head slowly. Apparently he had absorbed something of what they had said. Sofia looked at him with glistening eyes and sank down on the chair opposite him.

"Grandpa?" she whispered.

Fredrik hadn't said anything about Anders Traneus's car having been parked outside the house. There was absolutely no reason to bring that up just then. Sofia Traneus was worried enough as it was.

"Do you have any idea why your grandfather might think that?"

Sofia looked up at Fredrik and it was clear that she didn't have the slightest idea.

The girl crawled up into her lap without it occurring to Sofia to help her, and soon she was sitting there burdened with both children. The three-year-old leaned her head against her mother's chest, hugged her mother's arm and peered timidly at her great-grandfather.

"Mommy? Mommy?"

"Yes, sweetie, it's all right. Mommy just has to speak to these gentlemen here a little bit."

Fredrik looked at the three generations sitting around the table and gave up any ambitions he had of questioning the woman properly. This wasn't the right moment.

"Do you have a photograph of your father? A fairly recent one. That would be very helpful," he said and wondered at the same time if they would have much use of a photograph given the condition of the face.

Sofia nodded and stood up. The girl slid down from her lap and grabbed hold of her right leg with both arms.

"I should have something, I guess."

She shuffled out of the room with her daughter clinging to her leg like a monkey.

"Please, Emma," she said helplessly and shuffled on.

Fredrik and Gustav looked at each other, and just then came a loud crash from the kitchen table as Rune Traneus slammed his fists down full force onto the table.

"That bastard. He's a bastard. Him and that goddamn father of his. Murderers."

"Mommy!" Emma cried out in fright from the next room and then started sobbing loudly.

Rune Traneus had stood up and was glaring at Fredrik and Gustav, while he shouted out his words, only they didn't quite come out as real shouts. It was as if they had run into some kind of resistance, smothered by a deep and powerful anguish.

Gustav had already moved next to Rune in order to, if necessary, restrain an outbreak like the one they had witnessed earlier outside the house. But it was already over. Rune Traneus stood there rooted to the spot, his gaze confused, his blue lower lip trembling. An old, frail man. Gustav gently took hold of his extended left arm and helped him sit back down again.

"I'll go in there," said Fredrik softly.

When he entered the living room, Sofia Traneus was squatting on the floor, trying to comfort her clinging, sniveling daughter. The girl's cheeks were flushed from crying.

Sofia looked up at him with anxious, wide-open eyes.

"There's nothing to worry about," he said, "for the moment anyway . . . But Rune was very upset when he came to the house. Do you think you can manage this? Is there anyone who could come here and help you? Or else . . . maybe we should take him with us. To a doctor, I mean."

"I'll be all right," she said after thinking for a moment. "I'll call my husband. He can be here in five minutes."

"And Rune?"

"It's better if he stays here."

She fell silent.

"The photograph," Fredrik reminded her after a moment. "If it's not too much trouble?" he said glancing at the child. "We can always get a copy of his passport."

"Oh, no, I know where I've got one."

She managed to free herself from Emma and sat her down on the couch together with the baby. The girl stayed there while Sofia quickly walked over and unlocked the bottom cabinet of the bookcase.

"Here," said Sofia and returned with an open photo album in dark-red imitation leather.

It was a group photo with five people neatly lined up in front of the camera. Fredrik immediately recognized Sofia and Rune. In his eyes the woman next to him was little more than a girl in the picture, eighteen or nineteen maybe.

"It's five years old, but it's still a good likeness. Then there's my brother and my mother. It was taken at my father's birthday. Two months later they got divorced."

She worked one of her clear-coated nails in underneath the edge of the photograph.

"The only question is whether I can get it off."

Fredrik was about to suggest that they just borrow the whole album, so she didn't have to ruin it, when the photo ripped free from the black construction paper.

She handed over the picture. He took it and tried to avoid touching the glossy surface, more out of respect for Sofia than concern for the photograph.

"Does your father have any distinguishing marks that you know of? By that I mean scars, tattoos, that kind of thing?"

She let out a laugh.

"Tattoos?"

"For example," said Fredrik.

She shook her head and looked at him with a slightly dubious expression, as if he had asked her something inappropriate.

"It's better if you ask my mother about that."

Ninni was in the car, on her way from Havdhem to Hablingbo in the dirty gray twilight. The drizzle had made the road wet. The tires spattered loudly and the wipers swept across the windshield at the longest interval setting.

She was driving fast along the winding road, too fast she felt and lightened the pressure on the gas pedal. She didn't want anything to happen to her, too. She had to look after herself. Be strong. But where would she get the strength from?

She had left Simon and Joakim at Anneli's on Karlbergsvägen and taken the ferry back to Gotland to take care of a few things at work. Maybe also just to get a chance to breathe a little. Not to have to be strong for a moment. Maybe so she could have a breakdown. She wasn't sure. There was so much to think about, to take responsibility for. How long could they stay in Stockholm? What was best for the kids? How long could they be away from school? How long would it take before Fredrik was well enough to be moved to Visby? Would he even be able to receive the care that he needed there? Should she and the kids be moving up there instead?

She had climbed into the car at the Högby school parking lot. She had planned on driving home, but continued south and now she was on her way to Hablingbo. On her way? No, she wasn't on her way anywhere. She was just driving. She was *on the road* between Havdhem and Hablingbo, but that was all you could say with any certainty.

She had pinned her hair up behind her neck so that it wouldn't be so obvious how matted and dirty it was. It had been several days since she last put on any makeup, but there were faint shadows of smeared

mascara on her eyelids. She wished that she had a cigarette. She had
quit smoking eighteen years ago, but now she wished that she had a
full pack of wonderful cigarettes to light up and inhale to put a fog
between herself and reality.

The car rolled the last few feet up to the stop sign next to the electrical goods store in Hablingbo. If it had still been a supermarket she
could have stopped and bought cigarettes. But it seemed as if everything closed down on this godforsaken island. Everyone shut up shop,
moved away.

Ninni turned left out onto the coast road without really knowing
why, guided by a vague yet persistent feeling.

And how about that whole thing with Mother?! Ninni had asked her
for help. *How fucking stupid was that?* She should have known better
and spared herself the disappointment. Mother was playing a key role
at some conference or other, and then she would be flying off to Hel-
sinki for two days, and then her best friend was coming to visit her all
the way from Umeå—and that had already been booked a long time
ago—for about a week or so, at least over the weekend.

Ninni shuddered inside and nearly burst into tears, but she pulled
herself together, didn't let it get beyond a short sniveling.

Mother had made no attempt to hide her disappointment when
Ninni told her that she was moving to Gotland. She would have so far
to travel to see her and the kids. And Ninni had felt guilty, that she was
robbing her mother of something that meant a lot to her. It was only
after they had moved that she realized that her mother almost never
had time for them. On those rare occasions when she did have time, it
was always on her terms, when a little opening had appeared in her
chockablock schedule.

The wiper motor squeaked, the tires spattered. Where was she going? She didn't know.

She had a goal, she felt it, but she couldn't see it in front of her and after nearly an hour of driving around aimlessly, she pulled up in front of her own house. Pitch dark and deserted.

She unlocked the door, wriggled out of her coat, tossed it onto a chair in the kitchen, and sat down on another one. She stared vacantly at the dirty dishes in the sink.

The big question was whether the bleeding between his skull and brain had cut off the supply of oxygen before they had managed to reduce the pressure. The CAT scan looked good, but it didn't show everything the little woman doctor with the peppercorn eyes had explained. The more she had explained, the more Ninni sensed that the brain was unknown territory even for doctors. Wait and see, was the order of the day. There was nothing to suggest that Fredrik couldn't make a complete recovery, but at the same time they couldn't promise anything. In any case, she had to prepare herself for a long convalescence, at least six months, maybe even a year or more.

Maybe she just wanted to step out of her own life.

Easier said than done.

She sat in still silence as the minutes ticked by. Alone there in that empty house it was almost as if she was removed from her life. At least she could pretend that she was for a brief moment.

Then she suddenly understood where she had been on her way to. That vague persistent feeling in the pit of her stomach had been urging her to seek out a place of her own. Now she saw it: the low rocks beyond the pier where her parents had their summerhouse in the Stockholm archipelago. Bedrock that she had sat on every summer from when she was seven years old right up until they moved to Gotland. Or maybe the rocky outcrops at Hellas in Nacka, that she had swum from and set off on skating excursions with Jocke when he was little. She wanted to sit on solid, familiar bedrock and look out across the water, not on some brittle goddamn limestone that fell apart as soon as you looked at it.

She got up with a jolt and grabbed the first things she could get her hands on, a pepper mill of brushed steel that she had been given as a fortieth birthday present by distant relatives, and threw it with all her might at the kitchen cupboards.

"Goddamn you!" she screamed.

The pepper mill smashed a nasty hole in one of the cupboard doors and the little plastic container that kept the peppercorns in such a viewing-friendly manner, broke into pieces that went skittering across the floor with a rustling sound. Not unlike what you hear when a gust of wind shakes the water from a tree top after it's rained.

"Goddamn you!" she shouted again and threw a hot dish holder and the pile of newspapers immediately after it. "Don't you dare die on me now! And don't you dare become some fucking vegetable that I have to spoon-feed for the rest of my life! You hear me?"

She remained standing there with her hands clenched, fixing for a fight, as if she were ready to have it out with life itself.

It just couldn't end up that way. She had been dragged to this god-damn island half against her will. She had just started to feel a little bit at home—despite the drawbacks—thanks very much to her job and colleagues at the school. As a teacher you quickly worked your way into a community, made contacts, and gained stature. But it was also because of her job that they had ended up so far out in the country-side, over thirty miles from town.

What the hell was she doing here?

Was it her destiny to rot away in a limestone house in the middle of nowhere with a husband who couldn't wipe his own ass? It just couldn't end up that way.

11

The October sun had risen up higher into the sky. The day had become mild and clear.

"Wonderful day," said Gustav as they sat in the car. "First, two people cut to shreds, then a grandpa with a screw loose."

"Let's see how much fun we have at the ex-wife's house," said Fredrik and steered the car toward Södercentrum.

He was hungry, had eaten too little breakfast as usual.

"We'll have enough time to grab a quick lunch after Inger Traneus, right?" he asked and Gustav nodded.

"So what do you think?" Gustav then asked. "You think Rune Traneus is right?"

"Unless the guy's completely nuts, then I guess he must have a good reason for reacting the way he did. But we didn't get anything useful out of him.

"His son's car was parked outside, there's no escaping that. But it could just as well be Arvid Traneus lying hacked to pieces inside the house."

"More likely even," said Gustav.

"In which case Anders Traneus's car points in a different direction altogether."

INGER TRANEUS LOOKED like her daughter. Tall and slim with the same long hair, more gray than blonde, in a tight ponytail. A beautiful woman just over fifty.

Once again, Fredrik explained the reason for their visit, the sensitive

version, but was spared the trouble of having to try and make it incomprehensible to a three-year-old.

They were sitting crammed into an office at the Department of
Childcare and Education at Söderport. Fredrik had seen that office
innumerable times before, both at public agencies as well as in the
private sector: about seventy square feet, a desk in birch veneer, a
glass wall hung with thin cotton curtains looking out on the corridor.
It could have been his own office at the police station.

"Rune Traneus seems convinced that Anders is the dead man in
the house. Do you have any idea why he might think that?"

Inger Traneus lowered her head and looked down at her lap. Fredrik
thought he glimpsed a vague smile. She shook her head, then looked
up at them with a gaze that was somewhere else, tired, guarded.

"Why don't you ask him?"

"We already have," said Fredrik, "but now we're asking what you
think?"

His natural impulse was to be more open and forthright, show
more empathy, but if things were as Gustav had suggested, that the
answers were to be found within the family, it was better not to reveal
more than was necessary.

"I was together with Anders for twenty-two years. We were married and lived under the same roof for twenty of those. But I never got
to know him especially well. I thought I knew him, but then I discovered that I didn't know him at all."

There was that smile again, only it wasn't so much a smile as a
strained grimace.

"I'm not sure I understand," said Fredrik honestly.

"Well, what is there to understand?" said Inger Traneus inwardly
and stretched her neck. "I don't understand myself."

Fredrik decided to wait her out. The hard drive under the table
started whirring. The sound was drowned out a moment later by a loud
laugh out in the corridor, Inger's colleagues on their way out to lunch.

"If it is Anders lying . . . If it is him, then it's only logical that Kristina became the death of him. And he of her. Romantic, huh?" she said and moved her gaze back and forth between Fredrik and Gustav.

That didn't make things any clearer for Fredrik, and he was just about to ask what there was between Kristina Traneus and Anders when Inger's head fell forward again, and she started weeping.

She held her thumb and forefinger above her eyebrows as if she wanted to press back her tears. The long ponytail slid slowly down the front of her shoulder, strands of hair getting caught in her woolen sweater along the way.

"We don't know for certain," said Fredrik. "It's very possible that we've upset you completely unnecessarily."

They could just as well do this later, just concentrate on what was most important: finding out who it was lying sliced to pieces on the living room floor at Kristina and Arvid Traneus's house.

"We're heading back south. If you'd like we can give you a ride home?"

She shook her head.

"It's not Anders I'm crying about. It's all those wasted years. How you can waste your life so single-mindedly on someone who doesn't want you?"

They fell silent. What can you say? Fredrik wished that he could say something. Instead it was Gustav who broke through the gloom.

"It's better at least than single-mindedly staying together with someone you don't want."

Fredrik glanced at his colleague out of the corner of his eye. Sometimes he could surprise you. Inger Traneus also looked at Gustav and gave a little smile, a real one this time. Then she got up, turned her back to them, and wiped her tears.

"God how pathetic," she mumbled. "Me, that is," she added over her shoulder, in Gustav's direction.

"Our main reason for coming here was actually to ask you whether Anders has any distinguishing marks or scars, that could help us to identify him. If it is him."

She needed to think about it for a moment.

"He's got a brownish-red birthmark just above his right knee, about the size of a fifty-öre piece."

12.

Elin Traneus dropped a Treo Comp effervescent analgesic tablet into a glass of water on the bedside table. She didn't have a headache, yet, but could feel how it was lurking there ready to pounce. For the moment her entire world was wrapped up in a gray haze, but just the sound of the tablets dissolving made her feel perkier.

She looked out across the room in the ridiculously small apartment that she had been subletting since New Year's. The room where she would sleep, study, socialize, and look at TV was about fifty square feet. Beyond that there was a corridor of a kitchen, an intestine-like hallway, and a miniscule bathroom. The apartment was on the third floor of a building on Atterbomsvägen in Fredhäll. And Fredhäll was on the island of Kungsholmen, right in the center of Stockholm, although she had soon learned that it was the part of Kungsholmen that anyone living in the center of the capital didn't recognize as being part of Kungsholmen.

"Oh, I see, in Fred*häll*," they had corrected her with polite smiles when she had explained where exactly on Kungsholmen she was living. What inevitably followed was the obligatory, "It's a really neat area, Atterbomsvägen." That she had also learned. The inner suburbs were always "really neat." Totally unhip, but really neat. The outer suburbs weren't even really neat; "pretty nice" possibly, and when you got as far out as suburbs like Alby and Tensta they had nothing to say at all.

Her building was actually wonderfully situated on top of a high cliff with a view out over Riddarfjärden, even if the only thing Elin ever saw from her apartment was the light yellow facade of the building next door.

She was happy with her apartment, loved it in fact, even though she had grown up with closets that were as big. She couldn't care less what the inner-city crowd thought. It was her life, not theirs.

The Treo tablet had finished fizzing. Elin downed the contents of the glass and reached for her cell phone. She dialed her mother's number, but waited in vain for her to pick up.

"Damn it," she said out loud and threw off the blanket that she'd wrapped herself up in.

She had been trying to get hold of her mother since yesterday afternoon with no luck. It was as if her mother could sense that she was going to wriggle out of it and refused to answer. Elin checked the time on her cell phone. There was no way she was going to make it over there in time by ferry. She considered calling Ricky and letting him deal with it, but then decided to head out to Bromma airport and try to fly standby. That usually worked.

She slid out of her pajamas and stood naked in front of the hall mirror. Her hair was dyed black, but was actually a dull mousy blonde underneath. Her brother and sister had gotten real blond hair, while she'd ended up with her drab color. Otherwise, she looked pretty okay, she thought, even if her breasts were maybe a bit on the small side, and her stomach wasn't quite flat. And then she was short, of course. She could feel very unremarkable next to five-eight girls in four-inch fashion heels. But there were a lot of guys who liked small girls. It made them feel more manly.

Not that she'd had a lot of boyfriends. Her relationships were few and short-lived, and she was usually the one who broke them off. So she couldn't exactly complain. She wanted to be seduced. Always. Every time. Why did the guys she met always think they had free access to her body just because she had given in once? That she would want to make love to someone who wasn't ready to conquer her again each time he stepped through the door? Was that asking too much? Anyway, those were her conditions.

She felt the impulse to crawl back into bed and touch herself, but decided that she didn't have time. She climbed into the shower instead.

Mother had called and told her that Father was coming home. That was a week ago. More or less. Of course she had wanted Elin to come down. Elin had been noncommittal. Said that it depended on how her studies were going, and Mother had of course pointed out that she could bring her books with her and study down there. Because it would so nice if . . .

As if she could find enough peace and quiet in that house to read so much as two lines. But she didn't say that. They were going to speak later. And Mother called and pressured her and Elin had given in and promised to come, but then she had called to say that she couldn't come after all, but hadn't been able to get hold of her and couldn't get herself to just leave a message on the answering machine.

"It would be so nice to sit down at the same table all together. We haven't done that in so long."

How could she say something like that? Did she mean one single word of what she said?

Elin turned up the cold water and raised her face into the shower stream, felt how her skin got covered in goosebumps. The shampoo smelled of apple.

All together. Yes, it had been a long time since they had all sat down together at the same table. It was true. Maybe the only thing that was true. Ten years ago. And they would never be all together again. Did she realize what she was saying? Didn't she hear her own words? Never again would they ever be able to sit down, all together, at the same table. Elin pulled her fingers through her hair and down over her face as if she wanted to claw away the thoughts, then let the cool water run over her.

It felt good to have water that wet you right down to the skin, enveloped you, didn't just bounce off you like the hard water on Gotland.

Was it Mother's eternal duty to always try to make things better? Whatever the cost? Sure her intentions may have been good, but when your good intentions made you blind, what was the point?

Elin had been shocked when she heard that her father was coming home. Actually on his way. She wondered what her mother was thinking. She had wanted to ask, but hadn't had the courage, had tried to be as sensitive as possible, listen to every pause, every breath, but hadn't been able to detect anything that revealed what Mother was really feeling.

When Father first began spending more and more time away in Tokyo, Elin had taken the opportunity to get a room in Visby, like so many other kids her age who commuted to the high school there. Father hadn't said anything. She wasn't sure that he'd even been told.

Then, once she'd turned eighteen, there was nothing to stop her. She moved to Stockholm. Worked for a year in a café in the center of town, an awful place to work with a constant turnover of stressed customers you never saw twice, an obnoxious and sometimes downright mean boss who scared away his employees. When Elin quit after a year, none of the people working with her had been there for as long as she had. She went to Thailand on vacation, took a bus to Cambodia and saw Angkor Vat, had sex on a beach and got blisters, came home and enrolled at Stockholm University. She studied French for two semesters. She couldn't say that she regretted it, she spoke French fluently now, but it had still sort of been a waste of time and definitely a result of cowardice. She hadn't dared to make a serious start and now that she had finally chosen a five-year degree program it meant that she was no longer eligible for financial aid covering the full five years. She had heard that you could get a special dispensation, but she wasn't sure. People said so many things. Oh, well . . . She was just six weeks into her psychology degree and her financial aid wouldn't run out for another five years almost. She could survive one semester without financial aid one way or the other. There was no reason to get worked up about it.

Her father would most likely give her money, but he was the last person she wanted to ask. The last person on earth.

She turned off the water. She had been standing in the shower far too long. Her skin was so tight that you could almost hear it crackling. She put cream on, wrapped herself in a towel, and removed the wineglass that was still standing on the coffee table from last night. A dried film of red wine remained underneath.

She and Molly had drunk a couple of glasses of wine at El Mundo yesterday, before Molly was going off to meet her boyfriend. Elin had become friends with Molly after only a few weeks in French class. Molly was her closest friend in Stockholm and they met a few times a week, although it was a little less often now that Molly had a boyfriend. Or else the evenings became shorter, like yesterday, and Elin had to round things off by herself in front of the TV.

She tossed a change of clothes, some underwear, her vanity bag, and two psychology books into her black leather shoulder bag from Prada. Her father had brought it from Tokyo as a belated birthday present about a year ago. It was the third time she had used it.

Each time she boarded the ferry or the plane it was as if she shed her skin. She put on the clothes that her parents expected her to be wearing, wore purses and jewelry she never used otherwise. And started speaking in a Gotland dialect again.

She was going to stay two days max.

She put the opened Bag-in-Box wine into a plastic shopping bag, and then left.

THE YOUNG MAN who opened the door had short blond hair and light-blue eyes. He was tall, broad shouldered, and the skin on his lightly tanned face was almost unnaturally perfect. *Beautiful,* thought Sara Oskarsson. It wasn't often she thought that about a man. Good looking, attractive, sure, but seldom beautiful. At the same time there was a certain heaviness about him. As if he had been out partying or maybe had just slept badly.

The realization that there were two police officers standing outside the door seemed to perk Ricky Traneus up a little, but only a little.

And we don't exactly have very uplifting news to tell him, thought Sara.

Göran had already introduced himself, gestured at Sara and introduced her, too. Sara nodded and said hello. She tried to concentrate. That ought to have been easy, given their reason for being there, but she was still feeling a little off-kilter. She still hadn't had a chance to land properly after her vacation, had too many things on her mind: Douglas from Vancouver who had really given her life a spin just when she'd started seeing a guy in Visby; not a relationship yet, but sort of the awkward beginnings of one. What was the point of even thinking about a guy from Canada who certainly had no plans of moving to an island in the middle of the Baltic? And she for her part had no plans on emigrating.

It was just a few nights, a holiday adventure. Couldn't she just be her usual rational, single-minded self and draw a line through it? Stow it away like a pleasant little memory? Where Douglas himself was concerned, she had pretty much done that. But there was more to it . . . consequences . . . and the fact that she didn't know if it was the Canadian or the guy from Visby who was the father. Not that that really made any difference. Her mind was already made up, all she had to do was pick up the receiver and make the call. She couldn't

understand why she hadn't done that. Were there already some treacherous hormones defying her mind's authority?

She had lost control. Behaved . . . irresponsibly? Could you say
that? She bore no responsibility toward anyone but herself. She had
let go, let *herself* go. Become intoxicated, literally, but also in a broader
sense she had given into reckless abandon, followed her feelings; no,
gone chasing after them, been just as fast as them, no distance, no con-
sideration. It had been amazing.

Dangerous? Stupid even. The anxiety gnawed away at her. Was it
really worth it?

And now she was right in the middle of investigating a double murder, had to inform someone of the death of a loved one, and her thoughts
were just flapping around inside her head.

Sara, for Christ's sake, she thought.

The beautiful young man uttered something in response to a question from Göran and let them in. Sara spotted something that looked
like a Christmas decoration when she passed through the hall, but
considering that it was only October, she assumed that it was meant to
be ironic.

Ricky Traneus stopped irresolutely in front of the doorway leading
into the kitchen.

"Could we sit down?" asked Göran.

"Sure, sure," said Ricky Traneus and let them go in first.

The house was about three miles from the house where Ricky grew
up. He rented it from the farm's owner who lived a stone's throw away
in the new main farmhouse. Although "new," in this case, meant that it
was about a hundred years old.

The house Ricky was renting was easily two hundred years old, but
his furniture and possessions were anything but nineteenth century.
They sat down on black Ant chairs around a black superelipse table.
In the middle of the table stood a tall, red glass vase, and hanging on the

wall was a painting of three blurred figures sitting around a set dinner table.

"I'm afraid we have some bad news," said Sara. "It's about your mother, Kristina Traneus."

Ricky Traneus's eyes widened a little.

"She was found dead in her home, this morning."

Ricky sat there silently, didn't move. He stared straight at Sara without showing the slightest indication of having taken in what she just said.

"I'm very sorry to have to bring you such upsetting news," she said.

"Dead?" he said.

"Yes, I'm sorry. That's right. She's dead."

She saw how Ricky Traneus's eyes suddenly glistened over. He raised his hand to his face and bowed his head.

"My God, it can't be true," he said softly.

Sara waited before saying anything more.

"Why?" said Ricky and looked up. "How? She's healthy, not even fifty years old. Or has there been an accident?"

"Your mother didn't die of natural causes," Göran took over.

He was sitting there pitched slightly forward over the table with his hands loosely clasped and his forearms resting against the metal edge of the table.

Ricky stiffened.

"We have reason to believe that she's been murdered," Göran continued. "We don't know yet exactly what happened, but we're doing everything we can to find out."

Ricky let his hand drop from his face. He wasn't able to get a word out, just shook his head.

"Another person has been found dead in the house. A man. We haven't been able to identify him yet, but there is, as you may understand, at least a theoretical possibility that it could be your father, Arvid Traneus."

"No, no, no!"

Ricky Traneus stood up suddenly and took a few steps away from the table.

"No, no!" he repeated, ran his hands roughly through his hair and drew in a few deep, heavy breaths.

Sara and Göran also stood up, but did it slowly and quietly so as not to add to his distress.

"But that's not something we know for sure yet," Göran emphasized.

Sara walked over to Ricky.

"Wouldn't you like to sit down again?" she said and touched him gently as if to turn him back toward the table.

"Yeah, yes," he said softly without moving.

He hid his face once again with his hands and whimpered a word that Sara didn't quite make out. Was it *daddy*?

"Come and sit down," she said, took a firmer hold of Ricky Traneus's arm, and led him back to the chair. "I understand that this is a lot to take in all at once."

She asked the usual questions, if there was anyone who could come and be with him, so he wouldn't have to be alone. Said that they could stay there until then.

"My sister is on her way," said Ricky.

"Really?" said Sara in surprise, as if logic had been turned on its head.

"We were going to meet up tonight. The whole family that is. It was Mother who . . ."

Ricky looked at his watch.

"She's on her way over now, Elin that is. I'm supposed to pick her up at the bus station."

Sara nodded.

"Do you think you can manage that?"

"Sure. Yes, I think so. It'll be good to see her."

13

"A birthmark," said Eva Karlén who was down on all fours shining a flashlight underneath the gray velvet sofa, "that sounds good."

The memory of the two lacerated bodies was not something you could shake off easily, but the horrific sight had nonetheless had time to subside a little during the drive into Visby. But now the room threw itself over them once again. The bodies were covered, but the blood spatter on the furniture and walls screamed out its message even louder now that the bodies were hidden. Blood had spurted right out over the couch, hitting the wall behind it way up near the ceiling. The traces of blood were dark red where they were thickest, but almost pink further out toward the edges where they were just scattered dots on the light wallpaper.

"Just above the knee," Gustav specified.

"Right," said Eva and switched off the flashlight.

She sat up and looked at them.

"Göran and Sara are informing the son about his mother," she said and gestured at the covered female body.

She got up slowly as she continued:

"I've called in for a medical examiner. I hope she doesn't take too long getting here. It's starting to get a little ripe in here."

The smell was striking, but bearable. Like opening a refrigerator where something had gone past its use-by date.

"If this had been an ordinary October, we could have just turned down the heating, but it's eighteen degrees out," said Eva.

About a year ago, when Eva and Fredrik's passionate but short-lived fling had come to an end, he had found it literally painful to even be in the same room with her. Every morning when he stepped in through the front entrance to the police station he shuddered at the prospect of meeting up with her at a crime scene, at a run-through of the forensic details of a case, or just in the coffee room, which inevitably happened at least a few times a week. And each time he felt that same heavy doleful feeling inside, a strange mixture of longing and self-reproach.

Ninni and he had gone to see a family therapist a few times. Out of all the rehashing, there were a few words that had become etched in his mind, something the therapist had said: "There are always going to be other women, other men, temptations. Abstaining from them is part of what it means to be in a relationship."

That was right. At least it sounded right. Or proper. At the same time it sounded pretty harsh, demanding, like something a priest might have said. But it had stuck and he thought about it a lot. Especially when he and Eva Karlén ended up in the same room together.

After a few months the discomfort had disappeared and he had slowly started to realize that it might actually be good for them to work together. It left no room for fantasies, no chance that you could carry around a dream that wasn't real, that would otherwise have slowly but surely chafed a hole in his marriage. It was what it was. He was back with Ninni. Of course, she wasn't exactly pleased about his proximity to Eva Karlén, but that was something she had to live with as long as they chose to stay on the island. What Eva thought about the whole thing, he had no idea, since they never spoke about such matters anymore. For a while it seemed as if she and her husband had managed to patch things up between them, but it was apparently just temporary, if the rumors were true. Fredrik hadn't tried to find out any more.

Of course it wasn't completely without its complications. There were days when those impassioned spring months seemed like ancient history, but there were also days when it felt like yesterday. And those days were not good days.

"Okay, birthmark above the right knee, guess we might as well have a look-see," said Eva and pulled out a pair of scissors with angled blades from her bag.

"We were given this, too. It's Anders Traneus from five years ago, but it's supposed to be a good likeness," said Gustav and held up the photo Sofia Traneus had removed from her photo album.

Eva looked at the photo without touching it.

"I doubt it'll be of much help, but I guess we shouldn't leave any stone unturned," she said and walked up to the body in the corner.

She folded back a piece of the thin, white plastic sheet exposing the man's face. Gustav and Fredrik took a step forward. They were inclined to agree with her.

"I actually think I've never seen anything like this before, not in real life or in a photo," said Eva. "The blow across the eyes and the root of the nose has impacted so hard and deep that the eyes have been ripped out of their sockets. Then there's a deep gash in the middle of the skull, one across the neck, a superficial one across the chin, another to the side of the head that's sliced off part of the scalp and one ear. That's it lying over there."

Fredrik looked at what he had taken for a blood-drenched fold in the carpet, but saw now that it was a big slab of skin partially covered in hair with an ear attached to it that was still connected at the neck.

Eva reached out her hand for the photo, looked at it again and compared it carefully to the tattered and sunken tissue that had once been a human face.

"You can't even make out the hair color. He's got no distinctive features to go on. Not bad-looking, but a little ordinary, so to speak."

She handed back the photo.

"At best all you can say is that there's nothing in the photo to suggest that this *isn't* the same person lying here."

She covered the head, and instead pulled away the sheet to expose the legs and retrieved the pair of scissors that she'd put in her pocket.

She worked quickly but meticulously and soon the right pant leg was snipped open to the middle of the thigh. Eva reached for the flashlight and shined it at the knee. In the middle of the circle of light you could make out a faint reddish-brown birthmark.

"A-ha," said Gustav, "now we know. It might not be enough for a death certificate, but it's good enough for me."

"Of course it's Anders Traneus," said Fredrik.

Eva switched off the flashlight.

"Yup, it's as good as absolute certainty. The height fits, I checked with the passport database, and the shoe size matches a pair of jogging shoes lying in the backseat of the car."

Fredrik sighed. That means another trip into Visby and a definitive death notification this time.

"How does it look otherwise?" he asked and looked out over the room.

"I don't have much yet, not more than the obvious. Someone went berserk in here. What's really got my mind in a knot is the difference between the wounds inflicted on the man as opposed to the woman. He's been completely butchered, but she's just been hit with a single blow. Deadly, to be sure, but still."

"A crime of passion," said Gustav. "The lover takes out his rage and hate, but when he's going to go after the wife, his rage peters out after the first blow. Maybe he even starts feeling remorse."

"I don't know about that, I haven't found any convincing sign of remorse," said Eva who preferred to stick to what was concrete.

"Yeah, well, maybe I got a bit carried away there," Gustav said in his defense.

"There's another thing," said Eva. "It looks as if someone was sneaking around outside the house sometime over the past few days. Granholm has found distinct shoe prints in the flower bed, but I haven't had a chance to take a closer look at them yet."

"Is it true that he's being offered a full-time position?" Fredrik blurted out without thinking.

"Yes, starting next January," Eva answered.

Per Granholm wasn't one of Fredrik's favorite people and he had thought that Per would move away from the island once his temporary contract had come to an end. His antipathy was a little childish, he was aware of that, but he couldn't help it.

"Of course it could have been the husband spying on his wife, before he went inside to batter them to death," suggested Gustav.

"If those boats out in the hall belong to him then it should be pretty easy to determine," said Eva. "There can't be too many people out there clomping around in size forty-sevens."

GÖRAN SWITCHED ON his cell phone and listened to his messages. It was the first day of a murder investigation and he'd had his phone switched off for half an hour, so he didn't have to wait to hear the message alert to know that they were there.

He stood there silently with his cell phone pressed to his ear, then turned toward Sara.

"It's not the father," he said. "The dead man in the house, it's not the boy's father."

"Do we know who it is then?" asked Sara.

"An Anders Traneus, apparently he's Arvid Traneus's cousin. We have to head back."

He was on his way toward the house before he'd finished his sentence. Sara followed after him.

Ricky looked at them questioningly when he opened the door.

"I'm afraid it's us again," Göran apologized. "Could we go inside and sit down?"

Ricky followed them into the kitchen with an anxious expression. They sat down. Göran let out a quick cough.

"The dead man in your parents' house isn't your father," he said.

Ricky let out a deep sigh. His chest heaved convulsively a few times as if he were about to start laughing, and then calmed down.

"The dead man is your father's cousin, Anders Traneus. I'm sorry," said Göran.

Ricky didn't seem to react to the name.

"I don't know him," he said. "I mean I know who he is, but not much more than that."

"I'm sorry about this," said Göran.

"It's all right," said Ricky.

It sounded as if his mouth was dry. He smacked his lips once and looked at Göran.

"I realize that we've caused you a lot of anxiety, but . . . well, we didn't have much choice."

Ricky Traneus ran his hand over his eyes as if he was trying to wipe away tears that weren't there.

"My God," he said.

"I have to trouble you with a few questions," said Göran.

Ricky nodded.

"Your father, do you know where we can get hold of him?"

"My father?"

Ricky shook his head.

"I mean, until a moment ago I had thought he was the one that . . ."

"But that turned out not to be the case. The question is where we can find him. Because he is back on Gotland, right?"

"Yes," said Ricky slowly, as if he hadn't quite made the connection.

"You said that you were supposed to have dinner together tonight?"

"Yes. That was the plan."

"Any particular reason?"

Ricky shook his head again, but in a completely different way this time, more like someone trying to wake up rather than somebody who doesn't know what to think.

"Yes. Sure. Sorry. My father returned from Japan last Monday. He's been living there for . . . well, a good three years, I guess, but now he's moved back for good. So we were all going to have dinner together."

"And by all of you, you mean you, your sister, and your parents?" Ricky seemed to hesitate.

"Yes," he then said. "That's all of us."

"But your father, you have no idea where we can get hold of him? Does he work here on Gotland now?"

"No . . . well, he's a consultant you see. He works from the house when he's home. I thought he was home."

Göran Eide grasped his chin without taking his eyes off Ricky.

"When did you last see him?"

"Wow! Well, I guess it must have been five months ago, or so."

"Five months ago? So you mean you haven't seen him since he got home?"

"No."

"Why not?"

"Why not?"

"Your parents' house isn't that far away from here. It can't take very long by car. You never thought of popping by?"

"We spoke on the phone last Monday. He called and said that he was home, we chatted a little, and then he said that he'd see me on Friday," said Ricky and threw out his hands.

"And since then you've had no contact with him?"

"No."

"No idea where he might have gone?"

Ricky shook his head.

"It's strange. He said that he was going to take it easy for a while, stay home, that he didn't have to work again for the rest of his life, if he didn't want to."

"I see," said Göran Eide.

Not so strange if he'd just murdered your mother and his cousin, he thought. But if that thought hadn't occurred to Ricky Traneus, Göran wasn't about to ram it down his throat. At least not until he knew for sure that that was the case.

Göran stood up and the chair hopped backward on its narrow, steel pipe legs. He took out two business cards and handed them to Ricky.

"Give one to your sister and ask her to call me. We need to speak to her, too. And if it should occur to you where your father might be, please give us a call."

Ricky assured them that he would. He and Sara Oskarsson had also stood up and were heading toward the front door.

"Does she live here on the island, your sister, or . . . ?"

"On the mainland," Ricky filled in, "in Stockholm."

"So she may, in other words, not have seen your father, either, since he arrived home last Monday?"

Ricky was slow to answer, as if he didn't feel that it was up to him to speculate.

"No, in all likelihood she didn't," he said with a little grimace.

Sara who was leading the way, opened the door. The clear autumn light poured into the dark hall and turned her into a black silhouette. Göran got a sudden whiff of tobacco and couldn't resist taking a deep breath in through his nostrils. It hit him when he least expected it. Maybe he ought to start smoking a pipe. People said it was supposed to be less harmful to your health. No, they'd laugh at him. A detective with a pipe, that was just too ridiculous. Besides which, there was almost nowhere you could smoke anymore. He wasn't going to stand in the over-ventilated space beneath the stairs at the police station, like one of the prisoners in the pie-shaped holding cells up on the roof.

He sighed quietly and turned to Ricky.

"Anders Traneus, your father's cousin, what was his relationship to your parents like?"

"No idea. I didn't think they saw each other socially."

"Really? Why not?"

Ricky shrugged his shoulders.

"Do you socialize with all your cousins?"

14.

Elin's cell phone rang with a half-stifled ringtone. She had put it in her shoulder bag, which she had kicked in underneath the seat in front of her. She didn't want to flash it around. There was a good chance some old acquaintance might get on. After rummaging around for a moment, she found it. It was Molly.

"I'm on the bus now," she answered to the obligatory question, "should be there in about twenty minutes."

Elin groaned into the microphone and whispered:

"I really don't feel like doing this. A weekend with Mom and Dad. I'm gonna lose my mind."

"How about your brother, can't you stay with him?"

"I don't know. I mean, of course I could. I'd rather stay there, but then Mom would get all disappointed and go on about it endlessly. It's just as well I get it over and done with, then I'll be free until Christmas."

The bus was driving through the forest now. Tall, dark fir trees on either side. A long strip of cold blue sky above the road.

Elin had managed to share a cab from the airport to the bus station and gotten away with paying just fifty crowns. She had grabbed hold of a girl who seemed to be around the same age and who was about to climb into a taxi, and the girl had said yes straight off.

Money. Her father had spoken a lot about money when he'd called. About money, about the future, and about money. Almost like some kind of incantation. Hinted that one day it'll belong to her and Ricky.

She didn't want anything. She felt a twinge of pain in her stomach at the memory and put her foot over the Prada logo on her bag. She didn't want anything. She wanted to be her own person.

"Listen, I've gotta hang up now," she said to Molly, "I have to call Ricky and remind him to pick me up."

She snapped her cell phone shut, sat there with it in her hand, allowed herself to be rocked for a moment by the slight bounce in the movement of the bus, before she opened it up again and pressed R.

"Hi, it's me," she said when he picked up.

"Hi."

"How's it going?"

"All right. Should I come get you?"

Silence.

"Yes," said Elin.

"Okay."

"You sound like one of those computerized voices for blind people on the Internet. What's the matter?"

"Nah, nothing. I'm on my way. Something came up, that's all," he said.

He sounded like she'd just woken him up from a deep coma, Elin thought.

"Were you out partying last night?" she asked.

The bus pulled over and dropped off two people in Linde. No one got on.

"Out? Out where?" he said and laughed a little affectedly.

"In then, how should I know?" said Elin.

"We'll talk later, okay?"

"Okay. Hey, I brought along a Bag-in-Box," she said in a hushed voice. "Already opened but still, so we can prime ourselves before the dinner. Because you haven't been to the liquor store have you?"

"No, I had intended to go, but I didn't have time."

"Yeah, yeah, I heard something came up," she teased.

"I'll come get you."

"Okay, bye for now."

RICKY SQUEEZED THE cell phone between his hands. He remained sitting on the hall floor where he had sunk down after shutting the door behind the two police detectives. He couldn't get himself to say it over the phone. He just couldn't. But he had to tell her. Him. Ricky.

He tried to see Elin in front of him, how her expression would change once it had sunk in, and it struck him that he had no idea how she would react.

When should he tell her? As soon as possible of course. It wasn't something you put off. As soon as she stepped off the bus? No, better in the car, more private. Or maybe he should just wait till they got home? Maybe it would end up being strange in the car, if for example he suddenly had to break it off because something happened on the road that demanded his attention. On the other hand, what could possibly happen on the way from Hemse to Levide?

Ricky put the cell phone down on the hall floor and let his hands hang down along his sides, and felt a little clod of dirt under the fingernails of his left hand. He leaned his head back against the wall, closed his eyes, and tried to breathe deeply and rhythmically, crushing the clod of dirt between his fingers.

THE MEDICAL EXAMINER, Irma Silkeberg, put her used instruments into a bag of thick plastic, then backed away a few feet from the two bodies and regarded the mute scene.

"I think that the woman took the first blow," she said and pointed at Kristina Traneus's stiffened remains in front of the sofa.

Eva, who had stayed in the background to let the medical examiner work in peace, came up to her. Irma Silkeberg turned toward Eva and pulled off her gloves. She stuffed them into the plastic bag together with her instruments, and put the whole thing into her case.

"I have to analyze the blood in order to be a hundred percent sure, but I'll venture a conjecture. There's blood spatter on the woman's blouse that most likely did not come from her own wound and must have gotten there after she was struck in the chest."

"So the assailant hit the woman with a single blow and then went after the man and didn't stop until he was completely cut to shreds?" said Per Granholm without looking away from the butchered body in the corner.

"There's nothing that speaks against that scenario anyway. Then there's always the possibility that he, or she, first attacked the man, then for some reason broke it off, struck the woman once, and then continued to butcher the man," said Irma Silkeberg. "Those are the two possible conclusions that we can draw."

The madness, thought Eva Karlén, madness or rage, that the one who did this was carrying inside him, must have been horrendous. It must have taken over completely, impelled him, or her as Silkeberg said, not left any other way out. It was hard to imagine, hard also to understand the single blow to the woman. So clean and simple compared with the power and rage, the madness that turned this man into that . . . It must be the man who was important here, the man who was the focus of all this rage. The woman was just someone who got in the way. Or at least someone who didn't make the killer's blood boil to quite the same extent.

"You think it could just as well have been a woman, as a man?" she asked.

"Yes. You wouldn't have to be especially strong to achieve this, but

I guess you'd need to be reasonably steady on your feet, and be at least of medium height. So we can start by ruling out any short or feeble people."

"How about a crazed, absolutely enraged, feeble person?" Eva suggested.

"Possibly. But I doubt it," said Silkeberg and squinted through her glasses. "The murder weapon must have been relatively heavy. At first I thought a large kitchen knife or some kind of a samurai sword, but when I studied the wounds more closely, I noticed that the bone and cartilage, for example, which offer greater resistance, weren't just ripped apart, but also had been crushed."

"So you think it would more likely have been a . . . ?" Eva prompted.

Irma Silkeberg gave a slight smile, which probably meant that she didn't like being rushed.

"Something sharp, but not razor sharp, and heavy. A sword of some kind, perhaps a machete. Well, I can imagine a whole bunch of potential weapons, but something with a certain amount of weight to it. The man received over thirty wounds, probably all in quick succession. That requires a fair bit of strength and stamina. And the angle of the cuts rule out anyone under five-nine, say five-seven so you've got a bit of a safety margin."

"Thirty wounds," Eva repeated.

"Give or take," nodded Silkeberg. "Most of them must have been inflicted when the victim was already lying down, but a few of the wounds that were high up, around the neck and head, were inflicted while he was still standing. They must have been the first ones. The blow to the neck was presumably the immediate cause of death, but easily half of the injuries by themselves would have been enough to kill him within a few minutes."

15

Goddamn him! It was like some kind of disease. He just could not be on time.

Elin had been waiting at the bus station for ten minutes. Everyone else who had gotten off had quickly been picked up by cars or pedaled off on their own bicycles. For a few minutes, the idling bus had kept her company as it waited for the exact departure time, but once it had rounded the corner of the disused train station, she was all on her own. She stood there and stared at the big white ball with the old OK gasoline logo above the Lantmännen silo for about five minutes before she tired of it and sent off a text message. Told him that he could pick her up at Redners.

Now she was sitting in the bar with a glass of red wine in front of her, staring out through the window and crossing her fingers that the three squabbling winos who had sought out the darkest corner at the very back next to the emergency exit, wouldn't have a serious falling-out.

Her cell phone vibrated loudly against the tabletop.

> *Redners?! Are you*
> *out of your mind?*
> *On my way.*

Thanks for warning me, she thought, *it would have been even better if it had come before I'd made it over here.* Redners hadn't exactly been a first-choice hangout even back when Elin left the island over two years ago, but it had still been a potential second choice. Apparently not anymore.

The wine was rough and a little sour, but it was all right. It hadn't cost much. She took two quick gulps and tried to catch her own reflection in the window.

A man of around thirty came walking along outside. He stopped, leaned his forehead against the window and screened the light with one hand so he could see inside. His eyes moved around, peering into every corner of the place, then he disappeared as quickly as he came.

Elin was sure that it was someone she knew, but she couldn't come up with a name or a context. And yet he was so familiar.

She jumped up from the table and hurried toward the door. The waitress looked up from behind the counter when she heard the sound of the bell on the door. Elin stuck her head out through the doorway and looked down the street that ran straight through town. He was gone, must have disappeared down one of the side streets.

She walked back to her seat. Caught a whiff of rancid fryer grease from the kitchen. He had seemed so familiar. That long thin face and eyes that were somehow completely . . . wild.

She pushed her glass slowly back and forth across the laminated table in front of her. For some reason she came to think of Stefania. The last time she had seen her. She was sitting in the car and had raised her hand to wave, and just before the car began to roll, she had flashed a cautious smile.

Elin raised her glass and took a big gulp, tried to think of something else. She was going to take out one of the horses. Tomorrow she would go out for a ride. That was something to look forward to, at least.

Oh, what was she doing here? Dinner with Mom and Dad. Jesus Christ, please let it be bearable, she said to herself in feigned prayer, even though she didn't believe in anything. At least not in any god. She had rejected that possibility ten years ago. She may not have been one of God's little angels before, either, but after that day ten years ago she knew that for certain. There was no God. There couldn't be a God.

Because God doesn't like the poor. And God doesn't like blacks. And he sure as hell doesn't like you . . . Screw God! she sang silently in her head.

Where the hell was he? This was getting to be ridiculous.

BY THE TIME Ricky stepped in through the tinkling door, another fifteen minutes had passed and Elin was on her second glass of cheap red wine. In other words, he hadn't been on his way at all when he sent off that text message. But she was happy to see him, wasn't going to chew him out. She got up to give him a hug and accidentally bumped the table spilling some wine out. A bluish-red pool appeared at the foot of the glass.

There was something odd about him. He held her arms for a moment after the hug and looked at her gravely. She laughed and asked if he was okay. Ricky could be a bit sullen sometimes. He had periods like that.

He didn't answer and Elin sat down. Ricky slowly slid into the chair across from her.

"You want something?" she asked and nodded at the glass.

He shook his head.

"Have you seen him?" she asked.

Ricky looked at her that way again. Gravely, almost solemnly.

"What is it?"

"Something's happened," he said.

And when he said it she immediately understood that it certainly had. It knocked the breath out of her. All at once she felt terribly weak and all the sounds around her grew louder while Ricky slid away from her and became the size of an ant, far away at the other end of the table, which must have been at least thirty feet long. Please, could she be spared having to hear anymore, she didn't want this, please, please. And then she prayed again. How silly she was. A stupid little idiot. There was nobody listening.

And he sure as hell doesn't like you . . . Screw God!

"Something terrible has happened," he said. "I don't know how to tell you."

Then the earth split open.

Fredrik had shut his eyes. Sara was uncertain if this meant that he was sleeping, or if it had something to do with his condition. She was uncertain about almost everything, but deep down she had a hard time believing that he would ever be completely restored. She didn't want to think that, but it was difficult to come to any other conclusion. The pale skin, the dark rings under his eyes, the blood-red abrasions across his left cheek and temple, and the bloodshot eye, hidden for the moment behind the closed lid, did nothing to contradict her pessimistic prognosis.

She felt that he seemed worse today. He didn't talk at all. But the doctors had said that you had to be prepared for bad days. *One* bad day was okay. It didn't affect the diagnosis. But several bad days in a row wasn't good. But the doctors were optimistic. They really were. Or was that just an act they put on until all hope was gone? The white coats' fear of "failure"? It must be tough to see death as a defeat when you're in a line of work where every customer was ultimately doomed to die. It was a fight against time that sooner or later they always lost.

When Sara and her colleagues were given a new case to work on, there was seldom any hope left. Death had already been there and they could do nothing to help the deceased or anyone else. Their work was governed by a completely different set of laws. The Law. They did what had to be done and she often wondered if there was any point to it all, but she knew that it made little difference what she felt about the individual cases, or whether the apprehension of a criminal actually changed anything. It had never been about that. What was important was that they did what had to be done, always, because that's what had been agreed. Otherwise everything would come crashing down. Like a sand castle in the waves of a beach.

Sara looked at the transparent tube that wound its way down from the IV stand, and without warning a powerful fear dug its claws into her. She wanted to get up and rush out of the room, wanted to run out of the hospital to try and capture something, to start living, because she had become lulled into a prim conviction that such a thing was possible. Only she had no idea what it was she was chasing. Start living . . . How? What did that even mean? As if there was a life out there waiting for you, a life that you could just climb into like a hot tub full of essential oils.

"Damn it," she whispered, and got up and walked the short distance to the window. She leaned her head against the glass and looked out over the trees of Haga Park that were swaying in the wind, before she turned back toward Fredrik.

Fredrik's eyes opened very slowly. The movement was so slow that it almost didn't seem human. And then his gaze, that made no attempt to focus on her, or even look in her direction, but stared in the direction they had been in when the eyelids slid back, straight up at the ceiling.

She didn't know what to say any longer. It felt so foreign to her to stand there in front of a partner whom she no longer knew. It made her feel strange.

She breathed deeply.

"I better be going. Ninni will probably be here soon."

She took her bag.

"I'll come back."

Just as she said that, she felt that she couldn't handle it anymore, but that she would come back anyway. She took her bag.

Now he looked at her.

16.

Elin didn't remember anything more until they were sitting in the car. The engine was on, but they were still sitting in the parking lot outside the library.

She stared out through the windscreen and the first idiotic thought that went through her head was that you weren't allowed to park there. Not if you were at Redners drinking wine. Only if you were going to the library or some other municipal institution. Not if you had just found out that your mother was dead.

"Aren't you going to start driving?" she asked.

"Just calm down," said Ricky and sounded like he really was trying to calm her down. As if she had been carrying on or had berated him somehow.

Had she? Had she said things she didn't remember, words that were just as wiped clean from her memory as the steps out from the restaurant, across the street, and into the car?

She reached up and lowered the sun visor, the backside of which she knew had a mirror. She leaned forward, stretched her neck. Her face was flushed and her cheeks streaked with mascara. She must have been crying.

"What are you doing?" asked Ricky and ran his hands down the steering wheel.

She didn't answer, heard Ricky's breathing.

"Are you okay?" he asked.

She giggled in a way that sounded strange even to herself.

"Of course I'm not okay," she said.

Her voice failed her and her throat choked up into a painful little knot and she didn't know for sure if it was the grief or the pain that made her cry again.

"Can we please get the fuck out of here!" she shouted shrilly and kicked and stamped at the floor and around her.

"Okay okay, we're going," said Ricky and this time he sounded like he was afraid of her and that made her cry even more.

She wanted him to comfort her, be her big brother and not let his voice waver, but tell her instead that everything was going to be all right, that everything would work out.

Instead he slowly backed up the car so he could swing out of the parking lot. They were both younger siblings after all.

"This is so fucked up," she said looking down at the floor when they turned at the bank.

"I know," he said.

"Normal people don't get murdered, do they? Huh? Stuff like that doesn't happen."

The sun was hitting her in the eyes, but she couldn't be bothered to reach for the sun visor again. She squinted at the sun. She had traveled home reluctantly to see her father, mainly so as not to disappoint her mother. An obligatory dinner and hopefully a few nice hours with Ricky, that was what she had expected. Two wasted days of her life, but nothing she couldn't live with. And all of a sudden she was in hell.

17

Eva Karlén saw them at once when she examined the window above the flower bed. Two strands of hair that had gotten caught between the outdoor thermometer mounting and the window frame. They must have been plucked from the head of the person who had been standing there in the flower bed looking in.

She removed the strands of hair with a pair of tweezers—two long, black strands of hair—and put them carefully in an evidence bag. She was just writing a note on the outside of the bag when she heard someone approaching and turned around.

"How's it going with the shoe prints?"

Fredrik Broman. Couldn't he just stay away? Didn't he understand that it was better that way? She certainly tried to keep her distance as much as possible. He must have noticed that.

It bothered her, having him that close to her. She lost her concentration. Something was disturbed. It wasn't that she was still in love with him, not at all. She wasn't even sure if she had ever even been. Rather than love, it had been a wonderful intoxication that she had needed right there and then. But now it was just a memory. And yet. Her pulse quickened, and, when she had it bad, images could start flipping through her head: naked bodies, tender words. Isolated highlights that were easily cherished, but best forgotten.

Perhaps she wanted to become intoxicated again? Just for one day.

"These shoe prints weren't left by the same person as over there in that flower bed," she said and pointed over at the trampled red dahlias. "These are a size forty-two and those over there are forty-sevens."

"Arvid Traneus trudged right through the flower bed?"

"Presumably," said Eva.

"But someone else was standing over here snooping then?" he asked.

"Yes, and left behind two long, black strands of hair. Because I guess we can assume, given the shoe size, that it's a he," said Eva, "even if we can't rule out a large woman."

Fredrik nodded, stood there silently thinking.

Okay, you've got the forensic details. Now go! thought Eva Karlén.

WHEN ELIN STEPPED out of the car she didn't quite get a proper grip on the bag with the box wine. It tumbled out of the car and landed in the grass. She reached down for it, but fumbled and dropped it again and, without really understanding why, began stamping furiously on the pathetic little Bag-in-Box that she had schlepped with her all the way from Stockholm.

"Fuck," she gasped and jammed her heel into the box several times without anything happening. "Goddamn," she whimpered and wrenched the box out of the bag and pressed the spigot and spun around slowly as the wine gushed out onto the grass.

"What the hell are you doing?" asked Ricky and reached out to her with both arms, but she twisted free from his grasp and continued spreading the dark-red liquid across the ground.

"Stop it Elin, stop it," he said.

"What the hell's wrong with you, are you some kind of wino or what?" she cawed in a voice that was broken and didn't sound like her at all.

Ricky took two long steps forward and caught hold of her, forced her arms down to her sides. He put his arms around her, finally he put his arms around her.

The Bag-in-Box fell to the ground with a dull thud, just a third of the wine left inside.

"She's dead. Dead!"

She screamed out, and then her whole body started to shake as she broke down sobbing and went completely limp in his arms. Ricky had to hold her up to keep her from falling.

"It's him. It's gotta be him," she wailed through her bawling.

Ricky shook his head.

"Try to stand up now," he said. "Try. It'll be all right. Somehow things are going to turn out all right."

"But he's the one who did it. You've gotta admit it had to have been him."

The words bubbled through her sobs and gasps for air.

"Elin," whispered Ricky.

"It's gotta be him. It's gotta be Father. Father killed her. How could it be anyone else?"

"No, no, no. Stop it now, Elin. That's not true. Come on, try to stand up."

"It was him."

"No, Elin."

But that was the only thing she could think about. He had done it. That fucking son-of-a-bitch bastard had killed her beloved mother. Her beloved mother whom she'd turned her back on and left behind on Gotland.

"Come on. Stand up!" said Ricky, more firmly this time.

Her body was still shaking with sobs, but she was really trying.

"Let's go now."

He helped her step by step to the door. The Bag-in-Box and her black Prada bag would have to lie there for now in the wine-soaked grass.

THERE WAS A low, comforting rumble coming from the shiny, dark green tile stove. Elin sat curled up on the couch, wrapped up in a blanket, with an untouched cup of tea in front of her on the table. Outside the window a cold blue October twilight fell.

Ricky entered from the kitchen and sank down next to her without saying anything. She was surprised that he could be so thoughtful and caring. It didn't feel out of place exactly, but it was a side of him that she hadn't seen very often.

He actually didn't have to do all that—the fire, the blanket, the tea—but it felt good anyway. Something to hold onto. She could sit there forever, cocooned in her blanket, silently listening to the hiss and crackle of the fire while her thoughts went spinning around in her head. She didn't want to move, didn't want to speak, just wanted to sit there huddled up, sleep, wave, watch the light change.

"The police want to speak to you later. At some point. They left a phone number."

She closed her eyes.

If this had been one of her usual trips home, they first would have swung past the farm, she would have dropped off her things in her old room, maybe had coffee with Mother, then they would have gone over to Ricky's place for a drink or a glass of wine or two, and DWI-ed the short way back when it was time for dinner. If it wasn't too late she would have gone out and met up with an old friend. But not Ricky. He wasn't much of a party guy anymore. He'd become a homebody.

Now none of that would happen. Maybe she wouldn't even set foot on the farm.

"Do you know where she is? Is she still at the house or have they . . . ?" she asked.

He turned his head toward her and she could tell from his expression that he had been wondering the same thing. Mother. Where was she now?

"I don't know," he said.

She reached out for the cup of tea, but didn't have the energy to rise up far enough from her curled-up position to reach it. Ricky had to lean forward and give it to her. She took a few gulps because her mouth was dry, not because she wanted tea.

"It's strange to think of her."

"Yes," he mumbled.

"Lying somewhere."

She wanted to talk about this, but she was forced to do so with long pauses between sentences.

"On the floor at home inside one of those chalk outlines."

"I don't think they . . ."

"Or in a refrigerator in Visby. Or maybe she's on her way somewhere right now. Riding in an ambulance . . ."

"Elin."

Soon he would tell her to stop it again, but she wouldn't have any more outbursts, not right now anyway.

"Can they move her around as they please without consulting us? Don't they need to have some kind of permission?"

As if wanting to give her an immediate answer to her question, the cordless phone quivered with an indistinct ringtone.

18.

Wow, it's Saint Nicholas himself, thought Sara when she caught sight of the slouched figure with the long, white beard. *Or Saint Nicotine rather,* she corrected herself as the light hit the yellowed patch beneath his mouth.

Emrik Jansson's house smelled strongly of saturated smoke. Heavy, gloomy, pungent. Possibly you could pick up a slight whiff of fried food through the miasma of smoke. Everything was a yellowish brown: the walls, the ceiling, the woodwork, the hall ceiling lamp's pilled fabric shade that had been hanging there since at least the sixties.

"I was watching TV," said Emrik Jansson, "they're showing reruns of *Hem till byn*. You know it?"

Sara nodded. She knew the series, but she didn't follow it.

"I've heard about . . . well, all that up at the Traneus spread," said Emrik Jansson and pointed with his thumb over his shoulder toward the farm.

"Then you know why I'm here," said Sara.

Emrik Jansson's house was more a nest than a home. The jaundiced walls had something of a beeswax quality about them she thought, and decided to question him out in the hall. He'd have to come up with something really sensational for her to even consider sitting down anywhere in there. If it looked like a beehive already out there in the entrance, what must it look like in the living room, say, where he probably sat and did his smoking?

"Who is it?" asked the hunched chain-smoker in front of her. "Is it Kristina and Anders?"

Sara tried to hide her surprise. It wasn't all that surprising, in and of itself, for the news to have spread so quickly through the area. It would have been obvious to anyone who saw the steady stream of police cars and other vehicles heading back and forth to the farm that something serious had happened, but how he could be so informed about the details? After all, they had only just managed to establish the identity of the murdered man themselves.

"Has somebody suggested that?" she asked.

"No, not exactly. I just sort of assumed it," he said.

His voice was calm and pleasant and his gaze alert. He may have been living in a smoke-infused nest, but he was no insect. He wasn't even much of a freak. Maybe just too old to care.

"And why do you think that? Which Anders do you mean, by the way?" she hurried to say before Emrik Jansson had a chance to answer.

"Anders Traneus. The cousin."

He ran his fingers along the outer edge of his beard and she saw that the tips of his fingers were just as yellow as everything else in the house.

"And why?" she repeated.

He bowed his head forward and released a rattly cough into his clenched right hand. It never seemed to end and the coughs seemed to echo inside the old man. *He's going to keel over any minute,* she thought.

It ended abruptly and he continued as if nothing had happened, probably all too used to the convulsions to reflect upon the possibility that someone else might find them disturbing, if not downright disgusting. Sara was ready to sign up to the latter group.

"Well, I've seen him, haven't I. Many times. I suppose they've tried to be discreet about it, but . . . well, you know, you see what you see."

Emrik Jansson was the closest neighbor. That didn't mean that he lived close by, it was a long way from the Traneus's farm to the other houses in the area, but apparently it was close enough.

"I've also got plenty of time to observe my surroundings. I don't snoop around, definitely not, but I've got a lot of spare time and still a pretty good head," he said and put a finger to his right temple.

"So Anders Traneus has been a regular visitor to Kristina?" asked Sara.

"Yeah, I'd say so."

Emrik Jansson wobbled suddenly and put a hand up to the wall for support.

"Gosh, are you all right?" she asked.

"It's just the way it is," said Emrik and kept his hand against the drab brown wallpaper.

"We can go sit down," she said.

"I'm all right," he said and waved with his free hand.

"If you say so . . . Can you explain a little more in detail why you think that it was Anders Traneus who was killed up there?"

"Well, Arvid came home the other day, didn't he. Somehow I thought that maybe he caught them and, well . . ."

"Killed them?"

He paused before answering, as if he'd suddenly realized that his quick assumption amounted to a very serious accusation.

"Well, I can't possibly know anything about that, of course, but yes, I guess that's what I thought."

He smiled meekly and did a little gesture with his hand.

"A crime of passion."

"Is he the type who'd be able to kill over something like that, Arvid Traneus?"

"Sure he's the type. I think I could go so far as to say that."

"How would you describe him?"

"Adventurous, always in a hurry to get things done, hot tempered. I had him in school," said Emrik.

"That hot temper of his . . . did he used to get into fights? Do you remember?"

"Fights? Well, not fights exactly. I mean, you know what boys are like, some of them anyway. He threw the occasional punch I guess, but he wasn't the only one."

"But there must have been more to it than that to make you think that he killed his cousin out of jealously."

Emrik Jansson started to finger the edge of his beard again, a deeply ingrained habit.

"I'm starting to feel a little silly now," he said and coughed a dry, social cough this time, "but one reason of course is that there's a dead man lying up in that house together with Kristina, at least that's what I heard, and the fact that I've seen Anders coming and going. That I made the assumption that they'd had some kind of relationship. But then there are also the rumors about Arvid being abusive. Well, toward Kristina that is."

"Is that something that you've witnessed yourself at any point?" asked Sara.

"No, I can't say that I have. It could, of course, just be idle gossip."

"Well, if you haven't seen or heard anything concrete then . . ."
Sara agreed, but thought at the same time how gossip could sometimes be a criminal investigator's best friend. If you were lucky.

She rounded off with a question about whether Emrik Jansson had
seen Arvid Traneus since he got home. He had. He had seen him in
the car together with Kristina on Monday evening, presumably on
their way home from the airport. But not since.

EMRIK JANSSON FELT unsettled when he shut the door behind the
young woman from the Visby Police Department. His observations
and assumptions about what was going on in the houses around him,
conclusions that had seemed logical and sensible, appeared to fall
apart when they came under the scrutiny of something as serious as
justice. Were they, when it came down to it, nothing more than an old
man's excessive preoccupation with gossip and meaningless details?

He shuffled back to the TV and sat down slowly in his sunken armchair with threadbare armrests. The show he had been watching was
almost over. Normally he would have been peeved at having missed
half an episode, but all of a sudden he saw it as just a hollow attempt to
make time pass.

Arvid had been good at school, and yet wild somehow, not one of
the ones who sat at the front and raised his hand to each question. He
used to throw himself into any task with uncommon drive and energy, as if he wanted to get it over and done with quickly so he could
move on. He devoured school assignments as if someone had promised him a big delicious piece of cake if he'd just eat up that disgusting
plate of food first.

The other kids looked up to him, but were a little afraid of him at the
same time. And now he was out there somewhere. Maybe a murderer.

19

"I'm going to kill that son-of-a-bitch father of yours. And do you
know why? Well, I'll tell you, because he's not a human being. He's
an animal. A sick fucking animal who should be culled."

The words spurted out in angry gasps, so loudly that the voice in
the receiver was distorted to a grotesque croaking. Ricky felt how the
cordless phone became sweaty in his hand. He looked at Elin, but she
didn't meet his gaze. She had sunk back in the couch and was staring
vacantly at the ceiling.

"Hello?" Was all he managed to say.

"He won't get away. If the police don't get him, then I will. He's
gotta die!"

The last bit came out as an almost unintelligible howl that caused
Ricky to move the receiver two inches away from his ear.

Strange waves of heat billowed up through his body. He felt weak,
paralyzed, and terribly afraid. A feeling he had never experienced
before. It was an unpleasant combination that quickly caused his fear
to surge into panic.

"And if you try to protect him, then I'll fucking kill you, too! You
hear me? You don't stand a chance."

A click, and then the receiver was silent.

Ricky's heart was pounding so hard that his chest hurt, his tongue
was gummed up in his mouth. He felt like he wasn't getting enough air
even though he was actually panting as if he had just run a marathon.

"Ricky?"

Elin had sat up in the couch and looked at him, worry flickering in her eyes. Ricky gestured with the receiver. What could he say? How did you go about describing what just happened? What did just happen?

"He said he was going to kill me," he gasped between his heavy breaths.

"Who did? What do you mean?"

Ricky took a staggering step toward the couch and wobbled. His vision flickered, small colorful circles danced and spun around in a background that moved further and further away. His face had gone gray.

"Ricky!" shouted Elin, threw off the checkered blanket and leaped from the couch.

Quickly reaching her brother, she grabbed hold of his arm with both hands.

"Come and sit down. Sit down and listen to me."

She got him to the couch. His knees gave way when she gave him a gentle push and he fell backward with a heavy thud.

"Now you listen to me Ricky, listen to me."

FIVE MINUTES LATER she had managed to get him to calm down. His breathing was almost back to normal again.

"Worse comes to worst, we'll have to get you a paper bag to breathe into, but I think you're going to be all right," she said.

"What?"

"Take it easy, you're in good hands," she said and patted his leg, "I know all about panic attacks."

Her grimace made it abundantly clear that she hadn't come by this knowledge from studying psychology.

"But forget about that now," she said, "I want you to tell me who it was that called."

She sat at the very edge of the couch, turned toward him. Her eyes were dark and firm, and her cheeks flushed. A moment ago she had been lying under a blanket staring at the ceiling, but the grief and shock had at least temporarily been swept away by something much more powerful.

"I don't know," he said.

He recounted as best he could the threats that had been yelled at him over the phone.

She looked at him for a long moment without saying anything, her brow furrowed like a washboard.

"And that was it?"

Ricky nodded.

"He just started out like that, just straight off?"

"Yes. 'I'm going to kill that son-of-a-bitch father of yours.' "

"You didn't recognize the voice?"

"Not in the slightest."

"Jesus Christ, how scary."

Elin had to try hard not to show how shaken she was, but she knew that it was impossible to stop a panic attack in someone else, if you weren't calm yourself. Or at least appeared to be.

"Must be somebody who thinks Father is involved in . . ."

Maybe she ought to talk about something completely different, but she couldn't. She felt that she had to get to the bottom of this right away, if she wasn't going to freak out herself.

"Maybe we ought to call the police," she said.

"They gave me a card. Two actually. I was supposed to give one of them to you. Where did I put them now?"

"A card?"

"From the police who were here."

20

The high beams punched a hole in the dense blackness and lit up the reflectors at the side of the road.

"Do you think we can get anything useful out of that Rune character? He made it sound like this Arvid Traneus was some kind of devil," said Gustav.

"Maybe he's senile," said Fredrik who was driving.

"Probably just in shock."

"Or senile and in shock."

Lena, Ninni, and the children had eaten dinner without them hours ago. Ninni had called and said that they weren't going to wait.

"I'm hungry," said Gustav.

As soon as Gustav said that, Fredrik felt his stomach growl, too. They had wolfed down a quick lunch after questioning Inger Traneus, but that was two hours ago now.

They had tried to sum it all up on the way back. There was a lot pointing toward Arvid Traneus being the killer they were looking for. A witness had intimated that he beat his wife. He had been abroad for an extended period, his wife had some hanky-panky going on with his cousin, Arvid caught them at it and couldn't control his anger, especially not toward the cousin, whom he butchered beyond recognition. Then he ran off. Maybe he was even back in Japan by now. A country of almost 130 million inhabitants, 20 million in Tokyo alone, a city that that Arvid Traneus knew well after spending all those years there. Furthermore, he had virtually inexhaustible financial resources.

If he had made it that far, it wouldn't be easy to find him, but of course they had put out a nationwide APB, and alerted Interpol.

"But if the cousin was having an affair with Kristina Traneus, wouldn't he have stayed away from there once Arvid was back?" asked Fredrik. "What was he doing in the house?"

Gustav moved around in his seat and adjusted his shirt beneath his jacket.

"Yeah," he agreed, "but maybe something happened. Maybe Arvid Traneus started going after his wife, beat her or threatened her, and she called Anders for help."

"And he jumps into his car, drives over there, and then things don't turn out too well?"

"Yes. Or else Arvid invited his cousin over under some pretext, with the intention of confronting him."

"Maybe. But that doesn't really fit with how the body looked. I mean, would he really be so calculating at first and then totally lose control and make mincemeat out of him?"

"No, that's a good point."

"Beside which, it seems like they really didn't have any contact to speak of. Anders would have seen through him."

Fredrik turned off Road 142 and drove familiarly the last winding miles through the darkness back to his house. They bounced gently onto the grass in front of the old farm. There was an inviting glow in the windows and a flickering from the TV on the upper floor. They climbed out and slammed the doors shut behind them.

They felt both hungrier and more tired now that they were so close to their destination.

But then there were the footprints outside the window and the black strands of hair, thought Fredrik as he walked past the kitchen window with an outdoor glass thermometer that Ninni had recently put up. Neither the shoe prints, nor the hair matched Arvid Traneus. Of course they might not have anything to do with the murder. It could have been anyone, maybe one of the many visitors from the mainland searching for a summer sublet by shamelessly slipping ridiculous offers through people's letter boxes.

Fredrik felt the door. It was locked. It was always the same. They usually never locked the door until they went to bed, but with the start of every new murder investigation, Ninni would bolt the door until the killer was caught. Not so strange considering what happened to her their first summer on the island. It was more surprising that she hadn't had an alarm installed and put bars on the windows.

"Hello!" he shouted once he'd unlocked the door and stepped into the hall.

"We're in here," Ninni called out from the kitchen.

GÖRAN EIDE OPENED a bottle of Ramlösa mineral water and poured it into a Duralex glass he had taken from the cupboard. He felt the soda bubbles spray against his chin as he raised the glass to his mouth. He downed it in a few gulps and refilled it with what was left in the bottle.

Sonja was already asleep. She had lain there with a book in her hand, glasses on her nose, and a sixty-watt lightbulb shining right onto her face when he had come home five minutes ago.

He had switched out the light and removed the book and the glasses.

Quaffing the last of the mineral water but still feeling thirsty, he took out another bottle from the fridge and grabbed two round cheese crackers from the top cupboard that he started munching on.

He looked out through the window, out into Ekeby's autumn darkness. He was having a hard time shaking off the image of the two murder victims. He had seen many unpleasant things in his years as a police officer. He had learned how to handle the feelings of discomfort and disgust a long time ago. What still badly affected him were the traces of the murderer's rage, madness, and sometimes suffering. That this life could deform people to such an extent that they became capable of doing this kind of thing to their fellow human beings. Committing murder was one thing, often it was an accident, or at least wasn't altogether intentional, but sometimes it was more than that. In some cases the murderers were driven by seething hatred and a desire to cause injury and inflict as much pain and suffering as possible.

He sat down at the kitchen table, set the glass and bottle down. The dark wood surface was wiped spotlessly clean. Not a single bread crumb or coffee stain. He had never thought that it would happen, but he could miss the crumbs sometimes. It was as if his life with Sonja had been wiped just as spotlessly clean. Two weeks ago their youngest child had turned thirty. She was grown up now. Of course he still thought of her mostly as a teenager, but he had to admit that she wasn't and hadn't been for eleven years. A strange feeling. His son had taken a break from studying to become a teacher. Göran understood him. It's difficult to find the energy when you're studying for a career you don't really want.

He ran his hand over the table. In time your eyesight fades and your hands begin to shake, he thought, then the crumbs will come back. But life won't.

His cell phone began to vibrate on the crumb-free tabletop. Göran picked it up and answered.

"Hi, my name is Elin Traneus," said an anxious voice.

"THEN IT MUST be the husband, Arvid—isn't that almost always how it is?" said Lena more as a declaration than a question.

They remained sitting in the kitchen downstairs. An old country kitchen with deep window niches and floors of thick pinewood that forced you to wear rag socks or slippers when the weather turned cold. Lena leaned forward with her elbows propped on the table and looked at Fredrik and Gustav with curious blue eyes. She had recently shocked everyone around her by cutting off her long, blonde hair to a more manageable brush cut. At the care home where she worked she had been given the nickname "Self-confidence Now" because of a certain resemblance to a celebrity therapist who had published a number of books on the subject.

"Yes," Fredrik agreed, "unfortunately that is how it almost always is."

Lena replaced her pouch of smokeless tobacco, pressed the used pouch into the lid of the *snus* box and slipped a fresh one in under her lip.

"And he's taken off, too; it's gotta be him," she said after having adjusted the pouch exactly where she wanted it.

"Just bear in mind now," said Gustav, "that that's your theory. We didn't say that."

Lena made a face at her husband.

"I know the routine."

They were used to always talking to Ninni and Lena about new cases, at least if it was something spectacular enough to raise questions anyway. But they never said more than Göran Eide would be telling the press anyway. More or less. And they never told them about any theories or speculations that were being discussed down at the station.

Fredrik cleared the plates that were still on the table and set them down on the counter next to the sink.

"Traneus. Didn't they have a daughter who died?" said Lena and looked at Gustav and then at Fredrik.

They in turn looked at each other, but no one looked especially enlightened.

"Not that we know of," said Fredrik.

"I'm almost sure about it," said Lena and looked at Ninni this time.

"Don't look at me. When it comes to village gossip I don't have much to contribute."

They hadn't had a progress meeting with the rest of the team that day, and the next one wasn't scheduled until eight o'clock the following morning. Lennart Svensson had been in Visby checking through databases. He was sure to have a solid grasp of all the family constellations and any children that may have died.

"I think Karin knew her a little. Or maybe it was a friend of a friend of hers. But it must have been some time ago," said Lena.

Fredrik felt exhilarated, almost unnaturally awake despite the long day. A feeling that was familiar from the first days of an investigation, a kind of euphoria brought on by the challenge of solving the case. Completely different from the gray fatigue that would take over in four to five days if no perpetrator had been brought in.

He walked back and sat down at the table.

"How did she die?"

"I don't know," said Lena and fingered the box of smokeless tobacco, "there was something mysterious about the whole thing, a lot of talk, very hush-hush. I know that she was brought into the hospital on a number of different occasions. It may have been cancer, or else something psychological that made her commit suicide."

Lena threw her arms out in a quick gesture.

"But I really don't know. It all feels very distant now, but I remember my sister telling me about it at some point."

"How long ago was this?" asked Gustav.

"Seven, eight years ago, maybe more. She wasn't quite grown up yet, I don't think."

Ninni got up from the table and started clearing things away from the counter.

It was her way of saying that she was tired and wanted to go to bed. Fredrik would have liked to sit there a while longer.

"Is Simon still up?" he asked.

"I assume so," said Ninni, "unless he's fallen asleep in front of the TV. You'll have to go up and take a look."

"Well, there's no school tomorrow," said Fredrik.

"Yeah, but he always gets so grumpy when he doesn't get to bed."

A dead daughter, a murdered mother, probably killed by her own husband. *A lot of death in that family*, thought Fredrik.

"All right, I'll go up," he said.

21

Everything had changed. When Elin woke up it was as if she had woken up to a new life. The light was different, the colors, the air she breathed. *She* was different. Her skin, what was contained within it and that which defined her as a person, wherever that was.

She was used to being different when she came to the island. The moment she set foot on the quayside, she left a piece of her behind her on the ferry, took a big step back in time, pulled on an awkward overall, stiff with old complexes. Then when she'd climb back onboard again a few days later, she'd find herself again at the very back on one of the pilled seats in the pet area, sullen and disappointed, bored of being forced to waste two days traveling back and forth across the Baltic.

But now it was seriously different. Her mother was gone. Murdered. Her father was also gone. For some reason she thought of him onboard a big ship, far away. On the run, but satisfied.

She slowly sat up in the couch. There was a bed in Ricky's workroom, but she had always found that room to be so depressingly cold. She preferred to sleep on the couch in the living room.

All she had now was herself. And Ricky, of course, even if he wasn't much help. *Sorry!* she thought immediately, *I don't mean that*. She loved Ricky. And he was a help. Yesterday he had taken care of her. The thought of that made her feel that there was still something that survived after all.

It was getting lighter outside. There was a bluish glow coming in through the deep windows. She wrapped the blanket around her and walked barefoot across the cold floor up to one of the windows. She looked out across the little garden that without any visible boundary gave way to Ricky's landlord's extensive plot. To the left, however, there was an electrified fence around the well-grazed pasture where gray and black lambs stood motionless like little pruned juniper bushes in the sunrise. Then she caught sight of the Prada bag and the flattened Bag-in-Box in the middle of the lawn.

She quickly pulled on her clothes, slipped her feet into a pair of boots in the hall that were seven sizes to big, and went out to collect her things. It was hot outside and there was an unseasonably warm wind blowing in from the west.

She picked up her bag and slung it over her shoulder, took the box wine in her left hand. The purple plastic bag from the state liquor store that she had had it in, had blown away and was nowhere to be seen.

Elin straightened her back. It said something about yesterday that they had forgotten both the wine and the bag out in front of the house. She pushed her shoulders back and slowly turned to the left. There was a woman standing outside the house next door. She was standing there blatantly staring at her. Elin raised her free hand and waved, but then quickly turned her back on the woman and began walking toward the house. She didn't have the energy to answer any questions, could pretty much imagine what it would sound like. First sympathy, followed by fishing.

She took refuge inside the house with the oversized boots flopping and knocking around her feet. She stepped out of them and set down the Bag-in-Box on the bench next to the upright hall mirror. She stopped and regarded her reflection from head to toe. She felt as if she'd grown older since the night before, but you couldn't tell from looking at her. She leaned in closer and studied her face. A seam on the couch had left an impression on her cheek. She ran her finger along it.

The policeman she had spoken to the previous evening was going to call again. He had told her to call him if they received any more threats, or 911 if she couldn't get hold of him. He had sounded nice but tired, his voice not really clear. During the night it was also best to call 911, he had added. She had started to apologize, but he had cut her off telling her that there was no need. He had offered his condolences before explaining that he had some questions, but that it would be better to wait with them until tomorrow.

And now it was tomorrow. She went out into the kitchen and set her bag down on the glossy black table and poured herself a big glass of water. She was thirsty and emptied it in a few gulps. But she didn't feel the least bit hungry.

She saw the bag that lay deflated on the table like a punctured beach ball and it was only then that it dawned on her that she didn't need it anymore. She could throw it away, give it to the Salvation Army, or sell it on eBay. There was no longer anyone she had to lug it around for. Of course, her father was still out there somewhere, but she had never used the bag for his sake, not to please him because he had bought it for her. She had done it for her mother, because her mother felt that she ought to use it for his sake.

"It's only a bag after all," she said to herself and slowly emptied the contents onto the table.

HE WAS ALL wound up like a Duracell bunny, had hardly slept during the night. Beppo was still snoring in the bedroom when he pressed his nose against the kitchen window and looked out across the parking lot outside the Konsum supermarket. Downtown Hemse. It was light outside and people had started to appear along the sidewalks.

The apartment had two rooms. But the place was a fucking sty. Empty beer cans, liquor bottles, and dirty clothes jumbled up with hopelessly out-of-date home electronics, that Beppo had probably stolen from somewhere. The sink was piled high with dirty dishes and the floor was covered in grit and stained with ingrained crud. Not that he was particularly fussy, but whether he liked it or not, three-and-a-half years of prison discipline had made him accustomed to a certain degree of order.

Beppo and he had been in the same class since fourth grade and they had kept in touch since school. Sporadically, but still.

He lit a cigarette and decided to go down and buy the newspapers. He had watched the news all last night.

The local Gotland channel on digital TV had run the same news report over and over again: "A man and woman were found dead early Friday morning at a farm in southern Gotland. The police are currently very tight lipped about the circumstances surrounding the murders." Just think of all the things that happen when you've been gone for a few years.

Beppo had bragged all day about his digital TV box, how he had bought it under the counter for just four hundred. He had pretended to be impressed. *No shit?!* What did the guy think he was doing? Selling under-the-counter TV boxes in Hemse, what a fucking dead end.

He was about to light yet another cigarette when he realized that he already had one smoldering in his mouth. He put it down at the very edge of the table while he wriggled into his tracksuit jacket and pulled the zipper all the way up to his neck.

On the way out he caught sight of Beppo's hoodie hanging from a hook on the hall. He put it on over his tracksuit top and pulled up the hood. He didn't feel like being recognized. It had been many years since he'd last wandered around in Hemse. He had left the island long before he went to prison, but the people were essentially the same and many would recognize him. And some of them would put two and two together.

He took the last few drags from his cigarette on the way down the steps and tossed the butt into the boot scraper outside the front entrance. His hair hung outside the hood and he pushed it back and tried to shove it far back behind his neck.

He had kept it long throughout his incarceration. Many had cut their hair short or shaved their heads, but he had refused. His first month inside he had gotten into a fight. He wasn't the one who started it, and it really wouldn't have been that big of a deal, if it hadn't been for the fact that the guy who'd gone after him ripped a big tuft of hair out of his head when he'd gotten the upper hand. That punk-ass bastard.

Three days later he had caught sight of the hair-puller a ways ahead of him in the dinner line in the cafeteria. When the guy was busy getting his food, he had snuck up behind him and buried a fork in his ass as far as it would go. The guy had groaned like wounded musk ox.

He had been put in solitary for a few days, but after that nobody pulled his hair anymore.

It was hot with two jackets on, but he wasn't going far. The Hemse shopping center was just across the street. He walked into the tobacco shop and took a *DN* and a *GT* newspaper. There was one person ahead of him, a gray-haired old lady holding a newspaper.

"My goodness, this is awful, just ghastly," he heard her say as she waved the front page in front of the tobacconist, "why it's only a stone's throw away from here."

The tobacconist nodded behind the counter, a big, sturdy guy he didn't recognize and who hadn't been there the last time he had been on the island.

"But, misfortune visits rich and poor alike," said the old lady, and was handed her change, which it took her an eternity to put into her change purse. "Though I don't know how fortunate they were up there before, either. That big farm . . ."

She sighed a little and let her statement hang in the air a little. The tobacconist shifted his attention to him and he laid the newspapers onto the counter.

When he emerged from the tobacconist, the metal roller shutters of the state liquor store were just being raised, exposing the double-door entrance. He stopped with his back to the tobacconist's video shelf and looked through the window across the street at the racks full of cans and bottles. He thought for a while, but decided that he couldn't stand there gawking outside like an idiot this time, but decided to go ahead and enter the store.

That was another thing he'd promised himself before his release, that he would ease off on the sauce. So this was the second promise he'd broken in less than a week, he thought as he grabbed one of the gray plastic shopping baskets from the stack by the turnstile. But this would have to be written off as an exception, given the circumstances, and he could still take it easy even if he drank a little.

He veered off before he made it to the hard-liquor shelf, stopped in the beer section and quickly put four cans of Norrlands Guld into his basket. Four cans was nothing after all, and for that very reason maybe he wasn't going to take any more, he thought, but then realized that he couldn't get out of inviting Beppo to join him, and immediately doubled the number of cans in his basket.

Two guys his own age entered the store and stopped on the other side of the rack. One was wearing a blue T-shirt, the other a washed-out plaid flannel shirt and two-day beard. He didn't recognize either of them, but looked down at the floor just in case.

"It may sound harsh to say this, but if you ask me, if it was going to happen to anybody, it was going to happen to them," he heard one of them say.

He was heading off with his cans of beer when a man in his fifties came in through the turnstile. The older one called out and waved to the younger men and headed toward them.

"Did you hear about the Traneuses?" he said in a hushed voice when he'd gotten a little closer.

The other two nodded.

"Apparently it was a real bloodbath. Viktor knows the woman who does the cleaning up there, and it was no joke. The poor girl's a complete wreck, Amanda Wahlby, I don't know if you . . ."

The others shook their heads.

"There wasn't much left of them," he said and lowered his voice to just a whisper, "just mincemeat. She couldn't even tell who they were."

The younger man grimaced, but there was just as much curiosity reflected in their faces.

"It's like Stigge said just now, typical that it would happen to them."

"Yeah," said the older man, "it's almost spooky. It's like some people have a curse on them or something. I mean, how much shit can happen to one family? And it wouldn't surprise me if he's the one that did it, that Arvid."

"He's always been one cocky son of a bitch," said the one whose name was apparently Stigge.

"And a little crazy," said the other.

"But of course you gotta hand it to the guy, he's done well for himself, too. Not that I know much about it, but they say he was raking it in over there in Japan."

"He was rich before, too, wasn't he," said Stigge.

"Maybe things have gone *too* good for him," said his friend, then they went silent, suddenly aware that someone was listening.

Three pairs of eyes turned toward him questioningly. He realized that he had forgotten to look down at the floor, and instead had stood there for a long moment staring at them and listening to their conversation on the other side of the beer rack. He immediately looked down and turned his back to them. He headed toward the checkout, had to really force himself to walk at a normal pace, felt their eyes burning holes in the back of his neck.

He wasn't afraid of those bozos, he would have been able to take them all on, if it came to that, but the important thing right now wasn't to show off, but to keep a low profile. More than anything he just wanted to get out of there. Leave this goddamn shit hole of an island on the next ferry. But that wouldn't look very good, anyone could work that one out. Chill out with a few brews as if nothing had happened was probably the best thing he could do right now.

He lined up the cans on the checkout conveyor and forced a smile. He briefly met the cashier's gaze. He didn't like the way she looked at him. Not like he was just any other customer, not even like he was an oddball, but as if he reminded her of something.

22.

"If he has left the country, or the island for that matter, he certainly hasn't left any trace. We've checked the airports, Destination Gotland, national railroad, credit cards. Nothing."

The tall, almost completely gray-haired Lennart Svensson had dark circles under his eyes and his wrinkles seemed more numerous and deeper than usual, but he still looked buoyant. Lennart was legendary for his ability, when he was in that sort of mood, to exasperate his colleagues during briefings with bad jokes and trivial comments, but despite being the oldest detective at CID, he could put in more hours than anyone without either complaining or bragging about it.

Lennart Svensson liked to work, quite simply. Fredrik was convinced that he would fall down dead the moment he stepped out of the police station's front entrance with a gold watch in his hand, or whatever it was they gave you these days.

"He's no fool, Arvid Traneus," said Göran Eide, who looked both perkier and more worried. An emotional negative of Lennart Svensson.

"That's for sure; have you seen how much the guy's worth?" said

Lennart. "Unless he won it all on the lottery, I'd say he's pretty sharp. And if he's got that much in his registered investment portfolio and in ordinary bank accounts, then you can bet he's got ten times that stashed away on the Cayman Islands or some place like that. He could buy the entire Gotland Police Department if he wanted to."

"Good thing we're not for sale then," said Göran.

They held the briefing in the small conference room as always. The entire team was present. Prosecutor Peter Klint was also sitting in, but not the district police commissioner who was attending a course on the mainland.

Peter Klint had a deep tan, and sun-bleached hair that was in need of a trim. He had just returned a week ago from a sailing vacation in the Mediterranean and seemed more loose and laid back than his colleagues were used to seeing him. It might have had something to do with the fact that Klint, who was just over fifty, had left his wife that spring and, as rumor had it, moved in with a woman sixteen years his junior.

"So, the two victims have been identified as Kristina Traneus and Anders Traneus, both forty-seven years old," Göran continued. "Anders Traneus is the cousin of Kristina's husband Arvid Traneus, in case anyone missed that. Lennart, you're the expert on this, right?"

"Yeah, so, like you just heard, Arvid and Anders are cousins, Arvid is three years older."

Lennart got up feeling a little stiff and walked up to the whiteboard.

"It's all on the computer, but it might help to have it up on the board in front of you while we're talking about it," he said and wrote up the names that had already been mentioned. He ended up printing them in green marker since that was the only pen he could find. He grouped the names according to family and ended by underlining the names Kristina Traneus and Anders Traneus.

"Arvid and Kristina have two children, Oskar Traneus . . ."

"I think his first name is actually Rickard," said Sara.

"Okay, Rickard," said Lennart and changed it before he wrote the next name, "and Elin Victoria Traneus. They also had a third child, Stefania Traneus, who died ten years ago, at the age of nineteen."

"Do we know how she died?" asked Gustav fingering his blue Bic pen.

"Not yet," said Lennart. "So, starting with the cousin; he's divorced from Inger Traneus with whom he has two grown-up children, Sofia and Karl-Johan. The daughter lives in Visby and the son on the mainland. Rickard Traneus, by the way, lives here on the island, just a few miles from his parents' house in Levide. Göran and Sara were there yesterday. Elin, however, lives on the mainland, in Stockholm."

"But is currently staying with her brother in Levide," Göran interjected. "She came here to celebrate her father's return from his job abroad and only learned what happened when she stepped off the bus in Hemse."

"Well, I've checked with the property registry and apparently the cousins' grandfather left the farm to Arvid's father, who then passed it on to Arvid," said Lennart picking up the thread. "It's possible that Anders's part of the family felt passed over, but then we don't know anything about the original arrangements, and whether Rune Traneus received any kind of financial compensation for relinquishing any rights to the farm."

Lennart continued sorting through the family ties for a few minutes. He finished off by drawing a dotted line between Anders and Kristina Traneus and a question mark above it.

"Take this with you and keep it in the back of your mind when you're questioning these people," said Göran and pointed at the board.

Lennart returned to the table, but didn't sit down. It was a peculiar little habit he had developed because of his lumbago. Periodically he couldn't sit down for very long at all unless it was in the right chair.

"None of the people I've mentioned show up in our files," he said and rested his hands on the back of the chair. "But I called up an old acquaintance at social services. You sort of expect that big landowners and other muckety-mucks might stick in people's minds more than ordinary people."

"So there was a complaint filed?" said Ove.

"An anonymous complaint was filed eight years ago. Claiming that Arvid Traneus was abusing his wife. Social services made a few cautious inquiries, but didn't find anything. Then there are the phone calls. There we've uncovered a few items of interest," Lennart continued and picked up a sheet of paper from the table. "Listen to this; last Monday evening at ten-thirty-nine p.m. someone made a call from Kristina and Arvid Traneus's home phone to Anders Traneus's home phone. That is the only registered phone call between the two locations in the seventy-four days that we've been granted access to so far."

"Kristina contacts Anders, then they're killed," said Ove.

"Let me finish," said Lennart. "Like I said, there's only one call registered from Arvid and Kristina Traneus's phone to Anders Traneus, but there are upward of a hundred calls from Anders Traneus's home phone to an unregistered prepaid cell phone and essentially the same number of incoming calls to him from an anonymous phone number. Put them altogether and we're talking an average of two phone calls a day."

"So, Kristina had a special prepaid SIM card that she used to call her lover," suggested Fredrik, "a card that she got rid of before her husband returned. Then something happened where she needed to get hold of him, but then she didn't have the prepaid card anymore."

"Or else she got careless," Sara objected.

"It may also have been Arvid who called," said Fredrik. "If Kristina really did have an extra SIM card, then she was being very, if not extremely careful. Strange that she would suddenly start being careless."

"She may have destroyed the extra card, but she may also have been distressed, desperate. Maybe there was no time to fiddle around with different SIM cards."

Fredrik sat up in his chair and turned toward Sara.

"Let's say Arvid comes home from Japan and finds something that makes him suspicious that there's something going on. He becomes jealous, aggressive, and goes after Kristina. Kristina calls Anders, who heads over to the farm in Levide, but things don't quite turn out the way he'd intended."

"But there's a problem there," said Eva.

"I'm listening." said Fredrik and turned toward Eva.

"There's no way the bodies had been lying there since Monday. I'll be getting the preliminary autopsy report tomorrow, but in my opinion they were killed sometime on Wednesday."

"So the phone call can't have been what prompted Anders Traneus to go storming over to the house?" said Ove.

"No, definitely not storming over," said Eva.

She could have come out with that earlier, thought Fredrik, but said nothing.

Sara walked over to the shiny, spotlessly clean sink and filled a plastic cup with water. She had spoken for a long time and her throat was dry. The cup barely held four ounces, so she drank three of them before she felt satisfied.

"Blue," said Fredrik behind her.

Sara turned toward Fredrik in the hospital bed. She didn't know what to answer.

"Blue," he said again.

He seemed better, especially compared to yesterday's relapse. No dramatic changes, but definitely better. His power of speech had improved. The doctors described his power of speech in percentage terms. Sara didn't really understand how they calculated it, but obviously the higher the percentage the better, and it had gone up. He was speaking. For the most part, what came out of his mouth was unintelligible, but it was better than him not talking at all. "Blue" might well mean blue, but could just as well mean something else. Maybe it was an attempt to say, *telephone*. Or maybe: *What did the medical examiner's report say?*

Sara tossed the cup into the wastebasket next to the sink and slowly walked back to the window. Fredrik followed her with his eyes about halfway, but then lost track of her.

She looked out over the redbrick buildings of the hospital grounds. The sun hung low in the sky and beamed in streams of yellow light between the buildings.

"So anyway, then Göran told me that Rickard Traneus had been threatened late the previous night. It was somehow connected to the murders."

23.

"It was Elin Traneus who called me, but the threat was directed at her brother. The call went to his home phone and he was the one who answered."

"Could it have been Rune Traneus? Considering what happened outside the house yesterday it wouldn't come as any great surprise," said Fredrik.

"Did it seem to be an elderly person, did she say anything about that?" asked Gustav.

Göran Eide waited out the questions patiently and rubbed his eyes before he answered.

"According to his sister, Rickard understood it to be someone his own age."

"Then we've got another crank on our hands," said Lennart.

"We'll have to keep an eye on that," Peter Klint interrupted, "if it seems serious we'll have to arrange for protection. It's reasonable to assume that it could be a relative of one of the victims who made the threats, most likely someone related to Anders Traneus."

"Right," said Göran. "We'll have to pull Rickard Trancus's phone records and cross our fingers that this crank doesn't use a prepaid phone card. I guess that's it," he said and got up. "Everybody know what they have to do? Fredrik and Gustav take Anders Traneus's ex and the father, continue with the children if you don't hear anything else. Sara, you question Rickard Traneus. Check up on this threat. Ove, you check out the people closest to Kristina. If it's a case of infidelity, then there's bound to be at least one friend who knows about it. I'll question Elin Traneus, and then I'll see what we can glean from Arvid

Traneus's employers in Japan. The company is at least partially Swedish owned, so it shouldn't be completely impossible to communicate with them."

"One more thing," said Eva when everyone had already started to get up. "I found Kristina Traneus's diaries. I don't know if there's anything useful in them, but they're down in my office anyway. They're twelve books in all, with well-filled pages of difficult-to-read handwriting. I don't have time to sit down and plow through all of it myself, but maybe we can divide them up."

No one showed any spontaneous enthusiasm.

THEY HADN'T EXPECTED Inger Traneus to be at work, but that was where they found her. They let her decide if she wanted to be questioned there or at the police station. She chose the police station. They offered to come pick her up, but she said that she could walk. It wasn't far from Söderport.

When Fredrik met Inger down in the reception, he thought that she seemed unchanged from the day before. The same tone of voice, the same expressions and demeanor. The death of her ex-husband didn't seem to have affected her. Not on the surface.

The interview rooms on the ground floor were all occupied, so he took her to the video room up at CID.

"Whenever we have to interview children we usually do it in here," Gustav said explaining the teddy bears lined up on a little wall shelf.

Inger Traneus flashed a brief smile and then sat down on the chair Fredrik had pulled out for her. She adjusted her tight ponytail and drew two fingers along her forehead just below the hairline. Fredrik and Gustav sat down, too.

"What was your relationship with Anders like after the divorce?" Fredrik began.

"It was good," she said lingeringly and then added hastily, "lately it's been good. It been five years since we got divorced."

"Was it different then, five years ago?"

She looked at Fredrik with a pained expression and was about to say something, perhaps a plea not to have to talk about this of all things, but then reconsidered, as if she realized that it wasn't negotiable. She started again.

"I was the one who left him," she pointed out soberly. "We were going through what is euphemistically referred to as a rough patch, but I had never considered leaving him until just before I actually did it. Once I realized that he'd never really loved me, it was easy. Or, rather, it was awful, but it was easy to make the decision to move out. Over twenty years. Half an adult life with someone who doesn't love you. What a disaster."

She shook her head.

"That was what I was trying to tell you yesterday, but I was probably a little incoherent."

She breathed in through her nose and let out a little sigh. Fredrik sat there silently and waited, tried to concentrate on Inger and forget himself. Her words turned his insides upside down, both because he could imagine the abyss that must have opened up beneath her feet, how twenty years of life had suddenly been drained of all meaning, but also because there was something tragic in that absolute need for closeness, fusion almost. Was there anyone who escaped, who didn't sooner or later stand there at the edge of the abyss and realize that their lives were gone and that there was no time left to give it another go?

"Anders liked me. It wasn't that he didn't care, or treated me badly, but he was busy elsewhere," said Inger.

"You mean he was unfaithful?" asked Fredrik and felt clumsy.

Inger shook her head again.

"No. I'm sure he wasn't. As sure as it's possible to be," she said and paused, letting her right hand run over her hair. "Some people can't move on," she said. "Never. They're stuck in the past."

"Was there anything in particular that made you realize that he was *busy*, as you called it?" said Fredrik.

"Sure, you could say that. It was Rune who made me realize it. I don't think he intended to, it was just something he said. A little thoughtless, of course, but Rune can be like that, more honest than is really healthy, without realizing it himself. It was during the Christmas holidays. We'd been having difficulties for a while. It happened every so often, but this time it had gone on for a long time. I asked Rune straight out what he thought. About Anders, that is. Why he was so distant. We'd just finished dinner at our place. It may have been the day after Christmas, and Rune and I were still sitting at the table. First he nodded, as if it didn't come as much of a surprise, and then he began to talk about how Anders had always been a bit of a brooder and that . . ."

Inger stopped herself and looked at Fredrik stiffly.

"I'm sorry, I don't know why I'm telling you all these details. I'm not feeling very well. Maybe you can understand that? I doubt that this is the sort of thing you want to hear."

Strictly speaking that was probably true, thought Fredrik, but then again who was to say what was the best path to what they wanted to hear?

"Tell us in whatever way feels best for you," he said.

"Right, okay," said Inger and put her hands together again. " 'He's never quite gotten over Kristina.' That's what he said. Rune. 'He's never quite gotten over Kristina.' That's what he said to me, after I'd been married to his son for twenty years. I don't get what he was thinking, or I guess that's just what he wasn't doing. Thinking. He was a little drunk, too, so he was spinning around there in his own world ruminating over what he saw. It just slipped out of him. The stupid idiot! But Rune has always been clumsy. Not Anders, on the other hand. *That* he didn't inherit. An idiot, too, maybe, but not clumsy."

"You mean that Anders had a relationship with Kristina Traneus?"

"Yes, he did," she said and took a deep breath. "But that was over thirty years ago."

"That's a long time ago," said Fredrik.

"Yes, it's a very long time ago," said Inger and judging from her expression she thought it was more like an insanely long time ago.

"What do you know about their relationship?"

"Not much," she answered, calmer now. "Essentially nothing. They were together for a while before she met Arvid."

"But Anders never got over her, if I've understood you correctly?"

"You have."

"So the cousins were rivals?"

"I don't know about rivals. That sounds so serious. Anders wanted her, Arvid got her. I guess that makes them rivals, but whether or not it was an open rivalry . . . they had no contact with each other, after all."

"Was it because of Kristina that they didn't have any contact?" asked Fredrik.

"Among other things. Ask Rune."

"So there were other things, apart from Kristina?" said Fredrik.

"Yes, but I don't know anything about it. Ask Rune. You may have to drag it out of him. There are things in that family that don't get talked about. But he's the one who would know."

Fredrik decided to drop that line of questioning. They would have to come back to that after they had spoken to Rune, if it proved necessary.

"So when you decided to leave Anders there was nothing specific that had happened, nothing concrete that is, but rather . . ."

"No," said Inger, "nothing had happened in that sense."

Apparently she was in the habit of answering before the person asking the question had finished talking.

"But rather Rune's comment?"

"Not just that, of course. I spoke with Anders, threw it in his face as soon as the others had left. And for the first time he came clean. I knew about Kristina, of course, had even asked him about it several times, but he had always waved it off. This time he told me straight. Well, he wasn't actually very clear this time, either, but he spoke about it anyway. And what he said was enough for all the pieces to fall into place. After that, there was only one thing to do and that was to leave. The children were all grown up and had moved out, so it was easy, practically speaking. But it was difficult, very difficult after more than twenty years. I was angry, sad, and . . ."

She broke off in mid-sentence and looked first at Fredrik, then at Gustav.

"Anyway, I guess that's about what you needed to know?"

"Yes, I guess it is," said Fredrik. "I realize that this is difficult for you, but just one last thing."

Inger nodded weakly.

"After you got divorced, do you know if Anders reestablished contact with Kristina?"

"It sure looks that way. I mean, they died together. But, no, it was nothing I knew anything about. I understand that men are drawn to Kristina. She's like that. But I don't understand how anyone can cling to the memory of her for half a lifetime. She's not worth that. Maybe nobody is, but she definitely wasn't."

She paused for a moment and then continued clearly and resolutely:

"Kristina wasn't a good person. She wasn't worthy of all his longing."

24

"It seems as if Anders Traneus finally got what he wanted," said Gustav when Fredrik returned from having seen Inger Traneus out.

"Slow and steady wins the race," said Fredrik.

He stood there silently for a moment in the doorway to Gustav's room. Gustav didn't say anything, either. Cynicisms had no place here, they just felt sordid.

"What can you say?" said Fredrik.

"Yeah . . . what can you say?"

Fredrik leaned his shoulder against the doorjamb. Any attempt to sum it up or make a comment just felt petty. And the whole time he saw before him that abyss. Precipitous, dark, and impossible to cross.

"So what do we do now," asked Gustav, "should we go see the father?"

"Yeah, let's head over there and see how he's doing. If he seems okay, then we'll bring him back here. It'll probably be a little chaotic over there otherwise, what with children and grandchildren and everything."

ELIN TOOK THE heavy paper bag and carried it to the sink.

"Are you still shopping at ICA?" she said when he had untied his shoes and came into the kitchen.

"What?"

"ICA! You still don't dare shop anywhere except at ICA?"

"What do you mean, don't *dare*?" said Ricky and straightened his sweater that had been turned inside out down at the hem.

"You know what I mean. That Father always warned us about that pinko co-op Konsum."

"As it happens, I do shop at Konsum on occasion. Especially in the summer. The lines are much shorter there," said Ricky and took the tabloids that lay in the top of the bag.

"Sure," said Elin and started putting the groceries away.

The bag was neatly packed with milk at the bottom and vegetables at the top.

"I still don't understand if he meant that communists shopped there, or that Konsum itself was a bunch of communists who stole market share from private retailers."

Ricky held up both papers in front of him and scanned the front pages.

"Since when did you become such a lefty?" he asked, no longer fully engaged in the discussion.

"Ricky, it's not about politics. It's about the fact that I want to be able to go and buy a carton of milk without Father looking over my shoulder."

Ricky turned the newspapers around so that Elin could read.

MURDER DRAMA ON GOTLAND
MULTIMILLIONAIRE ON THE RUN FROM POLICE
DOUBLE MURDER A CRIME OF PASSION?
THEY LAY IN EACH OTHER'S ARMS

"Hemse wasn't a hell of a lot of fun. I didn't get a chance to think too much about which supermarket to go to."

Elin took the *Expressen* newspaper from him and quickly flipped through the pages dealing with the murder of their mother and her alleged lover. *They lay dead in each other's arms.*

"I can't read this."

She tossed aside the newspaper onto the table and wrapped her arms around herself, as far as she could. She was cold and everything seemed unreal.

"Strange that they haven't started pestering us yet," said Ricky with his nose in the *Aftonbladet*.

"Well, we pulled the phone jack out yesterday, after that . . ."

"Oh, yeah, that's right."

Elin left the kitchen, and went into the bedroom and started rooting around among Ricky's clothes.

"Could I borrow one of your sweaters?" she called out.

She pulled on a black fleece sweater that was far too big.

"Sure, but could you stop running around?"

"But I'm cold."

"Yeah, but can't you just sit down, or stand still at least."

Elin came back into the kitchen, sat down on a chair with her arms crossed.

"So how was it, in Hemse?"

"Strange. Fucking strange. First the news bills and then . . . well, you can imagine. People started coming up to me. And the ones that didn't stared. I was barely able to finish shopping. I just wanted to drop the basket and run away."

"Listen, I—"

She stopped short and looked out the window when she heard a car slow down. A red station wagon with the TV4 logo on the doors rolled slowly up to the gate while the driver pressed his nose up against the side window.

"Journalists," she said and nodded out the window.

"Really?"

Ricky turned around and looked out.

"Yeah, really. From TV. I can't believe this is happening to me. It's like being in a film."

"What do we do?" asked Ricky and pulled away from the window.

"Nothing," said Elin. "We don't open. I don't want to speak to anyone. I just don't have the energy."

Ricky looked around then rushed out to the entrance hall and locked the door.

"Let's go upstairs," he said, "then they won't see us."

They hurried up the stairs and slipped into the study.

"We'll be all right here," said Ricky.

They sat down on the guest bed, Elin farthest back in the corner, and Ricky in the middle.

The doorbell rang out through the house.

They looked at each other uneasily. The doorbell rang again. A moment later, a couple of insistent knocks were heard on the window of the front door. Ricky reached out and gave the study door a shove. They sat there silently, stared at the wall opposite them and listened. Somebody spoke, but they couldn't tell whether it was directed to them or if the ones standing outside the door were simply speaking among themselves.

"I called Åhlbergs," said Elin.

"Åhlbergs, you mean the undertak—"

"Yes."

"I see."

"I called while you were out shopping."

"Were they the ones who drove Mother to . . . well, wherever it was they took her?"

"No, apparently there's someone over in Kräklingbo who handles that kind of . . . transport. Anyway, I thought we ought to find out what's going on."

"Do they work on Saturdays?"

"I don't fucking know, I called home."

"Calm down."

"Yeah, well you're asking such stupid questions."

Elin sighed, but continued.

"They said that it might be a while before we can bury Mother, since the police have requested that she be taken to Stockholm for an autopsy."

"Do you have to say that?"

"What, autopsy? What am I supposed to say?"

Ricky didn't answer.

"You promised to take care of it. To keep after them so we know when they're done, so we don't have to think about it."

"All right," said Ricky mutedly.

They sat there quietly again. The doorbell rang.

25.

How old would he have been? Ten?

Could just as well have been eight or eleven. There was no time in the usual sense when the forty-four footer put out to sea from the pleasure boat harbor in Klinte, with its sails up, and soon enough the spinnaker, too, that swelled up like a huge multicolored beach ball against the deep-blue sky.

Ricky stood at the bow holding onto the railing that extended out beyond the pulpit. Like a figurehead: a roaring lion, a pirate, a mysterious mythical hero. There were thousands of games to play, like shipwreck, fending off pirates, or pretending they were being chased by a terrible deep-sea monster, but all the games had one thing in common: The island meant salvation.

Balmy winds swept around him, Mother and Father, Stefania, and Elin.

The summer sailing trips could be long or short, go to Finland,

Åland, or the Stockholm archipelago, sometimes all the way to Denmark, or the West Coast. But they always began the same way. With a counterclockwise lap around Gotland and a one-night sleepover on the island. Or actually they began when Father took out the sea charts the night before they were supposed to set off. Ricky got to locate the little island that lay all by itself just east of the much bigger Gotland. It wasn't much more than a speck on the charts. A speck with a thin promontory, like an appendix toward the south.

They never called it anything except the island, even though of course it had a name. That made it mysterious and full of secrets. The island belonged to them alone. That's how it had always been, ever since Stefania was a little girl, when the boat was also a lot smaller and the sailing trips rarely ever went farther out than to the island.

The first hours were always the same. Father at the helm. Mother and Stefania stretching their legs out in the cockpit, basking in the sun in their bikinis. Elin with a book, first on a mattress up on deck, then down in the cabin once she'd had enough of the sun, as long as the sea wasn't too rough, because then you got seasick down there.

Ricky would rush around, stand up at the pulpit, give Father a hand with things he didn't actually know how to do, but Father helped him and acted as if Ricky had done it. He got hoisted aloft in the boatswain's chair, or surfed behind the boat on a big black inner tube. Sometimes Elin was along, too.

The first day was always the best. And the island. On second thought it was probably the island that was the best, rather than the fact that it came first. It was another world. It was a big island, and there was nothing else there except for a few lambs, a couple of old ruins, and a lighthouse next to a little jetty. They used to anchor the *Adventure* with the bow facing the jetty. Elin and Ricky were the first to jump ashore, went dashing straight up to the lighthouse and pulled at the rusty iron door. Always the same ritual, always with the same result. Then they'd spend fifteen seconds looking for a key in the

seams of the limestone wall next to the base of the lighthouse before
setting off toward the opposite end of the island. They ran almost the
whole way and mother came after them and cried out telling them to
wait, sometimes Stefania, too. "I said wait, didn't you hear me?!"
They stumbled and jumped forward in flip-flops toward the scorch-
ing hot, chalk-white stone beaches and the big, dark limestone cave
that you could only enter by swimming.

As they moved toward the interior, the island became quieter. The
dry, tall grass rustled beneath their flip-flops, insects buzzed around
them, and from a distance they could hear the lambs bleating from within
the ruins of the old lighthouse keeper's quarters. That was the only place
where there was any shade when the sun was at its zenith. There and
in the cave. But the lambs couldn't make it in there, of course.

The sun beat down. It was hot. They marched past the overgrown
cluster of wind-battered junipers and dwarf birches where there were
fire ants, continued up the bluff as fast as they could and tried their
best to avoid stepping on the chalk-white bird skeletons that shone in
the low-cropped grass along with white flowers that were no bigger
than pinheads.

"I'm dying, water, water, I'm dying," they groaned one after the
other like two parched desert explorers, always at the same spot, where
they struggled up onto the ridge above the pebble beach. There they
collapsed onto the grass, lay there with their legs splayed and caught
their breath. But not for long, never long enough that Stefania caught
up to them. She was never as quick as they were. She came trudging
along at the same pace as Mother and Father. At least that was how he
remembered her, as being slightly in the background. But she was also
five years older than he was. Probably didn't want to have too much to
do with her romping little siblings.

They got back on their feet, saw the three figures slowly drawing
closer, almost camouflaged by the sun-bleached grass in their light
summer clothes. From down there, he and Elin must have stood out

like two steadfast little silhouettes up on the ridge. They started climbing down the steep, craggy bluff, heard a faint "be careful" behind them.

They reached the hot, blinding beach cauldron, teetered on chalk-white stones, and looked out across the endless sea. Then, they ripped off their clothes and threw themselves into the sometimes cold water, but they still threw themselves screaming into it and swam out toward the cave, into the dark, cool cave where the clucking of the waves echoed enchantingly against the rock walls, and reflections from the sun danced off the ceilings. Elin's hair lay pasted against her head and the water was like a wet film over her face. His heart pounded in his chest, the lurching surface of the water tickled his throat and Ricky felt warm all over his body, no matter how cold the water was.

There they were eternal. Time ceased. They were all immortal. He, Elin, Mother, Father, and Stefania.

26.

This day is turning out to be like walking backward in your own footprints, thought Fredrik as they pulled up in front of the row houses with the checkered pastel facades.

As soon as they'd climbed out of the car, the door at number 14 opened and Sofia Traneus pulled out a baby carriage where her youngest child lay fast asleep in a footmuff in the same dark-blue color as the carriage. The elder girl followed right behind and immediately took her mother's hand when she caught sight of Fredrik and Gustav.

"I'm sorry for your loss," said Fredrik. "I wish we could have brought you better news yesterday."

But someone had to get that news, he thought to himself. If it hadn't been Anders Traneus lying dead in the house, it would have been someone else. There was no getting around that.

Sofia Traneus nodded and rolled the baby carriage slowly back and forth.

"I was just going to take the kids out for a little walk," she said and glanced at the dozing infant. "Will it take long?"

"No, no, you go ahead. It's Rune we want to talk to. He is still here, isn't he?" Fredrik asked.

"Yes, Grandpa's inside."

"Then we'll do it here," said Gustav and looked at Fredrik.

"Yes, I think he'd feel better if he could stay here," said Sofia Traneus.

She headed off with the carriage and only once she'd disappeared around the corner did it strike Fredrik that she had been dressed in black from head to toe. Did people do that these days, or was it just a coincidence?

THE RUNE TRANEUS who was sitting across from them at the kitchen table was very different from the one they'd met the day before. He seemed calm, not the least bit confused and definitely responsive, but also subdued.

"We have to ask you a few things about Anders's background," Gustav began. "In a case like this, it is of the utmost importance to get as detailed a picture as possible of the relationships within the family, even going back in time, and you're perhaps the best person of all to tell us about it."

"That's possible. Yeah, that could be," Rune Traneus muttered.

Gustav's plan was to steer the conversation as little as possible and draw upon Rune Traneus's rage. Even if he wasn't shouting and screaming and wildly throwing his arms around anymore, the anger and hatred toward Arvid Traneus still had to be in there somewhere. That was the wellspring he wanted to tap into, there was a wealth of information that could be extracted from it.

"When you came to your nephew's farm yesterday morning, you seemed so certain that it was Anders lying in there. Something tells me you were pretty sure even before you spotted his car parked outside the house?"

Gustav saw how something flared up in the old man's eyes as his thoughts were brought back to the scene of the murder. *Just don't start howling about how Arvid is the devil again,* he thought to himself. But it was as if Rune Traneus just couldn't help himself.

"I realize that I went overboard yesterday," he said, "but I meant what I said. That man is the devil. Arvid Traneus is Satan himself."

Those last words came out with added emphasis and you could detect something of yesterday's fire in them, but he was far from uncontrolled. He said it more to himself than to Gustav and Fredrik, more like an incantation.

So far so good, thought Gustav, *but it would be great if you could be a little more specific.*

"I barely know where to start where that man's concerned," said Rune and twirled one of his bushy eyebrows.

"If you focus on Anders. How was Anders's relationship to his cousin and Kristina?"

"I understand that that's what you want to hear about, but it's still difficult to know where to begin. I sensed that something was amiss, and that made me . . . Well, it's impossible to describe."

Rune Traneus drew his hand across his mouth and shook his head. He had raisin-sized liver spots on his face and his eyes were pale somehow, diluted. He was an old man and his old age had all of a sudden become very hard to bear.

"What could I do? Anders was a grown man, and then some," said Rune and threw out the hand that he had just been holding over his mouth. "You can't . . . It becomes difficult to interfere."

"What was it that you sensed was amiss, as you put it?" asked Gustav.

"He was so busy all of a sudden, always had things to do, didn't answer the phone, and when you asked him where he was going or where he'd been, you never got a straight answer. It was like when he was a little boy and had gone and done something stupid. I recognized it. At first I just thought that he'd met someone new, you know, after Inger, and that he just didn't want to talk about it. You can understand that, if you're getting involved with someone new, and you're not sure yet where it's going."

Rune paused and breathed almost like he was a little short of breath, as if it had been physically strenuous to talk about.

"Then there was one day when he was over at my house; there was something in his eyes, an anxious look that I hadn't seen in a long time and the thought suddenly struck me like a bolt from the blue: *What if it's Kristina?* And the words just slipped out, before I had a chance to stop myself. 'You're not seeing Kristina are you?' He sat there silently for a long moment without looking at me. 'No,' he said then. That's it, just 'no.' I couldn't be more certain, short of him coming right out and admitting it."

"But he never did?" asked Gustav.

"No. If he'd done that, I probably would've told him what I thought, I don't care how grown up and middle aged he was, but I had asked him and he'd answered no. So what could I do?"

He panted softly again.

"I realized that it would end badly, one way or the other, but that it would end up like this . . ."

He looked at Gustav and Fredrik with big, lost eyes. Gustav met his gaze and felt how he went completely cold. There was a pleading look in those eyes that he couldn't face. He could only do his best to solve the case, but he understood that it wouldn't make a lot of difference. Not to Rune Traneus.

"You probably can't really understand this. But you see, Anders had a brother who died exactly thirty years ago. He died out there on the farm. He used to work for my brother sometimes in the afternoons. They said it was an accident. A horse accident. But it was my brother who had the answer. You don't let an inexperienced sixteen-year-old get onto a horse that's . . . It was said that my brother had a way with horses, but that wasn't true. Our father was a good horse breeder. He had a way with animals, with horses especially, but not my brother. His animals were tense and skittish. My son had to pay for my brother's mistreatment of animals with his life."

Rune Traneus clenched his right fist at the same time as his left hand pressed against his stomach.

"My brother and his offspring have taken away everything from us. It wasn't enough with Johan and Kristina, they had to take Anders, too. And now he's gone, Arvid. The question is whether you'll ever catch him? He's a devil, but he's a damn smart devil."

"Kristina? How do you mean that they took Kristina away from you?" asked Gustav without revealing that they had recently touched upon the same topic with Inger Traneus.

"Kristina," snorted Rune. "It was as if Arvid just had to do it. He saw how much she meant to Anders. But I'll tell you this much . . ."

He pointed a crooked forefinger at Gustav.

"If Arvid hadn't have married her, Anders would've been able to put the whole thing behind him in a completely different way, that I'm sure of. But he just had to do that, too. You might well ask why? I mean, why he even wanted to get married at all. He treated women just like his father treated horses. What does a man like that get married for?"

It wasn't a rhetorical question. He looked at Gustav as if he expected an answer. It hung there in the air.

"Can you tell us what happened?" asked Gustav.

Rune Traneus looked pained. He'd had enough.

"Yeah, I reckon I can, more or less," he said.

27

"Be gentle," she whispered through the hair that had fallen in front of her face and meant it in two ways, literally, but also hinting that there was another power at play, an alternative to being gentle that was both tempting and frightening and it was that power she was playing with when she gave her whisper a slightly syncopated quality akin to a gasp.

Arvid wasn't gentle. He turned her around and bent her over the couch that lay overturned on its side, with the back facing upward. It smelled of basement and mildew and the fabric felt damp through the sheer dress that she still had on, even if it was unbuttoned and hiked up around her hips.

He penetrated her from behind, purposefully and with surprising suddenness. He took a firm grip around her hair, not enough to make it hurt, but so that it drew taut, leaving no doubt about who was in charge. He got her to bend her spine backward, cupped an ample warm hand over her right breast, let go of her hair with the other, and let it slide in between her legs. He continued to fuck her from behind with long, hard thrusts. Hot waves shot through her body. Her skin was like an electrical field and no matter where he touched her, she was on the verge of coming. She had never experienced anything like it. It was as if Arvid was taking her virginity all over again down in that basement, there in the very back, in the room full of furniture and old junk.

It smelled of dampness, earth, and dank basement air and her body rocked and slammed against the rough fabric of the couch. She felt the dust and tiny pebbles beneath her bare feet, felt his cock sliding into her, and how his body smacked against her buttocks underneath the hiked-up dress. She squeezed the backrest with her right hand, actually wanted to grab hold of him, but had to content herself with the couch, felt that she had to hold on, tight.

Arvid was rampant, dangerous in that sense like nobody else she knew. He was strong. He didn't care. He was brazen. You could tell as soon as you saw him what he wanted, and he wasn't afraid to show it. He dared to fuck her in the basement while the party was in full swing out in the garden and someone could come looking for them at any moment, or come down there to fetch some cold beer or whatever.

The hairs on her arms stood up. She had goose bumps all over her body. Her nipples stood straight out in his cupped, squeezing hand. It was so powerful that it scared her. Were these feelings normal, or was something wrong? Was something happening inside her body that was completely twisted? Was she dying perhaps? It was as if she was being immersed into a scalding hot bath at the same time that she was floating, no, soaring, in the cool refreshing night air, way above the treetops, high up above, out among the stars.

And when she came it was if she had never come before. She fell completely limp across the back of the couch. Arvid continued to move inside her but she barely noticed, only had a slight sensation of her body being rocked back and forth, right up until his grip tightened around her hips and he came, too.

She turned her head to the side and looked up toward the grimy basement windows. Out in the lush garden she recognized Anders's pant leg slowly passing by. She closed her eyes, ashamed, embarrassed, and with a feeling of having been used. And she wanted more. She couldn't help it. Anders whom she'd come with; she had wondered a little why he wanted to bring her along to his uncle's party, but why not?

She had arrived together with her boyfriend—wonderful, handsome, caring Anders. It was a perfect love story: dreamy, romantic, and Anders was attentive and tender.

And now she lay half naked on a stinking couch down in the basement together with Anders's cousin. Fucked. Taken in a manner in which she hadn't even fantasized about. How had this happened? She didn't know. Getting fucked she could understand, that was the simple part. The last part. But how had she gone from being with Anders in the garden, to being down in this dingy room in the basement? She didn't know. She didn't have the slightest idea.

But she wanted more. That much she knew.

28.

The chromed, circular clothing racks were stuffed full of hangers. So tightly packed that you could barely get one out. Elin had already grabbed some socks and underwear. Now she took three T-shirts; one white, one black, and one lime green, the latter because there was a stupid voice droning on somewhere in the back of her head: "Take something with a bit of color, take something with a bit of color." She took one slightly thicker, long-sleeved cotton shirt that was meant to look like it was made out of wool. Black. She didn't care how it looked. There was little room for considerations like that. This was all about finding something that worked. Right size, right function.

The H&M on Öster lay virtually next door to the police station. She took out her cell phone to see what time it was. She didn't have to meet the detective for another twenty minutes. There was plenty of time.

She laid the clothes on the counter next to the cash register and pulled the money out of her front pocket. The clothes were cheap. Even for a student who was trying to get by on financial aid and part-time jobs, and proudly refused any help from Daddy. If it hadn't been

for that, she would have sold the Prada bag that she never used anyway. But she couldn't do that. It didn't work that way.

Once she had paid, she moved on to the sports store and bought a
fleece sweater on sale. It was almost the same as the one she was wearing, but in her own size. One hundred and ninety-nine crowns.

She had left Ricky's car in the parking lot outside the Coop Forum
department store. It was going to move, so they said, and it was going
to be turned into a shopping mall instead. Was that true? Were the
citizens of Visby finally going to blessed with a proper shopping mall?

She started the car and cut right across the empty parking spaces
toward the exit.

And he sure as hell doesn't like you. He forgot you long ago. Screw God!

Jesus, hell, it didn't mean anything, she just wanted to play the same
music her friends played, a little punk nostalgia that didn't mean shit,
not to her or to the others at Vibble who hadn't even been born back in
the day. And why did he have to come barging into her room like a
fucking maniac, almost destroy her CD player, and chuck her record
out the window. He who wasn't even religious. Not that she had ever
noticed anyway.

She had seen the record glinting out in the field for several weeks
afterward, until the farmer who leased the land came and plowed over
it, or a magpie took it, or whatever it was that happened. She stopped
and waited for an opening in the traffic and felt so tired and sad all of
a sudden. As if her heart had just fallen out of her chest. What was going to happen to everything? She wanted to stay at Ricky's place until
the funeral, but it could take time, the woman at Åhlbergs had said.
How long could she wait? She would fall behind with her course
work. But would she even be able to study if she went back?

Mother, who she'd seen so little of.

What would the casket look like? The flowers? Who would come?
Were they supposed to serve food? Coffee?

Then she thought about the farm, the land, and the money. She felt ashamed, but couldn't help it. What would happen to all that? Even if Father had . . . done it, then it was still his, right? How about Mother's estate? And whoever it belonged to, someone had to look after it. Father couldn't do it if he was locked up in prison, or had run off to Japan and was never coming back.

Ricky of course. He had always been puttering around over there, like some kind of house brownie. Doing chores and fixing things. Cutting the grass and helping Mother change the tires on the car. Which was totally ridiculous. You only had to take one look at his place to see that it wasn't him. Besides which, they could afford to hire someone to do all that. What did he think he could hold together with all his tinkering?

It made her depressed to think about it. He really needed to get away from here, he far more than she. Away from the farm, from Gotland, from everything. This wasn't his world. He'd be so much better off somewhere else.

Oh, for fuck's sake, she thought and shot out when there was finally an opening, he was only a few years older than she was. He needed to get his act together. Not just needed to, had to. He was the man in the house now.

She couldn't help but smile a little, despite all the hellishness.

On the E4 highway, just visible in the gap between the psychiatric department and the reddish-brown, increasingly sparse foliage, the northbound traffic crawled along at an almost depressingly slow speed. Sara was happy that she didn't need to sit in one of those cars.

"I had an abortion a week ago," she said without turning away from the window.

She felt that the words echoed in the austere hospital room. She hadn't intended to say anything, definitely hadn't intended to say anything to Fredrik. She was just as surprised that those words had slipped out of her as Fredrik might have been, assuming he could understand what she said, or even hear her for that matter.

She had revealed her secret to a colleague without really understanding how it had happened. She had intended to tell him about the investigation, about their work together, how Fredrik had ended up here. That was the plan.

The advantage, of course, was that this particular colleague couldn't pass her secret on.

Then it struck her, that she really couldn't be sure about that. Right now he could barely say a word, but what if he got better? What if he were to just blurt it out, like a parrot, in front of anyone. Maybe he had no control at all over what he said.

Sara felt how she began to sink down, how a gloom took hold inside her.

What difference does it make, she thought to herself then.

"This murder investigation came at a very bad time for me. I was supposed to . . . Well, I was planning to . . ."

152

Why the hell was it so difficult. She coughed. Only now did she turn away from the window. Fredrik looked at her. His gaze was unexpectedly intense and she felt that it contained a question. That didn't make it any easier.

Fredrik opened his mouth.

"Oops," he said.

Sara stiffened. Was that a comment, or just a random "oops"? She sat there silently waiting for more, but Fredrik lay there silently. She had to continue, she thought, and took a deep breath.

"I didn't want to keep the baby. But I couldn't very well take time off in the middle of a murder investigation, not without a very good excuse. And I wasn't looking forward to speaking to Göran about it. So I guess I was hoping that the investigation wouldn't drag on for too long, that Arvid Traneus would get caught in some passport control somewhere and confess to the murders, so that I could book a time for an abortion, preferably on the mainland, as I'm sure you understand. So I said nothing to Göran."

She hadn't wanted anyone to know and she didn't trust the patient-doctor confidentiality on Gotland. And even if the nurses didn't break their vow of silence it would have been enough for the wrong person to see her entering or leaving the hospital the same day that she took a day off work, for people to start talking.

Sara took the few steps up to the ergonomic visitor's chair clad in vinyl-like orange-brown upholstery.

"If I was ever going to get pregnant, this wasn't how I had envisioned it happening. I guess maybe I feel a little ashamed. In fact, I do. Not about getting pregnant. Not even about the fact that I don't know who the father is. At least not with any great certainty. The whole situation is just so ridiculous. Stupid, clumsy. It's not like I'm twenty years old."

The father could either have been a Canadian from Vancouver, whom she had met on Sardinia during her vacation, or, theoretically anyway, a guy from Gotland whom she didn't even know whether she was in love with. Not that love or the uncertainty regarding the baby's paternity had affected her decision. She wasn't interested in having kids, it was that simple. When she tried to imagine what it would be like to be a mother, the only thing she could think about was all the stuff she would no longer be able to do. Not travel, not socialize with whomever she wanted whenever she felt like it, not be able to just pick up and leave if she got tired of where she was, and of course not go to bed with strange men from other continents with no protection except a "safe period." Instead she would have to show up on time at the daycare, attend PTA meetings, fritter away her not especially generous income on designer jeans for a kid who's never satisfied and never knows what's good for him.

All those were perhaps petty and self-centered arguments, but it was for that very reason . . . It wasn't her, it was that simple. The decision hadn't been difficult.

And she had just said all that to a colleague with a head injury. Surprisingly enough, it felt pretty good. What Fredrik felt about it she had no idea.

29

"I appreciate your coming in," said Göran Eide and sat down opposite the young woman. The *girl*, he thought. She was hardly more than a child.

"That's all right. I had to come into town anyway."

She looked pale, but seemed strangely full of energy. She had sat down with her back straight and her gaze fixed intently on Göran.

"The phone call that you contacted me about yesterday, the one that you felt was threatening . . ."

"I didn't *feel* that it was threatening," she cut in. "It *was* threatening. It was a death threat."

"But it was your brother who received the call, if I understand correctly?"

"Yes. But it was still a fucking death threat."

Two pink splotches flared up on her white cheeks.

"Anyway," said Göran, "the call came from a number registered to a Karl-Johan Traneus. Does that name mean anything to you?"

"Yes," she said, "I mean, I think I know who it is at least. I've heard the name at some point, but not much more than that."

"And who is it?"

"My second cousin, I guess he'd be? My father's cousin's child, Anders's child."

She looked at Göran questioningly. He confirmed with a nod that second cousin was the proper term.

"You've never met him?"

"I suppose I must have seen him around in Hemse or Klinte at some point, but I've never met him. Though I guess that's about to change. Since he seems set on coming over to kill us."

She didn't sound the least bit afraid when she said it.

"Why do think he called and threatened your brother?" asked Göran.

"I guess he must be insane or something," answered Elin.

"Something must have set him off, even if he is, as you say, insane."

"Yeah, that's true," she confessed. "His father was killed in our house. He thinks our father did it, but he can't get hold of him, so in the absence of anything else, he's decided to come after us."

Göran Eide moved his shoulders subtly. He had a slight ache between his shoulder blades, but he didn't want Elin Traneus to see that he was in pain. It was also strange; that kind of ache usually only afflicted him late in the evening after a long shift, not already in the morning.

"How do you feel about that?"

"About what?" asked Elin.

"That your second cousin, Karl-Johan, thinks your father is the murderer."

"How do I feel about it?"

Her voice became light and questioning. She suddenly huddled up inside her big, black sweater, the sleeves of which she had rolled up several turns, laid her hands against her face and patted her cheeks a few times with the palms of her hands.

"I just can't believe that I'm sitting here talking about this. I just can't believe it. Can't I just go home and go to bed?" she whined shrilly.

"We can break it off if you like," said Göran.

He was rattled by her outburst, but was also unsure whether it was the start of a breakdown or just teenage petulance—well, she wasn't quite that young, but almost.

She pressed her finger against her cheeks and opened her eyes wide.

"No, it's okay," she said then.

"We can move on to some . . ."

"No, it's okay," she repeated, "I just have to think about it for a minute. It feels very strange sitting here talking about it."

"I understand that," said Göran.

"It feels as if I've become an orphan. Which I sort of have even though my father's still out there."

"I'm not sure I follow you."

"No. I'm probably a little confused. I came down here to celebrate my father's return, which I really didn't feel like doing. Now my mother's dead and my father's suspected of having killed her," said Elin.

"Is that what you think?" said Göran.

"It's what *you* think, isn't it?"

Göran didn't answer.

"What do *you* think?" he asked.

"I'm surprised that it took him this long."

She abruptly cupped her hand over her mouth.

"I'm sorry, Christ that was harsh," she mumbled through her fingers, "but it's true."

She lowered her hand and swallowed before continuing.

"I just started a very demanding, five-and-a-half-year degree program in Stockholm so I could stay away from here for as much as possible. Well, that wasn't the only reason, but it was a very welcome perk."

She fell silent without looking away. Göran said nothing. He had trouble finding a good way of responding to her. He thought that the best was perhaps to just let it show.

"Don't worry about me," she said after a moment. "It feels very strange talking about this."

"How were things between your parents?"

"They were . . ." she said and paused to think for a long moment. "He used to beat her," she said finally. "But I guess I already said that, in a way. He beat her, and if you ask me, I think he was the one who did it . . . the one who killed her. It's difficult to say it. I didn't think it would be, because I've really turned my back on him, I think he's a total fucking bastard, and yet it's still not easy for me to say it . . ."

She went quiet and bit down hard to keep back the tears. The white, cramped interview room was completely silent around them. It wasn't all that hard to understand that she must have found the whole situation very unreal.

"And Anders Traneus and your mother? How did they know each other?"

"That's what I just can't get my head around. Anyone but him, or any other relation for that matter. I hardly know who these people are. Anders Traneus and, what was his name now again . . . Karl-Johan. We've been like an island in our family, especially where relatives are concerned, but otherwise, too. I can't understand what he was doing here."

Göran Eide couldn't make heads or tails of this interview. It steered back and forth, produced information, but nothing concrete. Elin was virtually convinced that it was her father who had killed her mother, but it was a conviction that was based more on a feeling than anything else. She hadn't spent a lot of time with her family over the past few years, but neither had Arvid Traneus for that matter. How much did she really know about how things were between her parents?

"You say that your father beat your mother. I realize that it's difficult for you, but could you talk a bit more about that? How did you become aware of it?"

"I've never seen him do it. He never did it in front of us. But I understood it early on. And Stefania was older, smarter, she could handle him in a way that we couldn't. She could divert his attention. But she couldn't always be there."

"How did you come to understand that this was happening? Can you remember?"

"You just knew. We heard Mother crying, we saw the aftereffects, bruises sometimes, but mostly that Mother was just totally broken. She moved differently, became someone else."

"How often could you see those kinds of signs?" asked Göran.

"Often enough. But not so often that you understood it. Sometimes you could predict it, but mostly it was just something that exploded. You could sometimes convince yourself that we were a normal family, at least when I was little, but then when you got older and smarter, like Stefania, you realized that we'd never be a normal family. It always came back, things would never be hunky-dory."

30.

It was as if the entire community was holding its breath. Not out of shock, but for fear of missing something if they breathed too loudly. The evil that had taken place radiated, reeked, and resonated from the farm in Levide and if you just listened closely enough you soon knew everything. Anything that didn't appear in the newspaper or wasn't reported on the radio or on the TV news, you could soon pick up through the stealthy use of your own nose, eyes, and ears.

Kristina Traneus. Found dead next to her husband's cousin. And there were those who knew how everything had begun once upon a time. It was like a saga.

Arvid Traneus had come home and he had also used his nose, eyes, and ears to find out what was going on. But it was claimed that he didn't even have to do that. He had a sort of sixth sense; it was enough for him to just walk into a room. The way it worked was that people were afraid of him and when they became afraid they gave themselves away, whether they wanted to or not.

Oh, sure. There were a lot of people who knew all about it.

The day was gray, but mild. Two old ladies, still wearing light summer coats, were standing in front of the gray facade of Svahn's hardware shop in the middle of Hemse. Their hair was crimped, but hidden beneath a cherry-red beret and a white-knitted hat. They hugged their shopping bags and were engaged in lively conversation.

"What a way to end your days."

"And how, you wouldn't wish it on your worst enemy."

"And she who was such a refined woman. I remember her from when she was a young girl. It wasn't that long ago after all."

"She was willful, too, though."

They fell silent and looked at each other while they thought about what they had just said. Then the woman in the cherry beret sighed.

"Sufficient unto the day is the evil thereof."

The other woman nodded slowly.

"One today, and tomorrow another."

ELIN PULLED UP in front of the house, turned off the engine, and pulled the hand break. Just as she opened the door, two people came rushing toward the car. She had been keeping an eye out for the red TV4 van, but hadn't noticed the white rental Volvo that had been parked fifty-five yards farther down the road, in the shade of a big chestnut tree.

Her first instinct was to pull the door closed, lock it, and just remain sitting there, but that impulse only made it as far as a nervous twitch in her leg.

She climbed out and slammed the car door, activated the central locking system, and held the bags from H&M and the sporting goods shop in a tight grip.

They came up to her, two women of around thirty, close to each other in appearance, medium-length hair in a ponytail, one light, the other dark, both wearing trench coats, this year's fashion rage. The dark-haired one held up a camera that she trained on Elin, while the blonde one introduced herself and held out her hand. Elin said, "Hi," but didn't take her hand. She didn't want to appear rude, but she had decided to keep her distance, and continued walking resolutely toward the house.

"I'm really sorry for your loss," the blonde continued. "I lost my mother, too, recently, and I understand what a difficult time this must be for you right now. And I can really appreciate the fact that more than anything right now you'd probably just like to be left alone, but . . ."

Elin tried not to listen. She kept her gaze fixed on the door and hoped that Ricky was standing on the other side of it, ready to help her in. The two journalists walked on either side of her, the light-haired one babbling on and on, and Elin felt how she gave her a squeeze just above the elbow. And just at the moment when the woman touched her, something softened inside her, something opened up and she longed for the chance to just sit down and babble incoherently about what had happened with someone who didn't want to interview her, and someone who wasn't Ricky, no matter how great he was. Her chest and knees became weak, and she felt so goddamn alone.

But it didn't cross her mind her for a second that the blonde woman hurrying along next to her could be that person. She had only ignited that longing. The woman journalist was there to do a job, to get her to say useful things, not to listen.

When Elin was almost ten feet from the door, she suddenly rushed forward and at the exact right moment the door opened. She had no idea what happened behind her; just heard the door close and the lock turn.

"What timing," she gasped and dropped the bags onto the floor.

She thanked God for Ricky. Not just because he had guarded

the door so well, but because she had him, because she wasn't alone there. Otherwise she would never have managed it. Otherwise she would have been standing out there now, would have felt forced to talk about her feelings to those strangers.

There she was again, carrying on about God.

The journalist pleaded in a loud and friendly voice so that it could be heard clearly through the door.

THEY HAD FLED upstairs to the study and pulled the door closed. Ricky had wanted to turn on the radio to drown out the sound of the doorbell and the journalist's calls through the seam of the door, but Elin had stopped him. If she couldn't hear them she might start to imagine that they were breaking into the house. Not because she really thought they would try something like that, but you couldn't stop your imagination.

"The police were here again," said Ricky swaying slowly back and forth in the rockable office chair.

Elin stood in the middle of the room and looked out through the window, out over the meadow across the road. A pitch-black bull stared in her direction with bright-yellow tags dangling from its ears.

"But it was only the woman detective. The bald guy wasn't with her."

"The one named Eide, you mean. No, he was in Visby speaking to me," said Elin.

"What did he want?" asked Ricky.

He stopped rocking, looked down at his foot, and started to spin the chair around very slowly.

"He asked if I knew Karl-Johan Traneus."

Ricky looked up.

"He was the one who called yesterday. Anders's son."

Ricky looked away, stood up from the chair, and just then there was a knock on one of the windows downstairs.

"Oh, for fuck's sake! I'm going down there and—"

"There's no point."

Elin blocked his way to the study door

"It won't do any good. The more we communicate, the longer it'll take to get rid of them."

It didn't take much to get him to change his mind. Ricky turned around abruptly and dropped down on the bed.

"Is that what they teach you in psychology?" he said with a deep sigh.

"That particular trick I think I learned from working behind the bar."

Ricky gave her a quick smile.

"So, and what did she want with you?" she asked and took his seat in the office chair. He thought about it for a moment before he answered.

"She asked me about Mom and Dad. You know, how things were between them, that kind of thing," he said.

"And what did you say?"

They fell silent again. A different kind of silence this time. A silence between them.

"Well, I mean, what do you say to something like that? They had their share of ups and downs, but who doesn't? At least over such a long period of time. Besides which, Dad's barely even been home in the last three years."

"So that's what you said, 'They had their share of ups and downs, but who doesn't?' " asked Elin.

"Something like that."

"And that was it?" she persisted.

She looked at him intently, tried to hold back the anger, but noticed how her voice had already started to quaver.

"No, she asked me about what I'd done last Monday, what time I came home and—"

"About Mom and Dad," Elin interjected.

"No, that wasn't it," he sighed, "She harped on about that for a while."

"But you didn't say anything?"

"Like what?"

He looked at her vacantly and Elin felt how she wanted to rush up and scream at him, but faltered just as she was about to get up from her chair. There was something about his hunched figure on the bed and his confused, feigned confused, expression that made her anger so desperately sad. Ricky wasn't stupid. She knew that she had an intelligent brother, that he was really capable of so much more. And she wasn't talking about that boring accounting job that Father had set him up with. She meant more in every possible sense. But it was as if he couldn't get a hold of himself. He lived some kind of pretend life steered if not by lies, then at least a stubborn refusal to look life right in the eyes. It was easily done, it was comfortable and human, she knew that, but if you make a habit out of always directing your gaze a little off to the side, life starts to become a little fuzzy around the edges. And she didn't want to see him like that, meekly carving out a shapeless life.

She had to steel herself.

"He beat her, Ricky."

This time the answer came quickly.

"Did you say that to the guy in Visby?"

"Yes. Of course I did."

"Of course you did?" bounced right back at her.

He almost sounded hurt, as if he'd been one she informed on.

"Why wouldn't I tell them that? Mom's dead, why wouldn't I tell them what I know?"

Her voice barely held out till the end of the sentence.

"Did you ever see it? Did you ever see him hit Mother?"

"I saw the aftereffects, and so did you!"

She couldn't hold back any longer. She sobbed and whimpered her way through her words.

"You saw the *aftereffects* and that means he hit her. Give me a fucking break, Elin."

He sounded so damn cold, so unreasonable. So fucking . . . stupid.

"I said exactly what I'm saying to you now. That I've never seen him do it, but that I've seen the aftereffects and that's sure as hell good enough for me."

"I think it's pretty fucked up to talk about stuff you haven't even seen. Pretty damn fucked up," he said.

He had sat up in bed with his arms crossed, stubborn, sullen.

"She was murdered. Murdered, Ricky. We have to tell them what we know. What we've seen."

She sobbed, cried, and shouted out the words, and was surprised that he could even understand what she said.

"Then go downstairs and tell that to those journalists why don't you, if you think it's so important."

She flew up out of her chair, couldn't remain sitting down anymore, sent it skittering off on its wheels until it hit against the desktop with a dull thud. Elin stormed out of the room and slammed the door behind her. She heard how Ricky got to his feet.

"Elin!"

She spun around at the door.

"I'm not going downstairs," she screamed. "You think I'm a total fucking idiot?"

She continued into the bathroom, pulled the door closed behind her, and locked it.

What a fucking brother, what a fucking brother. He who was so good. She caught sight of herself in the bathroom mirror and looked away, sank down onto the toilet seat.

"Mommy," she sobbed, "I want my mommy."

Her feet thrummed involuntarily against the limestone floor tiles, lukewarm from the floor heating. The smell of citrus and vanilla wafted over from the soap dish by the sink.

"Mommy, Mommy, Mommy," she whispered softly through her sobbing, "my poor mommy."

She cried like a baby, but then again she was hardly much more than one. Her tears became big, dark-gray drops on the light-gray stone.

31.

There was a warm glow radiating from the windows of the houses. Each step he took across the paving stones exploded beneath him in a crisp echo.

The fog drifted in from the sea in thick sheets and the moisture settled onto the surface of the alleyways leaving them wet as if after a rain. But the cold didn't bother Ricky. He was sizzling, every movement sent warm waves through the cold night air, as if he were surrounded by a warm, protective field. As if he were a toaster. He giggled at the silly comparison.

He continued to make his way aimlessly through the warren of backstreets, through the damp darkness that was perforated from within by light, turning at random without reading the street signs' Gothic lettering. He stopped in front of a skewed gabled end of a house that sort of lunged out at him from the blackness. There was a cozy, welcoming glow emanating from its windows. He suddenly moved up so close that he was almost standing inside someone's living room. A man lying sprawled on a couch was languidly watching TV. On the floor above, a woman in a little kitchen. She was getting something from the sink, he could see the top of the faucet sticking up. She stood there for a moment with a glass in her hand, serene, looking out at nothing, in her own thoughts.

Were they dreams of home, rest, and security, as outdated as the city itself? Perhaps they weren't real. Perhaps they were just his dreams, his longing.

Slowly, hesitantly, he fished out his cell phone from his back pocket. He switched it on and followed the start-up ritual with exaggerated attentiveness, the dancing logo and signature melody that ended with a short vibration before it was time to log in. He punched in his PIN code and began looking for the number as soon as it would permit him.

ELIN WAS STANDING in the kitchen when it happened. It was dark outside. She was drinking a glass of water, so cold that it hurt her teeth and the hand that was holding the glass.

When she'd come out of the bathroom, Ricky wasn't there. She hadn't heard him leave, but it hadn't surprised her to find him gone. When she had stood up and unlocked the bathroom door, it had felt as though she had been sleeping. Her body had felt heavy, and her head empty. It had felt good, or at least much better. Like sleeping away an illness.

It had taken a while for her to realize that she was alone in the house. She had expected him to make his presence known one way or another once he'd heard her. But the house had been deathly quiet. She had peeked into his room, gone back upstairs to check the study, and had finally called out a few times.

He had to have forced his way past the journalists and driven off in his car, if they had still been out there when he left. There hadn't been any sign of them anyway when Elin came down. Maybe they had followed Ricky?

She hadn't minded being left alone for a while. It had felt good to be on her own with the feeling of being rested and calm. But when she put her glass down in the sink everything changed.

The doorbell exploded in a long series of aggressive rings, which, when they finally ceased, were followed by two violent shoves against the door, so heavy and hard that she thought that the door was going to give way.

"Come out here, you bastard! I'm gonna fucking kill you."

32.

Fredrik caught sight of the unmarked car with Gustav behind the wheel the moment he stepped out of Pettson's auto repair shop behind the police station. The white Volvo turned in toward the sidewalk and pulled up alongside him.

He crossed his fingers that his own, much older Volvo would make it through its service without any unpleasant surprises. The muffler was in the danger zone, that much he knew and was prepared for, but he couldn't afford much more than that. It was almost time to buy Christmas presents.

Stupid of him to turn it in now. It would have been better to wait until after Christmas, postpone the problem. Also stupid, but a better stupidity.

Fredrik opened the car door on the passenger side and climbed in.

They drove off at once. The garage smell hadn't quite had a chance to air out from the interior of the car and got mixed in with the scent of Gustav's aftershave.

"What the hell is wrong with people?" said Gustav.

"Sounds like deep thoughts for this early in the morning," said Fredrik as he put on his seatbelt.

Gustav let out a tired snort before continuing.

"This Karl-Johan character, he finds out that his father has been murdered. So he catches the first ferry over here, so far so good. But once he's made it over here, the first thing he does is head over to the other victim's children, who he's related to by the way, and threatens to kill them. I ask you?"

He looked at Fredrik with his already bulbous eyes flared open.

"People can do strange things when they get worked up," said Fredrik.

"I hope that it's just something like that. Sometimes I feel like I can't take any more. Isn't that enough? Isn't it enough for these two people to have died?"

Gustav sighed and they continued up the hill toward the traffic lights at Allégatan.

"I read something about some neuroscientist in the paper the other day," said Gustav. "He claimed that although we may occasionally act civilized, underneath it all we're nothing but apes. That's why we need police and prisons. He said that, '*That's why we need police.*'"

Fredrik uttered what he felt to be a chimpanzee-like sound and scratched at his armpit.

Gustav sighed silently and pretended to press the call button on his radio.

"Unit sixty to dispatch. Detective Wallin requesting reassignment, over."

He turned off toward Gråbo and soon afterward they bounced

up over the curb, and into the yard in front of Sofia Traneus's row house.

"Well, let's see what kind of an ape we've got here," Fredrik laughed as they got out of the car.

"Just forget I said anything," said Gustav and slammed the door.

"No, but you're right about that. Or that neuroscientist is. That's just what we do. Hunt down apes. People who can't act civilized."

They had tried to find Karl-Johan Traneus at his sister's house already during the night, but the sister simply said that he was out somewhere or over at a friend's place. Which friend she couldn't say. Considering that no one had actually seen him outside Rickard Traneus's house, it was hard to justify a search warrant. Besides which, the sister seemed credible.

It was Sofia Traneus who opened up when Gustav rang the doorbell and she showed them straight in when they asked for her brother. Karl-Johan Traneus was sitting in the living room couch with his youngest niece in his arms and looked up at them with a good-natured smile when they entered the room. He was wearing a pair of dark blue jeans and a black T-shirt with washed-out print. He had a red, straggly beard that the baby tried to grab hold of with one hand.

More of an orangutan than a chimpanzee, thought Fredrik.

"Could you take the baby, please," he asked Sofia Traneus.

She looked at him questioningly, but when he nodded at the little girl that her brother was holding, she did as she'd been asked.

"Visby Police Department," said Gustav and flashed his badge. "We have to ask you to accompany us to the police station."

Karl-Johan Traneus looked at them with an even wider smile.

"What, now, right away?" he asked and tried to sound cheerful.

Fredrik looked at him without saying anything, but thought that Karl-Johan Traneus was the last thing that this investigation needed right now.

———

THEY TOOK HIM into the interview room on the ground floor.

"What business did you have going over to Rickard Traneus's house?" said Gustav as soon as they sat down.

Karl-Johan Traneus face darkened slightly.

"He knows where Arvid is. I know it. He's hiding him."

"Threatening to kill someone is a serious crime. It carries a sentence of between six months and two years in prison."

Karl-Johan Traneus stiffened across the table.

"Threatening? I was just . . . I wanted to speak to him, that's all. Christ, all I want is for him to say what he knows."

Thank you for that, thought Fredrik. They had no witnesses who had seen him there, no plate number, nothing that tied him to the scene.

"Let us handle this," said Gustav, "it's our job, not yours. And if we don't have to waste time chasing after you, then we'll be able to find whoever murdered Kristina Traneus and your father that much faster."

"Whoever murdered my father?" said Karl-Johan Traneus. "It was Arvid who did it and Rickard knows where he is."

He was sounding really irate now, as if he could start making threats again any minute. Gustav ignored the comment.

"If you do that again, I guarantee you'll get slapped with a restraining order, which means that you'll be arrested and placed inside a sixty-five-square-foot cell over at our detention facility if you so much as stop your car outside Rickard Traneus's house."

Gustav rounded off his mostly truthful rundown by pointing up at the floor above.

"We appreciate the fact that you think that this is terrible and that you want to do something, but the best thing you can do is to stay out of the way. Look after your sister and your mother instead. Can we agree on that?"

Karl-Johan Traneus nodded reluctantly without looking at Gustav.

They got up and Fredrik asked if he needed a ride back, but Karl-Johan Traneus declined and quickly slipped out the door that Gustav held open for him.

"Do you think he'll do as he's told?" asked Fredrik as they went up to the meeting they were already late for.

"Don't know. But I don't think he's going to kill anyone at least," said Gustav.

LENNART SVENSSON WAS standing at the very back of the oblong room with his arms at his sides and his gaze directed toward the empty whiteboard at the far end of the room. He had days like that, when he couldn't sit down for more than a few minutes at a stretch. By rights he shouldn't even have to be at work on a day like that, but Lennart was old school. One of those dedicated older officers who stuck it out no matter what. He was a different breed altogether from those young slackers who took out comp time or called in sick as soon as they got half a chance.

"So, in other words it's completely unclear whether or not she was beaten?" Ove asked Eva, who had started to give them a rundown of the preliminary report from the medical examiner.

"There's nothing else in her life that could explain those injuries."

She was referring to the multitude of tiny fractures and scarring.

"I mean it's not like she was a professional hockey player," said Lennart.

Sara turned toward him demonstratively and glared at him.

"Oh, for crying out loud, I'm sorry, okay?" he said and would probably have thrown out his arms in an over-the-top gesture, if a sudden move like that wouldn't have risked sending pain shooting down his back.

"There were fresh injuries as well," Eva continued. "Kristina Traneus was subjected to violence about two days before she was murdered."

"Two days?" said Ove. "That makes it even more unlikely that Anders Traneus suddenly came rushing over to have it out with Arvid, or to protect Kristina."

"We shouldn't take for granted that he knew about the abuse already on the Monday," said Göran. "He may not have found out until Wednesday. But sure, in principle I agree with you."

"But then what did he want? I just can't figure it out," said Ove.

"There's another detail here, if I might continue," Eva interjected. "According to the medical examiner, neither Kristina nor Anders Traneus had eaten much over the past twenty-four hours. The first examination produced no physiological explanation, but they'll get back to us once the samples have been analyzed."

"If they had been going behind the back of a notorious wife-beater for a few years, then it wouldn't be strange for them to lose their appetite when he suddenly moves home again," Fredrik noted.

They moved on, went through witness statements and phone lists, but the picture of what happened Wednesday evening didn't become any clearer. Traneus's farm was a fair distance away from the closest neighbor, and the three possible approach roads didn't make it any easier. The murder weapon had not been found and they hadn't uncovered a single trace of Arvid Traneus. No witness reports, no phone calls, not one single credit card purchase, nor was he listed as a passenger on any airline or ferry operator since Monday.

"There ought to be something," said Gustav. "It's very strange. And damn irritating that he slipped through our fingers."

"Not that we had him in our hands to start with," said Lennart.

Göran clasped his hands loosely in the air and let them drop down in front of him onto the table. He started to worry that they had gotten stuck. That the lack of results came down to the fact that they weren't going about it the right way. Thinking too narrowly, too early.

He had been in contact with a Swedish-speaking representative of the international conglomerate that Arvid Traneus had worked for in

Tokyo. She had explained that Arvid's role in the company had been purely internal. Even if they seemed to be engaged in a highly competitive business, and that sometimes it could be a question of eat or be eaten, she had a hard time imagining that Arvid could have made any enemies. He wasn't a decision maker and nobody outside the company knew exactly what he did there.

If he had made enemies in Japan it would scarcely have been job related. At least, that was what she said.

"Let's hear something else," he said hopefully and looked around the table expectantly. "Don't think so 'investigatively.' Just throw something out there."

The room was silent. He leaned forward over the table and continued.

"Sure, he may have financial resources that we don't have any idea about, that don't leave any trace, he may have taken refuge in some old monastery in the mountains north of Sapporo, or maybe he's sitting on a beach somewhere in West Africa in a country where we'd have no chance of getting him extradited even if we found him. Leave that to National CID and Interpol. The question is what we can do here, right now."

Silence. *Well, just let it be silent then for a while,* he thought. Ove sat there hunched over staring down at the tabletop. He opened and closed the fingers of his left hand slowly. Was that just an unconscious mannerism or was it somehow a result of breaking his arm two years ago? Lennart wandered slowly across the room. A forced smile flashed across his face and caused Sara's to smile in the same way. Fredrik cleared his throat as if he was preparing to say something, but nothing came. Gustav ran his thumb along his beard.

"Here's what we'll do," said Göran, "we'll go through all the passenger lists from the ferries and flights again, from Wednesday up until we first started monitoring departures from the island on Friday afternoon. If we follow up on and can confirm all the names, then we know that in all likelihood he hasn't left the island under another name. Then, Eva, we're going to have to turn that house upside down. Every inch of the place—the basement, the car . . . There's got to be something in there that can give us a hint as to where he's gone. How's it going with those diaries, maybe they might give us something? Divide them up among yourselves and take them home for nighttime reading."

Göran mustered a smile.

"And then we'll continue questioning relatives, friends, acquaintances, colleagues. Anyone who might give us something."

"I was thinking about Karl-Johan Traneus," said Fredrik. "Could there be something in what he's saying, that Rickard knows something about his father's whereabouts?"

Göran turned toward Sara.

"What do you think? You want to give it a try?"

Sara squeezed her lips together and wrinkled her nose.

"No, huh?" said Göran.

"I've already been down that path. I haven't come straight out and accused him of knowing something, but I've covered all the possible angles."

"Even if Rickard Traneus doesn't know exactly where his father is hiding, he may be holding something back to protect him," said Fredrik.

"It might be worth letting someone else question him?" said Göran and looked at Fredrik and Sara.

"Fine by me," said Sara.

"Then that's what we'll do."

GÖRAN LEFT THE briefing feeling uneasy. He would have liked to shake them up a bit, get them to think in new directions. All he had succeeded in doing was making everyone feel discouraged. He tossed his papers onto the desk and sat down with his back to the door.

He tried to shake off the feeling of failure. It wasn't even a proper murder investigation. The case was crystal clear, they knew who the killer was, all they had to do was find him. Sooner or later they'd catch him. Tomorrow or in three years from now. There was no reason to feel discouraged.

But, if he turned it around, what did that have to do with his inability to inspire his investigators? He didn't get any further than that before there was a knock at the door. It was Lennart.

"Sit down," said Göran without thinking.

"No thanks," said Lennart.

"No, of course not. I noticed that you uhm . . . during the briefing. How are you doing?"

Lennart walked up to the window that didn't face outside, but looked out at the stairs leading down to the uniformed department, before he turned to Göran.

"I don't think it's gonna work anymore."

Even though it was clear what he was referring to, for a split second Göran thought he was talking about the investigation.

"Your back?" said Göran.

"Yeah. It's terrible."

"You should go on sick leave. That's all there is to it."

"Seems like really bad timing."

"Bah," said Göran and got up, "don't you worry about that. It is what it is. Besides . . . this investigation, it's only a question of time."

"Yeah, I guess you're right," said Lennart. "It's just so damn unpredictable. I can be fine for long periods, but then all I need is one little strain, and I'm out for the count. What kind of a police officer is that, who puts his back out just by lifting a phone book in the wrong way?"

"I thought you did all your number inquiries online," smiled Göran.

"Don't joke around with me," said Lennart.

He drew himself up slowly and gingerly and Göran could almost hear his vertebrae cracking.

"You do a lot of good here in the station," said Göran.

Lennart looked at him gravely without answering.

"There are a lot of us old hands who are a bit behind when it comes to working with computers."

"You can be proud of what you do," said Göran.

Lennart waved dismissively.

33.

Ricky woke up suddenly. He was looking up at an unfamiliar ceiling. Above him hung the extinguished red glass oval that had bathed yesterday evening in a warm and enchantingly unreal glow. Now the room was far more jarringly real. The sun shone in harshly behind the drawn curtains and the man sleeping beside him exuded a strong and unfamiliar scent. Ricky couldn't make out what it was. It wasn't perfume, it wasn't sweat, it wasn't sex, it was just unfamiliar. He knew that this smell would follow him around all day.

The body next to him was suntanned and hirsute unlike his own fair, hairless skin. Yesterday it had excited him to slide his fingers through the stiff, rustling body hair. Today it only seemed animal-like, in the basest sense.

It wasn't the first time he had woken up in this bed, but each time it ended the same way.

He cautiously slid one leg out over the edge of the bed, put his foot on the floor, and sat up. From experience he knew that the man next to him wouldn't wake up, or at least would pretend not to wake up, whichever it was.

Ricky gathered his clothes and got dressed in the living room. His body felt at once light and heavy and his skin almost hurt as he pulled on his rough jeans, as if every nerve ending was suffering from extreme oversensitivity. His head felt like it had pins and needles, as if his brain had actually fallen asleep, and his mouth felt so dry, like it had been glued shut. He filled a glass of water in the kitchen, also cautiously, no spattering stream against the metal sides of the sink, and raised it to his dry lips. He drank, slowly at first, but then with increasing thirst.

Then he was out on the street, bare feet against the leather of his shoes, the daylight cut straight through him like red-hot knives. Only now did he realize that it was still early in the morning. He headed down toward the sea. He was hit by a cold wind when he emerged from the sheltered back alleys, but the sun warmed his neck. Way out at sea, lined up in the shipping lane, the big cargo ships gleamed in the sunshine.

His feet were cold, so he bent down and tied his shoes. Everything was back the way it was. Cast out into reality. For a few hours the night before he had been released from everything, absorbed in the present and his own body. He had forged beautiful plans, but they had nothing to do with the future. It was only when time ceased that his thoughts about tomorrow could become so bright. Now he felt disheveled, burned out, and real. Real and completely repulsive.

He kicked away a rock that disappeared silently and imperceptibly into the choppy water. He had to think for a moment to remember where he had parked the car. Over by Söderport, he realized finally. Why all the way over there? Totally the wrong end of town. He sighed and started to walk along the seafront, turned up next to the big conference building, and passed between a deserted and yellowing Almedalen Park and the library's high glass facade. He glanced at a group of students, caught a few words in a foreign language. Polish, Russian?

I'm still young, he thought. It wasn't too late. He was still young.

LOW CLOUDS HUNG over the Karlsö Islands, but they seemed like they were about to dissolve, blown apart by the strengthening wind. The trees, still green in patches, jerked and shook in the gusts.

Fredrik drove south along the coast road and was just south of Västergarn when the phone rang. He didn't recognize the number on the display.

"Fredrik Broman," he answered.

It was from the repair shop. They had found a problem. Some kind of a grease seal on the right front axel was cracked. It wasn't very expensive to repair, but they wouldn't get any spares in until tomorrow morning.

"I see," he sighed, "well, I guess I don't have much choice. But are you sure you'll be getting one in tomorrow?"

The mechanic said that it was a sure thing and rambled on at length about their spare parts delivery routine, the night ferry, and other details Fredrik hadn't asked for. When he was finally done, Fredrik hung up and tried to call Gustav, but got no answer.

"A grease seal," he said out loud and at that same moment was overtaken by a black Opel Astra.

It was a bit of a reckless maneuver done well above the speed limit. The car hummed onward toward Klintehamn and was soon out of sight.

When Fredrik reached Levide only Elin Traneus was home.

"You can come in and wait if you want, but I've got no idea when he'll be back," she said.

She looked tired from lack of sleep, pale and with a murky gaze.

"Do you know where he is?" asked Fredrik.

"No. In Visby, I think, but other than that . . ."

She shrugged her shoulders.

"I'll have to come back later," he said and took a step down from the porch steps.

He nodded good-bye to her and was already on his way toward the car when she stopped him.

"Anything new on that Karl-Johan?"

Fredrik stopped and turned around.

"I spoke to him this morning together with another officer. If he comes here again he gets hit with a restraining order. He knows that. I doubt he'll be showing up here again."

"Are you sure?"

"About the restraining order you mean?"

"No, that he won't be coming around here again," she said.

She fiddled with the bolt on the door while she waited for his answer. Locked it, opened it again.

"Are you okay here?" he asked.

She shrugged her shoulders again.

"I guess so."

"Have you tried calling your brother?"

"Yes, but he's not answering."

Fredrik thought for a moment, then he took out a business card.

"There's something I have to take care of, but I'll be back in an hour, so we'll just have to see if Rickard has come back by then."

He handed her the card.

"Maybe you could give me a call when he shows up, or ask him to call me, so I know. I'd be very grateful."

Elin nodded.

Fredrik sat in the car and drove off, somehow relieved at having gotten away from there.

ALREADY ON THE way into Visby he had decided to swing past the crime scene to take a look around. It was only when he was pulling up in front of the farm that it struck him that Eva would be there.

He was about to turn the car around and drive away when she suddenly stepped out of the kitchen door. Eva immediately recognized him.

"Fuck!" he swore under his breath.

He had no choice but to stop and climb out of the car.

They said hi to each other. She with a certain tightness around the corners of her mouth, he thought. Couldn't she ever just relax? Only once had he called her up and been difficult, and that was a long time ago now. One single drunken pleading phone call a little too late at night. It ought to be stricken from the record by now.

"I didn't get hold of Rickard Traneus, so I decided to swing by here."

Why did that sound like a bad excuse?

"Okay," said Eva.

The kitchen door opened again and Granholm came out. He glared at Fredrik through his round glasses. *Granholm to the rescue*, thought Fredrik.

"Is there anything I can do?" he asked Eva. "I've got an hour to kill, give or take."

Eva looked a little at a loss, but then seemed to think of something.

"You can start in the basement if you like."

Relegated to the basement, he thought, when a minute later he walked down the basement steps and pulled on a pair of latex gloves. *Oh, well, nothing to do but grin and bear it.* No coldness or dank earthy smell hit him when he descended into the whitewashed cor-

ridor with no less than five doors on either side of it. It was warm
and clean.

To the right there was a sauna and something that he at first took to
be a jacuzzi made of stone and sunken into the floor. Then he saw that
it was some kind of a Japanese bath, given the small wooden stools
that were piled up by the wall. The next was a laundry room, opposite
that was the boiler room, and then adjacent to that, closest to the
stairs, there was a big storage room for clothes, shoes, skis, and other
sports equipment. At the far end of the corridor there was a food
cellar, or a big larder more like. It was cooler in there and there were
cans, jars of jam, pickled vegetables, and all sorts of different bottles
of liquor stacked on unpainted storage shelves. At the very back of the
larder, there was a narrow door and on the wall next to it some kind of
device with a little glimmering red light on it. It looked like an AC
unit, only smaller.

Fredrik opened the door and felt how the damp and cold swept over
him. There was a completely different climate in there, than in the
room outside. He switched on the light. Two dim bulbs cast a warm
glow over a room that was about double the size of the larder. It was a
wine cellar. The right wall was completely covered with cemented
clay pipes. Sticking out of virtually each one of them were foils in red,
green, and gold. His curiosity piqued, he moved closer and pulled out
a bottle at random, wiped off a little dust and peered at the label.

The bottle he was holding was a Château Pétrus from 1990. He
wasn't altogether sure whether wines like that were drunk at all, or if
they were just sold and bought at auctions. In any case, actually tast-
ing one was a pleasure afforded very few. A sixteen-year-old Pétrus
from a good year was worth quite a few thousand.

He stuck the bottle back into its clay pipe and realized that he
ought to have a flashlight to do a proper job down here. He was just
about to go upstairs and fetch one from the car when he caught sight
of something sticking out from among the wine catalogues and loose

sheets of paper on a little stained oak shelf to the left of the door. He
pulled out the shiny metal baton, which, just as he had guessed, turned
out to be a flashlight. With working batteries no less, he could confirm after having tested it.

He began the monotonous task of removing the bottles one by
one and shining the flashlight into each of the clay pipes. Over half
the cellar contained expensive Bordeauxs, although not all were of the
same breathtaking price class as the first one he had taken out. He also
found Bourgognes, Chablis, Meursaults, a few red Beaune wines, and
then Champagne of course, but nothing other than bottles stuck inside the pipes.

He examined the shelf where he had found the flashlight, quickly
flipped through the pile of catalogues and loose sheets of paper. In
among them he found a bound black A4 notebook, a cellar book. All
purchases were carefully entered in black ink on light-blue lines, as
well as when bottles had been taken upstairs to be drunk. He flipped
through it from the back. The last time something had been brought
into the cellar was two years ago.

Fredrik flipped forward, wanted to see if Arvid Traneus may have
taken out a bottle of Champagne or something else to celebrate coming home. He couldn't find any such entry, at least not after skimming
it so quickly. But another entry caught his eye. On the tenth of April,
2001, he had taken up two Winston Churchill 1985s. "Rickard 20"
was written next to it.

He heard footsteps in the corridor outside and stopped flipping the
pages. The door to the larder opened.

"Hello?" someone called out. "Fredrik, are you there?"

It was Eva.

"In here!" he shouted and tried to hide his surprise.

He thought she had sent him down to the basement so she wouldn't
have to see him.

Eva entered the wine cellar and pulled the door closed behind her.

"Hi, how's it going?" she asked and swept her eyes quickly across the bottle necks projecting from the clay pipes.

"Not bad . . . very nice wine collection, but nothing of interest, if that's what you mean?"

She took a few short steps toward him. Fredrik closed the cellar book and held it in his left hand.

"I see . . . well, I just wanted to see if you'd found anything."

What he had at first perceived as a capacious wine cellar, had suddenly turned into a very small room where two people ended up very close to each other, whether they liked it or not. He got the feeling that Eva had been struck by a similar thought. She seemed to have become distracted from whatever her original reason for coming down had been.

"I was just thinking . . ."

She fell silent, lowered her gaze, and sighed heavily.

"What?" he asked, just to puncture the silence.

"I don't really know what I was thinking," she said.

It looked like she was going to back out of the room any second, but now he didn't want to let her go.

"No, go ahead, say it."

When she still hesitated, he took a cautious step forward.

"Haven't we been silent long enough?"

That made her smile.

"I know that I've been a little . . . that I keep my distance. But I think it's better that way. Right?"

He suddenly became uncertain. Was that a *right* that demanded his agreement, or was it really asking him what he thought? There wasn't a lot of distance between them right now.

"I guess so," he said.

Eva looked at him, her gaze dark and solemn in the gloom of the cellar.

"It doesn't mean that there's nothing else there," she said.

"No," he said.

"But that's just how it is."

Fredrik walked slowly up to her. It wasn't more than two short steps.

She continued looking at him. What did she want with that look? Unyielding, insistent, and yet expressing some kind of desire? Or not?

He wasn't sure which of them touched the other first, but . . . No, that was a lie. It was he who touched her. He couldn't help it. But it was a completely innocent, virtually imperceptible touch. He raised his free hand and gently stroked the sleeve of her overall. She couldn't even have felt it through the fabric, but she continued to work him with that gaze, silent and unflinching.

Then suddenly they kissed, passionately and full of desire. Her smell was exactly as he had remembered it, her lips like coming home.

This is wrong. This is so fucking wrong, echoed in his head. But he couldn't help himself.

He let go of the black notebook, tore off the latex glove from his right hand, and dug his fingers into her cool, thick hair.

Then she broke away. Abruptly.

"Damn it," she whispered. "That was not good, that was not good at all. A bad idea, that's what it was."

Eva looked around furtively.

"Take it easy," he said. "I don't want to cause any trouble. If it was a bad idea then . . . well, then it was a bad idea."

He sought eye contact with her, but she wouldn't meet his gaze. Her chest was heaving in sync with her rapid breathing.

"Just take it easy," he said again.

She gave him a quick look, then she turned around and disappeared out through the door.

Fredrik looked after her stupidly, then bent down and picked up the cellar book from the floor while he tried to still the hurricane that was raging inside him.

"No, maybe that wasn't such a good idea," he whispered to himself.

34.

Elin felt how everything became easier once Ricky came back. Her fear disappeared from one moment to the next. It even became easier to breathe.

But she was angry at him, angry because he had accused her, angry because he had just run off without saying anything. But she didn't know how she was going to say that to him, if she even had any right to say it. And she was far too grateful to have him back in the house to risk starting another argument.

He had said, "Hi," looked at her with a glazed-over look, and then disappeared into his room.

Elin sank down into the sofa in the living room. She should go home. What was the point in her being there anymore? It would take weeks, maybe more, before they could bury mother. School was waiting, or rather wasn't waiting. The courses continued relentlessly without her and it would be hard for her to catch up once she had fallen behind.

It was like a nightmare. Had her father really killed her mother? That's what she thought, but she didn't want to believe it. Ricky couldn't understand it, couldn't understand the difference.

She leaned her head back and thought about dying. It was distant and incomprehensible and wasn't connected with any emotions. She couldn't picture the life that lay ahead of her or it coming to an end. But then all at once something sunk through her chest and everything around her became black and ice cold. She was completely alone and the world was neither good nor evil, and there was no point to anything. She jumped up from the couch to stave off the panic, walked over to the window, pressed her forehead and nose against the glass. A beautiful autumn sun shone above the lambs out in the pasture. She had to smile at the sight.

Once a long time ago, her father had spoken to her about the meaning of life. She didn't remember why, whether it had come out of nowhere or if she had asked him some naïve existential question. "There is no meaning to life," he had said, "no meaning other than the one you give it yourself." If that was true, her life right now was meaningless.

Then the doorbell rang. It was the police who had come back.

THERE WAS A large bouquet of white and red roses in a red glass vase on the black tabletop. There was a card attached to one of the stalks. Condolences from a relative, Fredrik guessed.

"What was it he was doing in Japan?" he asked Rickard, who was sitting opposite him at the big table.

"He's a consultant. He . . . helps companies make more money, you might say. In a nutshell." *Helps companies make more money*, thought Fredrik, *that sounds like something a father might say to his child*.

"Did he have a lot of clients?"

"He only had one in Japan, but he's got others in Sweden and Germany."

"Was it always the same one in Japan?"

"Yes, it was."

"Because that was quite an extended period if I've understood correctly?" said Fredrik.

"Ten years, if you count from the very beginning. But it's only the past two or three years that he's more or less been living there. It's become more and more intensive you might say."

Rickard Traneus looked tired. That was understandable. He had a jaundiced pallor beneath his eyes, and the eyes themselves seemed veiled.

"What sort of work do you do, or maybe you're studying?" asked Fredrik.

"No, not right now. I work part-time at an accounting firm."

"I see, where?"

"In Visby," Rickard Traneus answered and put his right hand on the chair's black backrest in what looked like a pretty uncomfortable position.

"What is it you do there, more precisely?" asked Fredrik.

"Accounting, ordinary bookkeeping. Not the greatest job in the world, stray hours here and there whenever they need me, but it usually ends up at around seventy percent for the most part. I studied economics up in Stockholm for a while, but I took a leave of absence after three semesters."

"Was that at Stockholm University?" asked Fredrik.

"That's right. My father went to the Stockholm School of Economics."

Fredrik nodded. He didn't want to plague Rickard with a follow-up question about why he had chosen Stockholm University instead. He was pretty sure of the answer.

Rickard Traneus sat with his back to the kitchen counter. It was thoroughly wiped off, spotlessly clean. On the left stood a shiny metal espresso machine and partially hidden behind Rickard a battery of olive oil, rapeseed oil, balsamic vinegar, oyster sauce, sherry, and other handy ingredients for the mildly ambitious home cook.

A part-time accounting assistant could hardly earn enough money for designer furniture, expensive kitchen appliances, and clothes that . . . well, Fredrik didn't know for sure, but they certainly didn't *look* cheap. He probably got help from his father, or in some other way. Either with cash, or else the chair and table were something that the parents had tired of and the son had taken over. But the kitchen and what he had caught a glimpse of in the other rooms, looked far too thought through to be the result of hand-me-down furniture.

"You have no idea where your father might be?" Fredrik asked.

Rickard Traneus let go of the backrest and laid his hand in his lap together with the other one. He didn't answer.

"If you were to guess," Fredrik proposed. "He has to have gone somewhere. Where do you think he'd go?"

Rickard's eyes narrowed almost imperceptibly.

"Are you taking Karl-Johan's angle now?" he asked.

"We're just trying to make progress. It's important that we get in touch with your father. Wouldn't you agree?"

Rickard looked down at his lap, then at Fredrik.

"I know that Elin has said a few things about our father. Things that she'll have to answer for herself. They're her interpretations."

"How do you mean?" said Fredrik, even though he knew very well what Rickard Traneus meant.

He could feel how Rickard held back a grimace.

"I have never seen my father hit my mother," he said.

After a short pause he added:

"And nor has Elin. She's just gotten it into her head that he did. My father isn't like that. He didn't hit her. Much less murder her."

The last bit came with added emphasis and it sounded like he believed what he said.

"The answers aren't self-evident, of course, but it's very hard for us to find out exactly what happened unless we get hold of your father," said Fredrik.

Rickard looked at him without batting an eyelid.

"I can't help you. I would if I could, but I have no idea where he is."

"But if your father had nothing to do with the murders, why do you think he's run off?"

To that, Rickard Traneus had no answer.

35.

Fredrik entered the café and immediately spotted Ove, who was sitting alone at a table right next to the glass wall with a crumpled up ice-cream wrapper in front of him. He sat down opposite him with a plain cup of coffee. Ove, who had been sitting hunched over the table with his head drilled down between his shoulders, straightened up slightly.

"I went down and questioned Rickard Traneus," said Fredrik.

"M-hm," said Ove.

"If it wasn't Arvid Traneus who killed his wife and cousin, how come he's disappeared?"

Ove stared at him.

"What?"

"Well, I mean if Arvid Traneus isn't the one who . . ."

"I heard what you said, but it's just doesn't compute. There's no answer to that question. It just doesn't make sense any other way. Arvid Traneus killed them and then made a run for it. How else can you explain it?"

When Fredrik couldn't answer Ove continued:

"But I have actually come up with another alternative. He may have committed suicide."

The light from the afternoon sky lit up the left half of Ove's face where the stubble that had been shaven in the morning had started to creep out again.

Fredrik rested his chin against his fist.

"Well, I agree that's not a totally unheard-of scenario, but in this particular case . . . I have a hard time seeing Arvid Traneus as the type to take his own life. Besides which, if he has, wouldn't we have found him somewhere in the house or nearby?"

"Maybe he ran off first," said Ove, "took the ferry and gave up half-way."

"Jumped overboard you mean?" said Fredrik.

Ove nodded.

"The night ferry. It's dark, stiff wind on deck, nobody would see him."

"No," said Fredrik, "this guy wouldn't give up. He'd do anything to avoid losing, as he sees it, live like a monk in some Japanese mountain monastery for the rest of his life, anything."

"A monk?" said Ove.

"Okay, that might not be Arvid Traneus's first choice. But if it came to that."

Fredrik didn't want to believe the suicide theory, but he had to admit that it wasn't completely unlikely, either. Arvid Traneus had killed his wife, the mother of his children, possibly by mistake, definitely without premeditation. What was left? Turn his back on everything just in order to survive? Never to be able to return. On the other hand, he hadn't been home for a long time. Maybe he already had another life that was easy to just keep on living?

Fredrik fended off the notion that Arvid Traneus might have climbed over the railing of a windswept ferry and disappeared forever in the waves with a faint splash that couldn't even be heard above the sound of the engines. That would somehow turn all their efforts over the past few days into meaningless gestures. There would be a conclusion to the tragic story, but the only contribution Fredrik and his colleagues would have made to the case would be mopping up and filing a report.

"If he has jumped into the sea, we'll have to hope that he floats ashore," he said.

"Or else we won't get any further than this," said Ove.

ONLY ONCE HE was on his way out to the parking lot did Fredrik realize that his car was still at the shop. By then it was too late to get a ride, Gustav had already left.

He emerged from McDonald's, not really sated and with a depressing greasy aftertaste in his mouth. He had the wine cellar book and two of Kristina Traneus's diaries in a plastic shopping bag that he carried in his right hand.

The sky was deep blue above the ring wall and the medieval town was strangely silent. He never really got used to the stillness that reigned during the long winter months, even during what should have been rush hour. It felt like a public holiday. There were only a few scattered people on the street, almost everybody seemed to be somewhere else, at home celebrating while the streets lay empty. He liked it, but he couldn't get used to it. He walked slowly over to the bus station and stood at the number 10 bus stop.

Standing around the number 41's glass bus shelter was a cluster of teenage boys with big, baggy down jackets and identical caps. They spat continuously on the ground around them.

The bus was almost completely full. Fredrik took out the cellar book from his bag and tried to read, but the reading lights were broken or switched off, and the glow from the strip lighting in the aisle was too dim for him to be able to make out Arvid Traneus's handwriting. He put the book away and looked out at the fading twilight, but soon there was nothing more to see. The view became pitch black,

except for a few short stretches with streetlamps that swept past at irregular intervals.

The bus pulled over in the impenetrable darkness and let off solitary passengers. Sometimes a car was waiting with the lights on to
pick up the person who'd gotten off. There was something pleasant
about the scene that was repeated along all the small roads that the
bus trundled its way onto. A secure feeling, maybe even of something
greater. Of belonging?

It had been a long time since he'd sat on this bus. He couldn't remember if he had ever taken it so late in the evening, after dark. He
almost started to feel sorry for the ones who got off with no one waiting for them. It was as if they stepped right out into a void.

When he got off himself just south of Hemse, there was only one
passenger left.

He stood there waiting outside the shuttered school while the bus
rumbled off. The damp night air smelled of wood fires and manure.
He had barely a mile to walk, two streetlamps, and then the night
took over. But he realized that it wouldn't be a good idea. If he walked
the other direction he could cut across the fields along the tractor
path. There at least he wouldn't get run over. Worse came to worst, he
could always light his way with the glow from his cell phone.

36.

They had eaten lunch. Spaghetti with homemade tomato sauce, grated
parmesan, and a few basil leaves from the pots around the back. Was
this really the first cooked meal she had eaten since . . . since she had
come to Gotland? It felt that way, but she had to be mistaken. Many

days had passed, a week maybe. Yes, a whole week. They couldn't very well have lived on coffee and sandwiches the whole time.

Elin scraped what was left into the garbage and put the dishes in the dishwasher. It was almost 2:30 p.m. She opened the larder and tested the Bag-in-Box. It felt light in her hand. She shook it. Empty. Had she taken the last of it?

She dropped down on her haunches and started rummaging among the liquor bottles at the bottom of the larder, selected a few that she took out.

"Would you like a drink?" she hollered.

"What?" she heard Ricky shout back from his room.

He had gotten up as soon as they'd finished eating, walked off with a bit of a vacant stare, and left her with the dishes.

"You heard what I said."

"Yeah, okay."

He sounded a little hesitant, as if she was forcing it on him. Hypocrite, she thought. He had gone into work one day but come back, said that he couldn't handle it. She had said to him that he ought to just take sick leave, but as far as she could tell he hadn't been to see a doctor.

So, if neither of them was working, what difference did it make, she thought and took out two glasses.

She had spoken to Molly. Once. It had disappointed her. In the midst of all the solicitude, Molly had seemed put out, as if she would have preferred to just hang up and get as far away as possible from Elin's murdered mother, grief and blood, and police questioning. Molly hadn't called back.

Ricky snuck into the kitchen, almost without a sound. He stopped and watched her work at the kitchen counter.

"There you go," she said and held out one of the glasses.

"Thanks," he replied taking it.

He studied the slices of lime that were floating among the pieces of ice in the golden-brown liquid.

"Did we have all this here?"

"Yeah, isn't that weird," said Elin. "I can't remember that we did any shopping, can't even remember eating anything. Can you?"

"No," he said.

Elin took a sip of the drink and shook her head.

"I have to go back, but I can't make up my mind. And nobody's been in touch from Åhlbergs, either."

Ricky didn't answer. He sipped at his drink.

"Tastes good," he said.

"M-hm, Markus taught me how to make this."

"Markus?"

Ricky took a bigger sip from his glass.

"This guy I was together with for a while."

"Oh, yeah? You never said anything about him before," he said and the corner of his mouth curled into a teasing little smile.

"There's not so much to say. It didn't last long."

Ricky's smile drew out into something else, more difficult to interpret.

"Yeah, sounds familiar . . ."

FATHER HAD LAID the sea chart out across the big walnut desk. The chart of Gotland always lay on top and sometimes it was the only one, unless they were sailing over to the mainland. Father had poured himself a glass of some brownish alcohol that he had set down dangerously close to the edge of the table on a round cork coaster. Looking back, Ricky guessed that it must have been whiskey, considering the design of the glass. On the floor, clustered around the legs of the desk, stood dark, tall bottles of wine that were coming along on the boat trip.

Outside the window the summer evening started to turn blue. The powerful reading lamp above the desk shut out the rest of the world, created a space where there was only room for two.

Ricky sat down on a chair next to him, or in father's lap when he was really small. Father showed him how to use a course plotter and divider and let Rickard measure out the distance from Klintehamn to the island. When he was old enough to understand, his father explained how if you had two out of the three variables—time, distance, and speed—you could always work out the third.

Those were important props and rituals, but the most important one of all was when his father ran his forefinger across the sea chart until it stopped on the island and they could start talking about all the treacherous challenges they would have to face to make it out there. He remembered Father's breath, a little sharp from the brown alcohol, and how his own silky, blond strands of hair got caught in Father's stubble.

Then of course it came to an end. Both the sitting with the charts the night before they set off, as well as the sailing trips themselves ceased. He couldn't say when that had happened or even why. Had he become too old for it, too much of a teenager, and thought that it was all a little childish? Or was it when Father had started going off to Japan? Maybe he wasn't home anymore during sailing season?

Somehow he disappeared, not just in time and space, but also inside himself. He came home and took care of things, organized, purchased, procured, handed out presents. For brief moments he could be exuberant, full of plans, tell stories with a glint in his eye, his entire being sort of bubbling with energy. Then you could reach him, then the feeling from the desk and the sea charts was there again. But it was fleeting and even if you could reach him, you could never reach up to him. He was forever beyond reach. Then he disappeared into his assignment and was swallowed up by Japan.

THE PLASTIC SHOPPING bag with the black cellar book and Kristina Traneus's diaries had lain there untouched for a few days. When Fredrik took them out and sat down with them up in the living room, his memory from the wine cellar came rushing over him.

He knew he shouldn't keep going back there, stirring it up, rekindling the emotions, but he couldn't help himself. At the same time, he knew that it was a waste of energy to keep mulling over what it meant. It wasn't going to lead anywhere anyway.

He lay Kristina Traneus's dairies aside, opened the cellar book and felt how decades of dampness and dust rose up from the paper. He flipped through Bourdeauxs, Bourgognes, Alsace wines, Italian red wines from Piedmont and white from Alto Adige. Many of the wines he recognized from his examination of the cellar. Arvid Traneus had kept meticulous records. When he removed a bottle he noted it down, sometimes even the occasion for which it had been selected, such as for example his son's birthday. Fredrik found more birthdays in the column all the way over to the right, but not the daughter's twentieth birthday. Did that mean she didn't come to Gotland to celebrate it? Or maybe that Arvid Traneus wasn't back in Sweden then? Kristina Traneus's fortieth birthday, she was born in the middle of summer, the second of July, was celebrated quietly with a single bottle of Beaujoulais. Or else perhaps they threw a bigger party with cheaper wines that never passed through the cellar and therefore were never entered into the book?

What was he really expecting to get out of this? If he was really honest about it, wasn't he sitting there perusing Arvid Traneus's cellar book mostly for the sake of his own enjoyment? To afford himself the opportunity of drooling a little over wines he would otherwise not even get within spitting distance of? Like yet another armchair traveler.

Yet he turned a few more pages and let his eyes wander down the entries. He stopped at four bottles of Riesling that had been taken out at the start of July, just a few days after Mrs. Traneus's birthday, but this one was an even earlier year, the seventh of July 1994. "Adventure" was jotted down next to the date. That was certainly an annotation that tickled the imagination. Fredrik flipped back and forth through the book a little at random and soon found more bottles that had been brought up for the "Adventure." All the notes were made in the summer, most of them in July, occasionally at the beginning of August. "Adventure," each time just that same singular noun. What sort of an adventure was that?

Fredrik set aside the cellar book, reached for one of the diaries and tried to find one of the dates that had been marked with "Adventure" in the margin of the cellar book. He soon discovered that the books he had brought with him didn't cover the corresponding periods. Instead he looked up another month of July and started scanning Kristina Traneus's neat and easy-to-read handwriting. When he didn't find anything he continued with the two other Julys included in the books, but there was no mention of any adventures there, either.

Kristina Traneus had kept records of virtually every single day. When Fredrik gave up searching for "Adventure" he started reading through the diaries more carefully. Kristina gave detailed accounts of every conceivable event, but they were at the same time terse and evasive. "Went up to Hemse to shop for weekend. Met Ingrid. They're going to Paris for a week in October. Took Elin's bicycle to Endrell's. Will be ready on Wednesday. Thinking about planting grapevines along southern gable, some hardy strain. Table grapes would be nice."

After reading through it for a while, it struck Fredrik that she basically never revealed anything about herself. She noted down the events of the day, impassively, as if she were recording the minutes of a board meeting. The short reference to wanting to plant table grapes was like a daring digression compared to the rest of it.

Was there any conclusion that could be drawn from what seemed to be missing? Wasn't a diary supposed to be like a safety valve for emotions, thoughts, and perhaps secrets? Fredrik had never kept a diary himself, but that was his take on it, anyway. In that case, was this the diary of a woman who was being closely watched by her husband, who was used to the fact that any comment that wasn't carefully thought through could be misinterpreted and set off her husband's rage? Or more to the point: one misplaced word and she risked a broken rib?

She couldn't even confide her deepest thoughts in her own diary. It just became a kind of account of the day's events. A memory aid that could be used to call other things to mind, things that she had to keep inside herself.

It was a kind of prison, he thought, being shut up inside yourself. In the end she had found someone she could talk to, someone she could confide in. The consequence had been death.

He searched on through the notes from three years ago, the last of the years that were included in the two volumes that he had taken with him. On the thirteenth of August he found the entry: "Laid flowers on Stefania's grave. Seven years old today." Nothing more.

Everything was clear now. Fredrik was there, he saw the room. Saw Sara in that ugly, ergonomically designed armchair. He heard everything she said. He knew who she was, recognized her, just as he recognized Ninni and the kids and a few friends who had been to see him with embarrassed smiles and nervous gazes they didn't know where to fix.

What Sara recounted, however, the investigation they were supposed to have worked on together, was completely new to him. It could just as well have been some old yarn, or one detective telling another about a case she was working on, which of course it was, but it should have been a lot more than that. It should have been something they had experienced together . . . but Fredrik could remember nothing.

Fredrik wanted her to hurry it up, wanted to ask her to focus on those bits that dealt with him specifically and hop over everything else. Somehow he sensed that somewhere in this account lay the explanation for why he was lying here in this hospital bed. He assumed that she wouldn't be sitting here rehashing the entire investigation if it didn't eventually lead up to whatever it was that erased his memory.

He wanted to ask her, but he couldn't. He had realized that the words he was capable of uttering were unintelligible. He was there, but only for himself, not for anyone else.

"They must have held an inquest into the accident with the horse, but we never managed to find any report," she said. "A thirty-three-year-old workplace injury . . . It had simply been weeded out. Or misplaced, for all I know, but there was no sign of it in our records."

Sara crossed her legs and sank down deeper in the armchair.

"But we did find a witness in the end. Ragnar Jonsson. He had been working on the farm when it happened. He hadn't seen the accident itself, but heard the commotion and the screaming and rushed into the stable. He hadn't wanted to believe that it was as bad as it sounded. He couldn't believe that Traneus had sent them to *that* horse. Arvid might conceivably have been able to handle Valdemar, he said, but not his cousin. Never. He was a complete stranger to that horse."

Fredrik was captivated by the scene that Sara depicted for him, and for a moment he forgot that more than anything he just wanted to fast-forward to whatever was about him. He was gripped by the sight that had met Ragnar Jonsson when he came charging into the stables so fast that he nearly slipped and fell on the concrete floor. The horse in the open box, glaring furiously yet stock still. The boy lying on the floor of the box, lifeless, stretched out along the wall, and next to him Arvid, in shock and unable to move, staring at his immobile cousin. Ragnar Jonsson had for a brief moment seen something in Arvid that he'd never seen before. Arvid, who otherwise never showed the slightest hesitation, was never at a loss, and never backed down from a challenge, peered for a few seconds into an abyss that he was completely unequipped to deal with. And the abyss stared back into him.

37.

Ricky couldn't remember what he had been doing down in the cellar, nor whether he was eleven or thirteen. Maybe it wasn't just on one occasion, but several. But he remembered Stefania.

He could see her in front of him, her long, blonde hair that had become brittle and rose up from her head like a flower when it was freshly washed. Like a dandelion ball when the sun shines through it. He remembered that image. Stefania hated it. She sprayed it and had all sorts of gels she used to make it lie flat.

He remembered her tall, frail frame hunched over the toilet. He could see her in front of him.

But had he really seen her?

The visual memory was so clear in his mind, but now eleven, twelve, maybe thirteen years later, he couldn't explain *how* he had seen her. What had he been doing down in the basement? Had he been spying on her? Snuck after her when she had silently disappeared down the steps?

He could have created the image in his own mind. It was quite possible. But not out of nothing. He had heard her. The reverberating echo of the porcelain from the toilet by the sauna. He had thought that she was sick, had a bad stomach, thought about how disgusting it was to throw up. How you wanted to avoid it at all costs at the same time that you were in a cold sweat and the feeling of nausea surged through your body in waves. He had thought about how it must feel like that for Stefania, that she couldn't hold it back any longer. In the end she had to sneak down into the cellar and give into it, let the stomach cramps take over, all that gross stuff that sort of assaulted you from within. Assaulted you and broke out at the same time. It was an odd force, that committed violence against you in order to escape from you. Did that mean that you fought against it? Yes, you did; he did anyway. It was wrong, it was awful, a waking nightmare, and not something you would ever voluntarily submit to. Once something was eaten, it wasn't supposed to leave the same way.

He had heard her, he was definitely sure about that. Once, maybe more. Probably more. Why would it otherwise have become etched in his memory like that, so powerfully that it had formed a visual image of something that he may have only heard? He had thought that she was sick. That was also quite possible. He was often sick to his stomach when he was little. It felt like as soon as he got sick he'd start vomiting. But, why did she need to sneak down into the basement then, like a sick animal seeking out a place to die? Why didn't she want to be looked after like he was when he was sick? Mother's hand on his forehead, a cool, damp washcloth that wiped away the sweat and vomit, a glass of water raised to your mouth so you could rinse away that disgusting, sour taste. But Stefania threw up alone in the basement. When he listened to the sounds from inside the sauna, he couldn't think of anything more terrible than throwing up alone.

SOMETHING CLATTERED, HACKED and rumbled its way into Fredrik's dreams. He tried to ignore the noise for as long as possible, pretend that nothing could bother him, right up until he couldn't sleep at all anymore, but lay there wide awake with his eyes closed. He rolled over onto his left side with a groan and peeked at the red lacquered alarm clock from Ikea. It said twenty-five minutes to eight. Göran had told him to sleep in for a few hours this morning, they all needed a bit of extra energy after almost two weeks of constant grind. He had even gone so far as to order Fredrik not to come in before eleven. And then this happens.

The straining lawn-mower engine raced somewhere close by, caused the panes in the old window frames to rattle, reminding Fredrik that they needed to be re-puttied. Only once he had wriggled into his robe, did he realize that it must be Jocke who was out with the mower, and that it was he himself who had been after him about cutting the grass, even promised him fifty crowns to do it.

The money had obviously got Joakim moving, but getting woken up by the lawn mower at 7:30 in the morning wasn't really what he had envisioned when he made the offer.

He tied the belt on his robe and walked down the steps, could hear Ninni hurrying Simon off to school in the kitchen. Suddenly the mower started scraping and screeching so loudly that it almost hurt your teeth. And then it cut out abruptly.

"Fucking piece of shit," Jocke cursed out in the garden, loud enough that their one neighbor definitely must have heard it.

Fredrik opened the front door and looked outside, but couldn't see Jocke anywhere. He must be around the corner of the house, toward the vegetable garden. Fredrik pulled the door closed and stepped into the room opposite the kitchen, the room that after a few years of dithering had become their joint workroom, even if it was mostly Ninni who used it.

He could see Jocke through the gable window, hunched over the lawn mower, which was tipped over on its side, his long body half kneeling and nearly doubled over. Fredrik managed to release the hasps on the window and pushed it open.

"How's it look?"

Joakim pointed at the blade underneath the tipped-over mower.

"Not too good."

He must have cut past the rock at the corner of the vegetable garden a bit too sharply. The long, black blade had been bent into a warped and scratched Z-shape.

"Make sure you disconnect the wire to the spark plug, before you start fiddling around with it," he said and felt a little glum about always having to be the one to chide him. But what were you supposed to do when your child's about to stick his fingers into a lawn mower that could chop them off in the blink of an eye?

"I've already done that," said Jocke, "*and* turned it over with the carburetor facing up."

Fredrik nodded and smiled, the latter more to himself than anything else.

"Okay, that's good," he said. "Looks like we'll have to junk it."

His gaze became fixed on the buckled blade that was still as sharp as a freshly honed knife where it hadn't touched the rock. A lawn mower blade. Why not? If you held it with a glove, otherwise you'd probably cut yourself. Or were they actually in fact looking for a murderer with injuries to his hand?

"You can just leave it there. I'll take care of it later," he said and shut the window.

His cell phone was still lying upstairs. He always slept with his mobile on the bedside table when he was in the middle of a murder investigation. He hurried up the stairs, but stopped short halfway up. He didn't want to call Eva from home.

"THAT'S TOTALLY FUCKING crazy. I mean, I just don't know what the hell you're talking about."

Ricky peered at Elin with a cold look in his eye, more distancing himself than aggressive. It frightened her, made her feel so terribly alone. She was on the verge of taking it all back, apologizing, anything to erase that coldness from his eyes. But she couldn't do it. When she opened her mouth to lie, or at least contradict her firm conviction, then she couldn't.

She hadn't been able to keep quiet, that was the whole thing. It was her own fault. They had been drinking, that had undoubtedly played a hand in it. Once she had tired of rummaging among Ricky's liquor leftovers, she had gone off to the state liquor store and bought a box wine.

She felt stupid. After three glasses of wine, the thoughts that had seemed so clear in her mind, hadn't come out that way.

"I don't understand how you can't see that," she said. "It's like you've turned the whole thing into some kind of dream world."

"You're the one who's dreaming here," said Ricky.

They were standing up, they had been sitting at the black table in the kitchen and had been having a really nice time, right up until Elin started to say the wrong things and they couldn't remain seated anymore. Ricky had gotten up first. She had thought that he was going to walk off and leave her there. But he had turned back to her after two steps, stood there and glared.

"Here's the thing, okay," said Elin. "Stefania was always there, always with the two of us whenever we were the whole family, always around you and me, at least as long as she still had the energy."

"Sure, she was . . ." he started and lost track of what he was going to say. He started again:

"She was always there. Stefania was always there. Sure. She took care of us, she did. We were good together."

He swallowed and fell silent, then he looked at Elin.

"Don't ruin it."

"I'm not trying to ruin it. Stefania was the best. And we were good together. That's great. The three of us. But have you ever thought about why she was always there, why she always kept us together, made sure we were together? A teenage girl who hangs out with her little brother and sister? Think about it. And why she was always prancing around so much in front of Father when he was along, why she was always so damn eager to keep him in a good mood, as if she wanted to get all his attention, make sure he was completely preoccupied with her?"

"Now see that right there is . . ."

Ricky reached his arms straight into the air as if he wanted to stop a huge weight from tumbling on top of him, then bent them back down and ruffled his hair.

"Didn't you see that? Didn't you understand?" she said.

She stood there bent forward slightly, gesticulating while she spoke.

"Understand? What did you understand?" he said and forced out a laugh. "How old could you have been? Eight, nine? What did you understand? Can't you see that these are just rationalizations you've come up with later on, things that you've dreamed up because you've been reading a bunch of psychology books?"

Ricky poked his forefinger against his temple and stared at her.

"It's all up here, what you're talking about. Inside your head and in those books."

"Take it easy," she said and felt how a drop of saliva hit her on the cheek when Ricky raised his voice.

He let his hands drop to his side.

"You're wrong," he said and then he walked off.

He turned his back on her and walked out of the kitchen, slowly and controlled to make it clear that he wasn't upset, but that this had gone far enough. They were done talking about it.

Elin went after him.

Why couldn't she just leave well enough alone, keep quiet? What difference did it make? But she couldn't. She couldn't stand the fact that he was trying to change the history, change what was true. She had to speak up, for Stefania's sake, for Mother's sake, and for her own sake.

Ricky continued out into the living room, picked up a newspaper from the coffee table, started flipping through it, busied himself. Elin went around him, stood a short distance away from him with her arms crossed. Face-to-face. Ricky hung his head over the newspaper, didn't want to see her.

"What do you think she was doing?" Elin asked.

"What?" he said without looking up.

"Everything that she did. What do you think it was for? You seem to think that you know. Why did she do it? Why was she behaving that way?"

Ricky put down his newspaper with a deep sigh.

"I don't understand what you want me to say. We've already spoken about this."

"But you can't explain to me, who was far too young back then to understand anything and blinded as I am by my reading, brainwashed by all that psychobabble as I must be after . . . *whooah* . . ."

She stopped short to make a trembling, flapping motion with her hands and then continued, "After six whole weeks of university."

Ricky's eyes flashed, it wasn't coldness this time, he was starting to get angry.

"She cared about us, we were good together, we've already . . ."

"And how about with Father? Why was she always carrying on like that and showing off in front of him, fooling around and wanting to sit in his lap all the time? What do you think the point of that was and what do you think it cost?"

It felt as if her voice ought to start trembling, but it didn't. The words came out steady and determined.

"What do you mean, *cost?*"

"The price. What price do you think she paid for trying to save Mother?"

Ricky shook his head. The room was silent, silent outside, no cars, no tractors, no animals or people, just a soundless flight of birds way off in the distance that seemed to stand still in the sky.

"You haven't understood anything. Okay, Dad may have his issues, his temper could really destroy a nice evening, that's happened a few times. But she just wanted everyone to be happy. It's not like you think at all."

Elin scowled at Ricky.

"She had to pay in a way that you just cannot imagine."

"You're out of your mind, you know that. I mean it. Next thing you'll be saying that you slept with him, too. That would just be so typical . . ."

"No, I'm not saying that. But she worked like a fucking slave to protect the rest of us from Father. You, me, but most of all Mother. So that he wouldn't beat her to death. Don't you see? She went mad from it. She died. He killed her."

She hadn't intended for it to sound so brutal. She hadn't wanted to shove it down his throat. She had wanted him to see it for himself, but his obstinate refusal forced her. She had to somehow punch a hole through that shield he was hiding behind. She succeeded. And he hit back. It landed low down on her cheek and across the jaw. It was just a slap, but he had wound up for it all the way from his shoulder. She stared at him speechlessly, her eyes welling up with tears. It was more paralysis than pain she was feeling, as if it was not just the right side of her face, but her entire body that had lost all sensation.

"Sorry, sorry, Elin, sorry, I don't know, I just . . . I just wasn't thinking. Sorry, Elin . . ."

Somewhere far away she heard the jabbering stream of excuses. So predictable, so clumsy; stale and pathetic. Then it ran over. She didn't cry, it was the tears that overflowed when the lower eyelid couldn't hold any more lacrimal fluid. A physiological phenomenon that couldn't be stopped. She didn't cry.

"Imagine that, you've become so good at defending him, that you've become just like him."

His face scrunched up as if he was the one who was suffering, as if it was she who had hit him.

38

Stefania holding a workbook from school. Her voice, rapid fire, cheerful. Dreaming about something that was coming up, a trip, a future. She imagined herself in the future, painted a picture of how it was going to be. Sometimes she sat on the edge of the bed, read a story to her younger siblings. The workbook comes back, a sheet of English vocabulary, a bare leg, a ribbed nightgown with a little ribbon at the front on the neckband. Her moving quickly through the rooms on long, powerful legs.

Ricky's own memories of her were mostly glimpses of that kind. When the end came, he was fourteen, that of course he remembered. The day she sat in the car next to Mother and then never came home again. Father had left for Japan, and the pale, whitish-yellow apples fell from the trees. Stefania was looking down at her lap, her face hidden by her long hair. He looked after her, but she never met his gaze. He remembered that, of course. But by then she was already far away. Even if she sometimes spoke of the future, spoke in that rapid-fire chatter, with a wide smile, it still wasn't like it had been before. Stefania was sick, Mother had explained and after that, the sickness was all you ever heard about. Any attempt to tell stories, to dream, was filtered through the illness. Even her movements and expressions were colored by her illness. She was sick above and beyond everything else, only after that was she Stefania.

The other times, with the healthy voice and the quick movements through the house, there were only brief glimpses of that left. She was so tall, he thought, but it may just have seemed that way because he was so small. Long, thin bare legs, he thought for some reason. Pale, bare legs, pale even in summer. But maybe that was a false picture, maybe he just didn't have any summer memories. Yes he did, on the way out to the island, with Mother in the cockpit of the *Adventure*. Stefania sunbathed her way through sailing trip after sailing trip. She must have been tanned, and yet he couldn't see that in front of him.

But with her workbook, or the vocabulary sheet, how she called out to Father as she skipped through the living room, so that he could see. She held out her workbook with a straight arm, at once demanding and pleading. Then those long, pale legs crawled up into his lap. And Father laid his arms around her and the book, or the vocabulary sheet, and considered the problem. The deep voice that guided her toward the solution. And how she sparkled and glowed, more alive than you could ever imagine was possible. Those broad lips smiling, that gaze that pierced right through you, and those words that whirled around in your head—plans, advice, things that were going to happen. Or was it because she later became different, that his real sister seemed to be so much more, as if she lived in her own world where you could bend the laws of nature?

He had two images of Stefania: a warm, living dream image, and a gray, silent, ghost image. But neither the one nor the other had anything to do with what Elin was talking about. If you combed through enough psychology theories, you could probably convince yourself that she was somehow flirting with Father and that he somehow was letting himself be flirted with. Or else maybe you didn't even need to comb through all that many, that was probably Exhibit A. Stefania had been the best, then she had become ill. The world wasn't fair.

He had heard her throw up in the basement, one single time he had seen it. He had seen her stick her hand into the vomit and taste it. It had almost made him throw up himself, but it was only now that he understood why she had tasted her own vomit. It was to make her vomit again.

39

It started to rain lightly as Fredrik passed Väte, but when he parked outside the police station it had already stopped and the clouds had begun to disperse. The asphalt was barely damp.

The first thing he did when he came into his office was pick up the receiver to call Eva about the mower blade, but he hesitated with his finger poised above the first number.

Was it really that bad? Had it gone from awkward to completely fucking impossible?

He solved the dilemma by sending a text message and at the same time asking her about Kristina Traneus's diaries. He got an answer almost immediately.

> *Blade was on the mower. Looked myself. Saw nothing loose, but can double-check. Easy to miss what you're not looking for. Don't know who has diaries. Better ask around.*
>
> */e*

He stared at the signature "/e". What was that supposed to mean?

After a bit of running around between offices and a few phone calls he concluded that it must have been Lennart who took the dairies home with him. He considered taking the car to go over and pick them up—Lennart didn't live more than fifteen minutes from the police station—but decided to call instead.

It took seven rings before Lennart picked up. Fredrik pictured

Lennart struggling up from the floor, where he had been lying on account of his back. Fredrik's father had spent a few summers like that, after having recklessly lifted some oversized rock in the yard of their summer cabin.

"How are you doing?" asked Fredrik and pulled at the receiver cord that had tangled itself up to half its length.

"Thanks, it's going in the right direction," said Lennart and coughed. He sounded hoarse.

"It's just a drag having to stay at home all day. You can hear for yourself, voice gets all gummed up. No one to talk to."

"You ought to borrow one of those language courses on CD at the library in Roma," said Fredrik and sat down so he wouldn't have to struggle with the cord. He grabbed a pen, wrote "phone cord" on a Post-it pad and knew that he wouldn't do anything about it. Not in the middle of a murder investigation.

"Maybe Japanese, what do you think?" answered Lennart. "Ella and I are going to Japan in February, two weeks. Tokyo, Kyoto, and Hiroshima."

Fredrik felt vaguely envious. It was the over-fifties with kids who'd left home, who had the time and money to travel around the world. If it wasn't Japan, it was China, Mexico, or Kenya. He hadn't made it past the Canaries since Simon was born. And not much further before that, either. On the other hand, who the hell wanted to be over fifty.

"You could see if you can track down Traneus while you're there," he said.

Lennart just laughed.

Fredrik explained his reason for calling and Lennart was quick to take out the diaries. It seemed as if he had them within arm's reach of the telephone.

"July 1994, you said?"

"That's right."

The line went silent for a moment while Lennart flipped through the book.

"Here we go."

"Can you see whether it says anything there about 'an adventure' or 'the adventure' on the sixth of July or after?"

"Let's see," said Lennart and hummed to himself as he scanned the text. "Nope, I can't see anything adventurous here. But if you give me fifteen minutes I can call you back?"

"So what does it say then? On the sixth of July?" asked Fredrik without answering the question.

"Want me to read it to you?" asked Lennart.

"Yeah."

"Okay. Sixth of July. 'Packed for Elin and Rickard. Had to go buy mosquito repellant and UHT milk. Arvid and Rickard were sitting with the sea charts as usual.' That's it."

"How about the seventh of July?" asked Fredrik.

"Seventh of July. 'Today we sailed out to the island. We put out early from Klintehamn. Good winds. We sailed the whole way. Arvid said that the gods were with us. I think so, too. An amazing day, clear blue sky, nice and balmy. We had a following wind the whole way from Hoburgen.'"

Lennart stopped.

"Want me to continue? It keeps on in the same style . . ."

"No, that's enough."

A boat. He should have been able to work that one out.

"Was that any help?" said Lennart.

"Maybe. We'll have to check it out."

IT HAD RAINED during the night. The air was cool and the dirt road between the fields and the pastures was dark gray and a little muddy. Johannes Klarberg had broken off a branch from a bush along the way and was walking with it in his hand. He whipped the ground with it with every fourth step or so. Little clouds of dust rose up when the branch ripped a hole in the damp road surface all the way through to the dry part underneath.

He had been sent out to look for two runaway pigs. He had been forced to do it. He was ashamed of his father's notion of happy pigs. The kids at school had gotten tired of shouting "happy pig" at him after just one week, but he still felt ashamed. And then they kept running away all the time; well, maybe not all the time, but this was the second time this month anyway.

He had tried to claim that this couldn't be considered a household chore that he could be expected to help out with. This was actually his father's job. But his father had waved him off saying that the day he really fulfilled his share of the chore list that was taped to the inside of the cleaning cupboard, he wouldn't have to run after any more pigs.

What the hell was he talking about? He had never asked for that list to be put up. It had just appeared there one day two years ago when they had been to visit his mother's cousin in Västerås, and his mother had been so impressed by all his second cousins running around like brainwashed boy scouts, clearing the table and doing the dishes and vacuum cleaning.

He whipped the ground extra hard with his stick, which spattered mud onto his black hoodie.

"Fuck!"

He brushed away the mud with his hand, but it left a gray spot that didn't come out.

Johannes knew just where to look. They were always in the same spot, some fifty to over a hundred yards in among the birch trees and oaks in the field next to the enclosure they had escaped from. He walked past the sign with the ridiculous message about happy pigs, tried not to see it when he looked out for cars before crossing the road and entering the field.

The dry branches and partially damp leaves rustled and cracked under his feet. It smelled of earth. He peered between the trees and stepped right into a fresh pile of pig shit. This was just so typical. He walked on, his sneakers becoming shiny with the dampness from the leaves and grass.

He spotted one of them. Brown spots against pink haunches, partially hidden behind the thick trunk of a beech tree. It was never difficult to get them to come along, not the fully grown ones, they didn't seem interested in fighting for their freedom. The same could not be said for the little pigs. You couldn't handle them on your own. They were totally crazy and fast as hell. But they had already been sent to slaughter.

The pigs had grubbed up a big hole in the ground, tossed up little piles of black dirt. The sow took a few steps to the side with her hindquarters when she suddenly became aware of his presence, gave him an indifferent glance. She had something in her mouth, covered in dirt and muck, limp, looked like a dead crow or some other little animal, maybe a squirrel.

He stopped. Stared at the sow and the thing it was holding in its tusks. That was no animal. What he had taken for a dead bird was something else altogether.

40.

The smell of tobacco was strong. Göran Eide could almost see the light-gray wisps of smoke above his desk. How could something that only existed inside your head tickle the senses so realistically? He felt tempted to wave his hand to see if he could affect the imaginary tobacco haze that defied the smoking ban.

Unfortunately, fantasizing about smoking didn't stay his craving for tobacco. If anything it increased it.

It had been twelve days since Kristina and Anders Traneus had been found murdered, two weeks since they had been killed. And still no trace of Arvid Traneus's whereabouts. Göran was sure of three things: that Arvid Traneus had killed his wife and her lover, that he was no longer in the country, but probably in Japan or possibly in some island nation with very lax banking and taxation laws, and that they would catch him. Not within the next few days, or weeks, most likely not even this year, but sooner or later, in a year or two, he would expose himself and could be arrested by the local police in whatever country he was currently in.

Arvid Traneus had had twelve days to get in touch, which he ought to have done if he wasn't guilty of the murders. The information couldn't possibly have escaped him. Every imaginable media had reported extensively on the double murder. And Arvid Traneus had last been seen on Gotland two days before his wife and cousin had been killed.

The phone rang. Göran picked up the receiver. It was the duty officer.

"We've got someone here who claims to have found human body parts."

"Where?" asked Göran.

"Somewhere between Etelhem and Hejde, out in the forest, or in some field," said the duty officer.

"So what is it, some old bones?"

The duty officer cleared his throat.

"According to the person filing the report, it looked like it was a man's penis," he said.

Göran's spirits sank a little. He wasn't in the mood for any pranks. He glanced at the calendar on the desk to make sure that he wasn't supposed to be celebrating some anniversary as chief inspector or as a police officer, or that there was some other reason he ought to be prepared to be the butt of his colleagues' jokes. He couldn't think of anything.

"I see," he said, "is there anyone other than the person filing the report who's seen this body part?"

"No," said the duty officer, "but I sent out a patrol. They ought to be there any minute."

"And the person who called it in, who is it?"

"It's a young kid, but he seemed credible, and very upset. He was out looking for a couple of runaway pigs when he found it. The pigs had dug up the ground and one of them apparently had this append-age in its mouth."

Göran was now in an even worse mood and feeling even more desperate for a smoke.

"Call back when it's been confirmed," he said and hung up.

OFFICER MATS LARSSON looked at Johannes Klarberg with a steady gaze as he listened to the boy's account. His considerably older part-ner, Leif Knutsson, stood next to him with his arms crossed and lis-tened, too.

The boy claimed that he'd found a human penis in among the trees at the side of the winding forest road. The problem was that there was no longer any penis—appendage, male sex organ, or whatever you chose to call it—left to see, because when he saw it, it had been dan-gling between the tusks of a pig. If the boy's story was correct, then it must have been dug out of the ground. When the boy had tried to get the pig to let go of the alleged organ, the pig had instead gobbled it up.

"Are you absolutely sure of what you saw?"

Johannes Klarberg nodded eagerly.

"As sure as can be. I can swear to it. I was this close," he said and illustrated by stretching out his arm to its full length and angling up his hand.

He looked like he was sixteen or seventeen years old, tall and thin and had dark, almost black hair that hung down in front of one eye.

"This isn't something you're making up is it? You do realize that submitting false information to the police can have serious consequences?" said Knutsson and managed to sound reassuring and a little threatening at the same time.

Johannes Klarberg didn't seem to understand what Knutsson meant.

"No, what would I do that for?" he gasped.

As for the two pigs, the boy had managed to get them across to the part of the pasture that currently wasn't being used. Knutsson and the boy could see them from the spot where they were standing. It didn't seem likely that Johannes Klarberg was lying, Mats Larsson thought. It was one thing to call 911 with a made-up story, but for him to stand there and lie to the faces of two police officers, that was hard to imagine. The boy didn't seem stupid, which of course didn't rule out the possibility that he may have been mistaken.

Knutsson sighed and took out his mobile. He called up the station and explained the situation to the duty officer, who in turn said that he would call back in a few minutes.

They stood there silently watching the pigs while they waited. They were a light grayish-pink against the green pasture and they weren't moving.

"If you think the kid's telling the truth, then those pigs will have to be put down," said the duty officer when he called back.

"Both of them?" said Knutsson.

"Yes, we can't rule out that there are or have been more body parts buried in the ground and that the pigs have found them and eaten them."

"So, what do we do?" said Knutsson, a furrow appearing between his eyebrows.

"I'll send over a vet."

"Okay."

"Do you know who owns the animals? You'll have to speak to the owner."

"It's the kid's father. He's tried calling him, but apparently he's at some meeting in town. He left a message."

"At least we know who it is anyway," said the duty officer. "Well, a vet will be along in a while."

"Okay."

"And for the time being we'll treat it as a body dump site, so you'll have to cordon it off."

Knutsson hung up.

"I'm afraid the pigs have to be put down," Knutsson told the boy.

Johannes Klarberg just nodded, as if he'd already worked that out himself.

LEIF KNUTSSON ACCOMPANIED the boy along the tractor path over toward the enclosure with the two pigs, while Mats Larsson opened the trunk of the patrol car and took out a roll of police ribbon.

He tied one end around a telephone pole and cordoned off over a hundred yards down the road. He continued up along the edge of the trees where it abutted the recently harvested sugar beet field. The beets were still lying in great piles in one corner of the field, awaiting transport to the mainland.

Better cordon off a large area, thought Mats Larsson. If there really were body parts buried in there, forensics would want to turn over every single leaf within a few thousand square yards. And if there really was a human body, or parts of one, buried in there, the place would be crawling with journalists and curious members of the general public as soon as news got out.

Twenty-five minutes later, a cherry-red Volkswagen Passat station wagon approached from the north. The site lay a few miles south of the road between Hejde and Buttle. Just a few farms beside an area of cultivated land, otherwise just forest, silence, and no witnesses.

The Passat slowed down as it approached the cordon and came to a complete stop when Mats Larsson stepped out from the tractor path and held out his hand to let the driver understand that this was the right place.

A middle-aged woman with short, dark hair with gray streaks and dressed in a green cotton overall, stepped out of the car carrying a big, black bag. Before she walked up to Mats Larsson, she opened the trunk and pulled out a folded-up blue plastic tarp that she wedged under her arm.

"I'm the vet, Ann-Charlotte Jansson," she said and shook his hand. Mats Larsson introduced himself.

"Do you need help with that?" he asked and nodded at the tarp.

"Sure, if you could grab it that would be great," she said with a smile and moved closer so that he could take if from her without her having to put down her bag.

Having relieved her of her rustling light-blue burden, Mats Larsson led the way over toward the enclosure. He opened the electric fence and let Ann-Charlotte Jansson go in first.

The vet continued toward Knutsson, who was waiting together with the boy.

"Which of the pigs is the one that may have ingested a penis?" she said after greeting them.

"It's that one," said Johannes Klarberg quickly and pointed at the pig closest to them.

"If it's true then I'm sure I'm going to remember this day," she said.

With the help of Mats Larsson, Knutsson, and the boy, she grabbed hold of the pig that had been pointed out and euthanized it with a bolt gun. It was over quickly and, as far as anyone could tell, painlessly. The procedure was then repeated on pig number two.

The sun was shining down over the landscape and the dead animals from between what remained of the dispersed rain clouds from last night. Many of the trees beyond the fields were still a lush green, but the birches had turned completely yellow.

Ann-Charlotte Jansson laid out the tarp and they heaved the first pig up as far as they could onto it.

The vet quickly tied on a disposable apron of thin plastic, took out a knife from her bag and started to slice open the pig from the neck on down. She sliced open the peritoneum and then, with a few well-placed incisions, freed the stomach and intestinal package, which she then pulled from the pig's body, out onto the tarp. Blood ran out of the disemboweled pig. It didn't bother the veterinarian, who was wearing boots, but the other three stepped out of the way. Johannes Klarberg followed the vet's work with great curiosity, eyes wide open, while Mats Larsson and his partner Knutsson regarded the entrails with not quite the same degree of enthusiasm.

Ann-Charlotte Jansson opened the large stomach and let the contents spill out onto the blue plastic. Among the indefinable, partially digested stomach contents lay a larger object that she carefully scraped over to the side using the knife she had used to open up the pig's belly. She took out a bottle with something that Mats Larsson guessed was salt solution and rinsed the object clean from the half-digested, greenish-yellow slurry.

All four of them stared in silence at the object for a few seconds.

"Well," said Ann-Charlotte Jansson after a moment, "guess you'd better call in a medical examiner. I'm just a veterinarian, but that looks to me like a human penis."

41

In addition to the wooded area, the private tractor path and the stretch of public road that ran past the trees were also cordoned off.

There were five cars parked along the road: Eva Karlén's forensics van, two patrol cars, and two unmarked police cars, and two civilian fleet vehicles. Claes Klarberg, Johannes's father and the pigs' owner, had arrived on the scene after checking his voice mail.

"Is this your land?" asked Fredrik pointing at the cordoned-off area.

Claes Klarberg shook his head. He was tall and dark haired, just like his son, not a gray hair on his head. He had come driving up on a big Japanese motorbike.

"Everything on this side of the road belongs to Bjersander," said Klarberg and unzipped his red-and-white leather jacket.

"Bjersander?"

"Lars Bjersander. The next farm up on the right-hand side," he said and pointed north.

Fredrik made a note of that before continuing:

"You didn't notice a car or other type of vehicle parked here lately?"

"No, but of course we live a mile over that way," said Claes Klarberg and nodded at the tractor path.

"You can't see over here, you mean?"

"Well, I can *see* over here I guess, but it's far away and then there's trees and things in the way."

"So nothing caught your eye as far as you can remember?"

Claes Klarberg thinks for a moment.

"It could have been anything. A light, a sound?"

"No. Of course you see cars driving along the road, but that's not something you think twice about."

You only had to turn your head around once to see that there was no one who lived close enough to get a good view of the wood. If they were going to find a witness, it would have to be a real stroke of luck.

"Listen, it would be good if I could go take care of my pigs now. Can't leave them lying out here."

Mats Larsson was still standing by the pig carcasses to keep the birds and other animals away. It hadn't taken long before a couple of gulls showed up with a cry and started circling above the enclosure. One of them had landed on the telephone pole just a few yards from Fredrik and Claes Klarberg, patiently waiting for an opportunity to dive down to feast on the viscera.

"Sure," said Fredrik, "that'll be fine. We'll be in touch if there's anything else."

"Just call me anytime," said Claes Klarberg.

THERE WAS A scratching along the bark as a squirrel skittered up the trunk and disappeared somewhere up in the crown of the oak tree. Both Eva Karlén and Johannes Klarberg looked up instinctively and followed the little animal with their eyes.

How could I have been so stupid? thought Eva and looked at the squirrel that suddenly popped its head out from a branch way up there. It shouldn't be that difficult for her to keep her hands off of Fredrik Broman? Sure she was attracted to him, she couldn't deny that, but he wasn't all that special. Besides which, he was married.

She hadn't lost any sleep over what happened in the basement, but it didn't take much for her to find herself reliving the memory of their kiss. It was exciting as well as frightening. What did it mean? What was the point? The best thing she could do was just forget the whole thing happened. Work and forget. Not think.

"So this is where it was?" she asked, turning her attention to the twenty-or-so-square-yard section of earth that had been dug up by the two pigs.

"Yes," said Johannes and pushed away the black hair from his face. "It was standing just behind that birch tree there."

Eva quickly put up a hand and stopped him when he was going to walk over and stand where the pig had been standing just a few hours before.

"Just point if you don't mind."

"One or two yards behind that birch tree over there," said Johannes Klarberg and pointed obediently.

"How about the other one, where did you find that?" asked Eva.

"It was further inside," he said and waved with his hand. "I can show you."

"Thanks. That would be great," said Eva.

She let Johannes go first. Their footsteps rustled through the tall grass. The trees stood far apart, but there were a few spots where thick patches of underbrush had grown up that they had to skirt around.

"Otherwise there are no animals being kept in this enclosure?" she asked.

"Not usually. I think Lasse puts his horses in here sometimes, mostly just so to stop it from getting too overgrown, but as you can see that's not really enough."

Beautiful, knotted oaks, thick grass, and the sun filtering down between the puffs of cloud. Eva followed a few yards behind Johannes and thought about how best to organize the extensive work that lay ahead. But first of all, she had to answer the most important question: Was there a human body buried here? In pieces?

42

It had taken Eva Karlén and Granholm over two hours to exhume the remains of a human body from the hole that the pigs had begun. On a piece of white plastic sheeting beneath the shelter of a tent, she had laid out two legs, two arms, and a torso with missing genitals. The legs had been severed from the rest of the body at the hip joints, chopped off so that the balls of the thigh bones remained in the sockets of the pelvis with a stump of bone. The arms, on the other hand, were broken off in such a way that the balls of the joints were exposed. The head was missing, as were the feet.

It was unusual for dismembered bodies to be buried without the individual parts being packaged in some way. Plastic bags sealed with tape was the most usual, but they could also be found wrapped in pieces of cloth. Of course they were much easier to handle that way. When they were not prepacked, as was the case here, it was possibly an attempt to accelerate the rate of decay. But in this sandy ground, the effect had almost been the opposite.

Göran, who had just arrived on the scene, regarded the dismembered body parts from the opening of the tent. He was reluctant to go inside, so instead he held aside the strip of tent fabric that formed the door with a cautious grip, his thumb partially covering the tent manufacturer's green and blue logo. Crumbs of black soil had scattered across the white sheeting around the body parts.

"We're still looking for the head and feet, but I don't think they're buried in the same spot, at least not the head," said Eva over her shoulder at him.

"Because . . . ?" said Göran.

"All these body parts lay concentrated within a limited radius. They were probably all buried in the same hole. It seems illogical to me for someone to dig a separate hole for the head in immediate proximity to the hole where the rest of the body is buried."

"Yeah, you're right about that, though I'm not sure how logical anyone who does something like this really is," said Göran and turned his back on the pale-gray, earth-covered remains.

"Who is it? Can you provide a basic description?" he then asked.

"Middle-aged male, good physical condition, but no manual laborer, about six-two to six-three. Not much more I can say," answered Eva.

"And the cause of death?"

Eva shook her head.

"I can't see any injuries other than the ones resulting from the actual dismemberment. It could of course have come from violent trauma to the head, but might just as well have been caused by poisoning, asphyxiation, or loss of blood. He may, for example, have had an artery severed in the armpit or groin, but as the body looks now it's impossible to say. For me, that is."

"I guess we'll have to assume that the head has been hidden somewhere in order to make it more difficult to determine the cause of death, or prevent the body from being identified. Worse comes to worst, it's been destroyed altogether," said Göran. "But the feet? I don't understand why they're missing."

"It may have had something to do with the identification. There are people with fused toes, stuff like that," said Granholm and adjusted his glasses with his forefinger against the root of his nose.

Göran sighed and looked up toward the treetops. The last of the clouds had dissolved and the sun was beaming from a clear blue sky. Airplanes on their way to and from Finland, Russia, and Northeast Asia drew white lines across the blueness. Seven hundred flights crossed above Gotland every day. You could make out a distant rumble from the jet engines.

He felt a slight dizziness, not so much from the body parts in the tent, as from the thought of what people were capable of doing to each other.

"Aside from the head and feet, it seems that all the body parts we found were lying in the same hole," he said, "but why would you cut up a body if you're going to put all the pieces in the same hole anyway?"

"It could have been due to the logistical difficulties associated with their subsequent transportation," said Granholm and Göran wondered silently why he couldn't speak like a normal human being.

"It would be easier to get them into the ground as well," said Eva. "Burying a big body like this one at a decent depth requires a whole lot of work. But if the body's in pieces . . ."

Göran drew himself up and adjusted his jacket. The irritation he felt earlier had given way to thoughts about how best to organize the new murder investigation. He had left Ove Gahnström in Visby as head of the investigation. That meant one less man out in the field and Lennart Svensson couldn't be counted on for at least another week.

He took a deep breath. *Tobacco*, he thought.

"There are two more spots where someone has been doing some digging recently, but it's hard to determine whether it's the pigs or something else," said Eva.

"Could be both," said Göran.

"Anyway, that's where we'll have to start."

"Nothing else? No clothing, objects?" said Göran.

"Not yet. We're prioritizing the head."

Göran nodded, sickened at the thought of the headless body lying inside the tent.

"How long do you think he's been lying here?" he asked.

"As I'm sure you noticed, there's not a lot of decay," said Eva.

He had noticed. The body parts hadn't smelled at all, either. Of course there had been an odor inside the tent. Of earth, dampness . . . humus. And a little plastic.

"It's hard to say because it's unclear how deep they were buried. The pigs' digging may have changed the position of the body parts," she continued. "We'll have to wait for the medical examiner. But if I say a month, tops, then I wouldn't be saying too much."

"A month. That's not good," said Göran.

"Tops," Eva repeated, "and at the low end I'd say at least a week, yeah, not less than a week."

"So we've got a span of three weeks?"

"The medical examiner will be able to shorten that. I've spoken with the medical examiner's office and we can get a preliminary report by tomorrow afternoon. But, we'll probably still have about a week to play around with."

"Okay," said Göran, "I better get back to the station. This is turning into a real mess. I'll see if I can get National CID to send over a few extra hands to manage the database, and then we've got a press conference this afternoon.

The last bit he said mainly to himself. He was already heading off when Eva hurried to catch up with him.

"We've found tire tracks from a car. I can tell you about it on the way, if you like," she said.

She adjusted the chief inspector's direction gently but firmly and they walked together twenty or so yards in among the trees before she stopped him.

"They start from the road and end up over there by the bushes," she said and pointed out the course for Göran. "You can't make out any tire pattern, but I've measured them. It has to be from a larger vehicle. A jeep, pickup, or small truck."

"If we're lucky that time span won't turn out to be all that big after all," said Göran. "We've found a witness who saw a car drive out of here late on the night of the second of October."

"Here, in the middle of the forest?"

"Yes. He was on his way home from dinner at his daughter's house in Etelhem. When he was just a short distance away from here," said Göran and pointed, "he saw a light in his rearview mirror. Someone pulled out, he was sure of that, and it wasn't from the farm right up here."

"The second of October is within my range anyway," said Eva.

"We'll have to wait and see then," said Göran and started heading down toward the road.

FREDRIK WAS SITTING in the car with the door ajar. He flipped through his notepad with his left hand and held his cell phone pressed against his ear with his right. A dog barked somewhere close by.

"I've got another witness, one Anette Larsson, who saw a truck standing parked by the field, but this was in the middle of the day and how long it had been standing there she had no idea. She just drove past. But she was sure that it was somewhere between the fifth and the eighth," he said on the phone.

"She didn't see any logo or anything?" Ove responded at the other end.

"No. It had a big light yellow or beige cargo box. That was all she could remember."

Fredrik continued flipping through his notepad.

"Otherwise there's not much here," he said.

"It's going out on local radio and the national news bulletin in an hour. We'll have to see what we get in then," said Ove.

Fredrik shut his notepad and had to switch hands on the phone in order to be able to put his notepad in his inner jacket pocket.

"I've been thinking about something," said Ove. "This may be the answer to your question."

"My question? What question is that?" said Fredrik.

"Where did Arvid Traneus disappear to? That question."

"You mean that this could be him . . ."

"Lying buried in the field, yeah. The head and feet are missing. Arvid Traneus wore a size forty-seven."

Fredrik didn't answer at once. He looked out at the farm where he had just questioned a witness. Five little black lambs were grazing around a dead, graying oak tree. At the very top of the severed trunk, someone had nailed up a birdhouse. The grass beneath the apple tree in front of the house was speckled red with fallen fruit.

"That would change everything."

"Might seem a bit of a stretch, but on the other hand, we've got someone who's been missing for fourteen days," said Ove.

"Which wouldn't be that strange if he'd killed his wife and her lover."

"Which he could still have done, even if he turns up at the bottom of a hole in the middle of a field."

"I can't quite get my head around it," said Fredrik and lay his free hand on the steering wheel. "Each of the murders is so different in character."

"We have to be ready to consider it. We could be looking at two completely unrelated crimes. The one doesn't have to be connected to the other," said Ove.

ELIN HAD PACKED her things. She could only blame the fact that she was still there out of some kind of inability to act. It was quickly done, stuffing the few items of clothing, her makeup, wallet, and psychology books into the little sports bag she had bought to replace the Prada bag that she had used for the last time. But packing a bag was just a gesture. It was harder to actually set off.

When darkness fell, it was as if she had lost whatever strength she had left. *Tomorrow,* she thought, *I have to get away from here tomorrow.*

How many days had she been thinking like that?

It was dark outside. There were lights on in the house next door, but otherwise it was completely pitch black. She couldn't understand how Ricky could live like this. When you looked out the window, you couldn't be sure that there was actually anything there. It could just as well be a great big void of nothingness.

She wondered if she was starting to become paranoid, or was about to suffer another panic attack. It wouldn't be very strange, anyway. What was she doing there? Why was she hanging around?

Ricky had stopped trying to apologize, while she had gone completely silent. They moved past each other in the house, alongside each other in the house, but without really taking any notice of each other. Neither of them knew how to talk to the other anymore. Maybe she lingered because she knew that she couldn't leave until they had somehow become reconciled, or at least had broken this silence. But how?

Ricky had slept late, then kept out of sight up in the study, and now he was sitting there sunken in front of the TV for the past half hour. He was staring intently at the silly variety talk show as if it were the most important thing in the world and yet it was obvious that he was just passing the time or hiding. It was childish, but she was grateful to him for doing that. As for her, she was hiding in the kitchen with a magazine that she couldn't get herself to actually read, with a dish that was already washed and a glass that was already empty, but which she could easily fill up again.

She ought to leave, stop swilling red wine, go home, and focus on her studies that had been set aside for the past two weeks. It was stupid to fall behind right from the start. How many times had she thought that thought? Stupid to fall behind. Yeah, it sure was. Tomorrow, when it was light and her strength had returned, then she would take her packed bag and get on a bus. If she took the number 10, she only had a mile to walk to the bus stop. She didn't even need to ask Ricky for a

ride. But maybe that was just what she should do. Find a practical opening. Ask him to drive her to the bus stop. One minute in the car and five
to ten minutes at the bus stop, before the bus came, it was all the time
they would have at their disposal, maybe all the time they needed.

And then she sank back inside herself again and everything was
just dismal and hopeless. She felt a sudden twinge of pain in her stomach. She sat down with her hand pressed against her diaphragm and
tried to think when the last time she'd had her period was. Maybe she
ought to ask Ricky for an aspirin instead. Or ask to borrow the car so
that she could drive in to buy some sanitary napkins. If that didn't
present an opening then at least she wouldn't have to sit on the bus
into Visby with a wad of toilet paper between her legs.

She got up and looked in the cupboard where she knew the pain-
killers were usually kept. She didn't need to ask for one, she could just
take one. She found a Treo effervescent tablet, dissolved it in water
and quaffed the bitter white flocculent liquid, rinsed the glass, and put
it in the dish drainer.

"Could I borrow the car for a bit?" she asked.

She stood in the doorway. Ricky looked at her for a second, then
over at the front door.

"Sure, the keys are on the table in the hall," he said and it sounded
so casual and free from all subtext, the way it only can when you're
really trying to make it sound that way.

She walked over and found the keys immediately.

The signature tune for the news trumpeted from the TV. She pulled
on her jacket, heard something about Angela Merkel and Jacques Chirac, then something about the south of Gotland, a dismembered body
had been found in southern Gotland. She turned toward the TV, couldn't
help herself, was drawn inexorably toward the couch where she slowly
sank down a few feet from Ricky.

"Did you hear that?" she said and looked at the TV.

"Yeah."

They were forced to sit through several minutes of Merkel and Chirac before the news anchor returned to the news about Gotland.

What the Visby Police Department was describing a likely homicide had been discovered when a runaway pig had exposed parts of a human body buried in a field in the vicinity of Etelhem in southern Gotland. The TV screen showed police cars parked along a road, a police cordon of blue-and-white striped ribbon in front of some trees. It could have been anywhere. The picture changed to a slightly stocky man with short black hair standing behind a rectangular lectern of light-colored wood. The caption along the lower edge of the screen indicated that he was Ove Gahnström, in charge of the investigation.

"No, the body has not yet been identified. All I can say for the moment, is that the victim is a middle-aged man, a little above average height," the policeman answered to a question that had been edited out.

"Do you have any suspects?"

"It's a little difficult to come up with any suspects until we've identified the body."

"You said that the body had been dismembered. Has that made the identification process more difficult?"

"Among other things, yes."

"Have all the body parts been recovered?"

"I can't comment on that," said the policeman.

The report rounded off with a request to the public to get in touch with the police with any observation they may have made in the area. Elin froze. The news had made her think of her mother and those horrific events that had taken place in her own family home. That had presumably also aired on TV, but she hadn't really reflected over it until now. But the last thing she had thought about doing that day was looking at TV.

She got up, felt weak, had to go and do some shopping anyway. She looked at Ricky. He followed her with his gaze.

"Where are you going?"

"Shopping."

He didn't answer.

43.

Eva Karlén and her team resumed the crime scene investigation early Thursday morning, at first light. There were four of them altogether, Eva and Granholm, and the two uniformed officers that had been assigned to help them. It had gotten colder. A damp mist hung over the landscape, touched the treetops, painted the branches black and wet.

Although they kept moving, the cold dug its way in, and after a few hours they were frozen through. During the coffee break they sat in Eva's van with the engine running and drank several cups of the hot coffee that one of the uniformed officers had brought with him in a red-lacquered steel thermos.

"How long can a body lie in the ground before it starts to rot?" asked that same officer with the cup of coffee steaming in front of his mouth.

Eva pretended not to hear the question, but Granholm enthusiastically undertook to answer it.

"It depends on the conditions in the ground and how deep the body is buried. And then the climate of course. This ground here is well drained and there's a lot of sand, so it can take eight or nine years if it's buried at normal grave depth."

"Eight or nine years?" the curious police officer exclaimed and lowered his cup.

"Before process of decay is complete, that is," said Granholm.

The officer nodded and seemed to be calmed somehow by the information.

"Then of course it also plays a role if the rotting process has gotten started before the body is put in the ground," Granholm continued.

The windows of the van had become fogged up. You couldn't see out.

"Drink up now and we'll get back to work," said Eva.

At a quarter to twelve they found a human head buried over thirty inches below the surface. As with the other body parts, it wasn't packaged in any way, but had been laid directly into the ground.

The head was buried four yards in among the trees that began behind the field. They had covered the entire field, gently raked away leaves to see if the earth underneath had been disturbed. When that hadn't produced any results they had continued out into the forest.

The officer who had been so interested in the rotting process had opened his eyes wide when Granholm lifted the head out of the ground. Eva was almost afraid that he was going to start touching it.

Granholm had been right. In the cool, tightly packed sand that took over once you dug past the top twelve inches of soil, the rotting process went slowly. The head might just as well have been in a refrigerator. There were three deep cuts in the back of the head from a blunt instrument and there was some discoloration, but otherwise it was intact.

Eva didn't need any help from the medical examiner and dental records to identify the dead man. She recognized him from the photographs.

THE BUS LEFT at 2:10 p.m. from Hemse. It would make it to the old shop by twenty past at the earliest. In other words, it would be enough if she left at two o'clock sharp. She didn't have anything heavy to carry after all.

Ricky wasn't home. Elin had heard him take the car out late the night before, after she had gone to bed. She hoped that he would show up before two, there were still a few hours to go, but if he didn't she would leave anyway. This was enough now. She had to get out of there.

She took an apple from the light-colored wooden bowl on the kitchen table, bit into the red fruit that was sweet and mealy. She heard a car pull up outside. It wasn't Ricky, she could hear that from the sound of the engine.

Elin was happy when she saw Göran Eide climb out of the car that had parked in the driveway. She had liked talking to him. When she told him those things that she'd never told anyone else before, he had received them without questioning any of it, almost as if it was obviously true, as if he had heard the same story many times before.

She opened the door before he had had time to ring the doorbell.

"Hi," he said and introduced the woman next to him as Sara Oskarsson. "Could we come in for a moment?"

"Sure, come on in," she said and backed into the hall.

She smiled, but it was as if they didn't really want to acknowledge her smile. There was something suppressed, almost embarrassed about the two officer's expressions when they tried to smile back. Elin couldn't understand what was wrong. Had she done something?

"Is your brother at home?" the chief inspector asked.

"No. I think he's gone to visit a friend," she said.

"I see. Here on the island you mean," said Göran.

"Yes," she nodded, "in Visby. I think anyway."

They sat in the living room, Elin on the couch, and the officers each on a chair.

"I'm afraid I have some bad news," said Göran.

Elin felt her heart start pounding faster. Bad news? What did they mean? She had gotten bad news two weeks ago. Could it be Ricky? Had something happened to Ricky? But they had asked about him. They wouldn't have done that would they, if something had happened to him?

She sat completely still and looked attentively at the middle-aged man across the table.

"Your father is dead."

Elin sat as motionless as before, without saying a word.

"He was found dead a few hours ago."

Elin sat there mutely.

"Can we get hold of your brother, do you think? It would be good if he could come here."

"I was just about to leave for home," said Elin. "The five-forty-five ferry, the bus leaves at twenty past two from the shop."

The chief inspector had a hard time finding the words.

"I'd be lying if I said that I understand how it feels. I can only imagine. It was less than two weeks ago that I sat here with your brother and told you about your mother. But we are going to do everything we can to help you. The best thing would be if we could get hold of Rickard and . . ."

"We're not getting along very well right now," said Elin.

"Is there anyone else you can call, who . . ."

"No," she cut him off again.

She didn't need to hear the rest of the question. There was no one left here.

"We could ask the priest here in Levide to . . ."

"No," she said abruptly, "no fucking priest. We've got to get hold of Ricky."

She got up from the couch with her fingers tightly clasped.

"We've got to get hold of Ricky," she repeated.

"Yes, we've got to do that," said Göran Eide and stood up, too, "but I still think that it might be good to—"

"No fucking priest," Elin interjected. "I'd rather just have something to help me sleep."

"We can call the district doctor," said Göran.

"Sure, why not," said Elin without great interest. Göran looked at his colleague.

"Could you . . . ?"

She got up and left the room. Elin sat there silently until she had gone out.

"Where did you find him? Was it in Tokyo? Had he committed suicide? Jumped from the seventieth-floor balcony?" she rambled off without looking at Göran.

I'll never get away from here, she thought. *Now there's Father, too. Another one to bury. Another call to the undertakers. I'll get stuck here. What's going to happen with everything? Is it just Ricky and me now?*

The chief inspector said something to her. She didn't hear what he said.

"What?"

"Wouldn't you rather sit down," he said.

"No, I don't want to sit down. I have a bus to catch," she said resolutely.

"I think it might best if you . . ."

"Aren't you allowed to catch a bus if your father's dead? Is it illegal or something?"

"No, but I think it would be better if you sat down. We need your help to get hold of your brother. We've got to get hold of Ricky, don't we?"

Elin sank down onto the couch. Felt how the down seat cushion gave way and drew her into a loose grip. She heard the female officer's mumbling voice out in the hall. Soon the cars full of journalists would be back. Wouldn't it be better to board that bus out of here after all?

"Was it in Tokyo?" she asked. "Did they find him in Tokyo?"

The chief inspector gave her one of those looks again, that was meant to be a calm, friendly expression, but that didn't quite know where to go.

"No," he said, "your father was found dead about twelve miles away from here, near Hejde."

"What?"

"Yes."

"Hejde?"

"Yes. It came as a surprise to us, too," said Göran.

Elin cupped her hand to her mouth, then stiffened and stared at Göran.

"Hejde. But . . . Wasn't that . . . the thing that was on the news yesterday? They said Etelhem."

"They weren't very precise."

"You mean that it was . . . that that's the same . . . that that was my father?"

Göran nodded.

"Yes," he said, "that's right. Unfortunately, it was only this afternoon that we were able to establish his identity."

44.

The sound of the car door slamming shut echoed through the station garage. Göran hurried across the cement floor, hauled out his access card, and held it against the reader before he punched in the code to enter the building. The front desk stood empty and his footsteps across the linoleum floor were quiet and dry.

He had been wrong about Arvid Traneus not still being in the country. He had been wrong about it taking months, perhaps years before they found him. He had been wrong about Traneus still being alive. Instead they found him dead, buried out in a field, not far from his home in Levide. It remained to be seen whether he had been wrong also about Arvid Traneus having killed his wife and her lover.

He walked past the pantry, nobody there, either, and opened the door to the cafeteria with his access card. There were only two staff members left. One was wiping off the tables and the other was just going to start counting the register, but they let him buy something anyway. He chose a Loka mineral water and a little bar of 70 percent chocolate, which was strategically placed right next to the cash register. Such was the life of a chief inspector who'd reached the meridian of life. Water, healthy candy, and no cigarettes.

He paid, opened the bottle, and left so that they could close. Outside the door he ran into Peter Klint. The prosecutor looked buoyant, but in an ominous way. He was glowing extra brightly, like a bulb does shortly before it goes out for good.

"So, our prime suspect is dead," said Klint. "Do you still think he did it?"

Göran wondered if Klint just wanted to discuss it, or if it was meant as a gibe, but it was impossible to tell from looking at the prosecutor's face. He did have a smug smile on his face, but he looked like that all the time these days.

"It's quite possible, but at this point your guess is as good as mine," said Göran and guzzled half his bottle of water.

He was hot and thirsty. They had ended up staying with Elin Traneus for longer than expected and it had been a stressful afternoon.

"Could it have been a robbery-killing?" asked Klint who looked cool and comfortable in his light-blue polo shirt.

"I've considered that. That someone may have come to the house in Levide, held Kristina and Anders hostage while someone else took Arvid Traneus out to force him to withdraw money from his bank account," said Göran.

"But then something went wrong," Peter Klint filled in.

"Very wrong. What speaks against it is the unlikelihood of all three of them—the husband, the wife, and her lover—being in the house at the same time. But of course it can't be ruled out that the robbers walked right into some kind of a confrontation between the three of them."

Klint pointed toward the stairs and they started to walk while Göran downed what was left in his bottle.

"Another possibility of course is that a person or persons unknown were out to get Arvid Traneus, but accidentally killed Anders instead," he said with a voice that was straining to keep down the bubbles that were on their way up again.

"And then corrected their mistake," the prosecutor filled in.

"Yes, but whichever it is, the question remains, why would they go through the trouble of burying Arvid Traneus, a time-consuming and pretty risky thing to do, especially when you consider that they left Anders and Kristina in the house anyway?"

"Maybe the killers knew about the rumors of domestic abuse," Peter Klint suggested.

He was walking diagonally in front of Göran and glanced back at him over his shoulder as he spoke.

"You mean they buried Arvid Traneus in order to make it look like he had killed his wife and her lover and then left the island?" said Göran.

"Exactly."

"Nice try, as they say in soccer, but . . ."

"You can say it went off the post if that's what you mean," said Peter Klint.

They shared a quick laugh together and Klint pushed open the door to the meeting room where everyone was already gathered.

Klint's idea wasn't a bad one, in fact it was very smart, which was just what made it seem less credible. Murderers' attempts to cover up their crimes were, in Göran's experience, seldom shrewd chess moves planned several steps in advance, but rather desperate actions taken to save their own skins. He and his fellow officers had misinterpreted the pieces to the puzzle, as had Klint. But what the prosecutor had now done was to construct a scenario to fit their misinterpretation. That was not a good way to develop a new approach to an investigation.

At the same time, he had to admit that he had trouble letting go of the notion that Arvid Traneus had killed his wife and her lover. But who, in that case, had killed Arvid Traneus? Was it a murder or a robbery-killing completely unrelated to the first event? Did it have to do with business, unpaid debts, someone he'd wronged somehow? He ought to make another attempt with the company in Tokyo, even if it seemed a bit implausible for Arvid Traneus's murder to have links stretching all the way over there. Or was it as simple as that; someone had caught Arvid red-handed and chosen to mete out their own form of justice? The son? They hadn't been able to reach him since last night.

Göran stopped short in the middle of that thought. Was he on the verge of making the same mistake all over again? The last time he had interpreted someone's absence to mean guilt and flight, it had turned out to mean the man's death.

He looked around the table, met district police commissioner Agneta Wilhelmsson's eyes momentarily. It was high time to get the meeting under way. Without thinking about it, he pushed the little bar of chocolate into his back pocket. He would find it there two hours later, mushed and melted.

OVE GAHNSTRÖM PICKED up.

"Hello, Ove speaking."

"Hi, it's Carina. I'm sending over a tip that came in that you should take a closer look at. There's a girl who works over at the state liquor store in Hemse who claims that she saw a guy who was together with one of the Traneus daughters years ago. She hadn't seen him for

years, but now he popped up in Hemse just around the same time as
the murders in Levide. Apparently she's seen him a few times, but it's
only now that she realized who it was. She seemed to think that he'd
had some kind of brush with the law, but she wasn't sure how."

"Wait," said Ove, "have you sent it already?"

"Yes."

"I'll just bring it up."

The computer had gone into sleep mode. Ove thrummed his mouse
impatiently with his fingers as he waited for the screen to come back
on, and could then bring up the tip. He quickly skimmed through the
text.

"You didn't take down a description?" he asked as his eyes scanned
the last few lines.

"Uh . . . no, I didn't think of it, since she was so certain of his name."

"She was sure about it?"

"Yeah, not the slightest hesitation," said Carina.

Leo Ringvall, Ove read from the screen.

"Thanks for letting me know," he said.

"Sure thing," said Carina and disappeared with a click in the receiver.

Ove hung up just as Fredrik swept past in the corridor. Ove called
out to him.

"What do you think of this," he said and pointed at the screen.
"Leo Ringvall, about thirty years of age, 'brush with the law,' some
kind of connection to the Traneus family from years back through the
now-deceased eldest daughter Stefania. Suddenly shows up in Hemse
around the same time as the murders."

Fredrik leaned forward over the desk in order to see better.

" 'A brush with the law,' whatever that means," he said.

"Seems a little unlikely, but interesting," said Ove. "Could you go
down and speak to the tipster?"

"Seeing as you're asking me so nicely, I can hardly refuse," he said and smiled.

Ove smiled widely back.

"Great, then it's agreed."

Fredrik looked at the screen again.

"If he spent time with the daughter then he knows that they've got plenty of cash. He gets into some money problems and comes up with the idea to pay them a visit."

"Let's see," said Ove, "Carina didn't pull his file, so I don't have his personal identity number, but it ought to be possible to limit the search anyway . . ."

Ove filled in a few of the fields in the search form and pressed return. They both silently looked through the list of hits that came up. Leo Ringvall had served out a three-year prison sentence for grievous assault that had ended just three weeks earlier.

"This might be something," said Fredrik.

Ove clicked up a photo. A long thin face framed by shoulder-length black hair stared vacantly from the screen with pale gray eyes.

"Long, black hair," said Ove.

He wrote down the witness's name in his pad, ripped out the page, stood up and handed it to Fredrik.

"Drive down there and speak to her, and I'll talk to Göran."

THE TYPICAL FRIDAY rush to buy alcohol for the weekend was nowhere to be seen at the state liquor store in Hemse. A few stray customers were slowly wandering around with gray shopping baskets hanging from their arms, scanning the racks of bottles. The premises had been refurbished as a self-service store a few years ago. Self-service state liquor stores seemed to go hand-in-hand with the rapid breakdown of the country's national alcohol policy, which had, for all intents and purposes, been doomed since the EEA agreement was signed in 1992.

Fredrik guessed that it would take at the most ten years before every Swedes' wettest dream came true: wine and liquor sold at regular supermarkets.

Sitting at the only open checkout was a young man with golden yellow streaks in his reddish-brown hair. Fredrik walked up to him and showed him his police badge.

"I'm looking for Marie Barsk."

"She's in the stockroom," said the man at the register and looked around uncertainly.

He reached for an intercom next to the register, but stopped short.

"Well, you can just go on back there, I guess; you are the police after all," he said and smiled wryly.

"I'll try to resist the temptation to swipe anything," said Fredrik.

"Just head straight into the stockroom and you'll find her," said the cashier.

He pointed to a gray door at the back of the store that was propped half open by a stack of wine boxes.

Fredrik entered a storage area with redbrick walls, full of pallets stacked with unopened boxes. Guided by the sound of ripping cardboard, he spotted a woman bent over a pallet of Spanish Navarra wines. She cut open the boxes with a light-green carpet knife.

"Are you Marie Barsk?" he called out to her across half the space.

The woman gave a start, straightened up, and looked at him questioningly.

"Yes, that's me."

"Fredrik Broman, Visby Police Department," he said and flashed his ID once again. "You called in with a tip. I'd like to talk to you about that."

Marie Barsk remained standing where she was holding the carpet knife. She looked put out, as if this wasn't at all what she had been expecting when she'd called the police hotline that had been published in the newspapers.

"Is there a problem?" asked Fredrik.

"No, no," she said and stayed where she was.

"Is there somewhere we could sit down for a moment?" he asked.

"We can go sit in the coffee room," said the woman and broke out of her paralysis.

She put the knife down on the one of the opened boxes and showed Fredrik into a room that lay immediately to the right of the entrance to the stockroom. He let her go in first and then pulled the door closed behind him.

It was a small room that was completely white, with a white laminated table, six white chairs, a kitchenette, and a window looking out onto the loading dock. On the stainless steel surface between the stove hotplates and the sink, stood three lavender-colored ceramic mugs.

They sat opposite each other at the table. Out of habit, Fredrik took the spot closest to the door.

"I'm here to talk to you about the person that you saw in the store," he said.

Marie Barsk had dirty blonde, naturally curly hair that spiraled a ways down her straight shoulders. There was something odd about her gaze and now that they were seated at the table Fredrik saw that she had a white spot in her right iris.

"You submitted a name. Are you sure that's his name?" he asked.

"Yes, of course I am. We went to the same school for five years," she said and looked at Fredrik.

Although her gaze was steady, he got the impression that there was something anxious about it. Maybe it just had to do with that spot.

"In the same grade?" he asked.

"No, he was one grade above me, here at Högby."

"Can you describe him?"

"Of course. He's got long, slightly mussed-up black hair. Down to about here," she said indicating with her hand at her shoulder. "Long thin face, looked pretty pale. He's not very big, but compact somehow, sort of strong without being hefty."

"How tall is he?"

"Well, I wouldn't say he's short exactly, but . . . I guess he's about medium height, a little less maybe. Whenever he's been in here, he's always been wearing a hoodie with the hood pulled up. That was why it took awhile before I recognized him."

Outside the windows behind Marie, cars were pulling into the customer parking lot of the Hemse shopping center.

"But you could see that he had long hair, even though he was wearing a hood?" asked Fredrik.

"Oh, sure. You could tell. But of course I also know from before that he had long hair," she said.

There was a faint clinking of bottles out in the stockroom.

"How many times have you seen him in the store?"

"Three, four times, maybe."

"And when was the last time?"

"The day before yesterday."

"Last Wednesday then," said Fredrik.

Marie Barsk nodded and tugged at the seam of her gray uniform shirt.

"Did you get any sense of whether he maybe lives close by or if he came by car? He wasn't holding a set of car keys or anything?"

"No, no idea. We only see a short stretch of the street from in here. And if you sit with your back to it, then you don't see anything."

She clasped her hands together in front of her and looked at Fredrik, waiting for the next question.

"What can you tell me about Leo Ringvall? What do you know about him?"

"Well, like I said we went to the same school for five years, but we never hung out. Except for maybe ending up at the same parties a few times. He started out at Säve, but then he left after first grade. But you'd still see him around here in Hemse even after junior high. First I think he lived in Klintehamn, but then he moved here, to Hemse, or his family did anyway, and then something happened and they all moved away some ten or twelve years ago maybe."

"Do you know where they moved to?" said Fredrik.

"To the mainland. Stockholm I think it was."

"You don't know what caused them to move?" asked Fredrik.

"I think his father lost his job. At the time people were saying that he stole something from his work, that that was the reason, but I've since heard that that wasn't true at all, that a number of people got laid off because the company was doing badly. I don't know."

"But Leo Ringvall had some kind of a relationship with Stefania Traneus?"

"Yes. That was when we were in ninth grade. Stefania and I were the same age. She was in the parallel class at Högby," said Marie Barsk.

"Sounds like a bit of a mismatched couple," said Fredrik.

"It didn't last very long, either. I think her father had something to do with it. That he banned her from seeing him. But she was very . . . how can I put it, almost obsessed with Leo. You can get like that at that age. Whatever your parents don't want you to do . . . well, you know."

How do you do that, Fredrik wondered to himself. How do you get a fifteen-year-old to stop seeing someone she really wants to see?

"But you're saying that it ended anyway?"

"There were a number people who said that Stefania's father had scared Leo away somehow. Though I can't say how you'd go about scaring off Leo. He was pretty wild as I remember."

"But still just a teenager," said Fredrik.

"Yeah, of course."

Marie smiled vaguely, as if she saw Leo in front of her as the boy he once was. Had Arvid Traneus gone after him, physically? Or had he gone after Stefania?

"Do you remember who Leo Ringvall hung out with back then?" he asked.

"Oh, sure, I probably remember pretty much everyone," said Marie Barsk without having to think about it.

"We can start with those closest to him," said Fredrik and smiled, and heard just then how someone called out for Marie from the stockroom.

"Then you can go," he added and started writing down the names that she gave him.

45.

Elin sat in the couch with the receiver pressed to her ear and listened to Molly's hoarse voice, hoarse because she had been speaking in such a low tone that her voice was on the verge of disappearing completely.

"I wish that I could be there," whispered Molly.

"I wish you could be here, too," said Elin and there was a long silence.

She felt clearer in the head, the painkiller had started to work. She had also gratefully taken the sleeping pills she had received from the district doctor that the police had sent for. They had allowed her to sleep straight through the night, but she had woken up with a heavy head and fuzzy thoughts. The painkiller helped, the way it helped with most things. She ran her left hand through her hair, felt that she needed to wash it. Her pale face was reflected in the empty TV screen.

"I don't know what to say," Molly hissed from receiver.

"You don't have to say anything," said Elin.

That was true and yet not. She needed someone who said something, who said a lot, but she didn't need any pity or someone to work through everything that had happened. She needed someone who called and talked about Freud's interpretation of dreams, about the pitfalls of CBT, about how drunk she had gotten at the last college pub crawl, about an incredible bargain they'd found at Tjallamalla, anything; even somebody calling up to complain about their pain-in-the-ass boyfriend.

Since she had told Molly that her mother had been murdered, Molly had called her once. One single time in two weeks. It made her angry. It made her even more angry since she realized that she had nobody on the island. There was nobody that she really cared about and who cared about her. Not anymore. Well, Ricky of course, but she hadn't seen him since yesterday night. And he wasn't calling, either.

"I'm gonna come home tomorrow," she said.

"Will they let you?" said Molly.

"You don't have to whisper," said Elin.

"Okay," said Molly after clearing her throat.

"They can hardly stop me," said Elin. "I can't wait to get home. I've been living at Ricky's place for two-and-a-half weeks now. It . . . I've just got to get home. It's too much over here."

"It must be awful," said Molly.

She started with a whisper, but caught herself and raised her voice on "awful."

"Try bizarre," said Elin.

She thought more about Mother than about Father. It was as if the news from yesterday had thrown her back in time, back to that moment at Redners when Ricky had told her that Mother was dead. She didn't remember it in detail, strangely enough, but she remembered the feeling, she was caught up in it. It was completely unbearable, and yet at the same time it enveloped her in a palliating silence. A great, white sea of mute stillness that helped her survive.

Her father. She didn't know what she felt about that. She wasn't there yet. The horrific circumstances of his death overshadowed the death itself. Elin couldn't understand that he was gone. Whatever that meant. She was caught up in the horror, the unreality of it all. Someone had murdered her parents. And she had believed that it was her father who had . . . She couldn't absorb it. It was too much.

"I'll be getting in at around nine. Do you have time to meet up?" she asked.

IT HAD BEEN raining for half an hour, a light resounding rain, the kind where every drop sounds like a soft but distinct tapping against the roofs and windows. They had gathered in Göran's office, Ove with some papers in his hand, the others restless, eager to finally be getting somewhere. After more than two weeks they were finally going to be able bring in a suspect for questioning.

"I've put together a profile of Leo Ringvall," said Ove. "It's true what the witness Marie Barsk said, that he moved to Stockholm with his parents in 1994. The assault charge in 2003 marks the first time he actually got convicted of anything, but if you ask around a little it seems that he's been involved in a whole bunch of other stuff. We're talking smuggling, selling illegal alcohol, receiving stolen goods, but he's always sort of on the sidelines, it's impossible to tie him conclusively to anything, not enough to arrest him."

"And probably no one has put much effort into finding anything, either, as long as he's careful and sticks to that kind of small-time stuff," said Sara and squirmed impatiently.

"Probably not," said Ove, "but then, *bang*, he gets put away for this assault. A nasty case. The victim was left severely disabled from a skull injury."

"Three years seems pretty light," said Gustav who was standing over by the door.

"Probably came down to the fact that it was his first offense and that the victim was a nasty piece of work himself, who started the whole thing by smashing Ringvall in the head with a beer bottle," Ove explained.

A resigned silence settled for a moment over the room.

"Some days you just want to give up and become a hermit," said Fredrik.

"Well, you moved here, that's a step in the right direction," said Sara.

They fell silent again. This time for a completely different reason.

"It was a joke," said Sara and looked unhappy.

Ove gently folded his papers together and clasped them between his thumb and forefinger. "Those who aren't planning on becoming hermits or stand-up comedians today, can head down to Hemse and bring in Ringvall. One of the guys that Marie Barsk said was an old buddy of Ringvall's is in our files. Per-Arne Hallman, better known as Beppo. And Hallman is registered as living on Ängsgatan in Hemse. I suggest that we start there."

Göran lifted the receiver, momentarily silenced the dial tone with his thumb against the cradle, and pointed at his detectives with the receiver in his fist.

"We'll go in as soon as we get the order, but you stay back. The SWAT team will go in first. If we're right about Ringvall then anything could happen and I don't want any detectives getting knifed. Lumbago is bad enough."

He removed his thumb from the cradle and dialed the number to the district police commissioner as the room quickly emptied. It took three seconds to break down Per-Arne Hallman's front door, another three for four men from the SWAT team to secure the little apartment on Ängsgatan in Hemse, with a view out across the parking lot outside the Konsum supermarket and municipal library.

A bleary-eyed Per-Arne Hallman, better known as Beppo, looked up from the couch where he'd been sitting before nodding off in front of a black-and-white matinee movie. Before he'd even woken up properly he was pushed down onto his stomach on the couch and was quickly frisked by a couple of rough gloved hands. There was no one else in the apartment.

The four officers dressed in protective gear, holstered their side-arms, which had been deemed adequate armament for the purposes of this takedown, and waved in the detectives from CID.

"He's all yours," said the SWAT team commander.

Gustav went in first, Fredrik and Sara entered behind him. The apartment reeked of cigarette smoke, which concealed a mixed odor of grime, garbage, dirty sheets, and sweaty socks. Piled next to the unmade bed was a stack of unopened boxes of amplifiers, DVD play-ers, and similar electronic devices.

"So, you haven't called it quits yet, huh?" said Sara and nudged the boxes with her foot.

Beppo had been cuffed and lifted back up to the couch where he was now sitting leaning forward because of the handcuffs behind his back.

"Watch it!" Beppo whined. "What, I'm not allowed to buy a new stereo?"

"Where's Leo Ringvall?" asked Gustav who'd pulled up a white steel-tube chair with a dirty red seat cushion and sat down in front of Beppo.

"What?" said Beppo.

Fredrik held up a green-and-yellow sleeping bag that he had found on the floor among the dirty laundry and empty beer cans.

"Looks like you've had company. Or are you going camping?"

"Where's Leo Ringvall?" Gustav asked again.

"I don't know."

Gustav looked up at Fredrik who had tossed aside the sleeping bag.

"Let's take him down to the station for starters."

"Yeah," said Fredrik and suddenly came to think of something else.

He took a pair of latex gloves out of his jacket pocket, pulled them on and squatted down next to the sleeping bag. He carefully folded it open and examined the lining, pinched his fingers together purposefully like a set of tweezers, and held up something that none of the others could see.

"One strand of hair, long and black," he said.

"I think Eva better take a look at this," said Gustav.

46.

Sara was standing outside the police station in Hemse looking at the ram and the banner on the shaft of the cross hewn in limestone above the entrance. She understood that all three of them couldn't question Hallman, but why did she have to be the one to step aside? Did it have to do with her hermit comment? She didn't understand how it could have caused such offense. It was completely harmless, not overly funny perhaps, that she could accept, but apart from that . . .

She pulled her gaze from the provincial coat of arms and took a few desultory steps along the whitewashed facade. The rain hadn't completely ceased. A light drizzle was drifting through the air. What was the deal with Ove anyway? She had always seen him as the most thoroughly good-natured person in the whole station; calm, dependable, knowledgeable, and nice. But as head of the investigation he had suddenly displayed a rather grumpy and uptight side that she hadn't seen before. Couldn't he handle the pressure? Wasn't he cut out to be a supervisor?

The drizzle had laid itself over her face like a thin layer of sweat.

She rubbed away the moisture from her forehead and cheeks and went back inside the station. On Tuesday at 3 p.m., she had an appointment at Stockholm South General Hospital. It had taken a whole lot of persistence and sustained badgering over the phone to get them to allow the procedure to be done in Stockholm rather than in Visby, but in the end she had gotten her way. For a while she had thought she was being silly, that it was just this fixed idea that she had gotten into her head, but after the uncomfortable silence that had followed her failed joke, she was happy that she hadn't given up.

As it happened, she had been given a time the same day that Arvid Traneus's remains had been uncovered in a field in Hejde. It was upsetting that it was going to clash with a new murder investigation, but she had no choice anymore. The clock was ticking. She had been forced to tell Göran. She hadn't said it straight out, but her prevarications had been transparent enough. She couldn't help noticing the shadow that had moved across Göran's face when it was clear that she would be away for at least three days. He had done his best to conceal his disappointment, but without success.

"YOU ARE UNDER arrest on suspicion of aiding and abetting a felon, and complicity to murder. You are also under suspicion for receiving stolen goods," said Gustav and looked at Per-Arne Hallman with his friendly gaze.

"What?" said Hallman and grasped the sides of the polished top of the old desk with both hands.

His face was harrowed from drugs and alcohol and his spiky hairdo hung down the back of his neck in a manner better suited to a rock star than a petty thief from Hemse. Fredrik wondered who had cut his hair. He had a hard time picturing Hallman paying someone to do it, but even a loser of his caliber could of course show some degree of vanity.

"You have the right to a lawyer. Do you want a lawyer now, or

would you consider continuing this interview without one present?"
Gustav asked.

"If you're going to talk about murder, then I want a lawyer, you
can be sure of that, because I sure as hell haven't been involved in any
murders," said Hallman and fingered the hair at the back of his neck
with his left hand.

"So you deny any crime?" said Gustav.

"I don't know nothing about no murders. You got the wrong guy,"
said Hallman who sat straight as an arrow in his chair and stared at
Gustav with eyes wide open.

"Primarily, we're interested in talking about Leo Ringvall. Could
we do that right here and now, or would you prefer to have a lawyer
present?"

Beppo Hallman was about to open his mouth, but Gustav interrupted him.

"If it's the latter, then we'd have to take you into Visby and put you
in a detention cell there while we find you a lawyer."

Hallman sat there stiffly as before and thought for about five seconds, then he slumped down and waved his right hand in resignedly.

"Sure, all right, ask away."

Fredrik took over after he had been read his rights, as they'd
agreed ahead of time.

"Have you known Leo Ringvall for very long?"

"Yeah, since school."

"And now he's been staying with you for a while?"

"Yeah."

"For how long?"

"A couple of weeks, three maybe."

"Could you be more precise?" asked Fredrik.

Hallman looked up at the ceiling at the oversized fluorescent light
fitting that cast a harsh, almost shadowless glare over the room, then
back at Fredrik again.

"It was a Saturday," he said.

"Three weeks ago?"

"Yeah. You can work the date out yourselves."

They heard the front door to the station slam shut. The closed door to the interview room gave a jolt from the backdraft.

"When was Leo Ringvall last at the apartment?"

"Yesterday," said Hallman.

"What time yesterday?" asked Fredrik.

"Around two o'clock."

"So he didn't sleep in the apartment last night?"

"No."

"So where is he now?"

"No idea," said Hallman.

Fredrik went silent and looked at Beppo Hallman with a slightly less patient expression. He let out a barely perceptible sigh and leaned forward across the table.

"A moment ago, it seemed as though you understood the seriousness of this situation, but now I'm starting to doubt it," he said.

"I really don't know," said Hallman quickly. "He went out yesterday afternoon, I haven't seen him since."

"You mean to say that he comes and stays with you for three weeks, and then just ups and leaves without telling you where he's going?"

Beppo Hallman nodded eagerly.

"Yeah."

"And he hasn't been in touch, either?"

"No."

"And you have no idea where he may have gone?"

"No."

"Well, what do you think?"

"Well, I mean, you can't help wondering. If something's happened to him, or whatnot."

Sure, thought Fredrik.

"We'll take a break," he said and gave Gustav a quick glance. "I'll wait here with Hallman. If you go, ask Sara to come in."

Gustav got up to go out and find Sara. The room where they were conducting the interview wasn't actually a proper interview room. You couldn't leave criminals like Hallman alone in here.

"I think Ringvall's gone. Hallman hasn't seen him since yesterday afternoon. Assuming he's telling the truth," said Fredrik when Sara took over from him.

Gunilla Borg looked up from behind her paper-laden desk, her blonde pigtails pinned up for the day at the nape of her neck.

"I don't think he's lying," she said and laid one arm on her desk, "Beppo is more the type to just keep silent."

"He's talking all right, but he's taking his time about it," said Fredrik. "Chances are Ringvall has already taken a boat out of here."

"He's gotta know something," said Gustav, "we might as well just keep at it."

Gunilla Borg leaned forward over the desk with her head cocked slightly to one side.

"I don't want to butt in," she said, "but I know Beppo pretty good. If you tell me what it is you want to know, I could give it a try."

Gustav and Fredrik looked at each other.

"Sure, why not," said Gustav. "Sounds like a sensible idea."

"Yeah," said Fredrik and made a gesture to Gustav, "you want to go with her, or you want me to?"

Gunilla Borg hemmed thoughtfully.

"Beppo usually works best with women during questioning, I should have said that from the start I guess, but the whole thing happened so quickly, and like I said, I didn't want to butt in, so really . . ."

Gunilla Borg's perky and slightly chirpy voice broke off in a smug pause for effect.

". . . it would probably be best if Sara sat in with me."

They fell silent for as long as it took Fredrik to realize that there was only one possible answer to that question.

"All right then, you two go ahead."

Gunilla Borg quickly got up and disappeared into the interview room containing Sara and Beppo Hallman. Gustav looked in astonishment at Fredrik who threw out his arms in response.

47.

Sara sat down on a chair over by the wall so as not to cause Hallman unnecessary stress. Gunilla Borg sat opposite him and looked at him for a long moment without saying anything. Those blue eyes above her freckled cheeks were steadfast and piercing, but not without empathy.

"Receipt of stolen property," she said at last.

Beppo looked away.

"Well, you know how it is, some old buddies show up and want you to do them a solid, and I tell them no can do, I don't do that kind of thing anymore, but then there's always somebody who, how can I put it, dumps shit on you anyway and . . ."

"Per-Arne," she interjected softly. "If your pal Leo has murdered these three people in Levide then we're talking, in all likelihood, lifetime imprisonment."

"He can't have done it. It's not him," said Hallman.

"There are a few things that suggest otherwise," said Gunilla Borg. "It's important that you tell us what you know, for his sake, for our sake, and especially for your own sake. Do you understand?"

"Sure, I don't know anything, but I'll answer all your questions, I swear."

"You're not just going to answer my questions. You're going to tell me everything you know, even if it seems totally unrelated and irrelevant. Okay?"

Beppo Hallman nodded and swallowed.

"Good," said Gunilla Borg without taking her eyes off him. "When Leo got in touch with you and wanted to come stay with you, what did he say?"

"He told me that he'd just been let out. He said that straight off, but of course I knew that, too, that it was coming up, so to speak. To tell you the truth, I wasn't really that thrilled about it. I mean, a guy who's just got out, you kind of don't really know what might happen, does he just want to take it easy for a while, sort of collect himself, or is there something else going down?"

"If we stick to what Leo said," Gunilla Borg interrupted Beppo's sudden rambling, "what was he doing here?"

"He never said," Beppo answered.

Gunilla Borg waited before asking her next question. She leaned her head back a little and her expression became what can best be described as concerned. Her eyes narrowed and a little furrow appeared between her eyebrows.

"Never?"

Beppo's mouth opened and closed indecisively.

"Okay, I believe you. So, Leo has just gotten out, you're old buddies, it's not so strange for him to get in touch, nor for you to let him stay with you. He may not have needed any other reason to come here. But . . . once he actually made it over here, maybe you guys started talking about the future, that would be a pretty natural thing to do after all, if you'd just been released from prison. Plans, maybe he had some ideas. Might not sound like anything he's really going to follow through with, mostly talk, as it often is. But I'd really like to hear it."

Beppo Hallman shifted nervously in his chair, scratched his upper arm.

"It was . . . he said it, but he only said it, you know, just like you're saying."

"And what was it that Leo said?" asked Gunilla Borg.

"That he was gonna go up there."

"Where?"

"He was going to go up to the farm. The Traneus farm in Levide."

Beppo Hallman looked dismayed.

"You can't say anything to Leo about my telling you this. If you're gonna tell him, then I'm not gonna say any more."

"He doesn't have to know anything," Gunilla Borg assured him.

What a pro, Sara Oskarsson thought as she sat there off to the side and watched her colleague, severe and impressive in that blue uniform shirt, free of any hint of insecurity. She reminded Sara of a teacher she had had in junior high who had possessed the unique ability to push the cockiest and most rowdy troublemakers up against a wall and stare them down, despite being a whole head shorter than most of them. She wished that she could understand the secret.

"He was going to head up to the farm and stand face-to-face with Arvid Traneus. He was going to stand there and look that bastard in the eye, that's what he said."

"And while he was standing there, what was going to happen?"

"He didn't know. He was going to stand there and then he was gonna see."

Gunilla Borg tried once again to wait Beppo out, but this time it didn't work.

"That was it. I swear. I asked him, even said that I thought he oughta just forget about it because it seemed, well, sort of pointless.

Chances were Traneus would just call the cops on him and he'd only make trouble for himself. But Leo never did it. He never went."

"How can you be so sure?"

"Not Leo. I know Leo."

"Your friend Leo just got out after three years in prison. He was in there for beating someone up so bad that they're disabled for life. You know about that right?"

"Yeah, but . . ."

"Yeah, but?" said Gunilla Borg and for the first time she didn't sound completely composed.

Hallman sat there quietly for a moment, absolutely still.

"I still don't think he did it."

"Well that's something else," said Gunilla Borg sounding more understanding.

Sara looked down at her lap in an effort to hide her smile.

"So you don't know, in other words, whether Leo went to see Traneus in Levide or not," said Gunilla Borg.

"No," said Hallman.

"Would it have been *possible* for him to have done it? Were you separated from each other for long enough that he could have made it over to Levide and back during that time?"

"I guess so. Yeah, we were," said Hallman with a deep sigh.

"Any particular occasion?" said Gunilla Borg.

"Well, I mean, he was out for a while every day. I have no idea where he went, other than that he'd been to the liquor store and did some shopping and whatnot."

"How about right after the weekend, when he'd just arrived?"

"Yeah, then, too. I don't remember the days exactly, but there were several occasions when he could have made it out to Levide if he'd wanted to."

"Did he have a car or any kind of vehicle?"

Beppo Hallman laughed.

"He'd just spent three years in the can. Where would he have gotten a car from? It's not like there was someone waiting for him outside the gates."

"He could have borrowed a car, stolen one, what do I know? But so he had no access to a car, moped, or even a bicycle maybe?"

"Not that I know of," said Hallman.

IT WAS ALMOST evening by the time they left Hemse. The onset of darkness was spurred on by the thickening cloud cover. The drizzle had given way to pouring rain that caused large puddles to form on the road through Hemse. The cars were tightly packed in the supermarket parking lot. People were hurrying out to their cars with their shopping carts filled with bags stuffed with chips, sodas, and Friday steaks, maybe the odd consciously chosen low-GI meal. And shoved down between the cartons of milk and clusters of bananas were latest issues of the tabloid newspapers filled with fresh details about the murders beneath bold black EXTRA headlines, that became wet from the rain and would be difficult to flip through. They sent a smell of wet paper and printer's ink wafting through the cars that were on their way home to celebrate the weekend.

Sara, Fredrik, and Gustav didn't have a free weekend to look forward to, they all understood that. Klint had decided to arrest Hallman on suspicion of receiving stolen goods. That was the safest bet. It was doubtful whether it would ever make it to court, but that was less important. The reason for keeping Hallman locked up, was so that he couldn't warn Leo Ringvall.

Gustav was driving, Sara was sitting next to him, and Fredrik was sitting in the back speaking to Ove on his cell phone. Per-Arne Hallman had been sent off to Visby in a patrol car. They were happy not to have to drive him themselves. When Hallman had realized that he was being taken to Visby, he had launched into a relentless whining about having been tricked. As he saw it, they'd had an agreement that he'd be released if he told them what he knew about Ringvall. But nobody had promised him any such thing. Though they may perhaps have hinted at something that could have been misconstrued to that effect.

Fredrik snapped his cell phone shut.

"Doesn't look too good for Ringvall," he said. "The DNA test isn't ready, but the strand of hair's a match. Plus the guy's got small feet."

"Looks like this is going to turn out to be a short stint of freedom for Leo Ringvall," said Sara.

They drove through a pool of water at high speed that sent up a great cascade of dirty water against the right side of the car.

"Let's hope so, so that we can put all this behind us," said Gustav.

PART THREE

He forgot you long ago
Screw God!

—EBBA GRÖN

"I'm leaving on the eleven o'clock ferry tomorrow. I'm starting work again on Monday," she said.

"Really?" said Ninni and looked up at her.

Ninni paused before continuing. Sara recognized her hesitation. The hospital room made everything so charged.

"Thanks for coming here, for spending time with Fredrik. It's been very helpful," said Ninni and looked at her husband.

Sara nodded quietly. She thought about all the visits she had made, the hours and days spent there in the room. She could hear herself speaking. She had revealed things that she would never have considered telling Fredrik if it hadn't been for the special circumstances. Things that he maybe wouldn't have wanted to hear, either. She felt how her cheeks heated up.

"Well, I'll leave you two in peace now," she said.

Ninni didn't seem to have any objections.

"See you," said Ninni when Sara slipped out through the door.

Fredrik had gotten a little better with every passing day, more words, more intelligible words, more eye contact. Better, but not good. Good still seemed a long way off. Sara didn't know what it was reasonable to hope for. The doctors still spoke about it being fully possible for him to make a complete recovery or very close to it. That sounded promising, of course, and she tried to stop thinking about what might be included in *or very close to it*.

She walked briskly down the corridor, but stopped short when she had passed the nurses' station. She thought for a moment and then walked back and stuck her head through the open door. A curly gray-haired nurse was busy at a medicine cabinet.

"Hello, my name is Sara Oskarsson," said Sara, "I'm a colleague of Fredrik Broman's."

The nurse put on a pair of purple-rimmed glasses that were hanging from a band around her neck.

"Hi," said the nurse once the glasses were in place. "Yes, I've seen you. You're the one who usually comes in here."

Sara smiled at the nurse.

"Yes, but this will be the last time. I'm going back to Visby to-morrow."

"I see," said the nurse and touched the medicine cabinet.

"I was wondering about something."

"Yes."

"Well, it seems like his memory is slowly coming back, that he's remembering more and more, or is it just that his speech is returning and that his memory has been there the whole time, but . . ."

Sara stopped short, realized that she was just making it more confusing. The nurse adjusted her glasses, waited.

"What I'm really asking," said Sara, "is whether you think that he'll remember anything from his time here at the hospital? I mean, has he even heard what I've been talking to him about, and can he remember it in that case?"

The nurse got a little wrinkle between her eyebrows.

"It's impossible to say," she said, "but it's possible. You'll have to ask him once he's gotten a little better."

48

He was alone in the dark. He felt the cold and damp against his face and the hard stone against his back where he was sitting curled up against the wall. No light, nothing, just the wind and the rain that buffeted the roof, whipped hard against the brickwork.

If the sleeping bag he'd crawled into couldn't keep out the damp and cold, he wouldn't last very long out here. He leaned his head back against the rough stone and shut his eyes. Might as well shut his eyes. There was nothing to see. He was blind when he opened his eyes. He closed them and tried to turn inward, feel his lungs rise and fall, to block out everything and focus solely on his own breathing.

Just when he thought that it was working, that he felt a relief of sorts, he suddenly got the distinct impression that someone was standing there leaning over him. He quickly opened his eyes and saw even less. The darkness just became blacker and thicker, but the figure in his head became ever more present. He saw something black within the blackness. A figure without a face, and yet he felt a pair of eyes staring at him, eyes filled with tears; no, eyes that were bleeding, a thick, red liquid that oozed from even redder eyeballs.

Madness, nonsense, a figment of his imagination, he told himself and quickly swiped his hand out in the empty void in front of him to prove his assertion. Nothing there, of course. And yet the figure remained, like an image etched into his mind following a blinding flash of light. A vague, rustling sound along the floor and suddenly the dark figure was gone, but had made way for something else. Another rustling. This was no figment of his imagination, no haunting apparition, there really was something out there in the darkness, that slithered across the gritty stone floor, rasping softly against it. A snake. He could hear it distinctly. He was alone in the darkness with a viper, a scaly, zigzag-pattered reptile, its flickering tongue sniffing him out just as clearly as he could see in broad daylight. Deadly and real.

He stamped down hard with both feet, but the effect was dampened by the cushioning effect of the sleeping bag. He threw out his left hand, groping along the wall, he tipped something over that rattled when it hit the floor, found his lighter and managed to get a flame. He got to his feet and held the lighter out at arms length. The flame flickered in the wind that was gusting through the building, but still did a decent job of lighting up the room. He moved it slowly from left to right, saw no snake. He moved slowly around the room with the lighter stretched out in front of him. No snake. No, of course there was no snake. It was just his mind playing tricks on him. When the frightening figure that had loomed over him proved so easy to drive away, his mind immediately came up with something else that was harder to fend off.

Why was he tormenting himself? Because it all came from inside, the snakes and the strange, bleeding figures. He detected a strong smell, turned around and saw that the camping stove that he had knocked over onto the floor was leaking alcohol onto the ground. A big, black pool was spreading across the floor. He swore under his breath, wriggled out of his sleeping bag, felt at once how the cold bit into him, hurried over and put it back upright, careful to keep his lighter well away. The stove was almost empty.

He moved his backpack with all his food and clothes, out of the way, the bag of bread rusks and the bottle of vodka that he'd un-packed. There was alcohol on the bag of rusks. He ripped it open and dumped the rusks straight into his backpack and tossed away the empty bag. He swore again. Luckily the backpack had been spared and he moved it even further away from the camping stove. His right hand was cold and dry from the alcohol.

The lighter was burning the thumb of his left hand. He crawled into his sleeping bag and let the flame on the lighter go out. He didn't know what to do with it, finally sticking it between his teeth as he drew up the zipper of his sleeping bag. He shuffled over to the wall, sat down, and set aside the lighter.

As soon as the stillness settled in, the visions returned. The darkness loomed over him, tightened around him, stared at him, grabbed at him. He stared back, steeled himself against the nonsense that was whirling around inside him, but no matter how hard he fought against it, he noticed how his heart pounded faster and harder in his chest, how his blood surged through his swollen, hardened arteries, and how his pulse finally seemed to flutter ceaselessly.

He grabbed the lighter again, had to flick the flint three times before the gas flame once again cast its dim light across the room. The round floor's dirty paving stones stared back at him vacantly. He reached for the vodka bottle and wished he'd had something more, something stronger, when he put it to his lips and took two deep gulps in quick succession. He wanted something that would knock him out completely until morning. He wasn't sure that the alcohol would help, but he drank it anyway.

He had felt that he was right. When he'd done it, he had felt that he'd been right to do it.

49

Detective Christer Eriksson pulled his thin, wrinkled raincoat more tightly around his grayish-green, one-size-too-big suit. It may have stopped raining, but there was still a cold wind blowing.

He had driven to Huddinge, south of Stockholm, in order to examine the scene of a shooting that had taken place over a week ago. When Christer Eriksson had started to sift through all the material that had been dumped onto him by a superior who was going on vacation, he hadn't quite been able to get the witness accounts to tally with the forensic evidence. So he had decided to head down there to see for himself. His personal theory was that someone had screwed up somewhere. Nobody had gotten hurt in the shooting and the intended victim had been an unemployed Chilean, no record, but had been under suspicion of making criminal threats. Low priority, in other words.

The shooting had taken place in a high-rise area up on a plateau not far from the Vårby Gård subway station. Instead of snaking his way up there by car along the endless winding loop roads, he had parked the car at the bottom of a long stairway that pretty much led straight to the crime scene.

The stairway was divided into three separate flights that cut up through a park. Christer Eriksson was trudging up the first one when he caught sight of a man walking along the asphalted path that intersected with the bottom and middle flights. Even though Christer saw him from the side, and his face was partially hidden beneath a gray hood, he was immediately sure of what he saw. Four years previously he had spent a few long, cold nights staking out Leo Ringvall. It hadn't paid off, but he wouldn't forget that face anytime soon. And he had been reminded of Ringvall this morning by the APB that district CID had issued.

The wind tossed Christer Eriksson's short but unruly bangs. He brushed them aside with his right hand and took an extra look while the motion concealed his probing gaze. He was absolutely certain. It was Leo Ringvall, the triple murderer from Gotland.

Ringvall veered off the park path onto the stairs ahead of Christer and continued up the green slope. Christer Eriksson, known to his colleagues as "Che" because of his station signature, had decided to arrest the man. The alternative would be to follow after him and call for backup, but he considered this to be a safe arrest both for himself and the public. If he could arrest Ringvall before he reached the plateau and he still had his hands where he could see them, then he'd do it.

He quickened his pace, let go of his raincoat and fixed his gaze on Ringvall's waist. He didn't like the whole "Che" thing, especially considering he had never voted for anyone left of the Center Party, but he had chosen to ignore it. Reacting against nicknames was a surefire way of getting it to catch on for good. A few of them had even taken to calling him "The Communist," but he didn't really care so much about them. They were the bad apples who thought you were an idiot for spending a calm Saturday morning at the station following up on an accidental shooting in the suburbs instead of sitting around scratching your ass in the coffee room. "Regards to the Cubans," they had hollered after him. It would feel pretty damn good to come back into town with a triple murderer in handcuffs.

When Leo Ringvall reached the top of the second flight of stairs, Christer Eriksson checked to make sure there was no one behind him, then he pulled out his service weapon, prepared it for firing, and aimed it at Ringvall's back in a quick, but controlled movement.

"Stop, police," he barked. "Put your hands on your head!"

Ringvall stopped short after the first shout, but remained standing where he was with his hands at his side.

"Hands on your head," Christer Eriksson repeated.

Ringvall glanced behind him, caught sight of the gun that Christer Eriksson had trained on him and slowly started to raise his hands.

"Don't move, eyes straight ahead. Hands on your head," Christer Eriksson ordered as he slowly moved up the stairs.

"Take it easy," Ringvall mumbled.

Christer Eriksson kept his gun aimed squarely at Ringvall's back the whole time. The suspected multiple killer took his time putting his hands on his head. Christer Eriksson wasn't about to make any mistakes. If Ringvall tried anything, he wouldn't hesitate to shoot.

"Clasp your hands on top of your head," he commanded once Ringvall had finally gotten his hands up.

He drew closer, and had nearly reached the landing between the flights of stairs. Just then, he caught sight of two teenage boys peering down from the crest of the hill.

"Police, get out of here!" he shouted without looking at them. "Not you," he said to Ringvall who glanced back over his shoulder questioningly.

He then told him to step to the side out onto the slope and get down to his knees. Ringvall did as he was told. As he was sinking to his knees, he instinctively lowered one hand to keep his balance, but Christer Eriksson immediately shouted at him to keep both his hands behind his head.

It was easy to shove Ringvall over onto the grass. Christer Eriksson approached him with the handcuffs and dropped down with his knee against Ringvall's back. Leo Ringvall was considered dangerous according to the APB, and this was a critical moment. His hand wasn't completely steady as he reached out toward Ringvall's arm with the cuffs. He fastened one cuff around Ringvall's left wrist, and brought that arm down behind his back, then he brought the right one down, too. At this point he should have holstered his weapon, but he could feel his hands shaking and how the adrenaline was causing his pulse to race. He didn't want to take any chances, risk being overpowered, or cut with a carpet knife or a razor blade that Ringvall might be hiding in his hand. The man beneath him had three lives on his conscience, and hadn't thought twice about dismembering his victims.

The pain that suddenly shot up the pinky of his left hand almost made him drop his gun, but that was nothing compared to what followed after a few seconds of stunned calm. It was as if someone had driven a spear right through his hand and on up into his forearm. Christer Eriksson screamed out.

It felt like he'd been out for a few seconds. He looked down at his left hand. Bright red blood was pumping out of his severed pinky. The burning, wrenching, pulsating pain was excruciating, but no longer completely overpowering. He steered the handcuffs around Ringvall's wrists. They were securely in place, but about an inch above his cuffed hands there was a hole in the fabric of his gray hoodie. Pressing his throbbing left hand against his body, he carefully turned Ringvall over. Off to the right, on the lower part of his chest, was an irregular and steadily growing bloodstain.

OVE GAVE A loose knock on Göran's open door.

"They got him in Stockholm."

Göran looked up from the desk, pulled off his glasses.

"Great. Where?"

"Somewhere in Huddinge. Some officer recognized him from the description. Apparently Ringvall was on his way home from a friend's house," said Ove and took a few steps into the room.

"Have they had a chance to question him yet?" asked Göran.

"Well, that just it," said Ove and crossed his arms. "Shots were fired during the arrest, both the officer and Ringvall were injured."

"Seriously?" asked Göran and tried to read the message in Ove's expression.

"The officer was hit in the hand, that probably wasn't serious. Ringvall was hit in the lungs."

Göran grimaced in dismay.

"What happened? Sounds like some kind of a shootout."

"The explanation I got was a little unclear, but apparently it was accidental. It seems the arresting officer didn't take proper care when he was going to cuff him and his gun went off. In any case, that means that we can't question him for at least forty-eight hours."

"Damn it."

Göran got up, pulled his pants up a few inches, and turned his back to Ove.

"Shit," he said and looked out the window.

"Yeah, and he won't be able to handle any lengthy interviews for another week or so," said Ove.

Göran turned back to Ove, put one hand on the back of the chair and the other on his hip.

"How can anyone be that clumsy?" he said. "So close and then this . . ."

"Well, now we've got him anyway," said Ove.

Göran raised his eyebrows tiredly.

"It's important that we not lose momentum now. We have to assume that we'll still get a chance to question him up in Stockholm. We have to prepare for that, see if we can find any other witnesses who saw him in Levide, check with the bus drivers who work that route and then we'll have to see if forensics can give us anything else. Are we still waiting for the DNA analysis and the autopsy report?"

Ove nodded.

"And then there's the son, Rickard Traneus. Nobody's seen hide nor hair of him in three days. That's gotta mean something and we have to find out what. Either he was involved in this somehow, or else he knows something that he doesn't want to divulge for some reason, or," said Göran and lingered a little before continuing, "or something's happened to him. To him, too."

50.

Tears in the cloud cover let in little specks of sunlight over the flat island and the surrounding sea. Sun, clouds, or rain, it didn't make any difference to him. He was grateful for daylight in whatever form it came.

He had slept a few short hours as morning approached, and woke up when the first gray rays of dawn had filtered through the round window. His body was in pain from the alcohol and the hard floor, and his tongue felt like a piece of cardboard stuck to the roof of his mouth.

He looked at the backpack, the camping stove, and the five-liter container of fresh water that was still standing inside the door. It looked like some kind of scout camp. What did he really think he was going to do?

He made his way out through the door that he had kept closed the night before with the help of a flat rock covered in gray and yellow lichen. You couldn't close the door properly from the outside and he was forced to leave it ajar.

He stood sheltered from the wind between the cylinder-shaped stone building and the roofless ruin on what had to be the island's highest point. It was here, right next to the long disused old lighthouse, that the otherwise low-lying island rose up to a steep cliff that plunged straight down into the sea a dozen or so yards below.

What had he really been thinking when he decided to come out here? He had imagined that he was running away from something, that he would be able to escape by hastily packing his bags and leaving, but the island was no place to escape to. It may have been true that no one would come looking for him there, but he wouldn't be able to survive there. If what he had hoped for was to get some breathing space, then he hadn't gotten that, either. Instead his thoughts had harried him worse than ever, appalling creatures from his imagination had grabbed at him in the darkness.

He left the wind-still spot between the limestone and cement-gray buildings, stood where he could look over toward the new black-and-white lighthouse at the other end of the island. Standing there, he could feel Elin close to him and in the distance he saw Stefania slowly walking toward him, about five yards in front of Mom and Dad. He saw the *Adventure*, the fire ants, the bird skeletons, the sea and the limestone cave, and he saw that everyone was alive. Stefania was alive, Mother was alive, Father was alive, and in the summer sailing trips they all lived together just like they could have lived, and he just couldn't understand why it hadn't been possible. He wanted to turn around and touch Elin, he wanted to have somebody by his side, but he understood that there was no one there, that there would never be anyone there ever again. He was completely alone in this, as alone as it was possible for a person to be. Beyond the island he saw the arc of the horizon. It was the curvature of the earth, the boundary of what was possible and there he was completely alone. And then the summer memories were also gone, and instead his father's head rose up out of a hole in the ground, and lurking behind his back were dark figures that he couldn't see, that wouldn't leave him in peace, and that you couldn't fight against since you couldn't touch them and because they only really came out in force once your eyes were closed.

Abruptly he turned his back on the lighthouse and the horizon in the southeast. He walked in the opposite direction, up to the precipice, stopped there with the wind blowing in his face.

He looked down. The already light-colored cliffs had been bleached by the salt from the sea. Was this what he had come here for? To step over the edge? Or was it so that he could see his parents and Stefania come walking through the dry yellowing grass?

Stefania hadn't died in the same way that other young people sometimes died of cancer or in car accidents. Stefania hadn't died; she had gone under. He had realized that. He wasn't sure when exactly, but it wasn't after her death, but long before. He had known long before she died what was in the process of happening. But he hadn't done anything. He hadn't helped her. He hadn't saved her. Instead he had convinced himself that everything was just as it should be. He hadn't lifted a finger when his sister was sacrificed.

He stood there with his toes sticking out beyond the edge of the cliff, but he couldn't do it. He couldn't bring himself to. It was quite possible that he lacked the courage, but there was something in those fragments of memory that was still beautiful. Not everything was ugly. Vivacious Stefania on her way through the grass that was buzzing with insects. When she walked there she was still alive, had not even begun to go downhill. She was strong, protective. He couldn't kill that.

51

Eva Karlén had put up a spotlight in the bathroom in order to have some decent light to work by. Once she had sprayed the floor, the Japanese bath, and the wall above it with luminol, she reached for the spotlight switch and plunged the room into darkness.

The entire bathtub shone a bluish green from the traces of blood.

It would have been difficult to wash away blood from an enamel bathtub thoroughly enough for the luminol not to react. In one made of stone with mortar seams it was impossible.

The camera was already set up and Eva hurried to take photographs of the bluish light before it faded away.

This was the third time that Eva was examining the same house. As she stood on her knees at the edge of the bathtub and took samples from the seams she heard a familiar voice lecturing her inside her head. It belonged to one of her CSI instructors. "Don't forget! You find what you look for." She tried to vindicate herself by saying that there hadn't been anything in the investigation to justify searching for traces of blood in the bathtub down in the basement. Nowhere else, either, for that matter. It was a reasonable defense, but it didn't quite hold up to scrutiny. That was just what the "you find what you look for" lecture was talking about. A bad crime scene investigation was one that worked on the basis of a single scenario. She shuddered, stood up, and set up the folding aluminum stool that she'd brought down there with her.

They had been through the house with a fine-tooth comb in search of Arvid Traneus, but they had been searching for something that could reveal where he'd gone, not for physical traces of his body. It was a let-down to discover that his life had run out right there in the bathtub. Either that or that he was dismembered there. Or both. Of course it remained to be seen whether it was Arvid Traneus's blood that had run out down there, but Eva was ready to hazard a qualified guess. It must be him, unless they butchered an animal down here, or took the lives of some other people who hadn't been missed by anybody.

FREDRIK SAT WITH the phone pressed to his ear about to call up a tipster when Ove came in holding a white A4 sheet of paper. He stopped inside the doorway and made sure that Fredrik wasn't in the middle of a conversation, before he began speaking.

"It looks as if Arvid Traneus was killed and dismembered at home in his own bathtub."

Fredrik slowly put the receiver back in its cradle without taking his eyes off Ove.

"That sunken stone thing?" he asked.

"Yeah, down in the basement. I just spoke to Eva. She's found extensive traces of blood in and around the bathtub, and a little splinter of bone from the skull behind the molding in the ceiling just above the bathtub."

Fredrik recoiled in his chair.

"The molding in the ceiling? It sounds like she's taken apart the whole house."

"Not far from it, I think," said Ove.

"Unbelievable."

"Yeah, I've never heard of that kind of a find before," said Ove.

He held out the sheet of paper to Fredrik who took it.

"What's this?"

"That," said Ove scratching his neck inside his collar, "is a list of Rickard Traneus's mail contacts that we retrieved from his computer.

They're organized according to the ones he was last in contact with or had the most frequent contact with, which, as it happens, are most often one and the same."

"So all we have to do is start at the top?" asked Fredrik and fixed his gaze on the top row.

"Jesper Mann, Ryska Gränd Four," he read.

"Yes. Sara and Gustav have also each been given one," said Ove.

"The same list?"

Ove did a double take and stopped scratching.

"No, not the same list."

Fredrik felt he detected an indulgent expression.

"But the same type of contacts," Ove continued. "I think you should go and pay a visit to any that are here on the island. I want to get as much as possible out of this. Even if they don't know where he is, they must be able to provide something that will make it easier for us to track him down. None of them has a record," said Ove and pointed at the list, "but it could be a good idea to read through the e-mails before you question them."

Fredrik nodded and quickly scanned the list again, noted that the second address also lay inside the ring walls. He could just as well walk there.

"Eva was right by the way," said Ove on his way out through the door, "forensics couldn't determine whether Arvid Traneus died before or after his wife and cousin."

"No help there in other words."

"Nope," said Ove and stopped in the doorway.

"Anything new on Ringvall? He is gonna make it isn't he?"

"Sure, he's out of danger, but it'll probably be at least another two days before you can question him. His lung was pretty badly damaged."

THERE WERE A lot of people milling around on the main shopping street even though it was three days before payday. Maybe it was the first signs of Christmas shopping. It was Saturday, everyone had credit cards and the money never ran out. A woman with curly gray hair and an orange Amnesty banner shook a collection box at them. He dropped a ten-crown piece into it.

By the time he'd reached Åhléns, his cell phone rang. It was Eva.

"Fredrik speaking," he answered and tried to sound as collegial and neutral as possible.

"Hi. I just wanted to let you know that I've checked Traneus's mower now. I've been pretty busy as I'm sure you can imagine."

"Yeah," he said.

"The blade is new."

"Oh, yeah?" he said and stopped for the bus that slowly rolled past.

"Straight out of the box. Never been used."

"Now it got more interesting," he said. "So, you mean it could be the murder weapon?"

"I've unscrewed it from the mower. It really looks like it came straight from the factory, but it's possible that slicing through a bit of bone and tissue wouldn't leave any visible marks. At the same time it's pretty crazy to imagine the murderer cleaning off the blade and then screwing it onto the mower."

"Ringvall definitely wouldn't have done that," Fredrik agreed, "but if it was Arvid Traneus then at least it might be conceivable."

"An old worn-out blade would hardly cause the injuries we saw on the victims."

"So you're saying that if the murderer did use a mower blade, that that has to be it?"

"Well, it would have to be a new one anyway," she answered.

"There's something else, too," he said, the sound of his voice changing as he passed through Österport. "If Arvid Traneus was killed in the bathtub down in the basement and a splinter of his skull bone . . ."

Fredrik broke off and looked around. This wasn't an appropriate topic to be discussing over a cell phone out in the street, especially not when you were mentioning people by name. Luckily, he had been alone beneath the arches.

"Hang on," he said and hurried past a family with little kids out on Hästgatan.

Once he had turned off onto Smittens Backe he was alone again.

"If a splinter of skull bone ended up behind one of the ceiling moldings and he had also been dismembered there," he said in a hushed voice, "well, you can just imagine how it must have looked. Someone did one hell of a thorough job cleaning it up."

"Not thorough enough for me," said Eva.

"What I'm trying to say is that it's not likely to have been the same murderer. Why put so much effort into cleaning up after the murder in the basement and then leave the living room looking like a slaughterhouse?"

"Maybe there wasn't time, but sure, I agree with you," said Eva. "It does seem strange."

"If it was a crime of passion, and Arvid killed his wife and cousin, let's say, with the new mower blade, then who killed him? Whoever killed him *had to* have caught him more or less in the act," said Fredrik and stopped at the beginning of Ryska Gränd.

"Why '*had to*'?" asked Eva.

"As I see it, he can't have had many choices in that situation. Either, turn himself in, or else make a run for it. I don't think he even considered trying to cover up the crime. They would soon have been missed and he would have been the prime suspect."

"You mean that whoever killed Arvid caught him literally red-handed?"

"Yes, if the murders are connected and took place in that order, then that almost has to be what happened," said Fredrik and took a few steps into the alley.

"Maybe you're right," said Eva.

"But then I think that maybe I've got it all wrong, that it's all one and the same murderer, and that we haven't understood the motive at all. There's a whole bunch of money after all. What if Rickard was also . . ."

He stopped short, stood there silently with the phone pressed against his ear. He could see Jesper Mann's door from the spot where he was standing, partially hidden behind a blue Saab.

"Never mind, it's just pure speculation . . . So, how are things otherwise?" he asked after another pause.

"I've still got work to do here. I'm sending the blade in for analysis anyway," said Eva.

"Okay, I'm just about to question someone," said Fredrik and was sorry he asked.

52.

Jesper Mann lived in a little two-room apartment in a crooked old house with a low ceiling. Fredrik could have easily reached up and touched it.

"So you want to talk about Rickard?" said Jesper Mann.

He sat sunken in a turquoise couch, dressed in a pair of shiny sweatpants, a T-shirt, and a pair of thin dark-brown leather slippers on his bare feet. The room they were sitting in looked cozy with green plants climbing along the windowsills and a big, cluttered shelf full of books perched upright or stacked at random. Two goldfish were swimming around in a fishbowl furnished with a single strand of Cabomba growing out of the white gravel at the bottom.

"Well. We haven't been able to get hold of Rickard for almost three days now. Do you know where he could be?"

Jesper Mann was half a head shorter than Fredrik and looked like he spent a lot of time at the gym. He had short, dark, naturally curly hair and self-consciously long, pointed sideburns. He worked behind the bar at Friheten, as he had told Fredrik earlier on the phone. Today he was free until five o'clock.

"I saw that you found his father," said Jesper Mann.

"Do you think it's connected?" asked Fredrik.

"I don't know. I mean . . . it would be strange if it wasn't, but I've no idea how. So he hasn't been home?"

"No, not since late Wednesday evening. His sister thought that he'd gone to see a friend in Visby, we thought that it might have been you."

"No, he hasn't been here," said Jesper.

"When did you last see him?"

"Over two weeks ago."

"But you've been in touch?"

"Not really."

"You sent him an e-mail just last Wednesday," said Fredrik.

Jesper Mann stiffened. The good-natured smile evaporated. It looked like he regretted sitting on the couch instead of on a chair like Fredrik. Maybe he also regretted his nonchalant dress and the slippers with his pale toes poking out.

He straightened up as best he could among all the cushions on the couch, threw out his hands with his elbows resting against his hips.

"I've got nothing to hide," he said.

"I don't think you do, either," said Fredrik, even though it wasn't quite true.

"If you've read our e-mails then you know that it was mostly just trivial Web chatter, the stuff you rattle off just to remind people that you're still alive," Jesper Mann continued.

"I understand."

"I didn't really count that as being in touch," he said.

"I understand," Fredrik assured him once again.

Jesper Mann dropped it, sank back down a little into the couch again.

"Any idea where he might be?" said Fredrik.

Jesper Mann thought for a moment, but couldn't come up with anything.

"To tell you the truth I don't know him very well . . . that is I know him, but I don't know so much about him."

"Is that how you perceive him then?" said Fredrik.

"How do you mean?"

"As being a little secretive? That he doesn't reveal too much about himself?"

"Not exactly, but we . . ."

He looked away and shrugged his shoulders.

"You . . . ?" said Fredrik.

"We didn't really socialize in that way," he said.

Fredrik wasn't sure he understood what that meant, or rather, he was sure that he didn't understand.

"How do you know each other?"

The apartment was at street-level and every now and then a diffuse shadow passed through the room whenever someone walked past in the narrow alleyway outside.

"We got to know each other last summer, out on the town. We've met up a little sporadically since then, but nothing I'd really call a relationship."

"A relationship?"

Jesper Mann smiled.

"You didn't know Rickard is gay?"

"No," said Fredrik.

"Not that strange really. He barely knows himself," said Jesper Mann.

He sank back into the couch and perched one foot up on his knee.

"You mean that he only recently discovered his orientation, or that he has difficulty accepting it?" asked Fredrik.

"The latter. Still stuck inside the closet with a double bolt. It's always the same pattern. He gets in touch, we meet, we have sex, then he leaves, and then you don't hear from him again for another month or two," said Jesper and looked as if he thought this was a wonderful arrangement.

"Except for the occasional e-mail," Fredrik corrected.

"Yeah, except for some casual e-mail chitchat."

They heard some voices outside the window, a few clipped words from a conversation that briefly gave way to a mumbling before fading away in the distance.

"But if you're so intimate with each other then surely you must have gotten to know him a little better than that, even if he does disappear after each time you meet. If you try and think back, there's no chance he could have mentioned some place he often goes, or where he has friends?"

"He said once that he wanted to travel to Japan to visit his father, but that's hardly likely now."

"Nothing closer to home?"

Jesper Mann shook his head.

"What do you know about Rickard and his father? What was their relationship like?" asked Fredrik.

"He didn't talk much about his family."

"He just said that he wanted to visit his father in Japan."

"That was pretty screwed up, too, if you ask me," said Jesper Mann and put his foot down on the floor again.

"Screwed up?"

"I mean on the part of his father."

He leaned forward, laid his arms against his thighs, and let his hands rest loosely in each other.

"He was working over there for a few years and not once did he invite Rickard, his daughter, or his wife to come visit. He was loaded, so money was certainly not the problem."

"Did you say that to Rickard?"

"Something like that."

"And how did he react?"

"He defended his father, almost became aggressive. I don't remember the details, but something about his father's work being so demanding, that he didn't have time for anything but work when he was in Tokyo, and whenever he could he came home to visit."

"Do think that was an accurate description?"

"No idea, but Ricky seemed to believe it anyway."

"And that was all he ever said about his father?" asked Fredrik.

There was a sudden glint in Jesper Mann's eyes.

"I just remembered something. I had blurted out something about my father, just as an aside, but something pretty negative, and Rickard started defending his father as if *he* were the one being attacked. My comment may well have been a bit sweeping, as if I had been talking about all fathers, but he got very upset."

"Do you remember what it was about?"

"No, but it probably had something to do with my father's attitude toward my choice of *lifestyle*. That's my pet peeve where he's concerned."

"Do you think it's his father's fault that Rickard hasn't come out of the closet?"

"Isn't it always?" said Jesper with a short laugh.

He straightened up and looked at his watch as if he thought that the questioning had gone on long enough. It almost looked like he was about to get up from the couch.

"What do you know about Rickard's drug habits?" said Fredrik and noticed how Jesper's eyes widened a little.

Fredrik couldn't help but feel a slight satisfaction at the sight of Jesper Mann's body language tightening up.

"Drugs? No idea. I don't think so. He drank of course, if that's what you mean?"

"If I had meant alcohol then I would've said so," said Fredrik.

"Oh. Well, no, he didn't do any drugs, as far as I know. But like I said, I really don't know him very well."

Fredrik gave him a questioning look and got a puzzled one in return.

"I've read your e-mails, and it doesn't take a rocket scientist to work out what all the little code words mean."

"Code words?" said Jesper Mann.

"Yes."

"The fact that you go in and read our e-mails, well that's just . . ."

He waved his right hand dismissively in the air.

"But that we shouldn't be allowed to express ourselves as we choose," he continued and let out a forced laugh.

"I think," said Fredrik, "that if I have this apartment searched, we'll find enough to detain you for a few days while we investigate the rest of the operation."

"Operation, I don't have an operation," said Jesper Mann looking shocked.

Fredrik wondered if he'd perhaps been a bit heavy-handed. The idea had been to scare him into answering, not to put the fear of God into him.

"We can't be sure of that until we've looked into it," he said dryly.

Jesper Mann looked a little less terrified, even if he was still gripping the turquoise seat cushion tightly with his left hand.

"He did a little party drugs."

"Like what?"

"E, amphetamines, coke on occasion."

"That sounds like a whole lot," said Fredrik.

"Look, I already told you that we've seen each other maybe once a month, max, since last summer, so really I can't say anything about his habits."

"But he took drugs on those occasions when you saw each other?"

"On those occasions he was usually high on something, yes."

"But you don't know whether he took anything otherwise?" asked Fredrik.

"No. But he doesn't seem like a serious junkie to me."

Fredrik thought it sounded like Jesper Mann had just described one, but they obviously lived in different worlds. The definition of junkie was apparently also a question of lifestyle.

"I'm not going to ask how he got hold of his drugs since I don't consider that to be relevant to this investigation," said Fredrik. "At least not at this time. But it may prove to be later on."

Jesper Mann said nothing.

WHEN FREDRIK EMERGED from the entrance to the building he wondered how far along Ryska Gränd he would get before Jesper went rushing into the bathroom to flush his stash of weekend drugs down the toilet.

When he had taken another thirty steps across the cobbled lane and passed the spot where he had stood with the cell phone pressed against his ear speaking to Eva half an hour earlier, he was struck by another thought entirely.

During the conversation with Eva he had argued that it wouldn't have done any good for Arvid Traneus to try and hide the murders of Kristina and Anders—if he, in fact, had committed them. They would have been missed soon after the murders and Arvid would have been the prime suspect even in that scenario. But who was it that would *miss* them? Who would miss Kristina? Who wouldn't get hold of her when he called? Who exactly would start to wonder if something was wrong and drive over to the farm in Levide to take a look, and then find them dead on the living room floor after having unlocked the door with his own key?

Rickard Traneus.

That ought to have been Rickard Traneus. Instead it was the cleaner who found them, two days after they had been murdered, when the blood had already congealed into black islands on the living room's parquet floor.

Fredrik had wondered why Rickard Traneus hadn't had more contact with his parents even though his father had just returned from Tokyo. His father had been away for three years, apart from a few short visits, and yet when he finally returns, his son only speaks to him briefly over the phone. A family dinner had been planned for Friday evening, the sister was coming all the way down from Stockholm for it. After Monday, Rickard doesn't hear a single word from his parents, nor does he try to call them. And he doesn't drop by to say hello to the father, even though he's only a few miles away. Isn't that strange?

It could of course be explained by the fact that they had a complicated relationship.

That wasn't implausible. But it could also be explained by the fact that Rickard Traneus knew there was no one to call.

53.

Göran received Elin Traneus in his office. She looked surprisingly composed and steady considering everything she'd been through over the past few weeks.

She took a seat in the visitor's chair with her back to the window. Göran sat down across from her at the long table with his back to the big safe.

"I appreciate your coming in like this. I thought it would be good to speak with you before you head off to the mainland," he said.

Elin sighed, but in what seemed to be a positive way, like a long restful exhalation.

"I have to go back. I think it's for the best. I can't do anything here anyway and we won't be able to hold the funeral for a while yet."

"It's completely up to you. But I'd be grateful if you would stay in touch so we know where we can reach you," said Göran.

"Well, I'm not going to disappear," said Elin. "I'm just going home to study. I'll be at my home address for the next five years."

She actually smiled. It was strange, but ever since Elin Traneus had come in through the door Göran had felt as if he was witnessing a conclusion. Although in reality they were in the middle of something. He couldn't really understand how it all fit together.

"Let's hope this whole thing gets resolved quicker than that," he said.

"Yes," said Elin and fingered the shoulder strap of the sports bag she had set down next to her chair.

Once again, he couldn't help but be surprised at how she managed to sit there and answer his questions. How could she handle that, when both her parents had been taken from her in a manner that might reasonably be expected to leave her no peace at all? He'd seen that before, people who managed to cope under the most appalling circumstances, but each time it was just as difficult for him to understand how they did it. You got up, did what you had to do. Life went on. A truism that contained some of life's greatness and its pettiness.

"When your sister, Stefania, was fifteen or sixteen, she was supposed to have had a boyfriend named Leo. Is that something you remember anything about?"

"Leo, sure I remember him," she said.

"You wouldn't have been very old. Eight or nine," said Göran.

"No, but it caused such . . . well, there was a lot of fuss over that."

"How so?"

"Mother didn't like her seeing him. Which is understandable. Only I don't know what he was really like, of course," she said.

"How do you mean?"

"Well, he was sort of going astray, but . . . I mean, maybe that came later."

"Did something happen between them, between Stefania and Leo?" asked Göran.

"Not that I know of," said Elin. "It was mostly that my parents didn't like him."

She let go of the shoulder strap which slid down onto the floor. Her expression revealed nothing about what she felt for her dead sister. Maybe she had put it behind her. Ten years ago.

"So your father didn't like it, either, that she was seeing Leo?" said Göran.

"No, but I think that it was more my mother who . . . I mean, this isn't something I understood back then, but more that I pieced it together later. My mother and I spoke about it. My father was more generally against it. He didn't like the idea of boyfriends period. But it was my mother who specifically didn't like Leo. I think she nagged my father about it and he finally put an end to it."

"How did he do that?"

"Leo wasn't allowed to come over."

"But surely there are other places they could've met?"

"Stefania was in ninth grade. I don't think she had the strength to stand up to him," said Elin.

"No . . ."

"My father wasn't the sort of person you talked back to," she added.

She looked up at the clock that hung above the table, positioned so that Göran could see it from his desk.

"I don't want to make you miss your ferry," he said.

"That's okay, I'll make it," she said.

Göran opened his mouth and then closed it again as he considered how to phrase his next question.

"You said that your father physically abused your mother. Did he hit Stefania, too?"

"No," she said firmly, "he didn't hit her, he didn't hit any of us."

She turned her gaze toward the door, longingly Göran thought, and he felt a little guilty for keeping her there.

"If you're going to make your ferry maybe we should . . ."

"He never hit us, but you always wondered if he was going to. When the first time was going be," she said and turned back to Göran. "I think Stefania thought a lot about it, but she's dead and now he's dead, too, so what difference does it make?"

A ray of sunlight flashed in the skylight. It hit Göran in the middle of his face and he shut his eyes involuntarily.

"I know, I'm studying psychology. Sometime I'm going to have to dig through all that. But not now and not here."

"No," said Göran and couldn't think of anything more to say.

He got up slowly to indicate that she was free to go now. Elin got up, and said good-bye with a short handshake. He saw her out. He would've preferred not to, but station regulations required it. It was difficult to say anything more, so they walked the whole way in silence.

"Look after yourself," he said a little too late when she was already on her way out the door.

SARA OSKARSSON KNOCKED three times on the door of Emrik Jansson's little house. The front porch was in the shade and her back felt cold. She turned to Fredrik.

"Don't count on this giving us anything."

"We'll have to see," said Fredrik.

It was silent on the other side of the door. Sara, who had seen how slowly he moved, waited without knocking again. At long last, the door finally opened.

"Sara Oskarsson, Visby Police Department," she introduced herself. "I was here a few weeks ago."

The dark blue eyes above the bushy beard looked at her for a brief moment before he nodded slowly twice.

"Yeah, I recognize you," said Emrik Jansson, "but not you," he added looking at Fredrik.

"Fredrik Broman," he said and held out his hand and felt his fingers get squeezed by a dry cold hand.

"We've got a few more questions," Sara explained.

"You'd better come inside," said Emrik. "I've got food on the stove."

"It'll only take a moment," she said.

"Oh, sure, that's all it takes to burn the food, too."

He gestured in toward the house, turned his back on them, and walked slowly into the kitchen. They followed after him and Fredrik pulled the door closed behind him. Sara was careful not to accidentally brush against any of the yellow-stained interior. She had warned Fredrik, but had gotten the feeling that he hadn't taken her seriously.

They entered the kitchen. There was a big cast-iron frying pan spattering and sizzling away on the stove. Not altogether surprisingly, the kitchen was even more encrusted with grime than the sections of the apartment that Sara had been able to see from the hall the last time she was there. The table and benches may have been wiped off, but seemed to have a layer of grease, dirt, and tobacco residue that no amount of cleaning had any real effect on. At least not Emrik's cleaning.

"It's wild rabbit," said Emrik Jansson and turned the two legs over in the frying pan with the help of a spatula and a wooden spoon. "The cat brings one in every so often. I usually take the legs and then he can make do with the rest."

Sara felt a look from Fredrik, but avoided meeting it. Here's one guy anyway, who eats what the cat dragged in, she thought, and couldn't help but stare at the rabbit legs that were frying in plenty of fat.

"When I was here last time you said that you had seen Arvid Traneus riding in the family car, a silver gray SUV."

"Driving, to be precise," said Emrik Jansson and looked up from his cooking.

"That's right, driving," said Sara. "It was in the evening, Monday, the second of October."

"Yes."

"And that was the last time you saw him?"

"Yup. Last time anyone saw him, I understand," said Emrik Jansson.

Teachers, thought Sara, they have an unfailing ability to make one feel like an idiot.

"And are you absolutely sure about that. You didn't see him after Monday evening?"

"No."

Emrik pressed one of the legs down into the frying pan with the wooden spoon.

"I think it's just about ready. They nibble on thyme and other herbs when they're hopping around out there, the occasional juniper berry maybe, so they come preseasoned. Salt is the only thing that's missing," he said glancing over his shoulder at Sara.

"Do you remember anything more from that week? Did you see Kristina Traneus or any other member of the family?"

"Kristina I saw midweek sometime, not sure what day it was. Before that I saw the car a few times, but I never saw who was sitting in it."

"You don't know which day?"

"Must've been on Tuesday."

"During the day?"

"Yes, it was. Sometime in the afternoon."

"So theoretically, Arvid Traneus could have been sitting in the car when you saw it on Tuesday?" asked Sara while Emrik Jansson served up his fried wild rabbit leg on a brown plate decorated with mustard-colored stripes.

"Theoretically anyone could've been sitting in the car," he answered.

You just keep it up, thought Sara.

"But all roads lead to Rome, know what I mean," he continued.

"I know the expression, but I'm not sure what it has to do with this case," said Sara and was about to put her hand on the kitchen counter to the right of her, but caught herself at the last second.

"There are several roads leading to that farm and there's only one of them that passes by my hunting grounds," said Emrik Jansson and grinned.

"Okay, now I'm with you," said Sara, "but if we just stick to what you saw? There's nothing else that you remember from those days; the second, third, fourth of October?"

"No," he said firmly.

He turned his back to Sara, lifted the frying pan with both hands and carried it over to the sink. There he stopped, and stared down into the frying pan that he rested against the edge of the counter, let go of it with one hand and stroked his beard.

"I think I saw the son, Rickard, drive past."

This time she met Fredrik's gaze that was urging her to keep going. Emrik let go of the frying pan, which clattered into the sink.

"You think you saw him?" she said.

"I mean, I did see him, but exactly when that would've been . . ."

He fell silent and turned toward Sara.

"You didn't mention this before," she pointed out.

"Rickard drives past here all the time. It's not something you think twice about."

Sara started to sense a slight feeling of irritation gnawing away inside her. She could have started to feel tired, but instead she was feeling annoyed.

"Was it after the second of October?"

The nicotine stained tuft of beard beneath his lip bobbed up and down as Emrik smacked thoughtfully a few times.

"I've seen him shoot past here so often. I don't know . . ."

"Do you know Rickard?" she asked.

"Know him? No, no I wasn't around long enough to have him in my class. I left before he made it into junior high. But then you get to hear a thing or two. I'm surprised that he ended up trying to go down the finance path. It really wasn't his thing," he said.

"So what was his 'thing' would you say?" asked Sara.

"He was good at school, as far as I know, it's not that, but he probably had more of a natural inclination toward the humanities."

Emrik Jansson ran his tongue across his lower lip.

"That is if you're going to believe what you hear," he added with a sheepish smile.

He took a few steps toward Sara and Fredrik and pointed at the table.

"Is it all right if I sit down?" he asked.

"Yes, of course," said Sara, ashamed that she hadn't thought of that before.

He had moved around with such domesticated ease in front of the stove that she had completely forgotten his unsteady legs. Fredrik pulled out a chair for him that he sank down onto with a quiet sigh.

"I've seen it before. Children who follow in their parents' footsteps. It can undermine their self-confidence. It's not a question of talent. Not primarily anyway. It's something else."

Emrik fingered his packet of rolling tobacco that lay on the kitchen table, but left it where it was unopened.

"It undermines their self-confidence," he repeated.

Sara nodded and made a final attempt:

"But it was around the second of October that you saw Rickard drive past on his way to the farm?"

"I can't say that for sure since I saw him all the time. He was always over there fixing things and doing stuff. But exactly when . . ."

"You were very sure when it was you saw Arvid Traneus in the car, that it was on the Monday," said Fredrik.

Emrik looked up at Fredrik. It felt strange that they were both standing, while Emrik was sitting, thought Sara, but she wasn't going to sacrifice herself for appearances.

"Sure, but that was different," Emrik answered in a tone of voice that suggested that that ought to be obvious. "Traneus had came home that day, after being away in Japan for a few years."

Emrik suddenly stopped short and turned back toward Sara purposefully.

"No, it was after Arvid had come back. That's right. Yes, I can see it in front of me. First Arvid in the car in the evening, then Rickard. And it wasn't the same day."

"Which day was it then?" she asked.

Emrik Jansson sat there in silence for a moment staring down at the table, then he shook his head.

"No, I can't say. Tuesday, Wednesday? Thursday? Can't have been any later than that."

"But it was after Arvid had come home? You're absolutely sure about that?"

Emrik nodded.

THE CAR WAS heading north, back toward Visby. The treetops were swaying uneasily along the coast road.

"Regardless of whether he remembers correctly or not, it's the second thing he said that's almost more important," said Fredrik who was behind the wheel.

"He said a whole lot," said Sara and opened the car window a little.

Cool air poured in over her face. Fredrik looked at her. It looked as if she was sweating.

"Are you all right?"

"Yeah, I'm fine," she answered.

Fredrik fixed his gaze on the road again and picked up where he left off.

"I mean the fact that Rickard was over there several times a week. That strengthens my theory that he knew. He stayed away and stopped calling since there was no one left there to call. He was involved somehow, unless he's actually the one who killed his father."

"And now he's run off?" said Sara and ran the tips of her fingers across her forehead.

"Yes."

"But, the fact that he stopped calling and didn't go over there could also have to do with the fact that his father had just come home. He went over there to help out his mother, then his father came. Pretty natural. And then maybe their relationship wasn't the best, either."

"I've thought about that," said Fredrik, "but we haven't actually found anything to suggest that. At least not to the extent that would explain why he wouldn't get in touch for a whole week."

"Don't be so sure," said Sara and then fell silent.

"What?" said Fredrik and looked at her.

Didn't she seem just a little pale?

"Are you sure you're okay?"

"Oh, yeah," she assured him, coughed gently a few times, and then continued. "Rickard was the only son out of three children. Maybe he felt a lot of pressure to live up to something that he wasn't suited for— Emrik hinted at something like that—and he's spoken himself about his failed studies. That can make things tense between a father and son, make you reluctant to get in touch, even if the relationship isn't exactly bad."

The landscape opened up to the dark-blue sea in the west. They fell silent and looked out over the jagged waves. It looked like the wind was starting to pick up. The smell of seaweed penetrated through the cracked-open window. Sara wrinkled her nose.

"Ugh," she whined and shut the window.

"You know, I've been thinking about those diaries," said Fredrik. "Kristina Traneus's diaries. You got a few of them to read, too, right?"

"Yeah."

"Did you look at them?"

"Sure, I read them," she said.

"Did you find any clues as to where we might be able to find him?"

"Rickard? No. I would have thought of that. I mean, at the time of course we were looking for his father, but still."

"There was something in one of the books, one of the ones that Lennart had, about a sailing trip. They had a boat called the *Adventure* that the whole family used to go sailing in together. It seemed to be a recurring event, something they did every summer with the kids."

"Oh, yeah?" said Sara and stared out through the window.

"That's the only place I've found any reference to, apart from the house, that seems to have had any significance, or emotional attachment for them. They never had a summerhouse, never kept coming back to some particular travel destination. The sailing trips on the *Adventure* were the only thing."

"So, what are you saying," said Sara, "that you want us to look for a sailboat?"

"No, there's no point in that. It doesn't even belong to the family anymore. But the notes in the diary said something about an island . . . I have to take another look at exactly what she wrote, but I think it might be worth checking out. Do you mind if we swing past Lennart's place? I think he still has the books," said Fredrik.

"Me? Are you crazy?" said Sara.

"Come on," said Fredrik, "he could do with a bit of cheering up."

"I understand if you don't want to go on your own, but . . ."

Sara suddenly got a strange look in her eye.

"Could you pull over?" she asked.

"What?"

"Can you stop the car?"

"Stop? Where? You mean here?" asked Fredrik and pointed out at the deserted landscape dotted with summer cabins that they were just passing.

"Just stop, anywhere!" she shouted in a shrill tone that made Fredrik jam on the brakes.

Sara had already taken off her safety belt, threw open the door, and was out of the car the moment it came to a halt. She took a few un-steady steps out across the shoulder, bent forward, and threw up in the ditch. A single, retching cascade, and then it was over.

She sank down onto her haunches and took a few deep breaths, steadied herself with one hand against the ground.

The whole thing had gone very fast and only now did it occur to Fredrik to get out. He rounded the car and hurried over to her. She waved at him to stay where he was.

"Can I do anything?" he asked.

Sara shook her head cautiously and wiped away the tears that had squeezed out of the corner of her eyes. Fredrik felt helpless, but man-aged to find a piece of paper that she could use to wipe her mouth. After a while he held his hand out to her. She took it and slowly rose to her feet.

"Want me to drive you home?" he asked when they were back in the car.

She shook her head again.

"I'm okay. Let's go see Lennart," she said.

"You're sure?"

"Yeah. It would be great if you could just stop somewhere so I can buy a bottle of water."

"Sure," he said and started the car.

He looked at her again as he pulled back out onto the road.

"I think it was the lunch," she said. "That's the last time I'm eating in the station cafeteria."

"You ought to call and complain."

"M-hm, definitely," Sara mumbled and looked out the window.

54.

Elin sat in one of the red armchairs in the stern lounge and watched Visby and Gotland slowly recede into the distance. The captain's welcome-aboard announcement droned from the ceiling's hidden loudspeakers. The voice fluctuated strangely between sincere enthusiasm and casual nonchalance. The winds were modest but increasing, and the crossing could be a little choppy if the wind continued in its current direction.

It could go ahead and blow, as far as Elin was concerned. She didn't easily get seasick. None of them ever had any trouble with seasickness. Not her, not Ricky, and not Stefania. Mother had been a little more sensitive. Especially if it was blowing the first day they were out, before she'd gotten used to it.

The distance between the ferry and the island grew ever larger.

She needed a sea between herself and him.

That was how she had always thought about it whenever she saw Gotland get swallowed up by the horizon, and the world, for a moment, consisted of nothing but water. She needed a sea. Two continents wasn't enough, she needed that sea, too. Used to need it.

He had returned from Tokyo. Ten years after he'd left for the first time he'd come back and was murdered in his own house.

Ten years after Stefania's death.

What did it mean for her that he didn't exist anymore? That he was dead, out of her life? It was too complicated for her to think about. The fact that Mother was also gone made it even more impossible.

If he had been the only one to die, then everything could have been different. They would have been able to breathe. For a moment they would have been able to take long, deep breaths. Mother would've been able to breathe, speak, move, look wherever she wanted. You couldn't think like that, wish for your own father's death. Sure you could, it was the most natural thing in the world, nothing to be ashamed of.

It wasn't complicated. It was only natural.

She fumbled for the lever that tipped the chair back, pulled it and pushed back against the chair. The glass with ice-cold, sour red wine vibrated on the tray table in front of her. There weren't many people in the stern lounge. A few rows to the left of her, a woman was trying to get a little baby to go to sleep that had a gray bonnet tied underneath its chin.

Father had flown back when the doctors had said that Stefania probably wouldn't make it. Mother had called and called and called. In the end, he had caught a plane. Stefania had fallen asleep for the last time when he was somewhere above Siberia, over six miles up in the air. He had stayed for three days, taken care of everything, spoken to the undertakers, set a date for the funeral, done everything that had to be done. Then he had left again, hadn't been able to stay any longer, but would be back for the funeral. It couldn't be done any other way.

The funeral had taken place three weeks later. A cold, clear day in November with just a few yellow leaves dangling from the sprawling tree branches. An empty day, completely empty and awful. Levide church felt wrong and unfamiliar, standing as it did wedged in among a few houses on the wrong side of the road. Elin remembered that she had thought that it was the wrong place for Stefania, that the entire funeral was one big betrayal.

She and Ricky had stood there on either side of Mother in front of the casket, laid down their flowers. The casket had been made of oak with brass handles. Father's choice. But he hadn't been there. They had stood there alone, by the casket. Something had come up. His situation had become completely untenable, he had explained to Mother. If he had left Tokyo at that moment, then he might just as well have given up altogether, packed his bags, and gone home for good, shut up shop. No one would have trusted him again after that. She remembered clearly how Mother screamed and sobbed on the phone. It was the one time that she could remember Mother raising her voice at him. She didn't know if there had been any consequences when he came home ten days after the funeral, but it didn't really make any difference. The consequences were of no consequence anyway.

Elin kicked off her shoes and put her heels up on the seat cushion of her chair. She flipped absentmindedly through the tabloid newspaper that she had bought at the same time she purchased the ice-cold glass of wine, but no longer had any interest in reading it. She rolled the thin pages diagonally from the upper right-hand corner, rolled them one by one into thin newspaper logs.

They had stood on either side of Mother, she and Ricky, and she had tried to imagine the whole time how it would feel to be lying dead there inside that casket. It was the only thing she could think of throughout the entire funeral service, what it would be like to be dead inside that casket. But it was impossible to imagine. She just got this strange image of herself lying naked beneath a wooden lid. She had imagined death as being naked, because no matter how many clothes you had on, you somehow could never be dressed anymore once you were dead. And the lid you were lying beneath could be pulled away at any moment, and you'd be lying there naked in front of the entire congregation. It was embarrassing and cold and threatening. Naked in a box in front of an audience, unable to cover yourself or run away. That was death.

Today of course she understood that it had nothing to do with death. That naked, frightened, and embarrassed girl underneath the lid of the casket lid was her. That was it.

Now it was her turn to choose the casket. Oak with brass handles? Speak to the undertakers, organize everything that had to be organized. She and nobody else. She wasn't surprised that Ricky had run away from it all. It wasn't the first time. She had told the police about the time he had run off when his studies broke down and Father had to transfer money to a bank in Portugal so he could fly home. God only knows what he had been doing down there. Partying? Having a panic attack? Feeling sorry for himself? Everything at once maybe? After three weeks anyway, his money had run out.

She wasn't worried about him. Well, of course, she was concerned that he felt so depressed, but not in any other way. She was expecting that she'd get a call. Because she was the one he had to call, now that everyone else was gone. It might take a week or two, but then he would call and tell her some convoluted and largely made-up story that would end with her having to send him money so that he could come home.

Elin pushed her feet into her shoes and grabbed the empty glass to go and fill it up. More cold, sour wine.

LENNART SVENSSON WAS sitting there looking at *The Misfits* with Marilyn Monroe when Fredrik and Sara rang the doorbell. He had paused the DVD and they could see Clark Gable's face frozen on the TV screen when they entered the house. A tall, straight-backed chair stood awkwardly placed between the couch and the TV.

"I got a Marilyn Monroe box set as a birthday present from my step-daughter," said Lennart and pointed at the TV screen. "But there are really only a couple of them that are any good. This one's one of the better ones I guess."

On a white-lacquered shelf underneath the TV stood two tightly packed rows of DVDs. Fredrik scanned the titles. They were mostly classics from the forties, fifties, and sixties along with the occasional colorful Walt Disney spine, which he guessed were to entertain visiting grandchildren.

"How's the back?" he asked.

"It's getting there," said Lennart.

He put his hands on his hips and stretched.

"When I can sit through an entire film without a break, then it's time to go back to work. But I'm not quite there yet."

"Poor bastard, having to sit here the whole day watching half a movie at a time," said Sara and nodded at the well-filled DVD shelf.

"Yeah, it's hell," said Lennart with a grin.

He turned his back to Sara and disappeared into an adjacent room where Fredrik saw a dining table through the doorway.

It was a modern house with light, but not especially big rooms. The living room was white with varying shades of blue. Thin curtains filtered the light from the high windows that looked out onto a deck made of pressure-treated wood. Fredrik had expected something else. He couldn't exactly say what, but something that was more . . . Lennart Svensson.

"Seriously kids, be happy as long as your backs are okay. It may look silly, but it's sure as hell no laughing matter," said Lennart when he returned with the two diaries in his hand.

"My grandfather's also got back trouble, so I know what it can be like," Sara said.

Lennart looked at her, narrowed his eyes slightly, then let out a short, almost silent laugh.

"That's it, kick a man when he's down."

He held out the diaries.

"Here you go."

Fredrik took the two books, which were bound in cloth with a black lace-patterned print.

"Maybe I should have come in with them, but I haven't wanted to get in the car if it wasn't absolutely necessary. The car is a killer for the back. And since you called, nobody's asked about them," said Lennart.

"Nah, I doubt if anyone's missed them," said Fredrik.

He handed one of the books to Sara.

"Check July and August," he said.

He opened the book he'd kept and flipped forward to the day that Lennart had read from over the phone.

"Here it is. 'The seventh of July. Today we sailed out to the island. We put out early from Klintehamn. Good winds. We sailed the whole way. Arvid said that the gods were with us. I think so, too. An amazing day, clear blue sky, nice and balmy. We had a following wind the whole way from Hoburgen.' "

He looked up at Sara and Lennart.

"Which island can she have meant? If you set sail from Klintehamn and head around Hoburgen, then you're headed north along the east coast, right?"

"Unless they were heading over to the Estonian archipelago?" said Sara.

"That's true, that's quite conceivable. That definitely sounds like more of an adventure, more to Arvid Traneus's taste maybe."

"But if we stick to Gotland, then Östergarnsholm is almost the only island on the east side," said Lennart. "There are a few small islets out there—flat patches of grass full of angry seagulls—but nothing that would really qualify as a final destination."

Fredrik continued reading.

"There's not much to go on here. She writes about the kids, the food, the weather. 'We went ashore next to the lighthouse. Rickard and Elin were ashore before Arvid even had time to moor the boat properly.' "

"Could be anywhere," said Lennart.

"Here," said Sara, "this is a year earlier, ninety-three. It says something here about the *Adventure*."

"Read it," said Lennart.

Sara gave him a quick look, but managed to refrain from saying what had been on the tip of her tongue. Instead she started to read.

" 'July twenty-first. The *Adventure* put out from Klintehamn at eight o'clock in the morning. Light breeze. Would we be able to make it without having to use the engine? We put up the spinnaker.' "

"Call the girl," Lennart interjected, "she must know."

"Elin Traneus?" Sara asked.

"Yeah," said Lennart. "That's the simplest solution isn't it. Unless you want to keep her out of it for some reason."

Sara and Fredrik looked at each other.

"Isn't there anything there?" asked Fredrik.

Sara scanned a few paragraphs mumblingly, then continued out loud.

" 'Dropped anchor alee of the headland. The sea report promised a calm night. Stefania can still show brief flashes of her old self when Elin and Rickard manage to draw her out of herself. A lively water fight broke out between the three of them. Went on for a long while before she suddenly caught herself and went and lay down with a book. Rickard and Elin stopped, too, and instead went to play cave explorers. I went along. Elin bobbed up and down inside the cave in her red life vest. Rickard took her in tow.' "

"Östergarnsholm," said Lennart. "I can bet you a hundred crowns."

"I'm in," said Sara in a flash without really thinking about it.

They shook on it.

"Easy money," said Lennart.

55

The trick was to stay warm and dry. He was wearing a union suit, a windproof Helly Hansen top, and a windbreaker on top of that. Waterproof shoes.

Father had taught him how to dress properly and what supplies to bring along. Even if he never managed to get his business degree he knew how to dress properly.

Apart from wearing the right clothes, there were only two ways to stay warm on the island; either by moving continuously or else crawling down into the sleeping bag in the alcohol-soaked room in the old lighthouse. He had walked over to the new lighthouse on the east end of the island and back again, had seen the distant tower grow ever larger until he finally had to bend his neck back in order to look up at the lantern room at the top with a crop of antennae on its roof. Then he turned toward the gray, can-like building where he had spent the night. He'd had to open his jacket and sweater a little at the neck on the way back. He was still hot, but the heat quickly radiated away when he stood still. His clothes could only retain it for short time.

His mouth tasted of fat and smoke from the sausage he had eaten for lunch.

Why had he come out here? Was it because there was no way out? No way out of himself?

The daylight wasn't enough anymore. It didn't help that the sun broke through the tears in the cloud cover. The visions left him no peace. No matter how light it was, he was sucked into a darkness of bleeding eyes staring at him. They bled forth the realization that there was no going back. He was what he was, something he had never thought he could be, and would remain forever.

When that realization grabbed hold of him, he wanted more than anything to run headlong up the bluff and throw himself off. But he didn't do it.

Was that what he was going to do? Was he building up his courage to overcome the last memories of Elin and Stefania, of the bleached-white bird skeletons and fire ants, the last fragments of a few happy summer days that seemed so distant that they might just as well have belonged to somebody else?

And maybe they did, too. He was someone else now, someone else entirely, about as far away from being an innocent child on a summer adventure as it was possible to be. The sun wasn't shining on him anymore. There was no light that could penetrate his darkness.

Father's head rose up out of a hole in the ground. It stared at him with empty eye sockets, the eyes eaten away by worms and insects.

The white skin smelled of smoked sausage. His silence had made Father into a murderer. For weeks he had been singled out as a murderer right up until he had been absolved by the remains of his own corpse. Only once his head had come out of the ground had his reputation been restored.

56.

"You shouldn't have taken him up on it," said Fredrik once they had pulled their car doors shut.

"I can't stand it when he acts so damn certain."

She glanced at Fredrik out of the corner of her eye.

"I guess I'll live to regret it?"

"Don't know," said Fredrik, "but I hope so."

It took them barely twenty minutes to drive to Herrvik from Lennart's house. The little fishing harbor looked deserted as it came into view below Grogarnsberget. There wasn't a person to be seen anywhere, but stacks of fishing crates, fishing nets, and other equipment hinted that it was still a working harbor. A fishing boat with a shimmering green hull was moored along the concrete quayside. Black net floats marked with bleached flags lay sprawled amidships. Along the pier over by the parking lot lay two older pleasure boats and a little fishing boat without any equipment. The red fishing huts were shuttered, except for one with the sign HARBOR OFFICE above the door.

Fredrik parked the car in the middle of the large asphalt parking lot where only two other cars were standing. He turned off the engine. The restaurant that lay on a little rise above the parking lot was also closed. It was in there that Eva Karlén had dumped him one Sunday in July a little over two years ago.

"What now?" said Sara next to him.

Fredrik looked out at the parking lot.

"We should run a check on those cars," he said. "Would be a shame if we missed something that easy. If you do that, I'll go and check with the harbor office."

"Okay," said Sara.

Fredrik climbed out of the car and walked the short distance over to the harbor office. The windows were dark. There was a handwritten note taped up to the windowpane directing inquiries to a cell phone number.

He turned his back to it as the phone began to ring at the other end. The flags on the fishing buoys flapped hard in the wind, but he was standing sheltered from the wind.

"Hello? Maj speaking," a woman answered out of breath after it had rung so many times that Fredrik ought to have hung up a long time ago.

He introduced himself and explained his reason for calling. He had heard that there was a fisherman who used to take people out to Östergarnsholm during the tourist season. Would it be possible to get hold of him?

"Sure," said Maj and gave him another cell phone number.

The fisherman's name was Evert Söderman. Sounded more like someone from Roslagen than from Gotland.

"He's usually quick to answer."

Fredrik went back to the car and slid into the driver's seat. It was muggy inside the car, so he kept the door ajar.

"Nothing of interest," said Sara, "both cars are registered to people around here. No Traneus."

"Okay," said Fredrik, "let's see if we have any luck with the fisherman."

He called the number he'd gotten from Maj and got an answer on the second ring.

"Evert Söderman," said an elderly man as if he'd read the name from a slip of paper.

Fredrik explained why he was calling.

"Are you in Herrvik right now?" said Evert Söderman.

"Yes," answered Fredrik.

"Are you the ones sitting in that Volvo?"

"We're sitting in *a* Volvo, if it's *that* Volvo or not I can't say," said Fredrik and peered toward the houses across the inlet's bluish-gray water, expecting to catch a glimpse of a man with a cell phone raised to his ear standing in one of the windows, but didn't see anyone.

Sara looked at him questioningly.

"In the parking lot, down by the harbor office?" said the voice on the cell phone.

"Yes," said Fredrik after a moment's hesitation.

"I'll be right down," said Evert Söderman.

"That won't be necessary," said Fredrik. "We can do this over the phone."

"I was on my way down to the boat anyway."

"Well, in that case," said Fredrik.

He flipped his phone shut.

"He's coming down," he said in answer to Sara's questioning look.

It didn't take long before an old, well maintained, former phone company Volvo came rolling down to the quayside. Bright orange. It stopped as close to the little fishing boat as was possible. The man who climbed out was white haired, tall, and slightly hunched, but more springy than slouched. He walked straight up to Fredrik and Sara, who met him halfway.

"Evert Söderman," he said and held out a hand that was knotted from a lifetime on the Baltic.

He greeted Sara first.

"You often take people out to Östergarnsholm, is that right?" asked Fredrik when they had shaken hands.

"That's right," said Evert Söderman and squinted at Fredrik as if the light bothered him.

"Have you taken anyone out there over the past few days?" he asked.

"No, no," said Evert Söderman and laughed. "Last time was a while ago. It's mostly tourists."

"When was the last one?"

"Must have been right at the beginning of September. Maj usually gives out my phone number when somebody asks," said Evert Söderman.

He smiled warmly at Fredrik, and glanced at Sara. The light from the breaks in the clouds flashed in his dark-gray eyes.

"Do you know if anyone else might have taken someone out there this week?" said Fredrik. "Or rented someone a boat?"

"No, I doubt it. Not that I've heard anything about, anyway."

"And nobody's had a boat stolen, a skiff or a dinghy that's been lying pulled up onshore somewhere?"

"Nah, I would've heard about that."

He turned out toward the sea and looked north.

"Of course, there are a few summer residents with small boats they keep up on land in the off-season. If one of those has disappeared, then it's likely to take a while before it gets discovered."

He turned to Fredrik again.

"So you're out hunting boat thieves?"

Fredrik excused himself and took Sara aside while Evert Söderman climbed nimbly aboard his boat, the *Anita*, and got busy with something.

"We could ask him to take us out there," he said to Sara.

"To look for Rickard?"

"Yes."

"You're thinking of what it said in the diary?"

"It's worth a try."

"Do you think that Rickard's the one who did it?"

"I think he knows something. He's protecting someone, or else he's directly involved. Maybe he needed money, tried to make some deal with Ringvall, but everything went wrong. Ringvall flipped out and killed all three. Or else it was Rickard who did it, although I have a hard time believing that."

"I have a hard time believing that, either. That kid's no maniac. But there's gotta be some reason why he disappeared," said Sara.

"Rickard is the key to this case. That I'm sure of."

Sara lay a hand on the roof of the car, looked over toward the fishing boat.

"Well," she said then, "why not? Let's go out there and take a look. Will you call Göran?"

———

SARA AND FREDRIK sat at the very front of the prow during the crossing. The boat didn't seem to be used for fishing at all, anymore. The net winch may have still been there, but the interior of the boat was scrubbed clean and freshly painted and cross benches had been added for people to sit on.

When they came out of the sheltered harbor inlet, the boat began to slam into the waves that were coming head-on. The occasional spray from the sea reached them in the form of a fine mist.

Evert Söderman stuck his head out from one of the windows on the side of the wheelhouse and hollered to them.

"You can squeeze in here with me if it's getting too cold for you out there."

"We're fine!" Sara shouted back. "We're protected from the wind here."

"One hell of a bumpy ride though," said Fredrik to Sara.

When the bow plunged down into the larger troughs they were lifted slightly off their bench and landed again a split second later with a hard bang.

Closer to the island, the waves settled down and the crossing became more pleasant. Evert Söderman steered in toward the thin headland that jutted straight out to the south. You could just make out a jetty at its midpoint, probably built to facilitate the maintenance of the lighthouse.

He stuck his head out the side window again.

"I usually take the tourists over to those cliffs over there," he shouted while pointing, "but in this wind it's better we go ashore at the jetty."

Söderman had wanted to take them out free of charge since it was police business. He didn't have much else to do just then anyway, he had said. In the end, Fredrik managed to convince him to accept payment. It was the police department that would be footing the bill anyway, he had argued, not him or Sara personally. That had worked and

Söderman had accepted. The question was whether that wasn't his intention all along.

Göran had said yes to the expense and urged them to be careful. "Look around; if you're right, you just stand by and call for backup." The *Anita* wasn't a fast boat and the headwind was slowing her down even more. It took nearly half an hour to reach the jetty. Evert Söderman put the throbbing diesel engine into neutral, threw out the fenders, and leaped ashore with a rope in his hand. It went so quickly and smoothly that neither Fredrik nor Sara had a chance to offer to help.

They stepped ashore. Evert Söderman held out a steadying hand to Sara, but Fredrik had to manage on his own. The surface of the jetty had recently been refurbished. The pressure-treated planking still shone green.

"I'll wait here," said Evert Söderman, "but if the wind turns northerly, then I've got to move. Then I'll have to head over to those cliffs, but you'll see that."

A narrow path led north from the jetty and beyond it loomed the Östergarnsholm's eastern lighthouse.

"So, if you were to come out here in a little outboard, where would you go ashore?" asked Fredrik.

"Well, there's a beach on the north side of the island. I guess I'd try over there. Then you could pull up the boat and tie it to a tree," said Söderman and slowly turned around as he spoke as if it helped him to visualize the island's topography.

"Maybe the stone beach on the west side," he continued, "but then you'd probably have to raise the engine and wade in with the boat. There's a whole bunch of rocks out in the water, almost like a reef, but you could probably make it in there somewhere."

THEY LEFT EVERT Söderman by the boat and started to walk toward the lighthouse. They didn't have a map with them, but had studied Söderman's sea chart before setting off from Herrvik. The lighthouse seemed the best place to start looking, and then head west by way of the north beach.

Fredrik glanced back toward Söderman who'd gotten back onboard his boat. He wondered if they were subjecting him to any kind of danger by letting him wait there. What if they did find Rickard Traneus, and he was armed and tried to escape from the island? No, he decided that the risk of that happening was slim. If Rickard Traneus really was out there he wouldn't run. Anyone who came out here, wasn't trying to get away, they were coming for something else. What that might be he could only guess.

After some thirty yards, they were no longer sheltered from the wind. There was a stiff breeze and they realized that the island must have provided them with some protection from the wind during the crossing. The waves were even higher on this side, with jaggedly spuming white caps. The wind was cold.

"If he's been holed up out here since last Thursday, he must have gone inside one of the buildings," said Sara. "It's cold as all hell."

"Yeah," Fredrik agreed, "or else brought a tent out with him."

He stuck his hands under his arms to warm them up and felt the skin on his face tighten.

"I have to admit, now that I'm out here, I'm starting to think I've taken you on a wild-goose chase."

"M-hm," said Sara and turned toward him in order to be heard in the wind, "but if we assume that he fled in panic and this place has a very strong positive association for him, something that is clearly connected with his family, then it's not such a bad idea."

They approached the towering lighthouse that rose up some sixty-five feet into the sky. Facing them was a solid door that was protected by an arch a few inches deep. Fredrik left Sara by the door and took a walk around the lighthouse, looked out across the flat terrain, and peered up at the windows of the lighthouse and the balcony-like platform fifteen or sixteen feet up.

"The door's locked, securely, and nobody's tried to get in," said Sara once Fredrik had circled the base.

"We'll continue down there," said Fredrik and pointed at a low structure a short distance away. The building had a tin roof and wood siding. The windows had metal shutters that were locked with padlocks, and the front door was shut with a heavy crossbar that was also fitted with a solid padlock. They repeated the same procedure. Fredrik headed around the building and checked that all the padlocks were secure. The metal felt heavy and rough in his fingers, pitted from salt and oxidation.

"No," he said when he came back, nobody's been here.

They continued west, turned up toward the beach that Evert Söderman had mentioned. A few trees and bushes partially blocked their view of the narrow beach. They separated and walked on either side of the vegetation, Sara on the sea side and Fredrik on the landward side. He walked through the tall grass that rustled softly as it got pressed against the ground. The bushes weren't big and soon he could see down across the beach, small rocks that gave way to coarse sand at the edge of the water. He stopped.

All the way up by the bushes lay a white plastic boat with light-green interior. Sara had stopped on the other side. She stuck out her hand and pointed at the tracks among the rocks. You could clearly see where the boat had been pulled up, blue bottom paint had been scraped off against the bigger rocks. It must have been tough going. A line attached to the bow had been lashed to a big rock just in front of the boat. It was secure there. The water wasn't likely to make it that far up the beach except in very heavy winds coming in straight from the north.

"Shit," Sara swore softly and stamped her feet repeatedly as she moved a few steps down across the beach. "Fucking hell."

"What is it?" said Fredrik.

"Fire ants," she hissed. "I stepped right onto an anthill."

She brushed along her shins with her hands.

Fredrik walked up to the boat. Inside it lay two graying wooden oars, but nothing else. He lifted the cover of one of the hollow thwarts. In the stern one lay a light-blue bailer, in the other nothing.

"If there was a gas tank then he's taken it with him, or else hidden it somewhere," he said.

"He can't have rowed out here in this weather," said Sara who was still eyeing the ground suspiciously.

"No, but it wasn't blowing that hard last Thursday, if that was when he came."

Sara rounded the boat and stood next to Fredrik. The waves were an ugly gray, as if the sea were made of mud. They looked toward the east end of the island where the cliffs rose up. Way at the top of them stood the old lighthouse, cement gray against an equally gray sky.

57.

Rickard was standing in the back entrance behind the kitchen, listening. He was listening just as he had listened to Mother and Father when he was little. Countless times he had stood behind a corner, listening to their voices as they rose and fell, sank to a mumble, and sometimes exploded. He had never really intended to eavesdrop. It had been more or less like now. He had rushed over to see them, filled with thoughts of his parents, of being together with them, when he heard something that caught his attention, a word, an intonation. He couldn't explain exactly what, but it had made him stop.

He had stood and listened like that so many times that he knew when Mother said the wrong thing. He couldn't understand why she did it. If he could understand when she said the wrong thing, then she must have known, too. Did she say the wrong thing on purpose? It ought to be so easy to avoid it. He knew just what she shouldn't say. He could have sat there like a prompter in a booth in the floor and helped her. He knew when she could still turn it around, and when it didn't matter what she said anymore, when she had crossed that invisible line that meant that it could only end one way. When it got to that point, he wouldn't stay, then he would sneak back to his room as quietly as he could.

Why did she do that? Everything could have been so much better if she just wouldn't do the wrong thing. Father would have been happy. Life would have been so much simpler for all of them. Especially for Mother. Why did she always say the wrong thing?

It wasn't something like that that stopped him this time. No discordant inflection or red-flagged word. It was the voice itself. The *voice* that was wrong.

The doorbell had echoed through the house without anyone coming to open, so he had unlocked the garage door and rolled his bicycle into the empty garage. He had checked the refrigerator to see if there was any beer. He had thought that there might be some now that Father was home again. But there hadn't been any. He must not have had time to buy any yet, or else had changed his habits while he'd been in Tokyo.

He had sat down at the kitchen table and flipped through the morning paper. When he had finished glancing through it, impatiently, without actually reading anything, and still no one had shown up, he had gone out to the garage again to replace the blade on the lawn mower. He had bought a new blade a week ago, but hadn't gotten around to putting it on yet.

At first he hadn't been able to find it, had thought that Father must already have done it, but then he had spotted it hanging from a hook on the wall, still in its unopened packaging.

He had heard the cars pull up the driveway. Two cars, one immediately behind the other. It was strange. He had heard them climb out and walk toward the front door, and he had stuck his head out the back entrance to call out to them when he heard the front door opening. But the voice had stopped him. It wasn't Father's voice. It was somebody else's. So he had stopped to listen.

Now he was standing there in the back entrance listening to the distressed voices that every so often became so hushed that he could only make out a word here and there. He stood with his head lowered, his gaze fixed on the large terra-cotta floor tiles, all his concentration focused on the voices.

"Well, what was I supposed to have done?" He heard his mother's voice, quivering and changed.

"You can't . . ."

The stranger's voice was angry, cut her off abruptly. It sounded like he swallowed the rest of his words.

"We mustn't see each other," he continued firmly. "Not now. We're going to be together, but not now."

"But . . ."

"You'll have to get a new phone, a new SIM card."

The voice vibrated as if it were being tightly controlled and could explode at any time.

"Aren't they going to find out anyway? About us, I mean. Sooner or later?" said his mother.

She sounded small and confused in a way that Ricky had never heard her before.

"It'll take them a while. We don't have to hand it to them on a silver platter. And we're going to get through this."

"But what if they ask me? Eventually they're going to come out here and ask me. I can't lie about it, can I?"

Ricky heard how she fumbled for something, stability, a way out . . . He stared vacantly into the wall, saw his mother in front of him, tried to imagine the other person.

"It'll take them a while. Right now we just have to take it easy. Not see each other. You certainly can't come rushing over like that."

"But I can't take it," she whimpered.

She sounded so pitiful now. The strange man breathed heavily.

"Now you listen to me. You can do this. You're going to stay here and you're going to handle it. You haven't done anything wrong."

His voice didn't sound nearly as encouraging as his words. It was hard, firm, on the verge of shouting. Ricky clenched his fists.

"No! Nobody can blame me, can they? Who could blame me?"

"Stop it!" the strange voice commanded. "It won't do you any good to . . ."

"I don't think many people would blame me," his mother interjected.

"Kristina, stop it!"

Ricky's heart was pounding hard. He could feel his pulse in his temples. His head was searing hot. He could hear her footsteps, anxiously pacing between the living room and the dining room. She was constantly in motion, spoke as she moved.

"It's terrible to have to say it, but he was the one who . . . he did this to himself . . . in the end . . . he did it. Maybe I sound like some kind of monster, but he did this to himself."

"That's right. He did it to himself. And you're not a monster."

Now the voice sounded enthusiastic, almost happy, had really found something, agreed.

"You set yourself free. You were a prisoner. He deserved it many times over. He wasn't a man, he was a coward; an abusive, vicious . . ."

The voice faltered, seemed unable to find the right words, words that were suitably scornful. For a long time Ricky couldn't hear anything but panicked breathing.

"Should I go to the police?"

"No!" The stranger bellowed. "What the hell are you saying? Haven't you been listening? It's like you said. He did this to himself. He deserved to die. You're no monster. He's the monster."

Rickard listened. He was wearing the work gloves. The new, razor-sharp mower blade was pointing at an angle toward the floor from his tightly clenched right hand.

58.

He had seen the fishing boat emerge from Herrvik harbor and pitch and roll its way through the waves. At first it had held a course that pointed straight at him. Whoever was at the helm must have used the old lighthouse as a landmark. Then when the boat changed course and started heading south, he had thought that it would continue on past, but as soon as he had realized that it was on its way to the jetty he had moved upstairs so that he could follow them more easily.

He was careful to stay well away from the window. He had to move sideways in the room in order not to lose sight of the two people who came ashore. They walked up toward the lighthouse and he assumed that that was the purpose of their visit. They disappeared from view for a moment but then suddenly reappeared, headed down toward the beach.

At that point he understood that they had come looking for him. Someone must've seen him on the way over. What else could have led them here? Elin? Could she have sensed it, worked it out?

As soon as they reached the beach they would know he was here. Was this the end approaching? There was no way out. The end washed up like black spume from the sea. He saw the bleeding eyes.

He saw his mother's gaze. Was it accusing him? No, that would have been so much easier. It was heartbroken, despairing, and dying. The long cut across her chest was bleeding profusely. It drenched him while she drowned in it.

He raised his heavy head and peered down at the two figures who were drawing closer. Now he recognized them.

59.

There weren't many glimpses of the sun left in the darkening cloud cover. They had the wind at their backs as they trudged up the bluff. There was a crunch beneath Fredrik's shoe. He looked down and discovered a little bird skeleton that he had just crushed with his foot.

Up on the bluff, they were completely exposed to the wind. Sara's straight black hair whipped back and forth across her face. She held it back with her left hand as she searched for a hair band in her jacket pocket and quickly put it up in a ponytail.

They hurried up to the lighthouse, Sara first, followed by Fredrik who kept a vigilant eye on the windows above.

"I think the door's open," she whispered.

The graying wooden door appeared to be closed at first glance, but when Fredrik looked more closely he noticed an inch-wide space between the door and the frame. In the middle of it a thin band of light-colored wood shone amid the gray. Sara had also seen it. The door had been broken open.

"I'll check these out," he said and nodded toward the crumbling remains of the stone buildings that stood next to the lighthouse.

While Sara stayed by the door to the lighthouse, Fredrik examined the closest ruin. The sturdy walls of mortared limestone remained standing there like empty shells, but the roof, windows, and doors had long since disappeared. No one was hiding there.

He wondered if it really was Rickard Traneus who had come to the island in the boat that lay down on the beach. There could also be other explanations. If it was Rickard, there was a strong likelihood that he had already spotted them. How would he react? Would he view them as a threat?

If Fredrik had been hiding out on the island, he wouldn't have stayed in the lighthouse if he'd seen that someone was coming to look for him. He would have moved around on the island, kept himself hidden behind bushes and crags in order to trick those who were looking for him. But was there was nothing to say that Rickard Traneus thought as he would.

He hurried over to the other ruin. It was in considerably worse shape than the first one, the gables had collapsed in on themselves and the stone had crumbled to pieces.

He stood up and threw a quick glance back toward the lighthouse. There was no window facing his direction. If Rickard Traneus was still inside there, he couldn't see Fredrik. He quickly circled around the ruin and peeked in through the empty window openings. There was nobody there, either.

Fredrik hurried back, approached from an angle where he couldn't be seen. He came up next to Sara.

"I think he's in there," he said, "if he hasn't managed to trick us."

"We can't go inside," said Sara.

"No," said Fredrik.

She was right. It was too dangerous and there was no pressing reason for it. If he was in there, then he was trapped. They could wait him out.

"Should I call it in?" she asked.

"We could try to make contact first."

Sara looked at him doubtfully, but didn't object when Fredrik took a few steps to the right so that he was standing on the other side of the door. He raised his hand and knocked hard three times.

"Rickard?"

He waited for a few seconds.

"Rickard? Are you in there?"

No answer, just the wind that was rumbling around his ears.

"Rickard," he tried again. "You know who we are. We came to your house. Fredrik Broman and Sara Oskarsson from the Visby Police Department."

It was silent inside the lighthouse. At least no sounds came out that could he heard above the wind.

"Maybe he can't hear," said Sara. "He could be lying inside there high on something, listening to his iPod."

"Or just high, or passed out from alcohol or pills or whatever," said Fredrik.

"We could try opening the door, just so he can hear us better," she suggested.

That shouldn't pose much of a risk, thought Fredrik. If he was in there, he would hardly be standing right inside the door ready to attack, but would probably have retreated as far up inside the lighthouse as possible.

"Okay," he said.

He cautiously tried the door. Something was blocking it, but then gave way a little.

"Rickard!" he shouted. "I'm going to open the door, but just so that you can hear us better. We're not coming in. Okay?"

"You sound like the big bad wolf," Sara whispered.

"You want to take over?" he hissed back at her.

She shook her head. Fredrik put his foot against the door. Sara pulled her weapon and stayed close to the wall. He gestured to her to keep it cool and shoved the door hard with his foot, but without kicking it. A rough rumbling could be heard from the other side as something was pushed out of the way. It sounded like a rock. As if the door was being held shut from the inside with a rock, which meant there was someone inside the lighthouse.

The door had opened a few inches. Both Sara and Fredrik kept away from the door opening.

"Rickard. Could you please answer. We're not going to go away until we get an answer."

It was silent. The door swung gently back and forth in the wind.

"Rickard. My name is Fredrik Broman and I'm from the Visby Police. We've met before. Sara Oskarsson, whom you've also met, is here with me. You know who we are, Rickard, so please answer."

It suddenly occurred to Fredrik that he may be dead. Had Rickard come there to end it all, to crawl away like an animal into a hole and swallow a jar of pills?

"Yes," came a soft echo from inside the lighthouse.

Fredrik looked at Sara on the other side of the doorway. The voice must have come from the floor above or even several floors up.

"Is that you, Rickard?"

"Yes," said the voice after a short pause.

It sounded steadier this time.

Sara let her pistol slide back into the holster, held up her cell phone so Fredrik could see it and pointed with it over her shoulder. Fredrik nodded back. He pulled his own gun instead and waited at the side of the door. Sara walked away a few yards and squatted down against the wall so that the wind wouldn't blow her conversation apart. The cold wind had made her pale, but she didn't look like she was cold in her dark-blue parka. She spoke into her cell phone for about a minute and then came back.

"They're sending people over," she whispered almost silently but clearly, mouthing the words slowly.

The wind brought a tear to the corner of one eye. She wiped it away with the outside of her forefinger.

Fredrik moved closer to the door.

"Are you alone out here?" he yelled in through opening.

"Yes."

"How did you get out here?" he asked.

"By boat."

No shit, thought Fredrik. It was uncomfortable trying to shout inside while standing with his back to the wall to the side of the door. He holstered his gun and stood in the middle of the doorway. Now that it was clear that Rickard wasn't down by the entrance it wasn't as important to be quite so cautious.

"The one that's been pulled up onto the beach?" he said.

He felt the grain of the wood beneath his fingers as he supported himself against the doorjamb, the softer portions hollowed out by the wind and rain.

"Yes. Is that what you came for?" asked Rickard Traneus.

Fredrik couldn't help but smile. Of course Rickard understood that they hadn't come out here over a stolen outboarder, but maybe he hoped they had. A last vain hope. His smile stiffened and faded away.

"No," he said, "the boat will sort itself out. I think you know why we've come."

No answer came but strictly speaking it wasn't a question, either.

"Are you all right?" asked Fredrik.

"I don't know. I'm cold. It's hard to think when you're cold."

"Do you have anything to eat?"

"Yeah, I do. So what do you want?"

"We need to talk to you. We'd like you to come with us, so we can sit down and talk to each other in peace and quiet."

There was no answer, but the silence was charged with deliberation. There was a loud creak from a floorboard and Fredrik instinctively pulled away a bit to the side.

"What is it you want to talk about?" said Rickard Traneus.

His voice was dragging, turned in on itself.

"The best thing would be if we could talk somewhere in peace and quiet instead of standing out here shouting," Fredrik yelled.

It was becoming increasingly difficult to shout above the wind, at least that's what he felt. He couldn't determine if that was because the wind had picked up or had changed direction. He looked away toward the headland and the jetty. Evert Söderman's boat was rolling and tugging at its moorings. Had it been doing that when they left it there about half an hour ago?

"Talk about what?" Rickard Traneus insisted.

There was a hint of irritation in his voice now. Fredrik looked at Sara before answering.

"We think that you can tell us something about your parents' murder, something that only you know and that could explain what happened to them. We think that you're the only one who can solve this for us."

Silence followed, the floor creaked a few times. With each step, dust was released from between the floorboards. In the dim light from the doorway, Fredrik could see how it slowly sprinkled to the floor. That meant Rickard was on the floor immediately above them.

"We're talking to each other now," said Rickard Traneus. "Why can't we just keep on talking like this?"

Fredrik paused for a moment before answering, in order to give the impression that he was considering Rickard's suggestion.

"Wouldn't it be better and more comfortable to come back to the main island, get inside where it's warm and dry? You can have a good sleep, eat something. Then we can talk."

"I can't sleep," he said quickly.

"We can get you a doctor. Maybe you need something to help you sleep."

The silence that followed was longer this time and Fredrik was almost certain that he would soon hear footsteps on the stairs, but instead again came:

"Can't we talk here?"

"But . . ."

Sara stopped Fredrik with a hand on his arm. He broke off, gestured for her to go ahead.

"Are you sure?" whispered Sara.

"Yeah, I think it might help. Give it a try," he whispered back.

Fredrik took a step to the side to make room in the doorway for Sara.

"Hi, Rickard," she began, "this is Sara Oskarsson. We've met as you know."

She looked away from the door for a moment, out toward the sea before she continued.

"Of course we can talk here. It works just as well. You're here, we're here, and like you said, we're already talking."

"Okay," came the lagging response. "Go ahead and ask."

"The best thing would be if you could just tell us. We think you can help us understand what happened."

Another silence. Sara looked at Fredrik, and then out toward the sea again.

"If you feel like it, you could tell us what happened."

Another look out to sea, as if it helped her think, find the right words.

"Do you know anything about what happened to your father?"

"I was there," said Rickard Traneus.

Sara and Fredrik quickly exchanged looks.

"Where?" said Sara.

"In the house."

"What house?"

"In the house. In Levide," said Rickard.

"Your parents' house in Levide?" asked Sara.

"Yes."

The tips of Fredrik's fingers were cold and he felt how his face tightened. The sea had become darker, grayish-blue, and punctured everywhere by foaming whitecaps.

Rickard had fallen silent again.

"What happened in the house?" Sara nudged him on.

"Nothing . . ."

Sara and Fredrik looked at each other again. Fredrik gave a look of resignation. He wondered how long before their backup made it out there, if it was coming by boat or if they were going to fly out there? It wasn't blowing too hard for a helicopter, was it? No, not yet, not by a long shot.

"I mean," Rickard continued suddenly, "I heard them talking about it."

"About what?" said Sara.

"They killed my father."

The words came out loud and clear, without hesitation.

"Who did?"

"My mother and that man, Anders."

Fredrik's heart was pounding faster. He looked at Sara, but all her attention was intently focused on the doorway and Rickard.

"You heard them say that?" asked Sara.

"I know that he got her to do it."

"Who?"

"Him, Anders."

Rickard's account was urged on bit by bit by Sara's questions. It had become an interview without his realizing. Or else he preferred answering questions.

"Do you know how the whole thing transpired?"

"I know that he got her to do it. Somehow he got her to do it."

"Do you know how?" said Sara.

"My mother would never have hurt my father. It was him . . ."

"Was that what they were talking about?"

Rickard didn't answer. The door got caught by the wind and was about to slam shut. Sara had to hold it open with her hand. She was halfway through the door.

"Did she say that?"

The interior of the lighthouse was still silent. Sara turned out toward the sea again, without looking at Fredrik. The wind pulled at the loose strands of hair along her forehead. To the east stood the new lighthouse, cold and unyielding, like a white line against the sea and sky.

"Rickard. What was it you heard your mother say? Did she accuse Anders of driving her to it?" she asked facing in toward the doorway.

"I know it," said Rickard.

Now it was Sara's turn to pause.

"Tell us what you heard," she said then. "Start with that. Just what they said, as far as you can remember. Just that."

60.

She struck him with the butt of the hatchet. Three times. The spot on her cheek and temple where he had hit her stung with each blow.

What had he hit her for? That same stupid old question that she had long known was completely pointless to ask. He hit because that's what he did. The reasons were within him. He was full of them.

When she lay in bed with her head numb and throbbing from the blows, it suddenly became clear to her why he had hit her this time. He had thought about the woman he had been together with in Tokyo. Kristina had sensed that there was one, sensed it to the point of knowing for certain. It hadn't bothered her. She had been happy that his attention was directed elsewhere. She was the one he had been thinking about, thinking about the fact that he'd had a mistress for a year or more, a woman that his wife had no idea existed. The thought that had flared up inside him soon afterward was that if he had secretly had a lover on the other side of the world, then his wife . . . could have had one, too . . . far beyond his control . . .

It wasn't that he had sensed the existence of a lover, that he had gotten wind of Anders. It was his own guilt, his own filth that had colored his thinking.

Her cheek and temple was throbbing, her head was burning up with a heat that soon spread to rest of her body. A searing hot wave of hate and rage. She had had so many years to prepare. She could have been so far away.

But she hadn't been able to. It was only now that the last drop of love was consumed that it was possible. There was nothing left. No love to get in the way. She would smite herself free.

She got up from the bed and walked barefoot out to the garage.

Not one more day, not one more minute.

She immediately spotted the hatchet. It looked like it had never been used. The handle in light-colored wood, the red-painted head, didn't have a single scratch. The gleaming blade covered by a leather cover was razor sharp. Frighteningly sharp. She put the little leather cover back on and fastened the strap that held it in place.

She slipped back into the house, tiptoed silently down the stairs.

He lay in the bath, his Japanese bath, facing the wall. He lay there stretched out after having fucked and beaten her. He had folded a towel into a pillow and rested his neck against the stone edge of the bathtub.

He didn't hear her coming. Only when she was standing right over him did he react and lazily turn his head.

She struck him, full of rage. Struck to set herself free. But she also struck to punish. She wanted to punish herself for all the years that had passed.

Three blows. Straight from above with all her might. As hard as she could. Three blows. It went so quickly that she didn't notice that he was dead already after the first hit.

61.

The windows rattled as the lighthouse was buffeted by the wind gusts. It was cold in there, colder than it ought to be, he thought, as if the air in the old lighthouse had been still for too long. Shut in, dead air. Colder than it should have been.

He wouldn't be staying out here till the end of the day, that much he realized. The police were standing down there, just outside the open door. It was as if they were right on top of him. He could almost feel their breath when they shouted their questions.

He couldn't understand why they didn't just come in and get him. Wasn't that what the police did? Not these ones maybe. No doubt they've got special units for that. Ones that didn't ask any questions, just came in and took you away. Maybe they were already on their way over. Or were they just going to stand here all night? The two of them down there, and him up here. They hadn't even asked if they could come in. He was happy about that. He didn't want them in there. Sooner or later, one way or the other, he had to finish this. That much he knew. But first he had to explain. He had started, tried, but it was as if they didn't really want to listen. He could explain how everything was connected, how one thing had led to another, but it was as if they weren't interested in the context.

"So your father was lying in the bathtub down in the basement?" he heard Sara Oskarsson's voice echo through the lighthouse.

"Yes," he said, "he was lying in the bath. That was where he was killed."

He had stood there in the back entrance and pieced everything together. But this wasn't just some made-up story, that was what they didn't seem to understand. It was only something that he could understand because he was there and because he heard what he heard, right there in the house where he grew up in Levide. He had grown up with Stefania, Elin, Mother, and Father, and Father's cousin who got kicked to death by a horse, and the island, and the *Adventure*. He could get it all to make sense. The police down there, on the other hand, hadn't even heard of him or his family before three weeks ago.

Stubbornly they asked the wrong questions.

62.

Blood. For the rest of her life she would dream about blood. She couldn't imagine that she would be seeing anything but blood, regardless of whether her eyes were open or closed. Whether she was asleep or awake.

She sat on the top step of the basement stairs. Her shoulders ached and her right hand hurt like it was cramping up. Wasn't it a little swollen compared to the left one?

How could what just a few short hours ago had felt like a deliverance now feel like the end of everything? "Who am I?" she had asked herself accusingly, because she hadn't seized the moment to change her life, because she hadn't made better use of the opportunity that fate had presented her with.

But who was she now?

She had been so strong when she'd raised the ax to deliver the blow. She had earned the right to do it. She was driven by something that was bigger than she was. She was strong. She would save herself. There was no doubt.

Now it was all over, gone. She tried to cling to the notion that she had been justified somehow. He had earned his death. Day by day, year by year, he had gradually tightened something inside her to the breaking point. Now it had snapped. She wanted to think that way, but it wasn't easy. She wanted to think that it was him, not her.

When Anders came they had first moved around each other like two caged animals without being able to say anything intelligible. They had circled, paced, reached for each other, but in the crushing gravity of the situation there was no place for tenderness.

After over an hour, Anders had told her to go into the bedroom and shut the door. She hadn't been able to, wanted to know, had clung on to him. Then all of a sudden Anders had broken free, taken her into the bedroom.

It's better that you not know anything, he had said. Then he had shut the door. You stay here, he had said.

She had sat there on the edge of the bed, heard him go up and down the stairs and then out to the garage, not much more than that. And yet she had been on tenterhooks and had listened. She hadn't wanted to, but couldn't do otherwise.

She had sat there on the edge of the bed where Arvid had taken her just a few hours before. Where he had beaten her. The same hand that had touched her between her legs and struck her in the face, right on her cheekbone. He had hit her with the back of his hand. It had probably hurt, because he delivered the next blow with a closed fist. It had connected with her temple and was harder, as if the pain in his hand was also her fault, as if it had been added to the thing that was already driving him.

He had taken her hard and suddenly, more as if out of some kind of compulsion than desire. The intercourse had been just as irrational as the beating that followed. She hadn't felt the slightest shiver run through her body. Everything was gone. Once upon a time, she had lusted after him beyond all else. She had been prepared to go to any lengths to get him, just to be able to touch his body again, just one more time. Weak-kneed, dizzy, and distraught, ready to do anything. And now there was nothing left, not so much as a distant echo. Just thinking about it felt foreign to her.

She had no idea how much time had passed when Anders pulled open the door. She looked at him, stared at him with big, questioning eyes. It's better that you not know anything, he had said again. He was going to drive off and he wouldn't return again today. It would be best for them not to see each other for a while, not to have any contact whatsoever.

But there was one thing left to do. She had to clean up. He had taken care of the worst of it, but she had to go down there and really scrub. The whole room had to be scoured with the most powerful cleaner there was. Every inch. She mustn't use the cleaning materials that the cleaning lady used. When she was done she should burn the brush, the rag, everything she had used. Stick it in the furnace, turn up the shunt overnight.

We'll get through this, he had said.

She didn't believe him. They would come looking for Arvid. They would find him.

No, he had said, you have to trust me.

They would find them out, find out how things were between her and Anders.

Let them find out how things are between us, he had said. We're going to get through this.

63.

Sara felt that she was starting to become hoarse. She had been standing there shouting into the lighthouse for a long while, the whole time with the wind whipping the right side of her face. She couldn't lose her voice now. This just couldn't fail because her voice gave out, right when she was finally getting somewhere.

Fredrik was standing to the side of the doorway, leaning against the lighthouse. He was frozen stiff. He had taken out his notepad and his aching fingers were struggling to write down what Rickard Traneus was answering to Sara's questions. It was logical, but also completely bizarre. This must have been the strangest interrogation she had ever done.

There was a lot going through Rickard Traneus's head. She didn't want to steer him too much and risk him getting annoyed and refusing to speak. While she asked her questions, she was also wondering in the back of her head how all this was going to end. They had to get him to come out, or else go in there and fetch him. Would he come out of his own volition once he'd said what he had to say? Would he resist? Was he armed?

"Did you go in to them? Did you go into the house or did you stay there at the entrance and listen?" she yelled gruffly.

Her vocal cords felt dry and rigid.

"They killed him," Rickard Traneus said softly from the upper floor.

They could barely hear him, but rather than ask him to speak louder, she leaned further in through the doorway. Fredrik gave her a wary look when she put her foot on the threshold. She gave him a dismissive wave.

"I understand," she said.

Somewhere she had already sensed what was coming and would really have preferred not to hear it. She wished that he didn't have to go through it. No one should have to suffer at their own hand like that. What sort of a future was there for Rickard Traneus? What would he do once he had served out his sentence? There was no punishment in the world that could atone for such a crime. Not in the eyes of the world, but above all not in his own eyes. He would always have to carry it around with him. He didn't think it was his own fault, but he would still have to carry it around.

"You went in to them, didn't you, Rickard?"

64.

He held the heavy blade tightly in his right hand. He felt the steel edges press through the glove's thick leather. He listened and he understood.

When the last piece fell into place there was nothing that could stop him. He became consumed with one single thought. That man had to die. That man who walked around in Father's house as if he'd already taken his place. He had never heard anything so sickening, never met anyone so despicable. That man wasn't a human being. He was an animal. A snake.

There was no deliberation. Once he had understood, everything happened in a split second. The fury engulfed him like a storm surge of fire.

He bolted from the spot where he had been hiding, rushed through the house with the steel blade raised in his right hand. He spotted him at once. He looked ridiculously ordinary. A man like any other. But when he met his gaze, there was no doubt. It was terrified and full of guilt, but above it was a look of absolute certainty. Anders Traneus knew that this was the end, that this was his punishment and that there was no escape.

Rickard roared at him, released a sound that expressed as much pain as it did rage. He raised the blade above his head, aimed his blow. The room was spinning around him, disappeared into a blur, but Anders remained clearly in focus in the middle of his field of vision. He was longing to drive that steel right through his throat, bury it into the chest that he glimpsed through the opening in his shirt, and extinguish his life.

And he hacked. Rickard brought down his blade.

Then all of a sudden she was there, her arms outstretched, not to protect herself, but to protect him, like a shield.

"Rickard! No!"

Her words cut into him, screamed inside him. But it was too late. The blade fell. Quick, heavy, and hard. Left a deep cut in her chest.

He stared at the red gash, saw how her limbs buckled and she sat down on the edge of the couch and slipped on down to the floor.

Beside himself, he turned toward Anders. He shoved the table out of the way, forced him into a corner of the room. Anders backed away, cravenly begging, knocking over furniture in his way.

The first blow cut through the tendons and veins of his arms, just beneath his hands that were raised toward him in a pleading gesture, or possibly just for protection. He stared in amazement at what he had brought about, blood that was pumping from the lacerated arms, hands that dangled limply when there were no longer any muscles or tendons to control them. But he didn't stop. He was burning inside, boiling with rage, hate, and despair. But it was more than emotions that drove him. He was beyond feelings. It was a searing primordial power that made him swing that keen, heavy blade that he was holding in his hand. A power that would annihilate and restore, that would put everything back in its place and make the world whole again.

The second blow hit him right across the bridge of his nose. The bone was crushed when the steel broke through and forced his bloody eyes out of his skull. With all his might he brought his arm down a third time, slicing the blade into his chest, cutting through bone and cartilage with little resistance. During the half second it took him to swing his arm back over his right shoulder he caught a glimpse of his heart through the blood-soaked cleft in his chest, beating hard and strenuously a few final times in its as-yet-undamaged grayish-blue sack.

He took a half step back as he smote for the forth time, and the blade sliced off his throat and the arteries on either side of his neck. His head shot backward in a surprising, grotesque motion and opened up a gaping fissure out of which blood spurted in copious but ever-weakening eruptions.

The body lay lifeless on the floor in front of him, but still he didn't stop. He raised his hand and hacked at it a fifth time, a sixth, a seventh . . .

65

The waves crashed against the rocky west side of the island. The air had become more humid, the clouds thicker and lower in the sky, but still no rain.

Fredrik thought about the pieces that had fallen into place. Kristina Traneus killed her husband, the lover buried him, and the son took his revenge on the lover and his mother. The latter possibly by mistake. And Leo Ringvall? He must have come to the farm, snooped around, looked in through the window, maybe even caught sight of the lacerated bodies. But he had nothing to do with what happened. Except in as far as he was yet another of a long line of people who wouldn't weep at Arvid Traneus's funeral.

The backup was taking a long time. Fredrik checked his cell phone to make sure that he hadn't missed a call. An hour and a half had gone by since Sara had contacted them.

Requisitioning a helicopter from the mainland was one option, but maybe it couldn't fly across the sea in this weather. It was impossible for Fredrik to judge from where he was. The coast guard in Slite was the more likely alternative. Had his colleagues chosen that route, then they ought to come into view off to the north at any minute.

The *Anita* plunged down and shot up in a repeating sequence as the waves grew ever higher. The car tires groaned between the hull and the edge of the jetty. It didn't look good.

"Rickard," shouted Sara, "you can't stay here. The weather's taking a real turn for the worse. I don't know how much longer the boat can stay here."

It sounded painful when Sara forced those words through her abused vocal cords.

"Yeah," Rickard answered.

Was that an answer or a question? thought Fredrik. It sounded like a question.

"Come down so we can leave!" Sara shouted.

He moved around up there. It was impossible to hear the creaking of the floorboards now, but they could still see the dust fall with each step. Fredrik thought for a moment that he was on his way down.

"Then what?" he asked.

"You come out. We'll take the fishing boat back to Herrvik."

"I mean what's going to happen?"

Sara was tired and cold, her voice was wrecked. She just wanted to get him out.

"You'll have to return with us to Visby," she said. "Since you've confessed to killing Anders and causing your mother's death, you'll be charged with murder or voluntary manslaughter . . ."

She stopped short and exchanged looks with Fredrik.

"And negligent homicide," she answered.

Peter Klint would probably go for voluntary manslaughter there, too, but just then it seemed like the right thing to say.

"Is there anything else you're wondering about?" she asked.

A long silence, then: "No."

"Okay, Rickard. Are you coming down?"

He didn't answer. No dust fell. Sara looked at Fredrik questioningly and a little hopelessly. The cold, wet wind grabbed at their clothes. There was a soft whistling sound inside the lighthouse whenever the wind blew through the half-open door and up into the stone tower.

"Are you coming down?" shouted Sara once again.

There was no answer, but they saw the dust. And then his feet came into view on the steps.

Fredrik stayed where he was by the doorjamb so that he could see Rickard. Sara moved to the side and stood out of sight with her gun drawn. Fredrik holstered his.

Rickard Traneus slowly walked down the steps. He was wearing black pants and a red-and-white windbreaker. His arms hung limply at his sides. When he'd come down far enough that they could make eye contact, he looked Fredrik right in the eye for a few seconds and then abruptly dropped his gaze. He walked straight toward the door and Fredrik backed away a little.

"Come out the door and stop next to the rock," said Fredrik and pointed at a round, flat rock that was conveniently sticking out of the ground outside the lighthouse.

Rickard Traneus stepped carefully over the high threshold and did as he'd been instructed. Fredrik moved in behind him and took hold of his left arm at the wrist.

"I'm going to cuff you and frisk you," he said to Rickard who just nodded silently.

Fredrik quickly put the handcuffs on him and as soon as that was done, Sara holstered her gun and came up to them.

"It was good that you came out," she said, "so we can leave."

Rickard turned his head toward Sara and looked at her, but said nothing. Fredrik ran his hands along Rickard's legs, back and across his sides and stomach. He found a Swiss army knife in one of the pockets of his windbreaker, which he confiscated.

"Okay, let's go," said Fredrik. "It'll take about a quarter of an hour to walk down to the boat."

Sara and Fredrik walked on either side of Rickard Traneus, Fredrik with a firm grip on his upper arm. Fredrik squinted toward the north as they descended the bluff. He expected to see the coast guard's blue ship surging forward through the gray sea, but still nothing.

Rickard Traneus hadn't said a word since he stepped out of the lighthouse. Fredrik couldn't help but wonder what he was thinking about. Was he somehow relieved that it was over, or wasn't it over for him? Was he just as trapped now as he was before, inside his own inferno of guilt and death? Was he peering into the gray, rain-laden storm thinking that there was no place left on this earth for him? Had he ever thought that he could get away? If nobody suspected him, if his father had never been found, what would he have done with his life then?

"Fredrik!" shouted Sara and pointed over toward the headland where they had come ashore.

He didn't have to ask what she was trying to tell him. The *Anita* was pulling away from the jetty, then turned slowly northward, pitching badly in the powerful waves.

"He couldn't stay there," said Sara.

"We'll have to turn around," said Fredrik.

Rickard Traneus glanced anxiously back and forth between them and Fredrik explained what had happened.

"There's a spot behind those cliffs that's sheltered from the wind. He can come ashore there."

He hoped that he was right, that the wind hadn't shifted even more and that they were stuck on the island.

"We'll have to head straight back up the way we came," he said.

Rickard Traneus turned around obediently and trudged off in the opposite direction. They plodded up the hill again. When they came up onto the bluff, Fredrik began to wonder what was best, to go with the fishing boat or wait for their own transportation.

"Can you call and find out what's happened to them?" he shouted to Sara. "If they're close by then maybe it's better we go with them."

But if they were delayed then maybe the fishing boat was their last chance to get off the island until the storm was over. He wasn't looking forward to spending a stormy night in the lighthouse, least of all with a double murderer.

Sara took out her cell phone.

"I don't know if I'll be able to hear anything in this!" she shouted back.

The wind was blowing even harder now. They had to really lean forward in the gusts. It was impossible to be heard in a normal tone of voice unless you were standing right up against the person you were speaking to.

"I'll give it a try, but I may have to go inside the lighthouse."

She cupped her hand around the cell phone in order to increase the chances that the duty officer would hear her though the gale.

Beyond the cliffs, the *Anita* was rolling violently. The boat seemed like it was on its way back to Herrvik, but Söderman was probably just circling out in order not to get too close to the rocks. Fredrik turned north, squinted into the wind. Didn't he see something there, way out in the distance? Were those breakers on a reef? No, it had the definite V-shape of a surging ship's prow plowing through the gray sea, and was heading straight toward the island. It was the coast guard cutter KBV 181 from Slite.

"They're coming!" he shouted to Sara. "There they are."

Just when Fredrik pointed north, Rickard Traneus suddenly jerked his body unexpectedly. He wrenched free of Fredrik's grip and started to run, trying to escape Fredrik thought at first, but Rickard Traneus was running straight toward the spot where the cliff plummeted most precipitously down into the raging sea.

Fredrik rushed after him.

"Rickard!" he screamed pointlessly into the wind.

Rickard had gotten a head start, but with his hands cuffed behind his back he couldn't run all that fast without running the risk of losing his balance. Fredrik quickly gained on him and heard how Sara in turn was following close behind him. Rickard Traneus stumbled and sort of lurched forward a little. Fredrik thought that he would fall headlong onto the rocks and clumps of grass, but with a quick, skipping maneuver he managed to stay on his feet and ran on toward the edge of the cliff.

Fredrik pushed himself closer and closer. He caught up with Rickard just as they approached the brink and threw out an arm to catch and tackle him. His arm got wedged underneath Rickard's arm just as he threw himself off, and as he twisted in the air Fredrik had no chance of freeing himself. Rickard disappeared over the edge and pulled him inexorably with him in his fall.

They plummeted. Fredrik grabbed hold of Rickard with his left hand, too, and they fell face-to-face. He fell from the cliff down toward a bluish-gray flat rock that rose out from the shingled shoreline below with Rickard Traneus's empty gaze staring into his.

He fell and saw himself in a bed, saw a woman in a long skirt come toward him from a pair of doors that opened out onto a brightly lit corridor. At first the image was unfamiliar, then he suddenly realized that it was from a British TV series that he had long since forgotten the name of. It was set in the 1800s and the man lying there in the bed was dying, the man whose gaze was now his. The woman in the doorway went double, the image went out of focus, the dying man went out of focus. Was that the last image that would flicker before his mind's eye? A scene from a TV series that wasn't even worth remembering?

Then nothing more.

66

Göran Eide was standing outside the ER entrance at Karolinska University Hospital smoking a cigarette. It tasted like shit and was completely irresistible.

When he had been informed about what had happened out on Östergarnsholm he had done three things. One: made sure that the ambulance helicopter was on its way out to the island. Two: made sure that Gustav drove down to inform Fredrik's wife about the accident and then drove her back to Visby. Three: politely asked a uniformed officer to run over to the supermarket to buy a pack of Camel Lights. That was over seven hours ago. Once the decision had been made to take Fredrik to Karolinska, Göran had flown up to Stockholm on the same plane as Ninni.

He didn't like to stand outside a hospital's emergency room and wait. He didn't actually like smoking, either. But right now he was doing both.

Two years earlier he had stood outside the entrance to Visby hospital after having visited an injured officer. Then he had stood there trying to work out what had gone wrong and what he could do to make sure that he would never have to stand there again.

Fredrik Broman had somehow been pulled over the edge of a cliff when he had tried to stop Rickard Traneus from throwing himself off it. Both of them had plunged down the precipice on Östergarnsholm and landed right on top of a slab of exposed bedrock below. Rickard Traneus on the bottom, had died instantly, with Fredrik on top of him. "They lay there as if they'd been sacrificed at some kind of altar,"

Sara had said in a quavering whisper when she returned to Visby deathly pale and frozen stiff.

Fredrik was badly injured. They had made a quick assessment in Visby, stabilized him and sent him on to Karolinska. It wasn't clear whether he would make it. This was considerably more serious than the incident two years ago. Göran shut his eyes. How the hell could things have gone so terribly wrong? Had Fredrik made a mistake, been careless or tried to play the hero? Or was it Sara? Or was it he himself? Or was it just one of those things?

To hell with it. The most important thing right now was that Fredrik pulled through.

Göran took a deep drag from his cigarette and noticed how the door to the ER opened. It was Ninni. She came up to him, walking with short, slow steps.

Without thinking about it he held out the pack of cigarettes to her. She took it without saying anything, shook out a cigarette, and let him light it. He made sure that it had really taken before he blew out the match.

They both smoked their cigarettes almost all the way down to the filter without saying a word to each other.

67.

Sara had added a few days of vacation to extend her three days of sick leave. Now that the investigation was over, it didn't really make any difference if she took a few extra days off. Her own procedure had been overshadowed by what had happened in the storm out on the island. It had just become something that had to be dealt with quickly. And nobody had asked any questions.

She had thought that she was well prepared for the meeting with Fredrik, had spoken to both Göran and Ninni, but she had still stopped short just inside the doorway, dumbstruck. The body lying on the bed was heavy and unresponsive, its gaze had no focus. He wasn't unconscious, and yet he wasn't there, either. Where was he in that case? Was he in there at all? Had the fall from the cliff expunged the person she knew as Fredrik Broman and just left behind a few remaining bodily functions such as breathing and a beating heart? The hospital had little useful to say about it.

They were told they just had to wait and see. It sounded vague, but the very vagueness itself inspired a kind of hope. Surely they wouldn't raise people's hopes for no reason?

Ninni was with him when Sara entered. She saw how her gaze clung to her oblivious husband's face, filled with despair but also something else, an involuntary loathing toward everything. The hospital room, the seemingly lifeless body, the bandages, and the IV. Well, maybe not toward everything, but above all toward that inert, limp, silent, helpless body. She saw it and understood her, didn't judge her.

She offered to sit with him for a while. Ninni could go down to the cafeteria for a bit, or go out for a walk, or whatever she needed to do. For a moment Sara was afraid that she had been too forward, crossed some line, but Ninni accepted her invitation with a grateful smile.

Ninni went off leaving her alone in the room with Fredrik. Sara regarded her colleague. Or that mute shell that bore a physical resemblance to him. What would she say to him? What would she do?

Elin Traneus looked out from her balcony on the sixth floor of the Hotel Okura. The hotel lay in Tokyo's Minato district, not many blocks from the building where her father had spent a large part of the last three years of his life.

It was the beginning of March. Tokyo was chilly and it was often raining. The rain came suddenly, was strangely silent and seldom lasted very long. When Elin had arrived in the city, she had gotten off the bus at the wrong stop. She had pulled her wheeled suitcase three blocks through one of those rain showers. Suddenly a man in uniform had appeared from out of the arcade beneath one of the hotels along the way. He had hurried up to her and given her a simple umbrella of see-through plastic. It had been such a beautiful gesture. She still felt moved every time she thought about it.

The Hotel Okura was built in the sixties and had appeared in one of the James Bond movies. She had read that in a brochure she had found in the lobby that was as cavernous as an aircraft hangar. The hotel also had a bar that served excellent dry martinis. She was going to try not to spend too much time in those gloomy rooms, among all the middle-aged, Japanese salarymen.

She didn't sleep much. The first three days she had mostly spent on her balcony looking out at the city. She had also wandered around in the immediate neighborhood that was ugly and drab. Despite the peculiar Japanese address system, she had eventually managed to find the building where her father had lived. The building was a graphite gray, anonymous high-rise of forty or so stories. Of course, she had no way of confirming that this was actually where he had lived.

Molly had gone with her to Gotland for the funeral. Elin was eternally grateful to her for that. She couldn't have handled it otherwise.

The funeral had taken place at Levide church one week before Christmas, in the unfamiliar church on the wrong side of the road. Or rather the *funerals*. No doubt there were those who felt that it was inappropriate, or downright offensive, to hold one joint funeral service. But for Elin it would have been unthinkable to do it any other way, no matter what had happened.

All three of them were buried together. Of the three people lying in the oak caskets with brass handles, two of them had each murdered one of the others. Her family. Now they were resting in peace with Stefania. That might not have been an altogether uncomplicated choice, either, but that was how it turned out.

Who was actually guilty of what? She couldn't bear to think about it like that. They were gone now, all of them, so what difference did it make?

The lights on the skyscrapers came on as the sky darkened. In the building opposite the hotel, men and women were still working away in an open office landscape beneath the fluorescent lighting. She stood out on the balcony looking at them while she thought about whether to order room service or head down to the gloomy bar.

Hotel Okura was an expensive hotel, but that wasn't a problem. It had turned out that she was the heir to a small fortune. The sole heir. In addition to the farm in Levide, which was worth at least 4 million, her father had left behind 320,000 in cash, plus stocks and funds worth about 2 million. There was also a company on the island of Jersey that owned shares and options with a combined value of 112 million crowns. In a yield account, the same company had over 3 million crowns worth of Eurodollars.

When she had spontaneously said that she would really prefer to just give it all away, the lawyer had looked shaken. She got the feeling that he was considering if there was any way to have her declared temporarily of unsound mind. Think it over, he had urged her. The money in Sweden couldn't be touched in any case until the estate was settled, and that couldn't be done until any wrongful death claims had been paid. The lawyer had been quick to reassure her on that point. Swedish courts never granted any large sums in cases like that. Regardless of the extent of the assets of the defendant. A few hundred thousand at most.

Think it over, he had asked her once again. She could start a foundation and put the assets in a fund if she was determined to give them away. Then the assets could grow and she could devote herself to donating the proceeds and if she were to change her mind one day, the money would still be there.

He didn't understand. She didn't want to devote herself to charity. She just wanted to get rid of the assets. But above all, she had other things to think about. And now she went traveling with the money. Father's money.

A soft, silent rain began to fall. Elin went inside from the balcony, but let the door stand open. It would soon stop.

She was unsure why, but the trip to Tokyo had been necessary. She had needed to stand outside father's anonymous skyscraper and feel that it meant nothing. She couldn't explain what it did to her exactly, but she felt that it did her good. He was far away now. There was a sea between them. Another kind of sea.

A loud, piercing shriek echoed outside. She looked out and just caught a glimpse of a black shadow in front of the lit-up facade. She had heard them the first time the night before, when she had lain awake on her bed and long since given up any hope of falling asleep. The awful shriek had given her a start and made her sit up. She had looked out through the window and wondered what it was. She had stared single-mindedly out into the night. Until she finally caught sight of them and understood that they were ravens. It was ravens that flew shrieking among Tokyo's skyscrapers after dark.